THE LIES YOU TOLD

Also by Harriet Tyce

Blood Orange

THE LIES YOU TOLD

HARRIET TYCE

NEW YORK BOSTON

Grand Central Publishing
Hachette Book Group
1290 Avenue of the Americas, New York, NY 10104
grandcentralpublishing.com
twitter.com/grandcentralpub

First published in 2020 by Wildfire, an imprint of Headline Publishing Group

First Grand Central Publishing edition: December 2020

Grand Central Publishing is a division of Hachette Book Group, Inc. The Grand Central Publishing name and logo is a trademark of Hachette Book Group, Inc.

The publisher is not responsible for websites (or their content) that are not owned by the publisher.
The Hachette Speakers Bureau provides a wide range of authors for speaking events. To find out more, go to www.hachettespeakersbureau.com or call (866) 376-6591.

Library of Congress Control Number: 2020946381

ISBNs: 978-1-5387-6275-2 (hardcover), 978-1-5387-6277-6 (ebook)

Printed in the United States of America

LSC-C

Printing 1, 2020

For Sarah Hughes—dearest of friends.
I'll never forget the Rimmel eyeshadow…

Part 1

1

It's the first time I've ever slept in my mother's room. That I can remember, anyway. It's cold. My arm is the only part of me out from under the covers and my skin feels clammy, my fingers chilled. I roll over, tucking myself in fully, leeching off Robin's warmth. She's snoring gently next to me. It's a couple of years since she's wanted to sleep in with me, but the temperature of the house defeated her. The first night we arrived, she walked into the room I made up for her and walked straight out again.

"It's freezing," she said, "and I don't like that weird painting on the wall."

"I'll move it," I said. But I didn't argue when Robin wanted to share my bed. I don't want to let her out of my sight.

The duvet is too thin. I piled our coats on top last night for extra warmth, but they slipped onto the floor while we slept. I reach over and pull them back on, trying not to disturb Robin, eking out her sleep for at least a few minutes more. It'll be cold when we get up.

The gas heater is still here. I remember sometimes in winter, the coldest days, that my mother let me dress beside it, warning me not to get too close. I was never allowed to touch it then. I'm scared to touch it now. It's brown, shiny, its corners sharp, gouges out of the paintwork. The ceramic burners are black with soot. I don't even know if it'll still work. The fireplace around it, once white, has yellowed, scorch marks above the fire. I looked away from the china ornaments on the mantelpiece last night, but in the dim light of the morning, I see they're still the same; smiling shepherdesses, a Pierrot with a vacuous grin, all crowded close along the narrow shelf.

Robin shifts next to me, sighs, subsides back into sleep. I don't want to wake her. Today is going to be hard enough for her. Anxiety spikes through me. The dank room lies heavy on me, thoughts haunting me of the warm house I've fled. The contrast between the spare room here, rejected by Robin, and her own bedroom that we've been forced to leave behind: the bed draped with pink hangings, the sheepskins on the floor. There are no sheepskins in my mother's house—only a ram's skull still displayed on the stairs, resplendent in his horns.

It's safe, though. Far away. Robin rolls over in bed, closer to me, her arm warm beside mine, the little knitted meerkat my best friend Zora made for her held tight in her hand. My breathing eases. After what happened, I would always have felt chilled in that house, despite the warmth. I shiver now at the thought, the shock still raw. Deep breath in, out. We're here now.

I reach over and pick up my phone from the bedside table—nothing. No messages. Its battery is nearly out—of course there aren't sockets beside the bed. But the electricity is at least still working. As long as we don't electrocute ourselves before I've had a chance to get the wiring checked. I lie back, listing all the jobs that are essential for the safety of the house, overwhelmed at the number of tasks ahead of me. At least there won't be time to think about anything else.

"What time is it?" Robin mutters, turning over to stretch her limbs.

"Nearly seven," I tell her. I pause. "We'd better get up."

For a moment longer we lie there, both reluctant to brave the cold. I steel myself, pushing the covers back in one go and jumping to my feet.

"You're so mean," Robin says, sitting up fast. "Do I have to have a shower? The bathroom's freezing."

"No, it's OK. I'll try and get it sorted for later."

She runs through to her room and I hear her thumping around as she gets ready. I throw on jeans and a sweater without giving my outfit any thought. It's too cold for vanity.

"I don't want to go," Robin says, a piece of toast in her hand that she puts back on the plate, uneaten. She sighs. My heart sinks.

"I know."

"I'm going to hate it," she says, turning away and putting her hair up into a bun twisted on the top of her head.

"It might not be that bad."

"Yes, it will," she says, staring at me. There's no arguing with her tone.

She's about to walk through the gates of a new school in Year 6, new uniform—box-fresh, crisp and stiff—years after everyone else has formed their gangs and factions. The uniform she's wearing doesn't even fit properly, collar too big around her throat, skirt too long. Her face is pale against the bright red of the new school cardigan, the stark white of the new shirt, everything we bought in a rush yesterday from the uniform shop up Finchley Road I remember from my own childhood. My throat tightens, but I make myself smile.

"It'll be OK," I say, an edge of desperation in my voice. "You'll make some lovely new friends." I pick up a piece of toast, look at it, put it down. I'm not hungry either.

"Maybe," Robin says, her voice full of doubt. She finishes dealing with her hair and pulls her phone out of her pocket, entranced immediately by the screen. I twitch, control myself. Is there a message from Andrew, wishing his daughter good luck at her new school? I don't know if Robin and her dad have spoken since we left…since we had to leave. Robin keeps scrolling down, eyes flickering.

"Anything interesting?" I say in the end, unable to stop myself, trying to keep my tone light. "Has your dad messaged?" Casually, I pick up my own phone and put it in my bag.

Robin looks up, her face still and pale, eyes dark as her hair. She shakes her head. "Not Dad," she says. "Haven't you spoken to him?"

I smile, neutral. I need to move the conversation on. She has to believe this is all normal. She doesn't need to know that the last contact between her dad and me was a hissed exchange on the phone before his number went dead. *Just go*, he'd said. *I don't want you here any more. Either of you.* Loathing in his voice I'd never heard before.

I've been silent too long. She's looking at me, a question starting to form on her face.

"Any gossip? You chatting to someone?" I say with an effort. Over the last couple of months, there's been a complicated spat between Robin's friends and people in her old class, and I've found the updates strangely compelling.

"Everyone's still asleep, Mum. It's the middle of the night back home."

"Sorry, yes. Of course. I wasn't thinking." The words hang in the air, before Robin relents.

"But there's a load of messages from last night while I was asleep. Tyler sat next to Addison on the bus on Friday instead of Emma and now no one is talking to Addison."

"Oh, lord..."

"I know. It's so stupid." She looks at her phone once more before tossing it down.

"Maybe it'll be easier being at an all-girls school," I say, striving for a tone of conviction. Failing.

Robin shrugs. "I guess I'll find out."

The last year of primary school. Memories of it, deep in my bones. Everyone turning eleven, some looking like teenagers, some still childlike. At least Robin sits in the middle of this spectrum, neither very tall nor very short, nothing extreme in her development that stands out. It'll be hard enough anyway. Suppressing a shudder, I remember the rejections, the spite. Whatever else I'm facing, at least I never have to go through fitting in to a new school again.

"I don't know how they're coping without you to mediate."

"I don't think they are," Robin says, her face serious. "They're falling out way more without me there. I'll never see the messages in time."

"I'm sure they'll work it out. And you'll see them soon. In the Christmas holidays, maybe."

Robin is silent. It's too much change to take in. Too much,

too fast. My world and Robin's turned upside down in a scurry of days. The air lies heavy.

"I know this is difficult," I say. "But we can make it work. We were lucky that this place came up. Your school back home was great, but we've always wanted you to go to school here, in London. You're going to love it." My voice falls off. I remember that last rushed day in Brooklyn as I threw clothes into bags, a smile fixed to my face as I lied through my teeth to Robin about why we had to leave. Right then. No time for goodbyes.

"And you were happy there? You're sure I'm going to like it?" Her face is pinched, suspicious.

"Yes," I say. Another lie. But only a small one this time.

"But you told me you didn't have the best childhood," Robin says. She's sharp, my daughter. Too much so.

I quickly gather myself. "That was more to do with home," I say. "Your grandmother. She wasn't very keen on kids—even her own. School was an escape. I mean, of course there were difficult bits, but I made some friends. I loved the library. They made me school captain in Year Six and put my name up on a board—that was pretty cool. It was definitely better than here." I gesture around me at the tired, cold kitchen.

Robin smiles. "At least it'll be warm," she says, attempting a joke. I reach across the table to hug her and after a moment she hugs me back. "Let's get out of here. You don't want to be late. Not on your first day."

Robin nods and crosses the room to pick up her bag and pull on a pair of gloves. I put on a wooly hat to hide the worst of my greasy hair, and we head out.

We walk to the bus stop, our footsteps slapping in time

against the pavement. I glance over at my daughter. Her face is set, her chin firm, almost grown-up yet still so young.

I don't know what lies ahead for us. I want to be calm. But I can't shift the fear at the pit of my stomach, heavy as our steps on the ground.

2

I sit next to the bus window, leaning my forehead against the glass. The 46 bus is full, and slow, lumbering from stop to stop from Camden to St. John's Wood. I remember the route so well I could walk it with my eyes closed. It's all different, all the same, layers of new builds, slicks of fresh paint on top of the old buildings.

I glance at Robin's profile—she's still entranced by her phone. She snorts with laughter, lifts her head.

"Emma sent me a big update. So much drama. I'm glad I'm not there having to deal with it all," Robin said, tucking her phone in her bag.

I almost believe her.

My stomach clenches as the familiar bus stop draws close. All of a sudden, I'm aware of the traffic noise around me. The screeching of brakes, horns sounding, a man yelling *fuck off* in the distance. Exhaust fumes leak in from the street, catch at my throat, a steady stream of black SUVs crowding past us. We'll be the only ones turning up to school on the bus.

The bus brakes unexpectedly and my head bangs against the glass. I shut my eyes against the memories.

* * *

"We'll never get a place," I'd said when I was first told of what my mother had done, two years earlier. "It's too late. It's too competitive. There's no way any spaces will come up now. Not at the beginning of Year Four, not in two years. There will be a waiting list as long as my arm. She thinks she can control everything, but she can't. Even if we were going to go along with it, we wouldn't be able to."

And this had been true, my delight great when the admissions officer gave my reluctant inquiry short shrift.

But that was before it all went wrong. My marriage with Andrew, collapsing in two short years. It was a surprise, then, to receive a call only a couple of weeks ago from the same admissions officer telling me there was a space now available if Robin could start immediately. I was about to say no again, but something gave me pause. *I'll think about it for a bit if that's OK.* Those words emerged instead.

Nothing could have prepared me for the desperation with which I'd call her forty-eight hours later, heart in mouth, to ask her—beg her—if the place was still available. *Please.* Just a standard offer to her, a way to fill an unexpected gap in the class. A miracle for me—everything I'd needed for our escape. An escape I never knew till then I'd need. The condition of my mother's controlling legacy met by sending Robin to Ashams—without her attendance, I wouldn't have been allowed this house or the small income from my mother's estate—just enough to live on now that I've left my marriage behind.

When I last left my mother's house, over a decade ago, I swore on my life I'd never go back. Never let my mother control me again.

But I'd break any promise for Robin.

* * *

Now we're at the school gates, and my hands are curled tight in my pockets. Even through the eyes of an adult, it still looks huge, imposing. Architecture fitting for the most prestigious girls' school in north London. I try not to imagine how intimidating it must be for my daughter.

There are two sets of iron gates, a formal flower bed in between with box hedges and cyclamen. From each gate the drive curves up to a wide flight of stairs that leads to the front entrance. Despite the grandeur of its fittings, it's not set back that far from the pavement—a carriage would have had to maneuver carefully around the gates rather than sweep majestically through. This place couldn't be more different from Robin's old school, a modern building on a quiet street. This school carries the weight of history, a gravity that seems to belie the presence of actual children behind those great doors.

I look down at Robin. Her face is tight, the color drained from her cheeks.

"It'll be OK," I say. I want to promise. I can't.

Robin looks about, her gaze unblinking. She clutches my arm. "This is an elementary school?"

"It is. It's a lot more friendly than it looks, I promise." I stop myself from crossing my fingers.

"Wow."

"We'd better go in," I say, and she nods. We walk slowly across the drive and up the stone steps. The doors are wide, wooden, with brass fittings polished to a high shine. I reach to open the door, but it's pushed back hard from the other side. A woman walks out briskly, bashing straight into me. I jump back, startled, only catching my balance by grabbing hold of Robin by the arm and nearly sending her flying, too. My ankle turns over, a sharp pain shooting up my leg.

"Watch where you're going!" The woman's scorn is sharp in her voice. "I could have fallen down the stairs." She pushes past us and marches off, her perfectly blow-dried hair bouncing on her shoulders with each step. I look after her, heart still pounding from the encounter. Tall, blonde. Hostile.

"Are you OK?" Robin says at the same moment another woman starts tutting and shouldering past us.

My throat tightens as though I might cry. Or scream at them all to fuck off. I brush moisture from my eyes with brisk fingers.

"I'm fine."

Once we're safely inside, and I've introduced Robin to the registrar and filled in the emergency contact forms, I stand next to Robin in an expectant manner.

"You can go now, Mom," Robin says, and the registrar laughs.

"She's safe with us, Mrs. Spence."

"That's my husband's name," I say. I can't bring myself to say ex-husband with Robin standing beside me. "My name is Roper. Sadie Roper."

"Of course, Ms. Roper," she says. They keep looking at me, waiting for me to leave.

Robin nods. "Go on, Mom."

I look at the registrar. "You don't need me for anything else? A tour, or meeting the form teacher, or something?"

She shakes her head. "Not today. You will meet Robin's form teacher in due course. We'll send you details of the parents' evening." She turns to Robin. "I'll take you to your classroom."

She whisks my daughter away from me before I can even say goodbye.

3

I head back fast to the bus stop on the other side of the road, the pain subsiding in my ankle as I go. I need to make some progress on the house and then get to chambers to see if there's any work available. The long years spent away from criminal practice yawn in front of me, but I refuse to let them put me off. I've braved worse in the last weeks. Far worse.

It shouldn't be this way. Anger courses through me: at Andrew for being such a bastard; at the rejection, the rage that's driven me clean across the Atlantic, straight back into the clutches of my mother and that wreck of a house. Thoughts of a tidy new-build apartment drift through my head. White walls and clean wooden floors, not the dark jumble of a neglected Victorian house, windows obscured by overgrown ivy. A toxic legacy.

The bus pulls up. No good thinking about this now. I'll wash, scrub, clean; bleach it all out. I take out my phone, ready to text Zora, invite her for dinner. My finger hovers over the screen for a moment before I write the message.

Surprise! Long story, but Robin and I are back and staying at the house. Dinner tomorrow? Lots to catch up on xx

Planning for the future, no looking back.

* * *

As soon as I'm home, I look at the boiler I was too tired to examine the night before, discovering to my surprise that it's relatively new. After a few minutes, it's up and running. Warmth, hot water—that'll chase away the demons.

Heartened, I get to it, scouring and scrubbing every surface in sight, not stopping for a second to let any thoughts of the past enter in, shutting myself off from any recognition of creaking floorboards or cracked tiles, the mark on the wall where my mother threw a book at me, the nail sticking out of the floor where I ripped countless pairs of tights, always forgetting it was there. As the dust lifts, so does the gloom in the house, and cold sunlight poking through the dirty glass of the kitchen window lifts my mood a little more.

After a couple of hours of frenzied activity, the kitchen is usable. It's still the same oven, the one I remember from all those years ago. I test it's working, remembering almost instinctively how long to hold the knob down before the gas catches light.

The old electric kettle is still here, its cord frayed, the metal of the wire exposed. I remember telling her to throw it away the last time I was here, fifteen years ago. I pick it up and turn it in my hands for a moment, tracing the marks of limescale etched on its surface, before my chest tightens and a sour taste rises in my mouth. *Why do you care if I get electrocuted?* rings in my ears. I dump it in a black bin bag, a smile lifting the corners of my mouth. Digging through the cupboards, I take out a small saucepan and fill it with water, put it on to boil.

Even though the house is on a busy road, there's no sound of traffic in the kitchen at the back. I'm unnerved by the silence. I look through the window of the back door onto the concrete patch outside. It's overshadowed by evergreen trees—a yew, chill and dark in the corner, all the plants my mother used to tend brown and withered, dead leaves lying in drifts in the corners. I'll cheer it up—geraniums, bulbs in big blue pots. I remember the time I brought a bunch of tulips home for Mother's Day, handed them to her. *So loud*, she said as she thrust them from her, petals crushed in the sink. *It's bad enough being a mother*, she said. *I don't need any reminders*. I remember how small I felt at that moment, how stupid, my feet too big for me as I stumbled backward and fled from the kitchen.

Time to plant daffodils, snowdrops. Crocuses. Parrot tulips, the brighter the better. I'll get Robin to help. Turning away from the door, I look again around the kitchen. It might be cleaner, but it's still bleak, still empty.

The water boils and I make tea, sitting back down again, nursing the warmth of the mug in my hands. It's nearly noon. Is it time yet for Robin's lunch? Maybe the food will be better now. I hope it's better now. I think about what we used to be served: lasagna swimming in grease, cold mashed potato, green-gray hardboiled eggs at the heart of a rock-hard veal and ham pie. I take in a deep breath, release it. Not now. I'm not going there. What lies beneath is worse, much worse, and I don't have time. My thoughts snap back to Robin.

It'll be OK, I'd said to Robin. *Really welcoming*. Reassuring phrases that rolled off my tongue. But in truth, it was never welcoming at all. Formal, assertive, utterly confident in itself. Sink or swim. That's how it was all those years ago. Maybe it's changed. I remember the grip of Robin's fingers on my arm, clutching so hard I'm surprised they didn't leave a mark. I hope it isn't as bad as Robin feared.

I fear it might be a lot worse.

My tea cools rapidly, and I drink it in gulps, pushing the mug away from me when I've finished. I need to change to go into chambers and ask the clerks if there's any work available for me. Realistically I know it might be tricky, but I can't let doubt creep in.

Before I go, I want to sort Robin's room out a bit more. It's the room my mother used for guests, few though they were. I shovel out piles of old newspapers and torn magazines, ruthless in my clearing. A chest of drawers emerges, a wardrobe, old coats and jackets, a moth-eaten fox fur, its tail held in its mouth with a tortoiseshell clip. It all goes into bin bags.

A message arrives from Zora. *Yes please to dinner tomo. I want to hear ALL about wtf is going on. I can't believe you're back tho can't wait to see you xx*

I feel my spirits lift, a small chink of light breaking through. It will be so good to see her. But it's going to be a long explanation. I send back a thumbs up emoji, unable to muster any more words.

4

Dressing for chambers feels like stepping back in time. I pull on underwear, black tights, a white shirt and black skirt and jacket, grateful for the sentiment that made me hang on to this suit through the years when I had no use for it. A tired black suit I used to wear in court over ten years ago.

The skirt does up easily. The jacket too—as if those years never intervened. I look at my silhouette, reflected in a dusty mirror on the back of the door. It could be nearly twenty years ago, my first day in chambers, before Andrew, before Robin, before my career gave way to a life I entirely failed to anticipate.

Despite everything, the forced nature of this new start, I feel a twinge of excitement. At least I'm finally going to be able to use my legal qualifications again. I'm going back to work.

I walk fast down Kentish Town Road to Camden Town tube, nerves rising, and sooner than I'd like I'm at Embankment, then Temple. I walk up Temple Place, cut through Milford Lane, the gloss paint on its black iron railing gleaming in the sun. I pause for a moment, looking from left to right.

I remember this alleyway well. I got off with Andrew here once, right at the start of our relationship, heady on cheap wine and the fire of early love.

That was a happy night, a good memory. Thoughts creep in of a time earlier than that, a darker night some months before, the older barrister who thought that young female pupils were his for the taking, his for the groping. I had to struggle hard, kick him harder still before I was able to break free. I stop at the place where it happened, to the left of the stairs, wiping my hands down my skirt. Nearly two decades ago but still fresh in my mind. I shake my head clear, keep walking, up the stairs and through the arch at the bottom of Essex Street into the ordered red brick of its parallel rows of barristers' chambers.

When I reach my old chambers, halfway up Essex Street, I stop for a moment and take a deep breath. Earlier, it felt that time had gone backward. It's happening again. I'm as ungainly and as clumsy as the first day I started pupilage, all elbows and knees, my hands hot. I take a deep breath, draw back my shoulders, and push open the door.

"Miss Roper," David Phelps says, and this time the years roll back and stay there.

"David," I say, damping down the supplicatory note that's creeping into my voice.

"To what do we owe the pleasure?"

He's standing behind reception, papers in hand. He must have been on the way to his desk as he would hardly have been answering the phones—as if in answer to this thought, a young woman slips past him and takes a seat at the desk next to the switchboard.

"Do you have an appointment?" she says to me in a neutral tone, scrutinizing me, her eyes sliding up and down me. I feel suddenly conscious of my outdated suit.

"No," I say, lifting my chin.

"Then how can I help you?"

"Miss Roper is an old member of chambers," David says, perhaps taking pity on me. Or perhaps not. I smile at him, and he looks through me with the eyes of a shark, dark and predatory, waiting for the first sign of blood.

"I was wanting to talk to you about restarting my practice," I say. "I know it would have been better if I'd written first, but everything has happened rather faster than I anticipated."

"I see," David says.

"I'm back in London now. My daughter is at school. There's nothing to stop me from starting up again." A note of defiance is creeping into my voice. I can feel my nerves stretched on edge but I won't let him drive me away.

"Hmm," David says. "The small matter of instructing solicitors, miss? I don't see them lining up, desperate to give you work." It's almost reassuring that he's still loading the word "miss" with more scorn than ought to be possible. Almost. Not entirely. At least I know where I am with him. I always did.

"I was hoping that there might be some junior work available, David, and through that I would be able to build up my practice in time."

"I'm terribly sorry, miss, but as any of our juniors would tell you, there's not exactly an abundance of work available these days. A lot has changed in the last few years, as no doubt you'll be aware." He pauses to smooth his hair down, a tic I remember from before. "Come to that, how many years is it now?"

"Nearly eleven." My chin is still up.

"It's not as if you can just walk back in, miss. There's also insurance, your practicing certificate, your continuing professional development. As I said, a lot has changed. It won't be possible."

"But I've done all of that already," I say. He thinks he's got one over me but he's wrong. "I have insurance. My practicing certificate and my CPD hours are up to date. I made sure I kept on top of all the legal developments online. I knew I'd be back one day."

"Miss—" David starts to say when he's interrupted.

"My eleven o'clock conference will be here shortly," a woman says from behind me, her voice imperious. Something familiar about it, tugging at my memory.

"Of course, Miss Carlisle. Would you like coffee to be brought to the conference room?" David sounds like a completely different person. Respectful. Obsequious, even. No wonder. I should have remembered immediately I heard her voice. Barbara Carlisle is one of the most senior Queen's Counsel in chambers. Powerful even when I was a tenant in chambers all those years ago.

I keep my head down.

"Naturally," she says. "For eight."

She does not say please. I keep my head averted, hoping she'll leave soon so that I can continue my conversation with David in private. He has a different idea.

"Miss Roper," he says, turning to me. "I understand your position. But it is simply not possible to turn up in chambers out of the blue after over a decade and expect to be given work. We have procedures. Regardless of your former tenancy our protocols still apply. If you write a letter in the correct format to the Tenancy Committee, they will consider your position in the fullness of time. I believe their next meeting is at the end of March."

Not for months. I nod, mute, swallowing my frustration. I turn again to go, walk toward the door when Barbara approaches me.

"Sadie," she says. "I remember you. You were the second junior on that fraud with me?"

"I was."

"And you left for America, isn't that right? Had a baby?"

"Yes, Robin's nearly eleven now," I say.

"And you're coming back to work?"

"I want to come back. I need to come back. But apparently there's nothing available." I glare at David who gives a self-satisfied smirk, eyebrow raised.

"I see..." Barbara says, but I don't hear the rest of her sentence. David's sneer has finished me off and I'm close to tears of humiliation or anger—I'm not sure which—but I'm damned if I'll let them see me crack. I march out of reception without looking back.

5

I wait for Robin outside school with my head down, focused on my phone, unwilling to catch anyone's eye. I know I'll have to engage at some point soon, but right now, I don't have room inside me. Too disappointed by my reception in chambers, too tired from trailing up and down on the tube. It takes me a minute to realize that Robin is right at my elbow. Her expression is still tense, though not so much so as this morning.

"How was it?" I say, leaning in to kiss her on the cheek. Robin pulls away.

"Can we just go? Please?" We walk swiftly toward the bus stop. It's only when we're on the bus, some ten minutes later, and Robin has looked around once, twice, as if to double-check that there's no one in the same uniform sitting anywhere near, that she's prepared to say anything about her day.

"It was OK," she says. "OK. The art department is really good."

"That's great. How were the other girls?"

Robin exhales sharply through her nose but doesn't otherwise reply. I open my mouth to ask the question again but stop myself. "Zora is coming over tomorrow. She wants to hear all about it."

"All about what?"

"All about why we're here so fast, why I've sent you to Ashams..."

"Maybe you can tell me while you're at it," she says with a withering look and turns back to the window. She's not a little girl any more. Only ten, but I can already see the teenager she'll become, no traces of the toddler she once was, her profile tense against the gray afternoon light.

As soon as we get into the house, Robin slams up to her bedroom. I leave her to it. A couple of hours later, she comes downstairs and gives me a hug.

"The house is feeling a bit warmer," she says. "And my room looks much better. Thank you. I've started putting my stuff away."

It's the reward that I wanted; more than I could expect. I've done my best with Robin's room. The room I'm sleeping in—my mother's old room—is still horrible, but I don't dare yet go upstairs to my childhood bedroom on the third floor, preferring to sleep on the same floor as Robin. Keen to avoid those ghosts.

"Do you fancy pizza for supper?"

Robin's pleasure at the suggestion wards off any further discussion about the house. Her face softens and she spends the rest of the evening chatting enthusiastically about her old friends and their tribulations. Not so grown-up after all.

The next evening, Zora bursts through the front door, grabbing me in a massive hug before letting go of me to take hold of Robin. Then she turns to me, hugs me again. She smells exactly the same as she's always done—fags and a vanilla-scented perfume. Most people I know have given up smoking—not Zora.

Her work as a busy criminal solicitor gives her too much stress for her to be able to give up, she always argues.

"Look at you both," she says. "I can't believe I've got you home again."

"It's…interesting to be back," I say.

"I can imagine," Zora says. "I know you never wanted to come back here. It must feel as though life's completely collapsed for you. Are you OK?"

Robin and I nod, wordless, before Robin mutters something and scoots out, running upstairs to her room.

"And Andrew? How's he coping?"

"Let's leave talking about Andrew," I say, turning and walking toward the kitchen. "It's really hard. Why don't you come and have a drink?"

Zora follows me through and sits down at the kitchen table. She looks around with an approving expression on her face.

"It looks a lot better in here," she says.

"Thanks for keeping an eye on the place," I say, pouring wine into two glasses and putting one in front of Zora.

"I was happy to help," Zora says.

"And thank you for not asking too many questions. It's taken me ages to process it." I remember the phone call to her, my voice tense, anxious, trying hard to be businesslike after the bombshell of discovering the provisions of my mother's will. No quick sale as I'd assumed—a long-protracted agony while we decided whether to comply with her terms for the legacy, or see it pass into someone else's hands. I didn't tell Zora then, unable to put into words how controlling my mother had been. It was hard enough to ask her to help look after this house.

"So tell me," Zora says. "Why *are* you here? And why have you sent poor little Robin to that awful school we hated so much?"

Her words are harsh, but her face is kind. Zora's face is always kind—open, welcoming, lit up by a smile. Though she's not smiling now, her eyes full of concern.

"There's no need to go on," I say, topping up our glasses.

"There's every need to go on," Zora says, taking a large swig. "You swore blind you wouldn't do this."

I take a sip of wine. I haven't drunk for a couple of weeks and it's helping, warmth spreading through me. "I didn't have a choice. I had to leave, and my mother had it all stitched up this end."

"What do you mean? What does your mother have to do with it? She can hardly be controlling you from beyond the grave." Zora starts to laugh. I don't join in. After a moment Zora stops. "Dear God, seriously? She's still got her claws in? How the fuck has she managed that?"

"It's complicated."

"I'm not in any rush."

"I'm doing my best," I say. "I'm doing my best to make the best of a shitty situation. That's what I want you to have in mind. OK?"

"OK," Zora says. "I have it in mind. Now spill."

"You know she cut me off when I got pregnant?"

Zora nods. "I remember."

"I really tried to sort it out. I thought she'd come round after Robin was born, but she stayed so angry with me. She kept telling me how much I'd ruined my life by having Robin, how much I would regret destroying my future in all the years to come. It was horrible. I couldn't deal with the way she was talking about her own granddaughter. And she hated Andrew, too."

"I remember," Zora says.

"Well, when Andrew was offered the job in New York—it was the end. We left, I never spoke to her again. In our last row, she said if I left, if I chose family over career, I was dead to her from that point onwards. And that she was cutting me out of any inheritance."

"Wow!" Zora says, with a sharp intake of breath. "You didn't tell me that. Her own daughter..."

"She was never exactly maternal. This is the woman who would only answer to the name Lydia, remember? Not Mummy or Mother. I didn't want to think about it, to be honest. I was out of here—I was never counting on any inheritance anyway." I get up to my feet and gesture around me. "I mean, look at the place. You remember what she was like—tight as tight could be. I always thought there was no money, not really." I pause, drink some more wine.

"But?"

"Well, there is money. Some, at least. And the house."

"And she left it to you?" Zora says.

"Not quite. That's where it gets complicated. She's left the whole lot in trust to Robin—some investments, an income, the house."

"That's good, isn't it?"

"It's not as simple as that," I say. "It's only on condition that Robin goes to Ashams. Primary and to the end of secondary school." I think about telling her the full story, the way it was all forced on me at the end. But I can't deal with it. Not yet—the fear is too great still, those hours when Robin was missing, when I couldn't reach her or Andrew. It's bubbling underneath.

I take a deep breath, hold it. She's safe. We're both safe. I'm not thinking about it. I continue. "The whole thing is mental, really. Everything hung on there being a place available at Ashams in the first place—something she knew would be near impossible. Those places don't come up—you need to put the girls' names down for the primary school before they're born, even. The admissions officer practically laughed at me when I called to ask about availability the first time."

"Wouldn't she have thought of that?" Zora says.

"Yes. I think it was her way of leaving the money to us without any intention of us actually getting hold of it. An elaborate act of posthumous spite."

"I wouldn't put it past her."

"Me neither," I say. "So when this place at Ashams came up now...That's why I've had to send Robin there. Otherwise there would be nothing at all."

There's a long pause. Zora is shaking her head. I can't blame her. "It's fucking archaic. You should try and break the trust."

I almost laugh at the horror on her face. "I was thinking about it. Her solicitor, the one who drew up the will—he's the trustee, too, and he's not that much behind it. As long as Robin is at Ashams, the house will be held in trust for her, with a small income to support us both, and once she finishes at the secondary school, she'll get full possession and the trust will end. But if she leaves, or doesn't get through to secondary school, the house is forfeit. It'll be sold and we won't see any of the inheritance. The solicitor doesn't like it.

Apparently, he told Lydia not to do it. He's pretty much told me what I'd need to do to overturn the will. At least now we don't have to bother."

At this moment Robin comes into the kitchen.

"And now I'm stuck at this horrible school where no one talks to me," she says, clearly having overheard. "And we have to live in this horrible house."

"Robin, please..."

"I'm hungry," Robin says, turning away. "Is there anything to eat?"

I stop my explanation and make supper, cooking spaghetti and reheating a sauce I'd prepared earlier. I can feel Zora's eyes, though, boring into the back of my skull, and I know the questions haven't gone away.

6

Robin's mood softens a little during the meal and she chats to Zora about her friends in America, but she stomps upstairs as soon as the meal is finished. I put the plates over by the sink and Zora and I go through to the front room to sit on the misshapen sofa, bottle of wine in my hand.

"Robin doesn't seem to be coping with it all that well," Zora says, finishing her wine before reaching over and filling her glass up again. "And we haven't even got on to Andrew yet."

I don't want to talk about Andrew. Not now. Not ever. I stay silent, hoping that Zora will get the message and leave it alone.

"It must be really hard for her," Zora says. She looks at me closely, and I try to meet her gaze, but after a few seconds I turn my head away, swallowing hard to dislodge the lump in my throat. "It must be hard on you, too." Her voice softens. *Yes*, I think. *Yes, it is, and you don't know the half of it.* Zora doesn't ask any more.

Instead, she wanders around the living room. I follow her with my eyes, looking at the tired floral wallpaper, the chipped paint. There are shelves in the alcove next to the fireplace, full of old photographs and ornaments.

"I've been meaning to ask—what is it with these? They're unbelievably ugly," Zora says, lifting a figurine. She carries it over to me. It's one of a pair of statuettes, similar to the ones I dislike upstairs. Zora's figurine is of a mother holding a basket of fruit in her arms, laughing as a little boy helps himself to an apple. The other statuette is of a father leaning to offer a sweet to a little girl with her apron outstretched. The colors are saccharine sweet, pastel shades of blue and pink and green, the expressions on their faces nearly as sickly.

"She was obsessed with them," I say. "I used to love them when I was a child, though I'm not that keen now. I remember sneaking in to stare at them when she wasn't looking. I even dared pick one up once. But she caught me in the act—she shouted so loudly I dropped it and the head broke clean off."

"Fuck," Zora says.

"Exactly. It was the man. If you look closely, you can see where it was mended."

Zora puts down the female statuette she's been holding and turns the male one over in her hands, tracing the line of the mend with her fingers. "Why on earth did she like them so much?"

"I don't know," I say, "but she had that strange streak of mawkishness. She loved kittens and pink bows and fluffy stuff. Dolores Umbridge, you know?"

Zora nods. "Well, I don't like it. Any of it. This house needs stripping out completely and starting again. You need to get rid of all those memories, start building your own. If you're going to stay here, that is. Which I don't think you should, if I hadn't made it clear."

"You've made it abundantly clear," I say. "I don't have much choice, though. The only money I have at the moment is through doing what she told me to do: sending Robin to Ashams. I can't afford to live anywhere else right now. I'm going to have to sort it out."

"I mean, Robin at that school we both hated so much—Sadie, honestly. I hope you know what you're doing."

I don't have any words. "I will explain, I promise. And you will understand. I honestly didn't have any choice. But I'm exhausted. Can we leave it? Can you trust me that I'm doing the best I can?"

Zora glares at me, her eyebrows furrowed, but after a moment she relents and changes the subject. "Look, have another drink. I'll trust you. Is there anything cheerful we can talk about? Have you any work lined up?"

I slump further. "I thought we were going to talk about something more positive. I did try. I went in yesterday to tell the clerks that I wanted to come back. I was sure they'd have some magistrates' court work, at least."

"And?"

"Not a chance. It's the same senior clerk, David—do you remember?"

"David? That shit?"

"He's not a shit. He's just...old-fashioned."

"I remember you talking about him back in the day. And I deal with him regularly now. I instructed a couple of barristers from there in a fraud trial I had recently," Zora says. "He is definitely a shit. Didn't he give you all that hassle when you kicked that QC in the bollocks, the one who was trying it on with you? Pretty much told you to go along with what more senior barristers wanted to do, not to make trouble?"

Zora's memory is too good sometimes. I'd chosen to forget about David's reaction to that particular incident. "He wasn't great when that happened, no. But I did get tenancy in the end, so...Not that that's worth anything now. I've been out of it for too long. I have to reapply in writing to the tenancy committee. They'll look at it in March when they make the decision on all the applications that have been made to chambers for membership."

"That's months away," Zora says. "Do you have enough to live on till then? Is Andrew giving you enough support?"

I look at her. "It's complicated." A voice from a week ago hisses in my head, one I've pushed down all day. *Get the fuck out of here, Sadie. I don't want you. I don't want Robin either.* Support? After what's happened I'm not even sure I'll ever see him again. I know I never want to. My hands are shaking and I push them deep into my pockets.

"Sadie," Zora is saying. "You OK?"

With an effort I relax my features into a smile. "Sorry, I'm just tired."

"Look, I know you don't want to ask. But I could always sort you out with something. I send a lot of work to that chambers of yours," she says.

"You're right," I say. "I didn't want to ask. You've already done so much."

"Bollocks," she says. "I checked this shithole every now and again, that's it. I'm serious—I'll have a think about it, see what we've got coming up in the office. I'm not going to leave you languishing."

"I don't need any favors," I say.

Zora looks at me, and I look back, but I'm the first to lower my gaze. We both know that a favor is exactly what I need, however little I like the fact.

"You were bloody good at your job," Zora says. "It wouldn't be charity. You'll have to earn it."

I smile at her, raising my glass, and the rest of the evening goes fast.

When she finally gets up to leave, she says, "It's so lovely to have you back, you know. You and Robin. Even if your life is a bit fucked up right now." She hugs me. There's comfort to be found in her familiar smell.

"And I'm going to make sure you tell me what's happening. You can't fob me off forever," she says, releasing me with a shake. "I'll let you know about work as soon as I can."

Once Zora has departed in a cab, I go upstairs. I check in Robin's room, but she's not there. She's tucked up in my bed, small under the thin duvet. I feel a twinge in my chest again, sharp and insistent.

"You OK, sweetheart?" I say, sitting down on the bed next to her and putting my hand on the lump under the duvet.

"I guess," Robin says. She pushes her face out from under the covers. "I wish we could go home."

I start to speak, but she keeps going. "I'm sorry I was mad. I just wish it was all different, that's all."

"I know. I wish it was different, too. But we can make it work. I promise." I lie down next to her and hug her. "Are you going to sleep here, or are you going to go back through?"

"I'll go back. I just wanted to see you when you came up."

She gets out of bed and pads through to her own room. After she's settled, I kiss her good night before I stand by the door and look at the room. The paintwork is stained, the carpet shabby. But it's clean now, and warm. I'm getting there. Early days, but it's progress.

"I love you," I say to Robin, softly, and shut the door behind me. Then I cross the hallway and climb back into my own bed, pushing my feet into the spot that Robin has warmed.

SUNDAY, 6:07 A.M.

A crash, glass shattering. Thuds up the stairs. I know something's badly wrong before he's even through the door, a smell of sweat and fear carried before him. I'm frozen, hands tight by my sides as he crosses the room in three easy steps, pulls me out of my chair, swings me around. Something cold at my neck, his voice rasping in my ear.

"Get the fuck out of here. Or you'll never see her again. Time you fucked off back home."

I start struggling, wrestling to be free, but his arms have stretched, grown, wrapped all the way down my legs, my feet. I can't fight my way out as he turns into a snake, an anaconda, coils wrapped around me. I thrash from side to side.

I wake, the sheets over my face, stifling me. I pull them off, gasping for air, my heart banging hard in my chest. It's OK. A dream. It's not real. It never happened.

I throw off the sheets, go to her room to see her, calm myself. It's OK. I'm still half in sleep, the dream lying heavy on me. This'll calm me, to see her safe in her own bed.

But she's not there. And although I remember immediately through my haze of sleep that she's not missing, she's not even meant to be here, that same panic lands on me from the afternoon before, those hours she was missing, when I swore I'd do whatever it took to keep her safe if I ever got her home again.

One hundred and twenty minutes of dread, each one stretching to infinity whenever I think back to them.

I know it's different this time. But it takes long moments before my heart rate goes back to normal, her bed cold and empty in front of me.

At last, I return to my own bed, breathing in, out, in again. She's safe. I know she's safe. All is well.

And in time, I sleep.

7

Time passes. Drop-off, pickup, cleaning, weekends an oasis of calm. There's a pattern emerging, a rhythm to my days. No one talks to me on the school run; I prefer it this way.

And being overlooked has its uses. Left undisturbed, I'm beginning to work out who's who in the hierarchy around the gates. The loudest group centers around a blonde woman whose hair is always immaculately styled; the woman who nearly ran into me on the first day. Different-colored gym kit every morning, jeans and a long gilet in the afternoon, the hint of a white shirt collar sticking up around the front. The women around her stand enrapt as she speaks, their laughter hanging in the air for perhaps a couple of seconds too long.

A gust of laughs ripples over from them now as we wait to collect our children, and my shoulders stiffen before I force them down. I take my phone out and scroll through the news, doing my best to ignore them. It's nothing to do with me. Surely they're not laughing at me.

"You'd think people would at least have the courtesy to respond," one woman says loudly.

"You put so much work into these events, Julia," says another.

"It's rude," says a third.

There's a flurry of agreement.

"We shouldn't judge," a voice says firmly, putting an end to the chorus. "Maybe it was done differently where they were before."

I don't understand why, but it feels more and more as if these comments are in some way being directed at me. I steal a glance over the top of my phone and, for the first time, make direct eye contact with the tall blonde. Her blue eyes glare at me over the heads of her acolytes.

"Not everyone knows that they're meant to RSVP if they're sent an invitation," the same voice says again. It's her. I look away, fast.

Another woman strikes up. "But it's pretty obvious from your emails. You use that invitation app—all anyone needs to do is click Yes or No. They don't even need to explain."

So, the tall woman is called Julia. I risk another glance. The blue eyes are still piercing me. I shift on my feet, turn a little so that I'm not directly facing the group.

"I'm going to say something," says the sharp-voiced woman. I look up to find myself confronted by someone dark-haired, small and snappish, sparks of anger almost visibly flying off her.

"You're the mother of that new girl, right?" the woman says.

I blink.

"Robin. Year Six. Yes?"

"Um, yes."

The woman doesn't let me say any more. "It's extremely rude to leave invitations unanswered."

"What invitation?" I say, trying not to sound angry. "I don't know what you're talking about."

"What invitation? Oh, come off it. The invitation to the

drinks tonight. Which Julia has been kind enough both to organize and to host. And which you can't even be bothered to respond to."

"I haven't received any invitation."

The woman isn't listening to a word I say. "You should be grateful to receive invitations from someone like Julia. You've no business ignoring them. It's unbelievably rude."

She spins on her heel and strides back into her group of friends. I'm left standing, my mouth slightly agape, unsure what has just happened.

"That told her," I hear someone say from the group, and I stare at her, incredulous, before I look away, hoping to God no one else will talk to me before Robin comes out.

"Daisy's mom is really angry with you," Robin says as we sit down on the bus.

"Who?"

"Daisy's mom. She's the head of the PT something."

"The PTA?"

"That," Robin says. "She's organizing a party tonight and you haven't replied."

The events in front of the school gate suddenly start to make more sense.

"Do you know what Daisy's mom's name is?"

Robin looks at me blankly.

"No, of course not," I say, reaching my hand out to touch Robin's face. "Was it a better day today?"

"I don't know. Maybe. They did talk to me. But only to say how rude you are." Robin shrugs, dislodging my hand. "Why haven't you replied to the invitation? You always tell me we have to."

"We do always have to. I just haven't received an invitation, that's all."

"Daisy said her mom sent it specially. She wouldn't make it up," Robin says with such certainty that I can't say any more.

I go through my emails. Nothing in the inbox. I check my junk mail folder, with little expectation of finding anything, but then I see it, a tightness building in my throat. Robin was right. I was invited. A week ago.

As form representative and head of the school PTA, it gives me great pleasure to welcome you to Ashams School. It may seem a little unusual to be arriving in Year 6 rather than earlier, but we will make every effort to ensure that you and your daughter, Robin, feel as welcome at the school as possible. I am hosting a small drinks reception on Tuesday evening at 7:30 to celebrate the new term—perhaps you might be able to join us? Please do let me know.

All best wishes,
Julia Burnet

I hold my phone out to Robin, mute. She reads through it and gives it back.

"I told you you'd been sent an invite," she says, smiling. Then, "Tuesday. That's tonight."

"No wonder they were cross. Oh dear..."

"Email back and tell them you're coming. It'll be fun for you to meet the other moms," Robin says.

I bite my tongue. I keep looking through my junk mail to

check I haven't missed anything else important, and as I do so, a new one appears at the top of the list. From Julia Burnet. The same email address as before. I click on it.

Sadie, it reads. *Given your lack of response to my invitation I will assume that you are unable to attend tonight's drinks. I won't trouble you with further correspondence as you are clearly extremely busy. Julia*

I swallow. Not a good start.

"You should go, Mom. Daisy's probably the most important girl in the year," Robin says. Her voice is pleading.

"I can't. We don't have a babysitter. I don't have anything to wear."

"I don't need a babysitter," Robin says with a groan. "I'm nearly eleven."

The tension I feel in my chest is lessened by Robin's expression of offended dignity. She looks even more offended when I laugh at the idea of leaving her on her own.

"OK, Mom—let's ask Zora. And it might make it easier for me if you get to know the moms. Then they can't be nasty to me about you being so unfriendly, too."

Suppressing the thought that if the mums get to know me, it might make Robin's position worse, not better, I lean over and hug her.

"OK. We'll ask Zora. But I'm not going if she can't come."

Robin rolls her eyes, turns back to her phone. I text Zora, disappointed to see the message immediately picked up, the gray dots moving as Zora texts her reply.

Sure. With you by seven xx

My heart sinks, but I text back my thanks and tell Robin. I'm rewarded with a smile.

* * *

I throw some food together for Robin and email Julia, trying to hit a balance between nonchalance—*silly me, hadn't checked my junk mail*—and apology for the last-minute nature of my reply. I check the address she's given at the end of the email—I know the road, an exclusive terrace in Belsize Park. Throwing on some smarter clothes, I rush to get ready. It's nearly seven by now and I don't have the time or the inclination to wash my hair so I twist it up into a bun and pin it on the top of my head. Then I go to a mirror and apply foundation and concealer. I look less tired, at least.

A few minutes later and I'm ready to go. I'm wearing jeans, boots and a black silk top. Not too formal, not too casual—just right for drinks at someone's house. I run downstairs as Zora knocks at the door. We go into the kitchen where Robin is doing her homework. She gets up and gives me an encouraging hug.

"You look pretty, Mom," Robin says.

"Yes, you do," Zora says. "Stunning. You'll knock them dead."

If only I could. I don't say it, though. I smile at them both and hug Robin back before heading out of the door.

8

I'm late. No time for the tube. As soon as I see a cab with its light on I stick out my hand and hail it. As we head toward Belsize Park, I look out of the window, trying to calm my nerves.

"This it, love?" the cabbie says, pulling up in front of a long white terrace of houses, pillars on each side of the doors.

"I guess so," I say, paying him with the final twenty in my purse. "Thanks."

I take a deep breath and stride up to the front door, ringing the bell. There's no answer. I wait for a little, ring it again. Nothing. There's a large brass knocker on the door and I start to raise my hand, when the door opens. I stumble forward, heavily, into a girl about Robin's age, dressed in a plain red dress.

"Sorry, sorry," I say, straightening up. At least I haven't knocked the girl over.

"It's OK. Are you invited?"

"Yes, I am. I'm invited. I have it on my phone." I start to grapple for it. "Do you want to see?"

"I don't need that," the girl says. "But my mother asked if I could take people's names."

I laugh. "Do you get many gatecrashers at school drinks?"

"Mum says we need to be careful," the girl says with an earnest tone, and I feel bad for teasing her.

"It's Sadie. Sadie Roper."

She picks a piece of paper up from the hall table and runs her finger down it. She's going a bit pink in the face, distress building.

"Roper? Are you sure?"

"Yes, I'm sure."

The girl looks up at me, back down at the list. Shakes her head. Even the end of her nose has turned pink.

"I can't find you," she says. "I'm really sorry..."

I scroll through the emails on my phone and open the email from Julia, triumphant.

"Look," I say. "I told you I was invited."

The girl looks at the email, then back at the list.

"My mum didn't tell me what to do if someone wasn't on the list," she says. I feel even more guilty that I'm putting the girl in this situation.

"Look, I totally understand what your mum has said. But I think there's been some misunderstanding. It's my fault—I didn't RSVP till very late, so she must have thought I wasn't coming. Do you think..."

The girl is shaking her head before I even get to the end of my sentence.

"I'm not allowed to let you in," she says. "Mum said."

"But this is absurd. It's a school drinks party. Who the hell is going to gatecrash a school drinks party? I've shown you the invitation."

The girl's eyes start to fill with tears.

"It's OK, I'll go. I'll email your mum and explain tomorrow,"

I say, and turn to leave. As I reach the bottom step, however, someone calls after me.

"What's going on?"

It's the woman from the school gate. Tall, blonde. Angular. Julia herself.

"This lady is invited, but I couldn't find her name on the list. I'm really sorry," the girl says, her words falling over each other.

Julia laughs. She puts her arm around the girl and squeezes. The girl flinches a little at her touch. It looks affectionate but Julia's knuckles are white on the girl's shoulder. "I think you've been a bit over-literal, darling. I wasn't telling you to turn people away."

"I'm sorry..." the girl says, her face by now entirely flushed. It clashes with the red dress. "I didn't mean to..."

"It's entirely my fault," I say, keen for the situation to de-escalate. "You were just doing what your mum said." I climb back up the stairs.

Julia gives her daughter one final squeeze and lets her go. "Right. Well. Please will you go through and fill the glasses? People are running short," Julia says, and the girl runs off. I look up and find myself caught in the steel blue gaze.

"Sadie," Julia says, cracks of ice in her voice.

"Sorry I didn't reply—your message went into my junk folder. Maybe that's what's caused the confusion..."

She doesn't reply, stalks away from me toward the sound of voices. I scuttle to keep up. We walk down a hall, long and marbled, with a staircase sweeping up from the left of the front door, passing through a set of double doors into a large reception space. I can't help but compare it with the squalor of my mother's house, and I wonder how Julia would react if she found herself transplanted from this palace, its walls hung with gilded paper, crystal chandeliers suspended at each end of the room, into my relic of a home.

It's not just the walls that are gilded, either. Before I enter the throng, a waitress arrives in front of me and holds out a tray of canapés, quails' eggs cut in half and topped with caviar and gold leaf. They look delicious. I pick up two, shoveling them both in my mouth, before registering that the tray of food is virtually untouched. Perhaps I'm the only person to have taken any food at any point this evening, I think with growing horror, and I try fast to swallow the evidence of my greed.

Too fast. A piece of egg sticks in my throat and I cough, my face reddening, my eyes watering. I'm beginning to panic—the food is stuck in the back of my throat; I can't breathe. I'm spluttering now, bent over, trying to loosen the piece of bloody egg, goddammit how *could* this happen and then there's a sharp bash on my back, a thump straight between the shoulder blades, and the egg flies out of my mouth, straight onto the floor. I straighten up, wiping under my eyes, my cheeks flushed.

"Ladies, ladies," Julia says smoothly, appearing beside me. It's as though the whole egg incident never happened, though a waitress kneels in front of me, mopping up the floor. "Let me introduce you to our newest mother. Sadie Spence, mother to Robin who has just joined us."

I'm trying to look collected, but I'm still recovering from the shock of nearly choking, my eyes streaming, snot coming out of my nose. I can't see who hit me on the back—no one is offering me any help now that I'm upright. A trio of women gathers around me, smiling politely. I feel the heat fade out of my cheeks, wipe under my eyes, remembering only too late about the mascara that I must now be wearing all down my face.

"We are all going to make sure you and your daughter feel very welcome," Julia says. Her words are kind, but a chill runs through me. Then she turns. "I'll introduce you to everyone."

The rest is a blur. Julia whisks me from group to group, introducing me so fast that they start to meld together. Everyone is dressed smartly. Shame is growing inside me, a gnawing sense that I've got it wrong; my outfit felt chic and understated earlier, but now it looks cheap and lazy in comparison to the silks and taffetas that rustle in the room. My coughing fit has dislodged my hair from its bun and when I put my hand up to push it back, I can feel the grease against my fingers.

The acoustics of the drawing room are harsh and everyone around me is talking so it's difficult to hear either the names that are muttered at me, or the names of the daughters, Robin's classmates. Someone hands me a glass of champagne at one stage and I sip at it with relief, but the slight buzz I start to feel does nothing to help me work out who is who. I place the glass on a passing waiter's tray and take some water instead.

No one is drinking much, that's evident, and the food is barely being touched. Every single woman is thin, restrained, eating half a canapé before leaving the rest discreetly at the side of a plate, or wrapped in a napkin. As they stand in their little groups, the women look longingly at the food for a moment as it passes, before one of them declines and the others follow. Even though I'm starving, I don't dare risk eating anything else.

The last person to whom I'm introduced is a woman called Jessica.

"Is this the one who took, um...the empty place?" she says to Julia, not acknowledging me.

"I don't—" Julia starts to say, when there's a crash. I jump as liquid splashes up me. The woman on the other side of me has dropped her glass.

"So sorry," she says, mopping ineffectually at my arm.

Julia walks off, perhaps to find someone to clear up.

Jessica turns her attention to me. "It's a bit odd to be starting a new school in Year Six," she says. "Can't be very comfortable for your daughter. She's hardly going to be properly prepared."

I blink, taken aback by the directness of the comment. "It wasn't the original plan, but we didn't have much choice in the end. Prepared for what?"

Jessica is in her early forties at a guess. There is a fixity to her gaze, which suggests a certain amount of cosmetic work. She ignores my question and persists with another of her own. "Have you relocated?"

"We've been living in the States for the last few years, for my husband's work. In Brooklyn. He's in investments. But then...Well, the place here came up very suddenly, so we moved over," I say. I know the explanation is full of holes, but Jessica's eyes are glazing over as I speak, her lack of interest only too evident.

"I see," she says, a beat too late.

"I'm doing everything I can to make the move easy on Robin," I say.

"With the entrance exam coming up for the senior school, it's going to be difficult. I hardly imagine she's up to the same academic standard as the others. I hope the school won't be diverting too many resources to helping her catch up." Jessica smiles, her lips stretched tight over her teeth.

I'm stung. How dare she? "Oh, she's very strong academically," I say. "She was at an excellent elementary school, and she's very good at maths."

Jessica blinks, her eyebrows moving fractionally. I think she might be trying to frown, though the Botox isn't letting her. "Well, I'm sure you know best. We've all been preparing our girls for the last couple of years for the exam. It's very selective, you know. Just because you've been at the primary school, there's no guarantee of a place in the senior school. We're all anxious."

It takes a moment before her words fully sink in. Our entire living situation is dependent on Robin staying at Ashams. I hadn't realized her transition through the school might not be automatic. Great, another thing to worry about. I twitch my lips in an approximation of a smile. I want to bare my teeth at her. But before I can respond, there's a polite chink of fork tines against crystal and Julia addresses the room.

"First of all, I'd like to thank my amazing daughter, Daisy, for all her help this evening. She's a fabulous waitress, and what's more, a fabulous sous chef, helping me make all the canapés beforehand." Applause ripples through the air. I crane my head to see the girl in the red dress standing beside Julia, her smile fixed as her mother hugs her close.

Julia starts to speak again. "As you know, ladies, despite the huge pressures awaiting us over the next few months, we mustn't let it dominate everything. It's so important to keep some balance for the children—they deserve our fullest support in times of such academic pressure. We have to remember that despite the demands of the senior school entrance exam, the competition for places, we're not competing with each other here—we have to work as a team."

I'm not sure, but I could swear that someone snorts behind me. When I look around, all I see is a row of bland faces, expressions neutral as Julia continues her speech.

"So, there will be lots of chances to volunteer for activities this term. We've got the bake sale, the used uniform sale, and of course the Christmas Fair. And as usual, I'll be looking for lots of support. Let's make this our highest fund-raising term yet!"

There's a burst of applause. I clap along too though I think Julia's overstating the case of the entrance exam. Huge pressures and troubled times? Jessica turns back to me, perhaps to give me a chance to redeem myself. "Volunteering will be beneficial for you," she says. "A good way to get to know people. I always think how marvelous it is that we have such an active parents' association."

"God, no!" I laugh. "I hate school fairs. I did loads at Robin's last school—too much. That's why I'm so desperate to get back to work."

As soon as the words emerge, I realize this was the wrong thing to say. And the decisive way in which Jessica turns from me and walks away leaves me in no doubt at all.

9

Zora is no comfort at all. She smirks as I tell her what happened. I'm almost tempted to thump her, cortisol still coursing through me from the strain of the evening. I drown the urge in a large slug of wine, having poured myself a glass from the bottle that Zora has open on the kitchen table in front of her.

After downing half the glass in one go, I start to see the funny side of the evening a little more, and my fury passes. Zora is still looking unbearably smug, though, and after a couple more sips, I lean forward.

"Why do you have that hideous *I told you so* expression on your face?"

"Because I did tell you so," Zora says. "It was obvious from the start that they'd be dreadful. I don't know why you thought this school was a good idea, I really don't. We hated it thirty years ago—it was hardly likely to have got any better, was it?"

"Leave it, Zora. You know I don't have any choice. I'm really not in the mood. Can we talk about this another time?"

"But you asked me why I was looking so smug!" She leans back in her chair and folds her arms. "When exactly are we going to talk properly? You didn't come here just because of your mother's will. Your daughter's miserable—you're hating it too. Why the hell are you doing this? What's happened with Andrew?"

Her expression is as serious as I've ever seen it. All the years I've known Zora, all the times we've talked through our problems together...this is the first time that I've felt so reluctant to tell her what's happened.

"Why don't you want me to know, Sadie?"

I look at my friend, memories of all the conversations we've had before crowding through my mind. The times Zora persuaded me not to run away from home, to stay calm in the face of the strongest provocation from Lydia. The comfort she gave me when Lydia made it clear that I had to choose between having her as a mother or becoming a mother myself, potential estrangement not a threat but a promise.

"I haven't told anyone what happened."

"I'm your best friend, Sadie. You know you can rely on me. And I know you—there's no way you'd break your family up over something trivial. It has to be something big. Did you find him in bed with someone else?"

I shake my head. "I wish it were that straightforward. I mean, I think there is something like that happening, his behavior has been so off. But that's not why I left..." I take another deep gulp of my wine. I find I'm suddenly desperate to share the burden of what's happened. But fear still holds me reticent.

"But this is Andrew we're talking about. Andrew, product of a broken home, the most loyal man on the surface of this planet."

"As everyone says."

"Look, I'm not trying to shut you down. What did he do?"

I shuffle on my chair. I can tell her how it started, at least. "He became more and more distant from me, over the last couple of years. I can't remember exactly when I first realized—it was quite difficult after my mother died."

Zora grunts in sympathy. "I remember."

"And I couldn't put my finger on it, exactly. He was making all these long phone calls at night, locked in his study. He never left his phone lying around. And then he stopped looking at me."

"You what?"

"He stopped looking at me. We had a huge row two years ago when I found out about the will, what conditions Lydia had imposed. He thought we should jump at it. I said no. He was so awful that I did contact Ashams in the end, but they didn't have any spaces—as I told you. And shortly after that, he stopped making eye contact with me. It was as if I had ceased to exist."

"I don't understand."

"For the last couple of years, Andrew has refused to look at me. He's turned into Teflon, an impermeable surface. Perfectly polite, perfectly helpful, doing all the stuff we normally do. But he won't look at me."

Zora is silent.

"See, I knew you wouldn't understand."

Zora sits silent for a while longer.

"Aren't you going to say anything?"

"I'm not sure quite what to say," Zora says. "He was giving you the silent treatment? Is that what was happening?"

"No. Not the silent treatment. He talked to me. Or rather, he talked *at* me. He just didn't have anything solid to say. It was all meaningless. Admin. Food shopping. Nothing substantive."

"But he was still talking to you?" Zora says.

"Yes. But it was like he wasn't there. I tried, Zora. I tried everything. I tried suggesting date nights, cooked gourmet meals—I even tried to seduce him a couple of times." I fall silent, shame flooding into me, remembering the way he'd almost looked at me, a resigned kindness in his gestures as he handed me a dressing gown to cover myself before he turned away.

"Oh God, you mean you stopped shagging, too?"

I take a deep breath, nod. "I put it down to work pressures. I tried to blame the late-night calls on work, too. But then..." I pause. "Then, there were a couple of nights when he didn't come home."

"And?" Zora takes a drink, another.

"I followed him. I sent Robin off on a sleepover and I waited for him to leave the office and I followed him. This was just last week."

"Did you see anything?"

I look at Zora, but it's not her I'm seeing. It's Andrew, the back of his neck, the slope of his shoulders as he walked in front of me through the subway, the way he took the stairs out of the final station two steps at a time, bounding as if he couldn't wait to get to his destination. And the blonde hair of the woman he was meeting, standing under a shop entrance in the rain, bright against the gray afternoon.

I focus back on Zora and nod, once. She doesn't ask again.

"So, he's having an affair," she says with finality. "Did you really have to leave? Shouldn't you have stayed and confronted him?"

I look at her, bleak. "I did. I did confront him."

"What did he say?"

"He laughed, Zora," I say. "He just laughed at me. Then he walked out of the house. He disappeared for a couple of hours. His phone was switched off. And when he came back it was like he was a different person. Like someone else had taken control of his body."

I feel a chill thinking about it now, the coldness in his eyes, the way he looked at me as if I were a stranger. The first eye contact we'd made in months, and I was shriveling under his contempt. *Yes, I'm fucking someone else. And I want you gone. If you don't leave this weekend, take Robin with you, I'm going to take her away somewhere and you'll never see her again.*

I take a deep breath, repeat his words to Zora.

"Oh, come on," she says. "That's such bollocks. He couldn't do that."

"Maybe not," I say. "But I believed him. I couldn't stop him. He showed me as much, the following day. Someone collected Robin out of school with his permission—a blonde woman, she told me afterward—delivered her to Andrew, and he kept her out for a couple of hours incommunicado. Both of their phones were off. No one had seen them. I was going spare."

"That sounds pretty bad," Zora says.

"It was the worst evening of my life," I say. "You'd think it would be amazing, seeing her come home safe, but that was almost the scariest moment of all. He had convinced her it was all entirely normal, just a treat at the cinema for the evening—he'd even persuaded her to switch off her phone so they could be uninterrupted. She came skipping in and I couldn't say anything I wanted to say. I didn't want to freak her out. That's when I realized I was going up against something I didn't even understand. By then, I'd had the offer of the place for Robin, the house—can you really blame me for coming here?"

She looks at me for a moment and sighs. "I guess I think you should have stood up to him. But at the same time... That must have been terrifying, not knowing where Robin was."

I shudder, remembering the way I ran back from the school when I realized Robin was missing, trying to call them both over and over again, my imagination running away with me at the thought of what might have happened to her.

"It was all designed to drive us here. That was the other thing—he'd spent the whole evening telling her about the brilliant new adventure she was about to have, that moving to the UK was going to be great, that it was all decided, and both he and I were really happy about it. So when she came back, she was resigned to the move. What could I do? I could hardly tell her what a bastard her dad is. It was the last straw. I've put up with him for ages. But it's not there. There's nothing there any more."

She keeps looking at me. "It just doesn't make any sense, though. Why would he behave like that?"

"I have no idea, Zora. Literally no idea. He's changed more than you would believe. He's not the man I married."

I stand up, straight in front of Zora. She averts her head.

"You're not looking at me either," I say, waiting for a response. Zora keeps her head down. The air lies solid between us. She sighs, leaning back into the sofa.

I turn my back, busy myself with a second bottle of wine. I don't turn around until I'm sure my expression is under control. When I've finally topped up her glass, I sit back down.

"Anyway," she says. "Let's change the subject. I think I've got you some work."

All my animosity slides away. "Really?"

"Really. There's a trial coming up, a grooming case at a school in central London. Male teacher, female pupil. He's the son of a judge and they're paying. Barbara Carlisle is leading the case. You remember, the QC?"

"I saw her the other day when I went into chambers," I say. "Though I kept my head down."

"Well, we've been served a whole load more evidence to go through. The case itself is straightforward enough, but someone needs to go through all of this, and it's not going to be Barbara. I was going to get someone in the office to look after it, but she's agreed that it might be helpful to get a junior, so..."

I've moved from wanting to shake Zora to giving her a big hug, slopping wine from her glass down my top as I do so. "When do I start?" I say.

"I'll take it that's a yes," she says, laughing.

"Yes. Yes, please," I say. "I'd love to. The only thing is, which court? I haven't organized any after-school childcare yet."

"You've only just got here," Zora says. "Give yourself a break. It's at Inner London. Straight down the Northern Line to Elephant and Castle—it'll be fine. I'm not sure when they'll want you, exactly. I'll send out the instructions tomorrow, and after that it'll be up to Barbara to get in touch with you. I imagine it'll be pretty soon, though. There's a lot of material to go through."

"I owe you for this," I say. "I really do. I can't wait to get back into court. I've missed it so much."

"It's about time. It's such a shame all you women barristers fuck off as soon as you have babies, you know."

"They don't make it easy," I say. "I could hardly go off at the drop of a hat to cover a two-week gun trial in Nottingham, could I? Andrew wouldn't give up work to stay at home."

"I suppose not," Zora says. "Anyway, it'll be good to have you back at the bar. I'm looking forward to working with you again."

"Me too," I say, and I hug her again. This time, I don't spill her wine.

SUNDAY, 9:35 A.M.

Another nightmare. Formless, shapeless; dread looming over me, swirling up over the horizon. I wake, my eyes heavy, horror close.

Coffee, shower, my senses twitching. Shouldn't they have called by now? Isn't it time she was home? I want her home, that's for sure. The house is too quiet without her.

Another coffee. Nerves still tingling.

If only I could press a button, see where she is on a screen... But, no. I won't be one of those mothers. I'm not a helicopter. No stealth reconnaissance for me—no tags, no trackers. I won't let what happened destroy my trust. Nor my peace of mind.

That's a joke. I'm a cat on a hot tin roof, skittering from room to room, the emptiness too loud. Once she's home I'm never letting her out of my sight again. Find My Friends, Life360—I'll get a tag implanted in her arm if I can.

Time passes. Slowly, slowly, no matter what I do to try and fill the time. I pick up my phone, put it down again. It's still early. Too early. It's not time to worry yet. It'll never be time to worry. That was then, this is now. She's had a lovely weekend away and she's on the way back home. Everything is fine.

A cat howls outside and I jump, resume pacing, one window to the next as I wait, and wait.

10

"You choked on a bit of egg?" Robin says as we sit on the bus to school the following day.

"Yes."

"And everyone else was in skirts and dresses?"

"Yes," I say. "You don't need to rub it in."

"Ouch," Robin says.

I laugh, and for the first time I feel better about the evening. *Ouch* is the best response.

"And Daisy's mom's house is really good?"

"Yes, it's lovely. I told you all this already," I say. I might be feeling a bit better about what happened, but it doesn't mean I want to dwell on it.

"Who did you talk to?"

"I'm really not sure. There were so many names. Someone called Jessica." The memory of Jessica's scorn scores straight through me.

"I think that's Portia's mom," Robin says. "Portia's one of The Group."

"Right," I say, storing the name away, still desperate for any information about school that Robin might give, while not wanting to show that desperation. "What is The Group?"

I wait for Robin to bite my head off rather than replying, but instead of a rebuff, Robin thinks about it for a moment. "They're the ones who decide who talks to who and who sits where."

"But you can't let other people tell you what to do!" The words burst out of me before I can stop them.

"Mom," Robin says, her face averted.

"Seriously, though. There can't be some central committee that decides who gets talked to. That can't be on. I'm going to speak to the school about this," I say. Panic is beginning to build, rage too, my breathing coming fast. "Are they telling people not to talk to you?"

Silence from Robin. Her face is still turned away from me.

"Robin, look at me. Are they telling people not to talk to you?"

"Promise me you won't go into school." Her tone is pleading and I give up.

We don't speak again until we're around the corner from school. Robin strides away from me without even saying goodbye. I'm left blinking, concern seeping up through my bones.

I take my phone out of my pocket, hoping to find that there's been a message from chambers about the trial, when two women walk past me, one of them catching my elbow so hard I drop my phone. As I bend to pick it up, I hear one of them laugh, another making a hushing sound. I get to my feet and stick my phone straight into my pocket, ready to blow up. The two women have turned to face me. One of them is Jessica from the party.

"There's a coffee morning tomorrow to discuss the Christmas Fair, amongst other things. But I don't suppose you'd be interested," she says, "as you hate volunteering." The woman to Jessica's left giggles.

I feel heat rising in my cheeks. I want to tell them to piss off, but the thought of Robin comes into my mind. I know she wants me to make more of an effort. "I'll be there. Where is it?"

Jessica and her friend look at each other, raising their eyebrows.

"Good of you," Jessica says. "I'll email. It's not fair on Julia that she has to do everything."

And without another word, the two women walk away. I stand on the corner, a little dazed, my hands clenched tight in my pocket. It's only when I feel a sudden pain in my palm that I realize that the glass of my phone must have shattered. I look at my hand—there's a small ooze of blood, nothing more. I need to be more careful.

By the time I've had the screen of my phone mended and tidied up the house, it's almost time to collect Robin from school. I'm getting my coat on when my phone starts to ring.

"Miss Roper? It's Kirsten Glynn. From chambers."

"Yes, this is Miss Roper. Hi, Kirsten."

There's a pause.

"The details are all sorted now, miss. Zora Gaunt has been in touch. Not sure how much you've been told, but you're going to be junior in this trial to Barbara Carlisle, QC—you remember her from your time in chambers?"

"Yes, I do." I can feel the tension drain out of me, my shoulders sinking down from where they were hunched tight up to my ears. At least one thing is going right.

"Well, she's doing an abuse of trust case. Defending a teacher accused of having a fling with one of his pupils."

"How old is the pupil?" I say.

"Seventeen," Kirsten says. "Barbara was going to do it on her own, but there's been a recent disclosure of a lot of extra material and someone needs to go through it. It's a good case. Starting next week."

"Yes, Zora filled me in a bit. That sounds great."

"Good. You OK to come tomorrow morning? About ten?"

"Yes. That's absolutely fine. I'll see you then," I say.

I sit at the kitchen table, triumphant. It's work. A proper trial. I'm going to be back in chambers. Back in court. From this case, other cases will follow. Maybe things are going to fall into place.

This positive feeling lasts me all the way through from picking Robin up, the journey home, and a basic meal of pasta and tomato sauce. It even survives Robin's silence, which lasts for the entirety of the evening, keen to avoid any conversation about her day as she hides in her room, only emerging to scoop the food up quickly from behind her hair before disappearing upstairs again. I know I should try to talk to her, but she so clearly wants to be left alone that I don't have the heart to force the issue. I stand outside her room and listen to her chatting on FaceTime to her old school friends, little chirps of noise with the occasional laugh, the worry fading from my mind.

All positive feelings leave me when I open an email, late in the evening, that spells out the details for the coffee morning.

> *8:30 a.m. at Café Marché, private room at the back. We will be discussing the Christmas Fair and other events—bring your thinking cap!*

8:30 a.m. When I'm due in chambers for ten. I've had so little to do, no appointments, nothing to do but drag poor Robin to and from school, and now, just when it's about to be sorted out, I have to be in two places at once. I hold my head in my hands for a moment, before shaking it clear. This isn't a problem. I can go to the coffee morning for twenty minutes, offer to look after a stall or whatever it is the parents are after, then nip down on the tube and I'll be in time. And if I phone chambers to let them know in advance, surely Barbara won't mind. It's not like I'm in court; it'll be fine. I almost believe my own reassurances.

But that night I barely sleep, torn between the two scenarios, an endless spiral of anxiety. At 4 a.m., when I've convinced myself that the other mothers are going to laugh me out of the café and that Barbara and Kirsten are going to link arms and prevent me from entering chambers in the first place, yelling *you're late, you're late*, I give up on the idea of sleep and get up, wrapping myself in a blanket on the hard sofa in the living room and staring at the wall until it's time to wake Robin.

11

Robin is chattier on the way in to school. I do my best to avoid asking any questions that might upset her, eggshell delicate. Even though most of what she says relates to her former school friends, not the current setup, I'm relieved that she's a bit more cheerful. Children are adaptable. Even her voice is starting to change, the slang from her elementary school employed less often, the slight American accent fading away. She leans closer to my arm than usual on the bus and I lean sideways against her a little, too, though not too much, trying hard to maintain the fragile balance between us.

I stand up first when the bus comes to the right stop, Robin close behind me, and as the bus pulls to a halt, she takes hold of the handrail directly in front of my face. I don't register anything at first, but then I focus more closely on Robin's fingernails. They're bitten to the quick, ragged and bloody around the edges, as if she's been pulling at the skin as well as chewing down on the nail. I put my hand out, covering her fingers, trying not to show Robin that I've noticed. Her fingers twitch and when the bus finally stops, she pulls her hand away. As soon as we get off the bus, she walks away without saying goodbye. Balance is restored. But not in a good way.

I sigh and make my way to the coffee morning, dread in my soul.

I sit in the private room at the back of the café, picking at a croissant I've taken from a huge pile arranged on the large wooden table. The table is surrounded by women I half recognize from the drinks party, though I don't remember many names. They clearly can't remember mine, either; only a couple of people said hello when I arrived. The only ones I can name for sure are Julia and Jessica, who's fussing around the plate of breakfast pastries, rearranging piles and moving items to fill in any gaps. Not that there are any gaps to fill—like two nights ago, I'm the only person eating.

The two women are sitting next to each other, discussing something between themselves, their voices low. I can't make out what they're saying, hard as I try to hear it across the table, but at one point it looks as if it might be a disagreement, Jessica's face is turning red, her lips pursed, as Julia speaks with what appears to be great emphasis, though her words are still inaudible.

I smile in a hopeful manner every time anyone so much as glances in my direction, but no one bothers to acknowledge me, their eyes sliding over me as if I'm not there. I take out my phone so as not to look like too much of a spare part and check the time. Twenty to nine already.

I clear my throat, screw up my nerve. "Sorry, excuse me for interrupting. I was just wondering…Are we likely to get started any time soon? Only I—"

"We are waiting for the others."

"Others?"

"There are still a couple of others to come. So sorry if we're keeping you from something more important," Julia says, her tone withering.

"It's very important that everyone is here," Jessica says. "We like to do everything together, in this year."

"Of course," I say, trying to sound placatory. Clearly without success. Jessica does not look placated, twitching her top lip and crossing her arms across her chest. She stares at me for a moment longer before her attention is drawn by a movement at the door.

"And here they are," she says.

The new arrivals lean in toward the food, lean away. Julia clears her throat and picks up a clipboard.

"First things first. I am suggesting that we make it an absolute rule that we do not discuss anything that relates to the considerable pressures we are facing. Nothing is more important than that we maintain unity for the sake of our girls. Are we agreed on this?"

Murmurs of assent. I glance discreetly at my mobile phone—fifteen minutes until I absolutely have to leave.

Julia continues. "As I said on Tuesday night, we have a big target to beat this year at the Christmas Fair. We will need to work extremely hard to ensure that we get there."

Another ripple of agreement emanates from around the table, precisely highlighted heads nodding in unison. But before Julia can continue, she's interrupted.

"I'm sorry, do we have a new parent here? There's someone I don't recognize."

I turn to look at the speaker, a woman with honeyed highlights wearing a sports top and leggings, Lycra hugging her close. The woman is looking aggrieved.

No one answers, and I slowly become aware that all eyes

are fixed on me. I shift in my chair, uneasy at the scrutiny, waiting for Julia to introduce me. No introduction comes. I try and sit it out but the suspense becomes unbearable.

"I'm Sadie. Robin's my daughter. She's just started," I say, my voice squeaking by the end.

"How did you manage to get a place? Was it because of—" More shushing. More forceful this time. I don't see who has asked the question.

"I, we had a change of situation. I've moved into town with Robin. We called, and it turned out there was a space. It was all very last minute," I say. "I've no idea why a place was available. I guess people move around." I gaze around at the faces watching me.

"I guess they do," Julia says. "Can we get back to the subject in hand, please?" She paints a smile on her face. "We've decided that the theme for this year's fair is going to be...Jingle Bells! It will be up to each of the stallholders as to how this is interpreted." Stirrings round the table. "I will be allocating stalls depending on school years, as usual—and I'll circulate a list in due course. As a new introduction, I am considering extending the fancy-dress competition to include a parents' category." The stirring becomes more noticeable.

It must be nearly nine by now. Julia is mid-flow. I feel utterly trapped. Of course it's more important that I get to chambers, but I've already got off to such a bad start with these people. I can hardly walk out mid-discussion. I pull my phone out to check the time again, when I become aware that the room is silent. I look up to find Julia staring straight at me, her eyebrows raised.

"No phones, please. We have a strict no-phones policy during these meetings," Julia says.

"Yes, sure, I was just—"

"Put it away, please," Julia says, a smile of great sweetness on her face, but with so much force that I do exactly what I'm told, pushing the phone far down into my jacket pocket.

Julia nods in approval, and keeps talking. "What we need to get together now are raffle prizes and also volunteers to head up each of the stalls. Form reps, will you be able to get names to me by the end of the week?"

The heads nod in unison, hands scribbling furiously in notebooks.

"Sadie, will you be able to coordinate raffle prizes? That should be reasonably straightforward for you, and it'll give you a good chance to talk to lots of people at school," Julia said.

"I couldn't possibly," I say, the words coming out before I can bite them back. So much for trying to make a good impression.

Everyone looks around at me again, skewering me with their glares. Jessica is so exercised she practically bounces in her chair: "I was hoping to do this. I've put together some fantastic ideas."

I attempt a smile. "Jessica would be much better than me. I don't have the first idea who to approach."

Julia looks over at me, then at Jessica, her expression thoughtful. "I was hoping you might take charge of the stall coordination, Jessica—you did such a good job last year. Perhaps you can discuss your ideas with Sadie and she can take it forward?" She looks at Jessica, who nods, evidently torn between delight at the compliment and fury that I've been offered the job she wanted. She shoots me a dirty look.

"Good, so that's settled," Julia says, moving on to the next job as if my involvement is a done deal. I deliberate for a moment, reluctant to be aggressive this early on. But I'm more reluctant still to get dragged into such a painful task with someone who so clearly does not want to work with me. I clear my throat and interrupt Julia.

"I'm sorry," I say, "but I'm not going to be able to help with this. I have a new job starting—today, actually. I'm going to sit this fair out and get a better idea of what to do and who people are. I'll definitely volunteer next term."

Julia looks at me in complete astonishment. I wonder when was the last time someone said no to her. She moves quickly on, handing more responsibilities to eager attendees, and calls the meeting to a close. I jump to my feet, keen to make a swift exit, though I look around to check I'm not too obviously the first to leave. The piles of food are still barely touched, but there's a woman on the opposite side of the table picking flakes off a croissant, crumbs on her lip. I'm transfixed, staring at the woman prepared to show the weakness of hunger to the group. The woman catches my eye and smiles. I flush, look away. There's laughter from another part of the table and I make a dash for it, nearly out of the door when Jessica calls me back.

"You haven't paid yet," she says.

"Oh sorry—I hadn't realized. Here. A fiver should cover it?" I dig in my bag and pull out a crumpled note. Jessica looks down her nose at it.

"It's thirty pounds, please."

"How much?"

"Thirty pounds. We need to cover the food."

"But no one ate the food..." I mutter. I dig around and find some more notes, thrust them into Jessica's hand. I turn to go, but as I do, I catch sight again of the mountains of uneaten pastries, and before I can control the urge, I pick up a napkin and stuff it full of croissants and pains aux chocolat. I hear the women murmuring around me, but I've had enough now, the thirty quid is the last straw—I'm bloody well going to take some away with me.

"Goodness," someone says behind me.

"What do you think you're doing?" Jessica says.

"Taking some of the pastries I've just paid for," I say, my chin jutting out. "Is that allowed?"

"Well, I mean, it's rather unusual. Not the kind of thing..." Jessica's words trail off. "Julia. Julia! This new mother wants to take a doggy bag."

"A doggy bag?" Julia says, her eyebrows raised. "I'm sorry?" She looks at me, disdain dripping from her. I clutch on to my napkin of patisserie, holding her gaze firm. After a moment, Julia looks away, flicking her hair with a gesture of contempt.

"Normally," she says, "our leftovers would be given to the homeless shelter. I know they are always extremely grateful. But perhaps your need is greater."

"I didn't want them to go to waste," I say. "But I don't want to cause any trouble."

"No trouble at all. Here—I have a bag with me. I'll empty out my papers. You must take more."

And with that, Julia picks up a bag emblazoned with designer labels and tips its contents out onto the table before shoveling pastries and bagels by the fistful into its capacious depths. She empties every platter on the table, filling the bag so full the food is spilling over the top. When it's about to burst, she hands it to me with a smile.

"Here. That should keep you going."

I smile back at her, but I can feel the blood rushing to my cheeks. Nodding a thank you, I reach over to take the bag, ready to walk out as if this is all perfectly normal. But as I'm about to take it, I hear a peal of laughter from a corner of the room. It breaks off quickly, but not quickly enough. As I take hold of the handle, my hand touches Julia's. My nerves are so on edge I jerk my hand, jump backward and the contents of the bag spill out all over the floor.

For a moment it's as if time has stopped; Julia and me standing over the ruins of the breakfast buffet. I open my mouth but all that comes out is an incoherent stutter, and I flee, not even bothering to try and dodge the debris all over the floor, still clutching the napkin full of food.

It's only when I'm outside that I realize a huge chunk of pastry is impaled on the heel of my shoe. I try to clean it off against the edge of the pavement, but a thick smear of chocolate wedges itself into the gap between shoe and heel, defying all my efforts to scrape it clean.

12

By the time that I get into chambers it's nearly half past ten. I've run from the bus stop and the blood is pounding behind my eyes. I greet Kirsten on reception with an apology, but the girl just laughs and tells me to sit down.

"Barbara isn't in yet, either. I won't take you up to her room until she's here, if you don't mind. She won't be far away."

The panic was wasted, then. I go over to the long leather sofa in the waiting area, still inexplicably clutching the napkin of pastries. I look around in vain for a bin before returning to the reception desk.

"Is there somewhere I could chuck these out?"

"Sure," Kirsten says. "I'll bin it."

She reaches over for the napkin and I hand it to her, suddenly reluctant to give up my prize. She looks at the food inside.

"What's wrong with these?" Kirsten says.

"Nothing, I guess. They're a bit squashed. I don't really have anywhere to put them, though."

"They look good to me. I'm going to make a coffee and have one—do you want to join me while you wait?"

I'm so defensive from the coffee morning that I'm about to say no, suspecting she's laying a trap for me, when I see that her expression is entirely without guile, enthusiasm lighting up her face. Something unknots inside me. "Yes, please. I'd love a coffee. Do you have any plates?"

There's an espresso maker at the side of reception, and Kirsten goes over and makes two coffees, grabbing saucers for the pastries. She joins me on the sofa and we eat together. Once I've finished, I wipe the crumbs off my mouth and drink some coffee before clearing my throat.

"Do you know anything about this trial? Have you met the defendant?"

"Oh, yes," Kirsten says. "He's been in for one conference already. Such a polite man. It seems like such a shame. I don't know how that girl can live with herself."

"That girl?"

"The victim. So-called. She should be ashamed of herself, destroying someone's life like this," Kirsten says. She's finished her first pain au chocolat and is tucking in to a second.

Before I can respond, the door into reception opens. Kirsten moves at a speed I wouldn't have thought possible to tidy away the plates and brush the crumbs from her lips, returning to her seat behind the desk with a polished smile.

Barbara Carlisle walks in. This time I'm not hiding from her—I face her straight on, looking at her properly this time. Taller than average, thinner too, she hasn't changed much at all in the last ten years, only her hair is steelier and the vertical lines around her mouth more pronounced. I try to tidy myself up, conscious of the flakes of pastry I'm wearing. I'm still shaking detritus off my skirt when she comes to stand in front of me, a smile lifting one side of her face.

"Sadie, I'm glad to have you aboard. You're not running away from chambers now, I hope!"

"Um, yes, sorry about that..."

"Why don't we go to my office and I'll get you up to speed with the case."

She turns and walks through the reception doors, not waiting to see if I'm behind her. I wave a hand at Kirsten, mouthing *thanks* at her as I trot to keep up with Barbara.

One flight of stairs, another. We turn down a corridor that I remember only too well from my earlier years in chambers—in this room on my left, I sat with my first pupil supervisor; in that, I prepared my first trial. I move swiftly past the memories, through the dark wooden door that Barbara is holding open for me at the very end of the corridor.

"Here we are," she says. "Forgive the mess. I've been trying to get on top of a couple of briefs. You can see why you're needed."

I look around. There are papers and books loose on every available surface; the floor is also covered. The room's reasonably light, at least, lit at one end by a high window looking out over Essex Street, but there's dust and several piles of books leaning precariously on the windowsill. Sounds of traffic permeate through the open window. And despite the ban on smoking, there's a strong smell of cigarettes in the air.

As if to answer my unspoken question, Barbara pushes the chair behind her desk over to the window and sits down, lighting a cigarette with a silver lighter and inhaling deeply before holding it out of the open window. I try to control my expression, but I'm not deadpan enough for her, trained as she is by years of examining witnesses to spot the smallest tell.

"Who do you think is going to tell me to stop?" Barbara says with a throaty laugh.

"No good my saying it's not good for you, I suppose," I say.

"Darling, I'm sixty-five. It hasn't killed me yet," she says, holding the pack out to me.

It's tempting. Almost. The rasp of the match, the flare of the flame as it catches, the sweet smell of the first fumes before they turn heavy and stale. But I can't. "No, no thanks. I don't. I gave up when I was pregnant. Never started again. I don't dare. I can't do it by halves."

"Ah yes, of course. You had a baby. Your career was about to take off, and you got pregnant and disappeared off to America. Don't you think it was rather a waste?"

I blink, surprised at the directness of the question. She couldn't be more different from the mothers I've left up in St. John's Wood, all done up tight in their sports gear.

"Come on," Barbara says. "Sit down and tell me all about it. I've never understood it in any of you girls. There you were, one of our brightest young tenants, crown court trials rolling in, and you chuck it all in for a baby. All seems rather a shame, if you ask me."

I clear papers from the second chair in the room, put them on the floor. I sit down, taking my time before I say anything. Though it's been well over ten years, Barbara's drawl is still so familiar. It's surreal being back in chambers. Even the smell of Barbara's cigarettes is the same, fighting for supremacy against the perfume with which the barrister has always doused herself; a powerful scent exactly the same as those years before. I open my mouth to speak, the years falling away.

"Yes. It was a shame. I'm not sure I'd make the same decision now."

"There's always something, every year," Barbara says. "One of the pupils cracks. Usually it's getting slaughtered and falling over in a chambers' party. Or telling the wrong person to fuck off. You were one of the sensible ones, though. I thought you'd be here for the duration."

My guard shoots back up. The waves of memory have receded. I remind myself of the cloud of malice that has always lurked not far behind Barbara's head.

"It's not the easiest, having a baby and having to travel so much to court. Besides, my partner got an offer too good to refuse in the States. That's why we moved."

Barbara's mouth twitches with disdain. "You were doing so well. I can't imagine what offer might be too good to refuse that required you giving up all those years of hard work. It's a shame his career had to take precedence over your vocation," she says with a snort. "At least you're back now. I assume he's going to take over the childcare?"

"He's still in the U.S.," I say. "We've separated."

Another snort. "I'm not surprised. You should have dumped him years ago—you've wasted the last decade of your life. At least you haven't left it too late to get back to work. Honestly, these women with so much promise, degrees from the best universities, brilliant practices, and they give it all up to go off and have children. We never see them again. Ridiculous."

I blink. I can see her point. I've raged about it silently over these years. But surely Barbara can't be so blind to the realities of the situation, the difficulties faced by parents in such an inflexible working environment, the demands of court and the cab-rank rule taking precedence over all other considerations.

"It's complicated," I say in the end. "I don't regret having my daughter in any way, but I'm glad to be back. And very grateful to have the opportunity to work on this case with you. Can you tell me anything about it?" It's time to move the conversation on.

Barbara snorts again, perhaps unsure as to whether she has finished her cross-examination of me, but I smile brightly, hoping that it might discourage her from going on any more. After a moment, she lights another cigarette and shuffles through some papers.

"I'll give you a brief chronology of the case. For what it's worth. I've never seen such nonsense in all my life," she says, settling back in her chair.

13

I pull a file at random out of one of the boxes that Barbara's given me to go through—screenshots from a Facebook page, a series of photographs of the complainant in the case. She's young, laughing, arm around a friend in one, posing in a fedora in another. I look more closely at the dates of the post. The girl would have been in her early teens. Just a child. In the third photo she's pouting, a feather boa draped seductively around her neck. But still just a child, playing dress-up.

I lean back in my chair, shut my eyes. As soon as Barbara finished her narrative, she headed out for lunch, so I have the room to myself. I need to piece together what I've been told, block out the feeling of compassion for the complainant that's crept up on me. I have to concentrate on finding the best way to serve our client's interests.

He's a lovely man, Kirsten said.

I feel very strongly about this case, Barbara said. *There's a significant danger of grave injustice here. We will have to fight very hard on this.*

I rehearse the facts as I've been given them in the papers and Barbara's brief account: Freya MacKinley, now seventeen, has had a troubled life, despite its brevity. She has been problematic for some time, both at school and at home: inattentive, undisciplined and very resistant to all authority. Her years at primary school passed without undue issue, and at one stage, she showed great academic promise. But she failed to gain a place at any of her preferred secondary schools, according to a report provided by her former headteacher, and she ended up at a private secondary school renowned more for its socializing than its academic standards. From Year 7 onward, her attitude at school deteriorated, and when her parents divorced when she was thirteen, the problems increased. She was the first in her year to experiment with cigarettes and alcohol, then cannabis, and harder drug use was suspected, though never established.

Freya narrowly avoided expulsion on a number of occasions, leniency only being shown in consideration of her parents' very hostile divorce. It's clear, though, that even by the school's lax standards, she was heading for academic disaster, when she was taken under the wing of Barbara's client, one Jeremy Taylor, a French and English teacher in his mid-twenties. He also taught drama, and through Freya's reluctant participation in a production of *The Taming of the Shrew*, he managed to create a good enough connection with her that she agreed to extra tuition from him. Through this, she managed to pull herself together enough to be heading toward a very creditable set of results in her GCSEs.

Up to this point, both prosecution and defense largely agree on the facts. But from here, the stories begin to diverge. According to the prosecution case, Taylor had been tutoring Freya in more than irregular verbs. They say that from the beginning, he had been grooming her for a sexual relationship, which came to fruition after her sixteenth birthday, and continued until he tried to end that relationship, whereupon she went straight to the police with her account, which forms the basis of the charges now laid against him.

On the other hand, the defense version of events is that Jeremy felt sorry for the girl and did his best to help her. She was persistent in making small advances toward him, but he was reluctant to give up on her as he felt that she had some potential, and was sorry for her. He ensured on all occasions that the tutor sessions were held in public places, and that her mother was copied in on all correspondence. Despite his best intentions to help her, however, the matter reached a head when during a tutorial session taking place in her house, she stripped off her clothes in an attempt to seduce him. At this point he terminated the arrangement, and in rage and hurt at the rejection, Freya went to the police with her allegations. He denies entirely any sexual or romantic relationship between them.

I rub my eyes. It's a simple story, a simple defense. It'll all come down to who is the most credible on the stand. I leaf through the photograph printouts until I find a more recent shot of Freya, from earlier this year. She's older, expression more wary, her eyes not quite looking into the camera. Still a child, though, still an air of inexperience, of innocence about her. I read again the description that Jeremy has given of her—it doesn't chime with the photograph. Perhaps the case won't be as simple after all…

Are there any photos of the defendant? I start to look through but give up, defeated by the paperwork. He inspires warmth, though, that much is clear from both Kirsten and Barbara's reactions to him. And I'll be able to judge for myself soon enough, when he next attends chambers for a conference with Barbara.

In the meantime, my job is clear. I have to go through the reams of messages from Freya's phone and computer, looking for any evidence to support the girl's contention that she and the defendant were in a relationship. Or rather, looking for the *absence* of evidence. Freya might claim that she was being discreet in how she and Jeremy were in touch, but there's no way that their relationship could exist as she says and there be no trace of it on any of her social media. Jeremy has said that there was never any external communication between the two of them. I need to make sure there's nothing to contradict that.

Three hours later and I've barely scratched the surface. It looks, at this stage at least, as if Freya joined Facebook first, when she was eleven years old. So close to Robin's age. I repress a shudder. I've managed to keep Robin off social media so far, instant messaging the only permitted stream of communication, but I know it'll only be a matter of time. As with Freya. By the time she was thirteen, Instagram and Twitter had followed, though Twitter doesn't seem to have been a site that held much interest for the child—the printout of Freya's profile page shows her following only a handful of people, two pop stars, a couple of teen magazines and the BBC news service. Then Snapchat, though I know that's unlikely to lead to any useful information, the automatic self-deletion of photographs its main appeal. I start noting down dates and times until it's time to leave and collect Robin. I take the first folder out of the box and put it in my bag, ready to work on later that evening.

I wait at the school gate with my head down, shoulders hunched against the chill of the autumn evening and the sneers of the mothers. I'm thinking about the case, wondering what sort of relationship Freya had with her mother that she was signing on to social media at such a young age. Then I chide myself. I shouldn't judge. For all I know, Robin is on half of them already, too. It's months since I checked her phone.

I'm still deep in thought when I feel a tap on my shoulder. I look up with a smile, assuming it's Robin. But it isn't. It's one of the mums. My face stiffens the moment I see her, but once I clock the smile on the woman's face, my jaw muscles unclench a tiny amount.

"I thought you were Robin," I say.

"Sorry to disturb you. You looked miles away, but I wanted to introduce myself. I saw you at the coffee morning earlier, but we didn't get the chance to speak."

I look at her more closely, now recognizing her—it's the dark-haired woman who was eating a croissant. The most normal-looking of the lot, fairly short, not that skinny, her hair showing the odd trace of gray. I feel my face relax a tiny bit more, but I'm still on high alert, nerves tingling.

"I had to get to work," I say. "It went on longer than I thought."

"It always does," the woman says, and laughs. I'm so taken aback that I laugh too, before sucking the sound back in. This woman might seem pleasant, but any minute now she's going to show her teeth.

"Anyway, it looks like the girls are coming now," I say.

"I think they'll be a couple of minutes yet," the woman says, glancing through the gates. "Let me introduce myself. I'm Nicole. I don't bite."

I feel my cheeks grow hot, the woman echoing my thoughts only too closely. "I'm Sadie," I say.

"Good to meet you properly, at last," Nicole says. "I'm Pippa's mum. I think she's in the same class as your daughter."

"Robin hasn't said."

"It must be a lot for her to take in," Nicole says, "with all these new people. Pippa says she seems quiet."

I sigh. "It's always hard to begin with. She's still finding her feet."

"I'm sure she'll be on top of it all really soon," Nicole says. "Kids are so resilient. So adaptable. Not like us. How are you finding it all? I felt for you when you choked on that canapé at the drinks."

She has a gentle note in her voice, a genuine sound of empathy, and it's been so long that anyone has spoken like that to me that tears prick my eyes. I swallow, hard.

"Sorry," I manage to get the word out past the lump in my throat. "Sorry. Was it you? Who helped me that evening? I never saw anyone to thank."

"Please don't apologize. And don't think you have to thank me—I was in the right place at the right time, that's all," Nicole says. She puts out a hand and places it on my arm, squeezing gently. "It's always difficult to adjust to a new place. Especially somewhere that seems as unfriendly as here. It isn't as bad as it looks, though. I promise."

I feel strangely reluctant to tell her I know exactly what it's like—that I came here myself. I try to muster a laugh, but it falls hollow. I'm feeling hot, my collar too tight, the backs of my hands starting to itch.

Nicole continues. "I feel like an outsider sometimes too, you know. This school is a real stretch for me, especially as I'm a single mum. But it's worth it. The girls are so happy. And they do so well."

"You really think the girls are happy?"

"Yes, definitely. It can take a bit of getting used to, but you'll get there. Robin too. This is just teething troubles. Give it a few weeks, and it'll be as if she's always been here." Nicole pats me on the arm again.

"Thank you. I really appreciate that."

"We'll have Robin round to spend some time with Pippa, if you like. I can catch you up with some of the gossip."

"That would be brilliant," I say, finally managing a smile.

SUNDAY, 11:05 A.M.

I pace up and down, up and down. Waiting. The house feels colder, more empty by the minute. Ten o'clock passes. Eleven. I make a phone call.

"I'm sure there's a good explanation," she says. "We need to stay calm."

"I'm doing my best to stay calm," I say. "But where the hell are they?"

"I don't know right now," she says, "but I'm sure they're on the way."

"I'm calling the police."

"Don't do that," she says. "Not yet. There's bound to be a good reason why they're not back yet. Maybe they've stopped for breakfast somewhere. Or there's been a breakdown. You can't go leaping to the worst conclusion. Just sit tight—they'll be bound to turn up soon enough."

"I can't just sit here and do nothing," I say.

"You need to stay at home," she says. "They might nearly be in London. You need to be there in case she comes home."

"I can't...I don't know what to do," I say. My head is spinning and I'm fighting a wave of nausea, panic and acid, sharp at the back of my throat.

"Sit tight," she says. "I'll call you back very soon. Just stay put. I promise you it'll be all right."

I'm trying to stay calm, go through all the rational explanations that I can muster, but pressure's building up in my head, higher and higher, louder and louder, scratching feet of insects marching around and around, scrabbling away in fear and self-recrimination. I start screaming, words at first, WHERE ARE YOU? *but the sound breaks into incoherence, a mess of shouted noise, until I slump down at the kitchen table, head in hands.*

Finally I can take in a breath. Fuck it, I'm calling the police. I punch 999 into my phone, wait in desperation for the operator to reply.

14

"What's Pippa like?" I ask Robin when we get home that afternoon.

"Pippa? She always seems a bit nervous. But she's OK. Why?"

"I was talking to her mum, that's all. She seems friendly, too. She chatted to me at the school gate. She said something about a playdate—would you be interested?"

"That would be really fun," Robin says.

"Great."

When Robin goes up to bed, I clear up the kitchen and pull out the file I took from chambers, ready to keep going with my search. I'm swiftly engrossed, surprised to find it's after ten when my phone pings with a message. It won't be Andrew—I know that without even looking. It might be Zora to check how the day has gone, though I know she's busy. But it isn't. It's a number I don't recognize.

Nicole here—how are you doing? Are you free next Friday for Robin to come over? Also ICYMI, costume needed for the girls' assembly tomorrow. Favorite character from Greek myth.

Ah, that's nice, is my first response. Maybe the situation is picking up. We'll have friends by the time it's half... Sorry, what? My brain does a sharp one-eighty. Costume? Favorite character from Greek myth? I rush upstairs to Robin's room, shake her awake.

"I told you," Robin says.

"You didn't. I would have remembered."

"It doesn't matter. I can just wear uniform."

"It does matter. I don't want it to look like we don't care. Who's your favorite character from Greek myth?"

"I don't know any Greek myths," Robin says. "I'm going back to sleep." She rolls over, back into oblivion.

My temper rising, I check my emails. In the midst of the multitude of start-of-term information I've received I find a calendar marked up with all the term's events and, sure enough, in very small text, it says *Year 6, assembly on Greek myths, costumes to be provided by parents.* How was I supposed to notice that? If only I'd started talking to Nicole a few days sooner…

After a few minutes looking on the internet at cardboard shields and masks, I turn off the phone. I'll do something with a bed sheet, and it will have to do. I get back to work with a sigh, suppressing the thought that sheets have more to do with togas and Romans than Greek myths.

Robin isn't happy the next morning with my bodged effort.

"I look really stupid," she says. "Everyone is going to laugh."

"They're not going to laugh. You'll all be wearing the same sort of thing."

"Bet we're not," she says, but she stops moaning.

I stand back and admire my work. A sheet draped in a classical way, pinned together at the shoulder, a wreath made out of some scraps of green material I found in a drawer. And the *pièce de résistance*, a stuffed owl that was living in a glass case in the hall, which Robin is now holding, though without any great enthusiasm.

"What happens if I drop it?" Robin says. "Or lose it? Or something bad happens to it?"

"Nothing bad is going to happen to it. Take it into the assembly, put it in your desk for safekeeping, then we'll bring it home at the end of the day."

"I don't want to," Robin says.

"If you don't have it, how will anyone know you're meant to be Athena, goddess of war? Goddess of wisdom? Not born a baby, but springing fully armed from her father Zeus's skull."

Robin looks blank. "If she's the goddess of war, shouldn't I have a sword or something?"

"We don't have any swords. We've got an owl. The sign of wisdom. It will have to do."

"You carry it to school then," Robin says. She zips her anorak up over the top of the sheet. The classical effect is spoiled, somewhat. But then they probably wouldn't have used floral sheets for their clothes, either, I think, ramming the owl into a plastic bag. Robin rolls her eyes and marches ahead of me toward the bus stop.

I say goodbye to Robin at the end of the road and watch her scurry away, head down, sheet beginning to trail on the ground. Once she's through the gates, I head toward the tube. Just as I'm about to go into the station I realize that I'm still carrying the damn owl. I know Robin would prefer not to have it, but that's not the point. Without it, she really is just draped in bedclothes—I turn on my heel and march back to school. When I get to the gates, I run into Nicole.

"Hi," Nicole says, with every air of being delighted to see me, her voice warm. "All set for assembly?"

"All set. Thanks for the heads up."

"Oh, any time. I do think sometimes that the form reps could be more on it, you know, with reminders, that kind of thing. If I were doing it..."

I try to keep my smile pinned to my mouth, but I can feel it slipping.

"I have to get this in to Robin," I say, waving the bag at Nicole.

"Aren't you coming in anyway?" Nicole says, her voice lifting at the end of her sentence with a note of surprise.

"I've got work. Are we supposed to come?"

"Of course we are," Nicole says, and takes me by the arm, drawing me through the gates into the school building before I can argue further.

It's the first time I've been properly inside the building for nearly thirty years. I brace myself, expecting a deluge of memories to drag me down, but it looks completely different, paintwork and flooring updated and clean. It always used to smell of pine disinfectant, but this has faded, too, a sweet, citrus scent there in its place. It's only when we get to the entrance to the hall that I recognize with a jolt a feature from the past, the wooden shields above the doors, filled in with the names of all the school captains and vice captains in gold lettering.

I pull away from Nicole's grasp and walk along, reading the dates at the top of the shields, searching for one in particular. It takes a minute until I find it, so many years have passed since I left, so many girls' names memorialized in this way. But there I am, Sadie Roper, Captain. I remember my mother sneering at it—*It's hardly Head Boy at Eton, is it? Feeble that they do this for a load of eleven-year-olds*—how it pricked the bubble of my pride, shriveled it with shame. I couldn't look at it after that, the pleasure I had in it tainted, like a stain.

Seeing it now I feel a twinge of that same shame before I push it away from me, imagining instead how pleased Robin will be when I show her. She won't think it's ridiculous.

"Aren't you coming in?" Nicole says, and I turn around, registering her presence again.

"Yes. I was just..." but she's gone ahead into the hall before I can finish my sentence.

I can tell the owl is a mistake from the moment I hand it over to a teacher to give to Robin.

"Is this real?" the woman says, holding it out at arm's length.

"Yes."

"A dead owl?"

"Yes. It's stuffed. Taxidermy."

"I'm a vegan," she says.

"I'm not asking you to eat it," I say, trying not to sound exasperated.

"What's it for, exactly?" the teacher asks.

"It's for my daughter Robin's costume. She just needs to hold it, and then she'll look the part—the goddess of wisdom."

"Right," the woman says, taking the owl from me with an expression of revulsion, holding it as gingerly as she can.

It doesn't get better when the girls come out on stage in front of the school in the assembly hall. Even from the back of the hall, I can see that there's a space around Robin, and that the girls are twitchy, not paying full attention to their performance. They are telling the story of Perseus and how he overcame Medusa, and the child playing the part of Medusa is in the best dress-up outfit of the morning, her skin all painted green and her head wreathed in a nest of multicolored snakes. All the girls are beautifully turned out, in fact, Bacchus with vines, Aphrodite with a golden apple, lots of nymphs in proper dresses. No one is wearing a sheet apart from Robin, and she looks very bedraggled by now. As does the owl, loose feathers following Robin around the stage.

Nor is Robin as fluent as the other girls whenever she has a line to speak, and I have to strain to hear her. I try not to let my paranoia run away with me, but I'm starting to get a distinct feeling that something is happening up on the stage to put her off. I ignore the feeling, try to rationalize it, but when it comes to the final section, I can't pretend it's not real any more. Robin is definitely being got at. She comes to the front of the stage, her mouth open as if for a declamation, when someone at the far left corner of the stage yells, "She's holding a dead bird. It *stinks*."

I clutch the sides of my chair as I watch the disaster play out as if in slow motion. There's a buzzing around me as the other parents start to notice, too. Robin's face turns red, redder than I've seen it since she was a baby. She starts to speak but hesitates, stops, holding up the owl in front of her as if in surprise, as if to ask: *How did this owl end up with me?* And then her mouth crumples, followed by the rest of her expression, and she looks at the owl one more time, her growing humiliation clear on her face, before she chucks it away from her, throwing it along the stage, straight into a group of nymphs and goddesses, and she turns, and she runs. But she can't even run because of the sheet, the shitty, shitty floral sheet. It falls down around her feet and trips her up, and between the cloud of feathers and screams in the audience and the sight of Robin, sprawling, before clambering to her feet and running off stage in her undershirt and sports shorts, I don't know where to look.

Before I can get up and go and retrieve Robin from the mess, someone pushes past me. It's Julia. She's sprinting up through the assembly hall, yelling and shoving her way past the teachers who have materialized on the stage.

"Daisy has allergies," Nicole says, her voice grave. "She's really allergic to feathers. This could be really serious. Julia's going to go spare."

"Where is Daisy?" I hope beyond hope that she's been on the periphery of the action, backstage even.

Nicole raises her hand and points, straight into the heart of the commotion. I peer at the stage. It's hard to make out which child is which from a distance. But as I squint, I start to distinguish one from the other. I can see which girl was hit by the owl, bits of his desiccated corpse all over her head and body. It's Medusa, her snakes broken and her green makeup smeared. And as Julia launches herself at this child, alternately picking bits of bird off her and hugging her, it becomes very apparent that Medusa is Daisy. A stone lodges itself in the pit of my stomach.

I steel myself and approach the stage, hoping to find Robin and take her away. She's hovering in the far corner, tears streaming down her face, no one paying any attention to her as they throng around Daisy. I'm nearly at Robin's side when Julia starts to scream.

"You! Hey, you there!" Julia says at the top of her voice. "New girl. Sadie."

I try to put a *Who, me?* expression on my face, but it's not even fooling me. I turn slowly to face Julia.

"Your stupid little scheme has nearly killed my daughter," Julia says. "Look at the state of her."

I look. It's not great. Daisy is a complete mess. She doesn't look close to death, though.

"I don't think there's any need to blow this out of proportion," I say. "Obviously we're both really sorry that this happened, but there's no question that anyone has nearly been killed."

"How dare you make light of this situation? She has serious asthma and an allergy to birds—there could be a delayed reaction. And if that, that *thing* had hit her at a different angle it could have had her eye out. I know you've done this on purpose, trying to hurt Daisy like this. Your sad little daughter is so pathetic. She's jealous. She's trying to undermine Daisy any way she can."

I nearly shout back at her to tell her to stop being so ridiculous. But I have just enough self-control to stop myself, looking at the state of Robin, her shoulders drooping, her face tear-stained, utterly bedraggled. I go to her and put my arm around her shoulders, but she stands stiff as a board, tremors running through her body.

"I consider this to be a deliberate act of sabotage," Julia says. She's standing right in front of me, veins throbbing in her neck, the tendons so tight they look like they're about to snap. "It's Friday, they've got their practice test today—you both know that. This is nothing but an attempt to distress Daisy, make sure she's not at peak performance. If it falls apart, I'm going to sue."

With that, she grabs hold of Daisy's arm and pulls her away. I try to hug Robin, but she pulls away, too.

"What tests?" I ask Robin.

"Practice tests for the entrance exams next term," Robin says. "They all care way too much."

"You haven't talked about the practice tests."

"They're not important, that's why."

"Robin..." I start to say, but she turns and marches away. I've no option but to follow.

15

The rest passes in a blur. Robin and I leave the stage and we're swept up by Nicole, who makes soothing noises and gets Robin a skirt and jumper from Lost Property to replace the fallen sheet. The headmistress looks at us both with a very serious expression before asking me if I'll come in at the end of the afternoon to discuss it. I nod. It's not like I can argue. Robin disappears out of the hall, and seeing Julia approaching me, I do the same. I walk fast, out of the front door and through the gates. But as soon as I turn the corner out of sight of school, I break into a sprint.

David Phelps is at the reception desk when I eventually get to chambers, but I'm too worked up to speak to him. I smile, the corners of my mouth barely lifting, and walk straight through and up the stairs into Barbara's room, where I throw myself into work, reading through pages and pages of messages.

By lunchtime, I've started to build up a clear picture of the complainant. She's sharp-tongued, arrogant, and quick to take offense. Lots of social media contacts. Perhaps not so many friends. There's an edge to her exchanges, a real *fuck you* attitude. I'm starting to like her. She's funny. She's also a liar, I remind myself, according to the instructions I've been given. At least there's no trace of communication with the accused. So far, so good.

I make my report to Barbara, who has been in court unexpectedly on another matter this morning.

"Good, that's what we like to hear," she says in response. "I'm certain there's nothing to be found, either, but it'll be good to have it confirmed. Anyway, wrap it up for now. The client will be here in a few minutes."

I go through to the loo and tidy up my face, brush my hair. Under the harsh strip lighting I can see that my jacket and skirt are covered with lots of tiny bits of feather, gray against the dark wool of the suit, and I brush my hand over them, trying to get them off, but after only a couple of minutes, Barbara sticks her head around the bathroom door and tells me to get a move on. At least the worst of it is off.

"Through here," Barbara says, gesturing me into the conference room. It's furnished with an oval table and several chairs. There's a sideboard laden with a coffee machine, water, and two large platters of sandwiches.

"How many people are coming?" I ask.

"Jeremy, his solicitor, Zora. I think you know her? And his mother," Barbara says.

I nod. "His mother?"

"His parents are being very supportive," Barbara says. Her tone is dry. "Almost competitively so."

I raise an eyebrow. There's a story in that dryness.

Barbara opens her mouth, about to speak, but she's interrupted by a phone call.

"Send them up," Barbara says down the line. "We're all set."

She turns to me. "Yes. The poor man, his parents don't speak to each other. There was a very bitter divorce some years ago. Father's paying for the fees, mother's the shoulder to cry on."

"That sounds complicated."

"All somewhat infantilizing. The client's perfectly pleasant, but rather wet. It's not entirely surprising," Barbara says. "Jeremy is their only child. They absolutely dote on him. This is putting them all through hell. As they tell me. Repeatedly. They will be keeping a close eye on how the defense is run."

I blink again. "Oh, lord."

"Quite," Barbara says.

There's a noise outside the door, and Kirsten walks in, the clients behind her. A woman in her late middle age comes in first behind Kirsten, then Zora, tidy in a black trouser suit, and bringing up the rear, a young man who must be Jeremy. The older woman is assured, almost arrogant in her movements, taking a seat immediately at the head of the table. She's dressed very smartly, dark trousers and a jacket, a silk scarf knotted at her throat. Jeremy hesitates at the door, a little stooped, his demeanor apologetic, his jacket tweed. He looks even younger than I expected.

Barbara welcomes Zora and Jeremy in and gestures to places at the table. Kirsten makes coffee and puts out the sandwiches. When she's left the room, Barbara begins.

"Jeremy, it's good to see you. Alexandra, you too. Thank you for coming in. I want to introduce you to Sadie. Sadie Roper, Alexandra Taylor, Jeremy Taylor." Barbara nods to them both in turn. "Sadie is my new junior on the case. She's just rejoined chambers after some time away."

"Some time away, eh? Hope you've kept your hand in," Alexandra says, her voice cold. She glares at me.

I reach across the table to shake hands, smiling, trying not to react. Jeremy's clasp is comfortable; warm, but not too hot. A reassuring handshake—not what I expected. Alexandra's hand lies limp and heavy in mine.

"Of course," Barbara says. "She's good. She gets it. And she looks the part. We need an all-female team, make sure he seems sympathetic. Yes?"

As if with reluctance, Alexandra's glare slowly transforms into an expression that's more measured, less hostile.

"Good point," she says. "You make a good point. I approve. Well done, Zora."

Zora smiles at me, winks. "Welcome aboard, Sadie."

As the conference continues, I sit back and take stock of the room. Barbara isn't asking questions of the client, at least not yet, but rather giving him an outline of where they are up to in the preparation of his case. They have obtained character witnesses from some highly illustrious personages, his father's connections shining through. There's even a bishop in there, and the chaplain from the school he attended, extolling his virtues.

It all sounds far too good to be true. I'm trying not to feel too cynical about it. Naturally he would be able to drum up all this support—he's establishment through and through. All the right places of education, the badges of privilege lined up in order. He doesn't come over badly, though, something guileless in the openness of his gaze. His brown hair is slicked back from his face but a lock of fringe keeps flopping down and he pushes it back, the movement automatic. It's hard to believe he's a fully qualified teacher—he looks like a student. He could even pass for a sixth former if the lights were low. It's not unappealing.

Once she's finished enumerating the references, Barbara turns to Jeremy.

"You're definitely going to be happy about giving evidence?" she says. "It'll be a very difficult environment."

I watch him carefully. His mouth is fixed but there's a wobble in his chin. He coughs, clears his throat.

"All I wanted to do was help," he says. "I had no idea it would come to this. Do you really think I'll need to take the stand?"

His voice is gentle, in keeping with the rest of him. My resistance to him is waning, even though I'd rather suss him out for a bit longer. He sounds very forlorn. It starts to seem plausible that he's more hapless than predatory.

"I think it's definitely going to be necessary," Barbara says, "if we can't get the case thrown out at half-time."

"Of course it'll be thrown out at half-time. There's no bloody evidence for this whatsoever," Alexandra interrupts.

Barbara nods but continues, "I would not always advise my clients to give evidence, but in this case you will definitely be your own best advocate."

Alexandra smiles, a movement that contains no warmth. "That's very true. Though we hope you'll be the best advocate that money can buy."

Barbara doesn't blink, though I feel a tremor in the air. "As you know," she continues, "we were successful in our application to go through Freya's phone and laptop. Sadie is searching through the girl's social media to ensure that there is no communication to be found between Jeremy and Freya."

"Well, of course there won't be," Alexandra interrupts with some force.

"That's the point," Barbara says. "It will reinforce the fact that there's no relationship between them other than one of strict professionalism, student and teacher. That's important for the jury to see. Given how much time teens spend on their devices, the absence of any mention of Jeremy is very telling."

"There are the emails," Jeremy says, his voice hesitant.

"Emails?" Barbara says.

"The emails between me and Freya," he says. "Although I always copied her mother in on those. They were to set homework, discuss assignments, arrange times."

"Yes," Barbara says, leafing through a file. "I have those."

"May I see them?" I say.

They all look at me as if surprised that I can speak.

"Yes, of course," Barbara says. "They're with the unused material that the prosecution served on us. The prosecution isn't relying on them because they don't show anything that advances their case. Helpful for us, though."

Zora opens a file and runs her finger down the page before pausing at a point and looking back up. "As you also know, we're set for trial shortly. We applied for an extension to the date to give us time to go through the extra material from the phone, but they haven't granted it. This explains why it's been necessary to engage a junior in the case." She glances at me. "You're going to have a lot to do in a very short period of time."

I nod.

"I understand from Barbara that you have children," Alexandra says.

"One child." I'm surprised this has come up in conversation.

"I hope you're not going to be one of those unreliable mothers, always having to take time off for a sickly child. Are you sure that you're going to be able to keep up with it all?"

"Yes. I am," I say. "I wouldn't have accepted the brief if I weren't able to fulfill my commitment."

"Well," says Alexandra, her lips pursed for a moment, eyes thoughtful. "I hope that's the case."

I don't reply. I catch Zora's eye and she winks again. My burst of anger passes and I try not to laugh.

The meeting over, Zora and Alexandra get into a huddle with Barbara, and I busy myself with tidying up plates and putting them on the side.

Jeremy reaches over with an empty plate and puts it into my hand. He smiles at me. "Thanks for taking the case on at such short notice."

"It's no trouble. I was very pleased to be asked. I've moved back here recently, so I've been keen to get my practice back up and running."

"Moved back from?"

"The U.S. Brooklyn. My husband's work..."

Jeremy nods as if this explains everything. "How long have you been back?"

"Not very long. It's taking time to settle in, but we're getting there."

"So your husband's job has moved back here, then?"

"No, Robin and I have come on our own."

"Right," he says. "Right. Well. Robin, that's a sweet name."

I twitch. Jeremy holds his hands up, his cheeks flushing. "That's the awful thing about a charge like this. It colors everything. I can't even make a comment on a child's name without it seeming inappropriate in some way." His mouth twists in disgust.

I feel bad. I didn't mean to react like that. "No, I'm sorry. Thank you for saying it's a sweet name. She is sweet. Though she's trying to adapt to a new Year Six at the moment, which isn't easy. There are entrance exams coming up next

January for the senior school which seem to be causing some tension."

"Oh God. Year Six. You have my sympathies."

"I'm beginning to think I haven't taken it seriously enough. I mean, after the craziness of New York school entry, I thought I'd seen everything. But everyone seems completely hysterical about it."

"The parents go mad. It's getting worse. So I'm told, anyway. I've never taught that age group," Jeremy says. "But anecdotally, it leads to a lot of pressure. Very high levels of competition."

I open my mouth to speak but Alexandra has turned her attention to our conversation.

"We must go," she says to Jeremy. "Good to meet you." This to me. Zora waves and they leave. Barbara tidies up her files.

"That went OK, all things considered," she says.

"What things?"

"Alexandra can be tricky. You might have noticed that," she says with one eyebrow raised. "The father is too. He's used to being in charge. I want to speak to my client on his own at some point, but so far one or other of them has barged into every conference. I've tried to point out that they're too closely involved to make the best decisions, but it's tricky." Barbara looks thoughtful. "Anyway, you'd best get back to work. Do feel free to take the material home with you so that you can get on with it in the evenings."

"I will do. Thanks. That'll make everything a lot simpler."

With a wave, I'm dismissed.

16

I've skimmed through another file's worth of printouts by early afternoon, and still found no sign of correspondence between the complainant and Jeremy.

"Is her evidence really all they're basing the case on?" I say to Barbara when I return to her room.

"Apparently so. And the testimony of a couple of friends who say she told them about it at the time. It's very weak. I anticipate that I'll be making an application to throw it out at half-time. I mean, I'm reluctant to give credence to the suggestion that the case is being brought as an attack, but one does have to wonder."

I nod. I shuffle papers together into a pile to put in my bag. "I'm going to have to make a move soon. I need to collect Robin."

Barbara's attention is now focused on her computer, before she snaps her gaze back to me.

"As long as you get on with it. I don't want us to miss anything. OK?"

"OK." I nod again.

I'm down in reception, saying goodbye to Kirsten, when

my phone rings. I look at the number for a moment before answering with reluctance.

"Yes...of course...I understand it's necessary...four o'clock."

The voice at the other end of the call was cool, dispassionate. A complaint received, teething issues, best to meet and talk it through, all very easily settled. I don't share the school secretary's confidence. If it's so easily settled, why do I need to meet the head? I had hoped the whole fuss would blow over. I put the phone in my pocket and stand for a moment, unwilling to leave the calm of chambers to deal with the drama.

"All well?" Kirsten says.

"Yes. Well, no. Not really. There was a...situation this morning at assembly, and one of the mothers has made a complaint. I have to go in and see the head."

Kirsten's face is sympathetic. "One of those professional school-gate mothers?"

"Maybe a bit."

"The head will calm it down," she says. "She'll look like she's listening to the woman, make all the right noises, but won't do anything to you. Don't worry about it."

"You think?"

"We've had our fill of run-ins at school with my kids. Those mothers who don't work are the worst—they don't have anything better to do than magnify every little thing into a massive drama, just for the sake of it. I'm sure it'll be OK. Don't stress."

I'm taken through to a waiting room once I arrive at school. I ask the secretary about Robin and whether any arrangements have been made for her, given that it's time for pickup, but she waves off my concerns. "It's taken care of," she says, walking out of the room.

I sit staring at the door of the head's office. I'm a fully qualified barrister, was a tenant in a good set of chambers, and dealing with an important trial; mother to a daughter of ten. None of it matters. I'm also a seven-year-old girl, waiting to be told off for stealing an exercise book from the stationery cupboard. I'm nine, my knuckles still sore from where I punched Carole because she wouldn't stop teasing me about my father being dead. My palms are slick with sweat, my heart hammering in my chest. My windpipe is tightening in anticipation, amygdala fully hijacked, flight or fight.

Silence stretches out in the antechamber, a clock ticking loud from the mantelpiece on the opposite wall, a petal dropping from a vase of roses next to it. A rhythm beats out in my mind—*get on with it, get on with it*—and I try to bring my breath in time with the tick of the clock. Three counts in, three counts out, four, five.

It's working, I'm calming, though the wait is stretching out unbearably long, the big hand of the clock moving from one minute past, to two, to three. No sound from behind the office door. No sound from anywhere else in the building. No evidence of the presence of hundreds of children just past the other door. *Jesus, can't they just open the fucking door and GET ON WITH IT.* Despite the breathing, pressure is building in my head, the silence almost too much to bear, when it's broken by an imperious screech.

"It's utterly outrageous that I have to come in too. Totally unnecessary. A complete waste of my time. All you need to do is tell that new girl and her dreadful mother how to behave and there won't be any more of a problem."

The secretary returns to the waiting room, Julia behind her. She's changed for the occasion, no longer in sportswear, now in dark fitted jeans, white shirt and what looks like a Chanel jacket. She jangles with long chains of gold and pearls adorned with interlocking C shapes. Definitely Chanel. I doubt it's knock-off. An image flashes into my mind of this woman poking around market stalls looking for fake designer goods and despite the tension I'm feeling—maybe because of it—a snort of laughter escapes me.

"And what the hell are you laughing at?" Julia strides over to where I'm sitting. Her porcelain face is mottled red and spittle flies from her mouth, speckling my cheek.

There's a split second in which it could go either way. She really looks as if she's about to hit me. I keep my cool. I've been faced with worse than this down the cells in the magistrates' court. Waiting to see the headmistress might resurrect my childhood insecurities but not a woman like this, entitlement and the superiority of privilege erupting from every well-tended pore. I rise slowly to my feet, jaw set, shoulders squared.

Julia's shoulders are squared too. I stand right in her face, eyeball to eyeball, loathing running in a current between us. I'm resolute, unmoving, letting Julia's contempt wash over me, rocklike against the scorn.

"Ladies," a voice says, and the spell is broken. Julia shifts, moves back. I take a deep breath.

"Ladies," the voice says again, and now the door to the inner sanctum opens and it's the head, her smile beatific. "Thank you for coming in."

SUNDAY, 11:09 A.M.

"What's the address of the emergency? Where are you?" says the emergency service operator.

"I don't know what the address is," I say. "Somewhere else. It's my daughter."

"I hear you, madam, but I need you to give me an address and the phone number you're calling from."

"It doesn't matter what my address is," I say. "She's not gone from here."

"I still need to have a phone number, please," says the voice at the other end.

I reel off my address and phone number. I know the operator is only doing their job. I understand the need for the questions. But it's pointless. It doesn't matter where I am. It matters where my daughter is, and it's too complicated to explain. Not when I can't put into words my fears. Not even to myself.

"What is the nature of your emergency?"

"It's my daughter. She was away staying with friends last night. And they said she was being brought home, but she isn't here yet."

"Do you have the address where she was staying?"

"No, I don't. But she won't have run away."

"Let's just go through this in order. Can you tell me exactly what's happened?"

I take a deep breath. I'm trying to calm myself down. I can't start screaming at the operator even though it's all I want to do.

"My daughter was taken by some friends to stay in a holiday cottage. They told me hours ago that she was being driven home by someone, but she's not here and I can't get hold of anyone. I thought I should call 999. Get the police involved."

"Do you have the address where your daughter is staying?"

"I've already told you, no," I say. Before I can stop it, I break into sobs, my crying hysterical now. I jab at the red button to end the call, overwhelmed with the futility of trying to explain something I don't understand, throwing the phone away in frustration.

At last I get myself back under control and drop to my knees to retrieve my phone. There's a missed call notification from an unknown number—it must be the emergency operator. I delete it—there's no point. No point at all.

I get up and sit at the table for a few moments, breathing in and out, regaining some calm. Then I stand up. I'm going to the London house now. Right now. See if they're there. And if there's no answer, I'm going to break down the door with my bare hands.

17

The head gestures us to two chairs set at an angle to each other in front of a large mahogany desk, behind which she lowers herself onto her own chair. I sit down immediately, having parked my bag of papers against the wall near the door. Julia continues to stand.

"Do sit down," the head tells her, the words dropping through the room like a stone. I watch in fascination as the command works its way through Julia. She's clearly torn between the desire to assert herself, and the recognition of an authority greater than her own. If I weren't so hyped up, I'd laugh.

The headmistress gestures once more, and says, "Sit down please, Mrs. Burnet." There's a chill in her voice that wasn't there before. Still resistant, Julia stands for a moment more before giving up the fight and throwing herself down into the chair behind her.

"That's better," the head says. "Now, Ms. Roper, we haven't met as yet. I'm Florence Grayson." She offers her hand to me. Her grip is firm and her gaze steady. A woman in her late fifties, she has a sensible air to her and, despite the circumstances, I feel reassured. She turns to Julia and nods. "Mrs. Burnet."

"Can we cut to the chase?" Julia says. "We all know why

we're here. That new girl did her best to sabotage my daughter's performance in assembly this morning. It was a deliberate attempt to undermine her before she had to sit the practice test today."

"That's not true," I burst out. Mrs. Grayson's upheld hand silences me.

"Mrs. Burnet, I need you to calm down. The incident this morning is part of the reason for this meeting, but not all of it."

"What more can there be?" Julia says with huge indignation.

"I thought that this would be a good opportunity to bring you both together, see if we can bring some calm to the situation." She looks pointedly between us. "It's far from ideal that there should be a shouting match of this sort in front of the children. I appreciate that tensions are running high in the run-up to the senior school exams, but it's not advisable to throw around accusations of sabotage."

Julia doesn't reply. I take advantage of her silence.

"Robin has no interest in sabotaging anyone, honestly. She doesn't even understand what the exams are about. And the owl was my fault, not hers—I wasn't organized about the costume for this morning and had to throw something together at the last minute."

"That's because you're too busy working to look after your daughter properly," Julia says.

"I'm sorry, what did you say?" I'm getting angry, but again Mrs. Grayson interrupts.

"Let us steer clear of any kind of personal attack," she says. "There is no room for prejudice in this school, whether against working or stay-at-home parents. We all support each other."

Julia's lips are clenched tight, her eyes narrowed. Her face is strangely smooth and expressionless, though, despite her obvious emotion—an ageless mask, full of Botox and fillers.

"I don't understand why the school keeps doing it," Julia says. "Why do you keep bringing in new girls so late in the day? You did it before and you know what happened. You've made the same mistake again, but this time it's too close to the exams for us to ignore it. It's ruined the dynamic of the class. Daisy is really unhappy."

"Daisy is a fine, resilient girl who can cope with a new addition to her class," Mrs. Grayson says firmly. "And that's why I wanted to speak to you both. You should not let personal differences play out in front of the girls like this. It's destabilizing for them. They are looking to us to be positive role models, not examples of behavior that they should avoid."

"How dare you speak to me like that?" Julia spits.

"I'm not speaking to you like anything," Mrs. Grayson says. "I'm telling you that Daisy is absolutely fine. I've had the test results from this morning and she got seventy-five percent."

"Only seventy-five?" Julia says. "You see! How can you say she's not disrupted? I would be expecting over eighty percent at this stage. She's more than capable."

"Well, we wouldn't. There's no need for her to be scoring more highly than that—it's already a very high score and you need to trust both us and Daisy that we know what we're doing. You know perfectly well that she's going to get into the senior school with no trouble at all."

"She should be winning the scholarship. You know she's earned it. And I don't trust anyone but myself," Julia says. "What score did *her* daughter get?"

Mrs. Grayson looks at me. I shrug. She goes through the

papers on her desk and looks up. “Eighty-two percent. The first maths paper. It’s a very good score. Both of them are.”

By now Julia is bright red. “This. *This* is what I mean. It’s outrageous. It’s going to be unbelievably unsettling for Daisy to have someone challenging her in this way. How am I going to calm her down now?”

I’m trying to show no expression on my face, but I’m aghast at the performance that Julia is giving. I look over at Mrs. Grayson and for a moment our eyes meet. For the first time since I’ve had anything to do with the school, I feel in perfect accord with one of its players. Then she looks away and the sense of agreement between us fades.

“Mrs. Burnet, I understand that you’re anxious about these test results, but I can assure you that you don’t need to be concerned. Daisy is performing very well indeed. She just needs to be left to get on with it. We really do know what we’re doing, you know.”

“Looking at that result, I doubt it very much,” Julia says, pushing herself up to her feet. “I am extremely unhappy about the situation. The school had no right to introduce any new pupils so late into the process, and I will hold you entirely responsible if she doesn’t go through with flying colors. She should be first in line for the scholarship. And if this, this *interloper* takes it from her, you can expect to hear from my solicitor.”

“We haven’t applied for any scholarship,” I interrupt. “I don’t know what you’re talking about.”

“You don’t apply,” Julia says with fury. “It goes to the girl at the top of the class. Daisy’s rightful place.”

Mrs. Grayson raises an eyebrow. “I would seriously recommend that you calm down and stop shouting in this way.”

Julia actually snorts at this comment. She tosses her head and storms out of the room, slamming the door behind her. But a split second later, she charges back into the room.

"I'm going to make sure she's a social pariah for the rest of her time here." She glares straight at me. "No one is going to give you the time of day by the time I've finished with you. They won't even know you exist." She swirls around to face the headmistress. "And you—you should be ashamed of yourself, too, letting this girl join so late. Ruining everything. I don't know how you can live with yourself."

"That's quite enough, Mrs. Burnet. You're taking this too far now. I must insist that you calm down," Mrs. Grayson says.

Julia snorts and turns on her heel, flouncing out of the room for a second time, the door again closing with a loud bang.

Mrs. Grayson looks down at her hands for a moment, then up at me.

"I hope that Robin is starting to settle in well," she says, "and that she won't let this unfortunate business upset her. We are not going to let her feel isolated at any stage, I can assure you."

"Does someone coming in late spoil everything for the rest of the class?"

There's a very long pause. "Mrs. Burnet has an unfortunate turn of phrase on occasion," she says. "It really doesn't. It's fine for children to join us at any stage—the class is completely adaptable. And, of course, you're an old girl too. We always like to continue family associations in this way."

I force a smile. "It doesn't feel like my old school, I have to say. It's changed a lot."

"For the better, I hope," Mrs. Grayson says.

Just then, there's a knock at the door and the receptionist

sticks her head round. The headmistress nods at her, turns to me. "Well, I'm afraid I'm going to have to get on. Try not to worry about this too much. It's just noise, you know," she says, leaning forward with an earnest expression. "They don't mean half of what they say. It's heat of the moment. They get terribly worked up, and then it passes."

"I haven't seen anything like it before," I say. I want to feel reassured, but I don't. Other than Nicole, every time I've had anything to do with the other mothers, it's been a disaster, and now Robin is even more out in the cold, as if things weren't bad enough already.

"Should I be worrying about the senior school entrance exam?" I ask. "It all seems very stressful. I need Robin to be able to stay on here."

Mrs. Grayson leans forward. "You have nothing to worry about at all. I can assure you of that. Robin's marks speak for themselves—she will certainly be going through to the senior school."

I nod, reassured in this, at least.

"If you have any problems, please don't hesitate to let us know," Mrs. Grayson says, "but I would advise keeping your head down for a bit, and it will all pass. It always does."

She's looking at a piece of paper in front of her as she speaks, and I know I've lost her attention. With a feeling of dread lying heavy in my gut, I leave the room.

Robin is sitting on her own in the waiting room. She looks tired but not overly tearstained. I go over and take her hand, pulling her up.

"You OK?"

"Can we go home now?"

"Yes. Let's get out of here."

We leave. The school is empty now, everyone else gone home already at the end of Friday afternoon. The feeling of dread starts to shift a little inside me. At least we can get out of here without any further interaction, have the whole weekend to ourselves.

I look at Robin. She is still in the uniform Nicole found for her. "I guess we'll need to wash that kit and bring it back," I say.

Robin shrugs. "At least it was better than spending the day in that sheet. I should have had my uniform with me in a bag," she says.

"Oh, God, I am really sorry. I've made a complete mess of it all. I thought it might be a good costume. Today's been a bit of a fail."

"It has a bit," Robin says. "I'm sorry, Mom, but please don't have any more good ideas about owls." She stops and takes hold of my arm again. "It was funny, though, in a way. Did you see Daisy's face when the feathers exploded?"

"Robin..." I say, ready to lecture her about the potential severity of allergies, but Robin's laughter is infectious, and Julia's reaction was so ridiculous that I start laughing too. Together we walk out of the school gates, arm in arm, two days of peace stretching before us till the next Monday.

18

Saturday morning is calm. No school run. We do more work on the house together, clearing bags of junk out into the back garden, leaving shelves and surfaces clear at last from the clutter that's built up over decades. Afterward, Robin gets on with her homework, and as she sits at the kitchen table, I wash the crockery she's found piled in the back of the living-room dresser.

"This is pretty," I say, holding a flowery bowl up to Robin, who smiles when she sees it. "I don't know why your grandmother kept it squirreled away."

"I like it," Robin says. "It's starting to feel like home. Though I wish Dad was here."

I don't have a reply to that. I keep washing up and Robin keeps working. We have pizza for lunch, and when we've finished, Robin goes upstairs before immediately coming down again.

"Can I have a look in your old bedroom?" she says. I jump, dropping one of the teacups into the sink with a splash.

"Why do you want to go up there? It's going to be grim."

"I want to see where you slept when you were my age," Robin says. "And I want to see what toys there are."

It's unanswerable. Although I desperately want to say no, Robin's words are still ringing in my ears. *I wish Dad was here.* I don't want to disappoint her any more.

"I'm not sure there will be any toys still there. But OK. We can go up. Let me just finish this."

I wash up the rest of the cups in the sink, moving slowly, putting it off. But try as I might, I can't ignore Robin's presence behind me, hovering with intent.

"OK," I say again. "OK, let's go."

Robin runs up the stairs first. I'm behind, my steps slow. Again, it's like I've gone back thirty years, running upstairs to hide after Lydia yelled at me again for not doing well enough at school. I arrive on the landing and gaze up at the second set of stairs. I last climbed them over ten years ago, the time Lydia told me to choose; having a baby, or her. It wasn't a hard choice.

I had climbed to my room, packed the few possessions I'd brought with me for the short visit, and walked out of the front door without saying goodbye. I knew it was the last time I'd see my mother. I thought it would be the last time I'd set foot in the house. But here I am.

Robin's at the top of the stairs now. I'm a flight behind, every part of me wanting to turn and walk away. But Robin's opening the door. I hear the turn of the knob and the creak of the door as it opens, instantly recognizable, the familiar sound running deep into my core. I steel myself. But then, sounds I'm not expecting. A gasp, sobs. Robin flings herself headlong down the stairs, straight into me. I stumble backward, grabbing on to the banister with both hands.

"What on earth is the matter?"

"Your room, Mom. Your room..." Robin forces the words

out before starting to cry in earnest. "It's horrible." She runs down to her own bedroom. I'm about to follow her but something draws me up the last stairs, remembering by instinct which creaking board to avoid. I stand on the threshold of the low doorway, liminal, caught between then and now, a hurt child—a scared adult. I look ahead.

It's carnage. Dust lies over everything, thick layers of it. There are spiderwebs in the corners, dead flies speckled black across the floor. But that's not what catches at my throat, chills my fingers as I close them into fists, arms rigid at my sides. Everything in the room has been destroyed. Every book, every piece of paper, every toy; all of it, all my childhood, has been torn into tiny shreds, ornaments smashed, clothes ripped.

On top of the pile, like a grim parody of the toys left at the sites of fatal accidents, there's the head of my favorite old teddy bear, the torso lying separate, stuffing spilled out from its slashed guts. I wanted to take it that last time before I left the house for good, but I didn't have room in my bag. I reach my hand out toward it, then pull it back, unwilling to touch anything in the pile.

The air is thick and musty, unaired for years, but heavier still is the sense of malice that overlies it all, palpable in the gloom. My mother standing behind me, her breath heavy on my neck. *Thought you'd get away, did you? No chance.*

The pile of destruction is a red scrawl on the manuscript of my past—the desk I worked at, the bed I lay on, the window I stared out of for hours. But the original is still there, underneath all of this, despite Lydia's best efforts to score it all out. I decide then and there. I'll clear the ruins of my childhood, shovel it all into bin bags, reclaim the space and start again.

My vision clears as I continue to assess the damage. My

old doll's house is over in the far corner of the room, still intact. Some warmth returns to my face, hope springing that perhaps there's something to be salvaged. I go over, picking my way through the detritus on the floor, and kneel in front of it. I used to play with it all the time when I was small, arranging and rearranging the figures inside on their miniature furniture. A mother, a father, two children and a cat, the family structure I longed for so much.

I reach out and put my hand to the front of the doll's house, ready to open the panel to reveal the rooms within. But the moment that I set my hand on it, the structure collapses. Inside, every tiny item of furniture has been smashed, and the heads ripped off the four human figures.

The malice is back, Lydia's breath heavier still, a cold blast that's now too strong to withstand. I bolt from the room.

Robin is tucked underneath her duvet reading a book. Or at least, pretending to read, holding the book in front of her face when I enter the room.

"That was horrible," she says. "Why was it like that?"

"I don't know. But your grandmother could get quite angry." I've recovered myself a little now, though the chill of it still runs through my bones. I take hold of Robin's hand, the warmth of it comforting.

"Why?"

"She wasn't a very happy person." I pick my words with care. "She wanted to be a barrister, you see, but she got married and had me instead. I don't think she ever forgave me for it. She had to give up her career—that's how it was. So she was really keen for me to be a barrister instead. She hoped I'd go all the way to becoming a QC and then a judge. Do it for her. But I met your dad and we decided to get married and then we had you and moved to the States, so being a barrister stopped happening."

"What did she do?"

I take a deep breath. I can't tell her the full truth, that her grandmother was so angry about Robin's very existence that she cut me off when I said I was going through with the pregnancy.

"Well, when I said I was going to marry your dad, she made me choose. She said if I married him, I could never talk to her again."

"Wow."

"Yes, wow. So I guess she did that to my room sometime after that."

Robin is looking distressed now, her face flushed. "I think it's a horrible thing to do," she bursts out, almost at a shout. "I think it's really mean."

"Yes, I suppose it is. Sometimes when people are unhappy, they do nasty things. They don't mean them, but they get so emotional they can't control it."

"I don't care," Robin says. "I think it's horrible."

"It is," I say. "You know, it's not the first time she's smashed something up of mine. There was a Russian doll, you know, those nesting dolls? My father had got it for me on a visit to Moscow when I was a baby. I loved that doll—one of the few things my father gave to me before he died. Anyway, I failed an exam. Just a normal test. And she took it and she smashed it into pieces in front of me, with a hammer..." My voice trails off as I remember the expression on Lydia's face as she wielded the hammer, a combination of satisfaction and grim determination. Robin reaches forward and touches me on the knee, nothing but sympathy to be seen in her expression. "That's when she told me to call her Lydia. She didn't want me to call her Mummy any more."

I hug Robin, the child solid in my arms. For a moment I inhale the warm familiar smell of her scalp, and the tightness in my chest subsides, warmth rising back in my cheeks as the blood returns. But only for a moment. Maybe it wasn't when I got married that she smashed up the room. Maybe it was when she found out I had given birth to Robin, all her dreams for my future career then broken for good.

19

I call Zora.

"Why didn't you tell me?"

"Why didn't I tell you what?"

"What Lydia did."

"What has she done?"

"My...my bedroom. It's...it's completely smashed up. I think it was Lydia."

"Jesus. I'm sorry. I never looked up there. Do you want me to come over?"

We agree on lunch the following day. I decide to do some work for a bit, to distract myself, but it's hard going; images from the destruction keep jumping up unbidden in my mind. Digging through Freya's life is beginning to get under my skin, my hands grimy as I paw through her messages.

I don't even understand the language properly, all the strange abbreviations and the failure to properly punctuate or use capital letters, emojis scattered across the pages like grapeshot on the screenshots of Facebook messages that comprise one of the files. There must be a key to teen speak, a way of understanding. I grit my teeth and get on with it.

As I delve deeper into the files, and my nerves calm, the

sense that I'm being intrusive fades. I'm interested in nothing but the evidence. And after a while, I've broken the back of two more files; still nothing to tie Jeremy to the girl, still nothing to tie Freya to any man or boy whatsoever. I yawn. I should pause now, make some dinner for Robin—I've done quite a bit, it wouldn't be unreasonable to stop, but now I've started...I open a third file and start reading.

By half past seven my eyes are dry and itchy. Fifty thousand messages printed out onto over two thousand pages. Page after page, I skim down the text in front of me, words dancing one into the other. I'm about to give up for the evening, when my attention is well and truly caught. I've struck gold. Marking the section with Post-it notes, I take a careful note of the page, relief coursing through me. I might not know much about teenagers' use of acronyms, but I do know when I've read an exchange that will go a long way to undermining Freya's credibility.

I make a coffee and keep reading, time forgotten, until Robin comes down complaining of hunger, and I realize with a start that it's nearly nine o'clock. I put together one of Robin's favorites, pasta and pesto and peas, and we eat it in front of a rerun of *Friends* on Netflix, neither making much conversation, the tension of the day seeping away.

All through Sunday we both pretend that Monday isn't going to come, don't mention the shut door upstairs. We go out to the supermarket and buy food to cook a roast for Zora for lunch. I take special care over the meal, parboiling potatoes and making batter for Yorkshire puddings.

I wash and dry Robin's uniform at the same time. When it's done, I fold it up and take it in to her. She's lying on her bed, looking at her phone. When she sees the clothes in my hands her face falls.

"I don't want to go in tomorrow. I hate it."

"It will get better. I promise."

"You can't promise that," Robin says. "I know it's not going to happen. It's a horrible place and the people are horrible, too."

"Just give it a bit more time, darling. It might improve," I say, but I don't expect her to believe it. I don't believe it myself. Robin's face is pale, sad, and a rush of anger surges through me.

"OK," I say with such decision that Robin sits bolt upright. "OK. Till the end of term. You are going to give it to the end of term. And if it keeps being as bad, then we are getting you out of there. I don't care about it being such a good school. There are loads of others. And I can teach you at home in the meantime. We will sort you out."

"But what about the will? This house? I thought we couldn't live here if I don't go to that school."

"I'll take it to court if I have to. And we can stay at Zora's if we get kicked out. But we won't."

"Really?"

"I will do my absolute best, I promise. I'm not having you so miserable—it's awful to watch. I can't promise it's going to get better, but I can promise that if it doesn't get better by the end of term, I will take you out. Deal?"

Robin's face has lit up, pink back in her cheeks.

"Thanks, Mom."

Zora arrives at this point and we take her upstairs to look at the carnage in my old room.

"I never wanted to come up." Zora shudders. "I once took a couple of steps up, then I felt something turn me back."

I roll my eyes. "Don't listen to a word of it," I say to Robin. "Zora has always had a taste for melodrama."

"OK, maybe that's a bit much, but I didn't like the vibe. The house didn't feel great, you know?"

"It still doesn't. Though we're getting there. Making it our own, aren't we, Robin?" I say and Robin laughs, almost convinced, and the conversation moves straight on to the incident with the owl, which Zora finds funny.

Robin then takes Zora to show her the recent improvements in her own room—a new rug and some big floral stickers on the wall.

When Zora comes back downstairs she's encouraging.

"It's coming together," she says. "Robin likes her room, at least. I'm so pleased she still has that punk meerkat I knitted her—I never thought it would survive this long."

"She loves that meerkat. She won't be parted from it," I say. "It was always the nicest bedroom—I think because it didn't get as filled with my mother's stuff."

"It must be tough for you being in her old room."

"It's OK, actually. I guess I've got used to it. Or I don't let myself think about it. That's probably closer to the truth."

"I can't believe you've done this, you know," Zora says, sitting down heavily.

"You made your feelings pretty clear the other night," I say. "Clear enough. I don't need you to say it again."

"I wasn't going to," Zora says. "I just worry about you. You didn't see your mother for the last few years of her life—you didn't even come to her funeral." She catches my eye, holds up her hand. "Sorry. I know it was her decision to cut you off. I know she barred you from the funeral. But now you're back, sleeping in her bed, sending your daughter to your old school. How did it come to this? Was it really so bad with Andrew?"

I nod, look at Zora. Hold her gaze until Zora looks down.

"OK," Zora says. "OK. But look, you've a miserable little girl upstairs who misses her dad. Do you think you could try to talk to him again? See if you can work things out?"

I could laugh. "No chance. This is on him, Zora. This is what he wants."

Zora looks over at me. There's a moment's hesitation. "You can't know that."

"Can you just take it from me? I know what I'm talking about. This is exactly where he wants to be, and there's no other way. Anyway, it's good for my work, isn't it? You've lectured me enough about it. All those years I gave up after having Robin, living in a place where I couldn't use my qualifications, all for Andrew's job. At least I'm back in court—thanks to you. A school place for Robin, a place to live, enough money from the trust to keep us so that I've got time to build up a practice. We'll make it work."

"I still think you're wrong about Andrew, though. I think there must be something else going on, something that isn't to do with you. It's just too odd otherwise," Zora says.

I shake my head. "You don't know, Zora. Stop standing up for him. He's checked out. It's over."

"I don't believe that's true," Zora says. "You can't just give up on him like that. Think about Robin."

"They speak to each other," I say. "This is what he wanted." Anger flashes through me for a moment, fury in my eyes, before it subsides and I shrug, helpless. Zora gets the message. We move on to discussing the evidence I've been going through, and we don't mention Andrew again.

20

I'm in the middle of a dream about a crash, my car flipping across three lanes of oncoming traffic, when the alarm cuts through it, just as I'm thrown from the vehicle. I wake to discover that I'm caught up in my sheets, sweaty and hot, heart pounding. As the rate of my breathing subsides, I look at my phone: 6:30. Monday morning. I only got to sleep at four and now it's time to go.

I thought Robin was nervous on the first day of term. That was nothing. Today, the poor child is pale, lethargic. I have to tell her to get up three times before she emerges, and the face of desolation on her would melt a heart of stone.

"My tummy hurts," Robin says. "I feel really sick."

"Robin."

"Seriously, Mom. I think I'm going to throw up everywhere."

I walk around the table and hug her, before sitting down next to her, my hand on her arm.

"Running away isn't going to sort it out."

"I'm not running away. I can't help it if I feel sick." Robin's air of lethargy is overtaken by indignation.

"You weren't feeling sick when you got through that massive Yorkshire pudding yesterday."

"Maybe it's because I ate too much junk in the evening? I had all those sweets. You said I'd make myself sick," Robin says, sitting bolt upright in triumph at her comeback before remembering the dying-duck-in-a-thunderstorm act, head drooping again against my shoulder.

"I know you don't want to go to school," I say. "I completely understand that. I don't want to face them either. But you did nothing wrong. Daisy and her mum are being completely unreasonable."

"I just hate the way no one will talk to me," Robin says. "It's miserable. I sit there and it's as if I don't exist."

"Wasn't Pippa being a bit friendly at least? Her mum is organizing for us to go over, remember?"

"I suppose. But even Pippa will only talk to me if no one is looking. I hate it."

"I know you do. And I totally understand it. Just a bit longer. Let's see how it goes. And then we'll take it from there."

Robin makes a grumpy noise through her nose, but she sits up and eats her toast.

"You can do this," I say. "I know you can. It could turn out to be the best school you've ever been to."

Robin crunches down on the final mouthful of toast before looking at me with a withering expression, and I raise a hand and laugh, backing off.

I'm not laughing when we get off the bus near school. Nor when at least three mothers I recognize from the coffee morning walk past me, faces averted. Robin hunches down, her face pinched, and it takes all the self-control that I possess to continue walking toward the school, not to pull Robin by the hand and take her away from this terrible place.

Even the weather is muted to match our mood, a pathetic fallacy of heavy gray clouds and a deadening light.

"Here goes," Robin says, when we arrive at the school gates. "Wish me luck."

"Good luck," I say. "Just give it a go."

I watch Robin stomp up the steps before turning away. Walking back from the school, I see Julia on the other side of the road and I put my head down, determined to avoid a further confrontation. I'm not fast enough, though. Julia darts across the road and stops me dead in my tracks.

"Your daughter had better keep away from mine," Julia says, standing right in my face. I take a step back, not keen for the situation to escalate, but Julia follows, cornering me against the railings. "If I hear one more complaint from Daisy about anything that girl does, I swear to God I will not be responsible for my actions."

She's so close that I can see the small red veins in her eyes, the pores on her nose where her makeup has caked. Cracks in the mask. The flaws give me a jolt of courage and I set my jaw, pushing my face in closer to Julia instead of following my initial instinct and pulling away.

"I don't know who the fuck you think you are, but I've had enough of this. You're behaving like an absolute cow, and your precious daughter is too. She had better stay well away from Robin," I hiss. "Or you won't be the only one taking action."

"Who the fuck do I think I am? I'm head of the PTA, that's who I am," Julia says. "And I'm an old girl. I know this school. This school is mine."

"So fucking what? I'm an old girl too. And you know what? I hated it then and it's no fucking better now, thanks to people like you."

We stand nose to nose, motionless for a few long moments.

"*Mummy!*" a voice calls and the spell is broken. I loosen my fist and step back. It's not Robin, though the note of panic could have been hers. It's Daisy, Julia's daughter. She's run up to us and is now clutching hold of her mother's arm.

"Just leave my daughter alone," Julia hisses, and pivots away from me so sharply she nearly pulls Daisy over. The girl lets go of her mother and staggers before regaining her footing. Julia's already meters ahead of her, striding away down the road toward the gates. For a short moment, Daisy looks at me, an expression almost of pleading on her face, before she turns and runs after her mother, schoolbag banging on her back.

I walk to the tube, feet heavy, heart heavier. The week couldn't have got off to a worse start.

21

Every day this week proceeds in the same way. Violence doesn't threaten again, but I feel there's tension whenever I get close to the school building. Groups of mothers huddle tight or part like the Red Sea at my passing. I'm doing my best not to be paranoid, but I'm sure I'm not imagining it. I might as well be swinging a bell in front of me and intoning, *Unclean! Unclean!*

That's not the worst, though. The worst is Robin. She's growing paler, the strain of the ostracism preying on her. She's bitten her nails down into bloody little stumps, and a dry patch of skin by her mouth is spreading. But she won't talk about it.

"It was fine," she says to me on Wednesday evening when I ask about her day, picking at her pizza. She won't look at me.

"Did anyone talk to you?" I say.

A long pause. She gets under the edge of a big bit of cheese and peels it off in one go from the pizza base. She opens her mouth as if she's about to say something, closes it again. She shakes her head.

"How about netball?" I'm going to persevere with this until I get something out of her. She's quiet for a moment longer, before she shakes her head, the motion slight, but enough.

"They won't pass to me, Mom. I was in just the right place for Daisy to pass and she let the other team have the ball deliberately rather than let me have it. And her mom didn't even tell her off. She just laughed."

"Her mum was at games?"

"Yes, she likes coming to watch practices as well. She's got lots of coaching tips."

"For netball?" I can't keep the incredulity out of my voice.

"Grown-ups play it too, Mum," Robin says. There's a pause. "She shouts a lot, though. She made Daisy cry earlier."

"How did she make her cry?"

"She missed a shot at the net and her mom got really mad at her. Kept telling her how useless she was and how she'd never get into the A team."

"That's horrible," I say. "How stupid to care so much about Year Six netball."

"Mom," Robin says. "It's important."

"Oh, I know it's important, but you know what I mean. It's not that important—not important enough to make someone cry about it. I didn't even realize parents could come and watch practices."

"Daisy's mom is the only one."

"Doesn't the teacher try and stop her when she's shouting?"

Robin looks at me as if I've lost my mind. "The teacher's scared of her, too. She shouts a lot." She pushes the rest of the pizza aside and stomps off upstairs. I want to follow her and get her to talk more, but I restrain myself, sitting on the sofa downstairs trying to read a book, leafing through the pages though I don't take in a word in front of me, images of the violence I'd like to wreak on Julia swimming in front of my eyes.

It's nearly eight when I decide to go upstairs to make sure that Robin is getting ready for bed. I'm halfway up the stairs when I hear a muffled cry from her room. I run the rest of the flight, taking the steps two at a time.

She's sitting on the floor beside her bed, the contents of her schoolbag spread out around her. There's a box in her hand that I don't recognize, square and blue, the color of a duck's egg. It looks just like a Tiffany box and, as I move closer, I see the logo on the lid on the floor beside her. That's exactly what it is.

Robin looks up at me, the box in her hands. I realize she can't move. I go and gently take the box from her. Then I look inside. I can't make out what it is at first, an indistinct mass of brown and white in the bottom. I look more closely. It looks like bits of rice. But they're moving. I'm as frozen as Robin for a moment, looking at this without fully grasping what it is I have in my hand. But then the realization hits properly.

"Maggots! It's full of maggots!" I scream and throw it away from me and watch in horror as the maggots shower out over Robin, the box landing on her bed. She starts screaming and runs frantically into the bathroom and I hear the water start running in the shower, her screams continuing until they subside into sobs.

I'm screaming too, brushing my hands down myself, trying to get rid of any that might have landed on me, until I suddenly remember it's Robin I need to look after. I go to the bathroom door and shout through, asking if she's OK. She's stopped sobbing now, and all I can hear is water from the shower, the occasional splashing. I leave her to it, run downstairs to get cleaning stuff, a rubbish bag.

Rubber gloves at the ready, I grit my teeth and get down to clearing it up. At first, I'm loath to pick up the maggots, even wearing the gloves, but the thought of Robin stiffens my nerve and soon I'm over it, picking them up one by one with grim determination.

Robin has finished by now and she stands at her bedroom door, wrapped in a towel. The shock seems to have worn off a little, but she still looks very shaken, refusing to come anywhere near where the maggots landed. I clear the floor as much as I can and move over to the bed where the box landed. It's on its side and I tip it back onto its base. I'm really trying to overcome my disgust but it's hard. I look at Robin, her misery, and it spurs me on. I look back inside the box, poking the contents gingerly, trying to shift the maggots to see what's underneath. There's a small body, not much of it left now, and some feathers. Brown feathers. And red.

It's a robin. The remains of a dead robin.

"What is it, Mom?" Robin says from the door and I push as much of the mess as I can back into the box and shove the lid back on. She doesn't need to see this.

"It's a dead bird," I say. "Where did you find this?"

"Someone must have put the box in the bottom of my bag. I only found it now."

"Where was your schoolbag?"

"In the changing room at netball. Anyone could have done it."

I nod. Anyone could.

I've scraped up every maggot I can see now. I put the box into a plastic bag and tie it up firmly. Then I strip the sheets off the bed—I'm going to put them through a boil wash.

"Can I sleep in your room?" she asks.

"Of course you can," I say. She pads off through. I take the sealed bag downstairs, and the sheets, sticking them straight into the washing machine, adding bleach to the detergent. Then I go back up to check that I've got rid of all the mess. I pick through the things on the floor, the books from the schoolbag and the pencil case, piling them up neatly. Then I get hold of Robin's bag and look inside it before turning it inside out to make sure there's nothing else nasty lurking in there.

No more maggots. But a folded piece of paper falls out. I pick it up in my gloved hand and unfold it. It's A4, from a spiral notebook, one edge torn. And scrawled on it in uneven capital letters:

A ROBIN FOR ROBIN. HOPE YOU ENJOY MY PLACE.

My scalp is prickling. I fold the note carefully, go through to my room to find Robin curled up in my bed.

"Has anyone talked about you taking someone's place at school?" I ask. I try to keep my tone light. I don't want to tell her what else is written on the note.

She sits up and rubs her eyes. "No. Someone called me a vampire, feeding off the dead. I didn't want to tell you, but that's all they say now. Daisy had garlic with her today—she kept waving it at me whenever I went near her. I don't know why, though."

"Oh, sweetheart..."

"I know it's stupid. But I don't like it."

"I don't like it either. You know I'm going to have to tell Mrs. Grayson about this, don't you?"

She jerks upright, her face distraught.

"Mom, no. Please, no. Please can we just ignore it? It'll only make things worse. Please. You have to promise not to tell anyone." Robin starts crying, her sobs increasing in intensity until I acquiesce, albeit with reluctance.

I lean forward and hug her until she quiets, lie beside her until she goes to sleep. I'm desperate to email the school and report what's happened, but I've promised Robin not to…Besides, I don't even know who I'm accusing. Julia seems the most likely suspect, or her daughter, but it could have been anyone with access to the changing room. Surely this is just malicious teasing, not anything more sinister. Maybe whoever did it was only meaning to give Robin the bird, didn't realize that maggots might hatch out of it, giving such a sinister edge to it all.

I'm shaken. I lie awake for most of the night, regretting my promise to Robin, my brain whirring, trying to work out the best approach. Trying not to remember the feeling of the maggots squirming in my gloved fingers as I picked them up, one by one, from the floor.

SUNDAY, 12:15 P.M.

I'm out of the house and running, keys in one hand, phone in the other. I keep checking it every few moments in case anyone calls, but nothing. I look again as I'm turning the corner of my street toward the main road when I trip on the curb. I stumble and fall headfirst to the ground, thumping the edge of my glasses into the top of my right eye socket.

My phone has flown out of my hand, landing with a thud just out of reach. I push myself up and reach to get hold of it, but my head hurts and I'm dizzy and I nearly stumble again. My head is aching, with a sharp stinging where the glasses have been forced into my face.

I don't have time to care. It doesn't matter—I'll let it hurt later. Right now, I have to find a cab, get there as fast as I can. I bend down slowly, carefully, picking up my phone. Before I can check it again I see a bus approaching and I run toward it, holding out my hand. It might be ages before a cab comes and I can't bear to stand still. The bus comes to a halt and I climb on, tapping my card against the reader.

It's only half full and I find a seat easily. Once I'm sitting down I turn my phone over. The damage is bad. Worse than

I realized. The screen is entirely cracked, little shards of glass falling off the center of the damaged area.

I want to throw it away from me. I want to start screaming at the top of my voice, tell the bus driver to go faster, get a fucking move on. Despite my efforts to control myself, a sob escapes my compressed lips. I see people turn toward me, and I duck my head down, unwilling to engage with anyone. If I have to speak I know I'll lose control.

Too late, a woman in a headscarf has moved over next to me. She puts her hand on my arm, concern in her face.

"You OK?"

"Fine," I say, shoulders hunched against her.

"You look like you've hurt yourself," she persists.

"I'm fine," I say. "Please can you leave me alone."

"Is there anyone I can call? Do you need some help?"

"Please, leave me alone," I say. "I promise you I'm fine. Thank you, but really, I'm OK."

She looks at me, her face troubled, but after a moment she moves away from me. She's being kind, but I wish people would mind their own business. The bus can't move fast enough.

There's something trickling down my face, down my neck, and I put my hand up to wipe it away. The bus judders unsteadily over a pothole and I push against the back of the seat in front to keep myself steady. When the bus comes to a halt at the next stop I take my hands away. I've left a print behind. A red handprint. A handprint in blood.

My head throbs again but the adrenaline drives me on. I grit my teeth. I have to get there. That's all that matters now.

22

No good answer has presented itself by the time we get up the following day. Robin seems a little more cheerful after some sleep, no suggestion that she shouldn't go into school, though I'm braced for complaints of a tummy ache, or worse. She isn't keen to go into her room but I assure her I've got rid of all the maggots, and eventually she consents, getting dressed without incident.

I'm torn about how best to approach the dead bird. Should I make no further mention of it? I don't want to freak her out. But I do want her to be on her guard. Before I can work out what to say, she brings it up herself.

"I texted Dad this morning and told him about the bird," she says. "He says I need to be brave and stand up to any bullies. So that's what I'm going to do."

The irony of his words is so strong that I could almost laugh, before a wave of fury engulfs me and I have to leave the room rather than show Robin how I feel. Stand up to bullies? I wish to God I had stood up to him and his manipulations, what he did to get rid of me, of Robin too. Andrew is the biggest bully I know, killing off our marriage, banishing us here with his threats.

I can't resist. For the first time since we've got here, my resolve cracks. I need to tell him how I feel.

Stand up to bullies? That's a fucking joke. You fucking bastard.

So much more I could say. But I don't. I press send then turn off my phone. I've had enough. We travel to school in silence, and I watch Robin walk in through the school gates with a knot in my chest.

The trip down to chambers is a good distraction. I'm due to show Barbara the evidence that I unearthed at the weekend.

"This is brilliant," she says when I lay it out in front of her. "It shreds her credibility." There's such glee in her voice that I feel almost alarmed.

"I thought there might be something to it," I say, "but do you think it's going to make that much difference?"

"Yes, of course it will. It's the whole case in miniature; shows once and for all what a little liar she is."

I turn it over in my mind. I'm conflicted. On the one hand, I'm delighted to have found something that assists the defense. I've proved my place on the team. It'll lead to better work in future—my place in chambers is more assured. But on the other, there's a crawling feeling of guilt in my gut. What Freya is saying about Jeremy could ruin his life, sure, but she's ruined her own life too, in the process, all her petty shames and fears exposed like this to hostile eyes.

I run through it again, cringing at the way it plays out on the pages in front of me.

It was about a year ago, from the dates on the messages, an exchange between Freya and someone called Susie. It spanned two weeks, give or take, starting with Freya's breathless account of how she'd met a boy at a party and they'd kissed and exchanged numbers. He was at one of the big south London private schools, their pupils socializing frequently with the pupils from Freya's school in central London.

They met the next weekend, which was when the relationship (such as it was) seemed to sour, culminating in Freya's comments to her friend Susie that he had tried it on with her. This led to a flurry of messages and overuse of the acronyms OMG and OMFG, and many expressions of support, then Susie went suddenly quiet. A long string of messages from Freya went unanswered, until Susie abruptly came back to her, a week later. She said that she'd spoken to boys at the other school, that Freya's allegation of pushing it "too far" was entirely false, that, in fact, Susie knew that Freya had tried to seduce the boy, been rebuffed, and was now making up this story to cover her own shame and embarrassment at the rejection. Freya needed to be more careful about what she said. *You can't go round throwing accusations and lies out about people.*

Freya had written one message in reply—bleak.

He choked me and he wanted anal and I said no. He made me give him head. I was crying. He didn't stop.

Unfortunately for her, Susie wasn't going down the sisterhood route. *We all know you don't say no to anyone. Stop telling lies. He didn't want it because you're such a slag and now you're talking shit to get back at him. Don't DM me again.*

"I can't believe the police didn't pick up on this earlier," I say to Barbara. "Surely it goes to the heart of her credibility, if she's done it before. Did she take this one to the police?"

"Not that we know of. And, in general, they're overworked,

underresourced, understaffed. That's why so many rape trials are falling by the wayside—a girl makes an allegation, the defense finally get to go through her phone and, boom! In whatever way, she shows she isn't purer than the driven snow. The jury won't convict."

"You seem very philosophical about it," I say.

"It's a boon for defense lawyers," Barbara says. "And you know how we feel about it—it's better that ten guilty men go free than one innocent man is wrongly convicted. Also, look at it rationally. Jeremy has his whole future ahead of him. He doesn't deserve to have his career blighted by something as trivial as this."

"Do you think he did it?" I say, the words bursting out before I can stop them.

Barbara looks at me with scorn, and shame crawls over me at the gaucheness of the question. The worst question of all to ask a defense barrister. I know better than that. But I've been too long out of the game, lost my nerve. After a long moment, Barbara laughs.

"Surely I don't need to remind you that what I think is completely irrelevant? The only question with which we need concern ourselves is whether the prosecution is able to prove it."

I laugh too, apologize. Of course that's the only relevant question. But that clarity of thought is escaping me, a slight feeling of guilt growing that I'm complicit in something shameful, a nebulous sense of wrongdoing that's hard to shake off.

I shouldn't be having any feelings at all about the complainant. I should just be doing my job. But Freya isn't so much older than Robin—the idea that in a few short years Robin will be negotiating these choppy waters is terrifying, and that Robin could herself be met with such lack of empathy is sadder still.

Jeremy's career might be at risk, his reputation.

But what about Freya's?

23

The last days of the week follow the same pattern. Robin drags her feet going into school, I harden myself not to take her straight home again. On Thursday morning I see Julia on the other side of the road, and I quicken my step to get out of there before there's any further confrontation. On Thursday afternoon, I see Jessica in the distance. She seems to wave at me. I turn my head, trying to blink away the image of the dead robin that's swum before them.

But as we walk away from school, I hear someone calling my name, and I look around. It's Jessica, Portia at her side.

"Hi," she says.

"Hi." I look at her blankly, waiting for her to speak. I'm about to walk away when she finally starts talking, the words falling out in a rush.

"Apparently you said you were an old girl—you said you went to this school?"

"Yes, I did say that."

"Is it true?"

I look at her with total scorn. "Do you really think I'd lie about it? It's not exactly something I'm proud of. I wasn't happy here."

"It's just. Well. We don't remember you. We've talked about it, and we don't remember you at all. So..."

I look at her, shaking my head. I can't actually believe that she's questioning me like this.

Robin pulls at my hand. "Show her the board. The one with your name on it."

"What board?" Jessica says. There's contempt in her voice, or something close to it, and the fact that she dares to speak to my daughter like that sends me raging.

"OK, yes. That's a good idea, Robin. A very good idea. My name is on the board inside. The list of school captains and vice captains. I'm up on that bloody board and I'm going to show you right now."

I start marching straight back toward school, not bothering to look around to see if they're following, though the sound of rapid footsteps behind me suggests they are. I push through the front door of the school building and stand at reception.

"I'd like to look at the board above the doors to the hall, please."

The receptionist looks at me blankly. Jessica is now beside me, Robin and Portia a little behind.

"I'm sorry, what do you..."

"I want to go through to the entrance of the hall and show this lady my name on the list of former school captains. She doesn't seem to believe that I am an old girl."

I turn and go straight on through, Jessica hot on my heels. I find the boards and locate my name immediately.

"Look. There I am. Look. Sadie Roper, Vice Captain. Straight up there."

"That's not your name, though. Isn't your name Sadie Spence?"

"Oh, for fuck's sake, have you never heard of the concept of a married name? Spence is my husband's name. Roper is my maiden name. The name I use."

"There's no need to swear," Jessica says, but she lacks conviction. She's looking uncomfortable.

"There's every need to swear," I say. "I've had enough of this. You've all behaved appallingly for weeks. It's not on. Anyway, where are your bloody names? I don't remember you at all either."

She gestures up at the shield to the right. I look up and read down the list from the years below me. Four years after me I see the name Jessica Morton, Vice Captain. I turn and look at her.

"You were four years below me, then," I say. "I don't see Julia, though."

"Have you never heard of the concept of a married name?" she sneers back at me, though without conviction, before pointing above her own name. I squint and see the name Julia Brumfitt, three years below me.

"Is that this Julia, then?" I say. Jessica nods. "You were both much younger. No wonder you don't recognize me. I don't remember anything about either of you."

She's still looking uncomfortable. I examine her face closely, looking to see if I can place her after all this time. But I can't. Not even the name rings a bell.

Finally, she speaks. "I owe you an apology." She doesn't sound sorry. She sounds cross. "I shouldn't have accused you of lying."

"No, you shouldn't. I have no recollection of either of you whatsoever," I say. "I'm surprised, I have to be honest. It wasn't exactly the coolest thing to be school captain—didn't they only hand it out to the people they were sorry for, the ones with no friends? Or people whose behavior they were trying to influence?"

Jessica is shaking her head. "Oh no, not at all. It was definitely a badge of honor. Only the most popular girls were chosen. By the time I was doing it, certainly."

I look at her with skepticism. "Maybe they changed their policy. It was certainly the case for me," I say. "And look, nothing has changed. Anyway, that's quite enough reminiscing for one day. Do ensure that the message makes it through to the rest of your little gang, please. Since it seems to be important to you all. God only knows why."

I walk off without saying anything else, Robin at my side. In tacit agreement we keep going without talking until we're safely on the bus, at which point we both burst out laughing. The discomfiture of Jessica keeps me going for the rest of the day. I even forget about the dead bird.

Later that evening I text Zora. *Do you remember Julia Brumfitt or Jessica Morton from school? Three or four years below us?* Then I go to sleep, still smiling at the look on Jessica's face.

24

Finally, it's three o'clock on Friday. I've worked from home today, a list of demands from Barbara at my elbow. She's getting edgy as the date of the trial approaches, despite the advances that I've made in reinforcing the defense case. I look through the list, tick off what I've managed to achieve so far, looking at the other four files with a sigh.

I've found more nuggets of information. Other times when Freya has thrown accusations at her interlocutors, once suggesting one has got off with a boy she fancied and another time asserting that a girl called Priya has stolen her makeup bag from her locker. Each time, there's a strong pushback, and counteraccusations of Freya being a drama queen—someone who makes up stories to get attention.

My qualms have faded. The more I see this pattern of behavior, the more I'm beginning to doubt the complainant's credibility. Which is the point of the exercise, after all. I set up a document on my computer, saving it under the title *Lies Freya Told*. Three entries so far, but with another six months' worth of messages to plow through, I'm pretty sure we're going to get more material to add, all fuel for

Barbara's cross-examination of the girl. I'm going to have to work over the weekend.

Zora texts just as I finish working.

I don't remember Jessica. Wasn't there some drama around that Julia? Something to do with bullying? I'll ask around, see if anyone remembers xx

Despite my intention not to bother, not to make any effort at all, I shower before going to collect Robin. Then I dress and apply makeup with more care than usual. I'm fed up with feeling shit whenever I go near the school gates. They've only seen me in my old black suit, dull work stuff—it's time to break out some less formal clothes. I put on a slick of red lipstick, wipe it off, put it back on again, and slam out of the house without looking in the mirror.

I see Nicole as she leaves the tube. The woman looks around once, twice, before coming up to me.

"Hi," she says. "I almost didn't recognize you. You look... different."

"Oh yes?"

"Good, I mean. You look good. Younger. Sorry, I didn't mean..." Her face flushes. I don't reply for a moment, leaving her hanging. Then I relent, a little. At least Nicole is making an effort.

"Thanks," I say, a small concession. Still not making it easy for her.

"Um, I was wondering. I know I said I'd call about us meeting up with the kids. Sorry I haven't, it's..." Her words trail off.

"Complicated?" I say brightly.

"Yes. Complicated." A long pause before words start rushing

out, tumbling over each other. "Look, I know how Julia must seem. But she's all right, really. She was so good to me when my husband left. She doesn't realize how she comes across, she's so focused on Daisy. I mean, her husband left her, too. It's really difficult for her. It can make her seem quite…hard. But once you get to know her—"

"She's made it quite clear she doesn't want to get to know me," I interrupt.

"She'll get there," Nicole says. "Just give her time. Especially now she knows you're an old girl. Honestly, she's really lovely underneath. I owe her so much." Her voice breaks. She looks close to tears, pink around her eyes.

I'm mute, a jangling sound in my ears. I know Nicole is trying to be kind, to be helpful, but I won't bring my defenses down just like that. I don't dare, not after everything that's happened. I take a deep breath, calm myself. Smile.

"I'm sure it'll all work out," I say. Nicole smiles back, and we walk together the rest of the way to school.

"You look nice," Robin says and hugs me. My doubts about the brightness of my lipstick fall away. I draw Robin close for a moment then pull away, keeping my hands on her shoulders.

"How was it?" I say.

Robin rolls her eyes. "Awful. But I did really well in the comprehension test."

"I'm sorry, I totally forgot to say good luck."

"It's OK. I'm not too bothered. Though it's good to do well."

"How did it go down with the others?" I take Robin's hand and we walk away from school, my lipstick a shield against any dirty looks and mutters.

Robin laughs. "We're not meant to share our marks. But

Daisy stole my paper when I got it back. When she saw what I got she went bright red and burst into tears."

"Oh no, why? Had she done badly?"

"Not at all. She got seventy-six percent this time. But her mom wants her to get over eighty percent each time."

I shake my head at this. "Nuts. I don't understand it. Did she actually talk to you?"

"No. I overheard her talking to Pippa. They're still ignoring me."

At that moment the bus pulls up and we climb onto it, the conversation ending. It's time to focus on the weekend ahead.

25

There's a lasagna bubbling golden in the oven, its aroma enticing. With the lights dimmed, in the twilight, the house looks almost inviting. We've come a long way. Robin is actually happy—the combination of her favorite dinner and the weekend stretching ahead.

I chop up the salad, the knife cutting clean through the tomatoes and the cucumber. I revel in the calm. It's lovely that, for once, Robin isn't miserable. We're about to sit down for food when there's a knock at the door.

Robin sprints to answer it. I'm expecting her to come back, but there's no sound. I suddenly panic—has someone grabbed her? Has she been overpowered at the door in a home invasion? I dash through to the front before stopping. Andrew is standing in the doorway holding Robin tight. She's clutching him around his middle—it looks like she might never let him go. They don't notice me.

I pull myself together.

"I didn't expect to see you," I say with some effort. I want to start screaming. As soon as Andrew hears me, he jumps like a cat, letting go of Robin.

"Come in, Dad. Come and have supper. Mom's made lasagna.

There's loads. Why didn't you tell me you were coming? I've missed you so much," Robin says, pulling him inside before I can say anything else.

Robin talks nonstop all the way through the meal, Andrew's contribution only a few noises of encouragement as Robin fills him in on every detail of the last few weeks. The owl, the ostracism, all the hurts and slights she's suffered. The maggots. There are shafts of light, though; she likes the teachers, the art department. But overall, it's a litany of woe. I swallow down my lasagna with difficulty, shifting the lumps in my throat with constant sips of wine, water. I'm trying not to get drunk, afraid that I'll break, start screaming abuse at Andrew and never stop.

"Mom hates it too," Robin says. "The moms are all horrible."

"It'll all get better soon," Andrew says, his first full sentence for some time. He's leaning in my general direction, but his glance slides past my ear, over my shoulder.

"Mom says if it doesn't, I can leave at the end of term," Robin says.

"I don't think that's the best attitude," Andrew says. "What happened to my little fighter? Remember that time you were being bullied in elementary school and you stood up to him and told him to leave you alone? You need to channel some of that here."

My fingers have curled into fists under the table, fingernails jabbing sharp into the palms of my hands. I am not going to start yelling. It's not fair on Robin.

"Dad," Robin says. "It's horrible."

"I bet you can turn it around," he says. "You're brilliant at making friends. Don't give up. That's not the way to do it."

I can't look at him. I want to thump him, sitting there at

my table, eating my food, when it's his fucking fault we're here.

"Well, that's not the worst thing. You should see what Grandma did to Mom's old room," Robin says, clearly not ready to stop complaining. I protest, trying to stop it, but it's too late, Robin is leading Andrew out of the kitchen and up the stairs. I sit with my head bowed, picking at the skin around my nails, picturing the scene as Andrew looks at the destruction Lydia has wrought. Will he feel sympathy? Or will he view it without surprise, this confirmation that I'm fundamentally unlovable, rejected both by my mother and by him.

After a while I hear their footsteps coming back down the stairs. Robin first, light on the treads. And Andrew's. Heavy, slow. Will he even come back into the kitchen or is he going to leave right now?

But he comes through to the kitchen, stands in the doorway. Robin's not with him. I look up at him, and for the first time in months, he actually makes eye contact with me. We hold our gaze for a few long seconds, and I'm not sure, but there's a spark of something, a connection that's made, or renewed.

"I'm taking Robin with me for the weekend. I'm staying in a hotel; it's a twin room. I'm sure you could do with a break. I'll take her into school on Monday, see the place. You can pick her up in the afternoon," he says. The connection is broken.

"What if I don't want you to do that?"

"Then let's ask Robin what she wants, shall we? Do you want to tell her she can't spend time with me?"

I take a deep breath. He's got me.

"How can I possibly trust you, that you'll take her in to school? How do I know that you're not going to take her back to the U.S. instead?"

He looks at me with surprise. "Why would I do that?"

"I don't know what you're capable of anymore. I don't even know who you are." I can't be arsed dancing round it. "What the fuck are you doing here, Andrew?"

"I wanted to see Robin. Of course. And I wanted to see..."

"What? What did you want to see?"

"I wanted to see that you were doing OK without me," he says. "And you are."

We look at each other. The text I sent lies heavy between us, unmentioned, as is so much else. I can't do this any more. "Why the fuck would you care? You forced this on me in the first place. Fuck you, Andrew. Just get out. I never want to see you again."

He stands for a moment, looking at the floor, before going to find Robin. I hear his footsteps as he climbs the stairs, his voice in the distance. She'll be packing her weekend clothes, her uniform. Any minute now she'll come and ask for my help. She can never find everything she needs. I'm ready for her call, but it never comes. I sit in the kitchen and wait until Robin comes in to say goodbye, her farewell distracted, so excited is she at the prospect of a weekend with her dad that she's practically bouncing with each step. Andrew leaves without coming in to see me again, Robin skipping at his heels. The rest of the weekend is dark.

26

It's the first day of the trial. I wash the weekend off me and dress in my black suit. At least I don't have to deal with the school run. I think about whether I should call the school, make sure that Andrew has actually delivered her there rather than doing a run for it with her, but I control myself. They'll let me know soon enough if she hasn't arrived. If he ever moves back to the UK, I'll have to get used to this.

Once through Security, I see Barbara in the robing room and hand her the work I've done.

"As suspected, no evidence of communication between the client and the complainant at all," I say. "And there's some more examples of her making stuff up to try and impress her friends. I'm making a list. Lies she told."

"Excellent," Barbara says. "Good work. Is there much more to go?"

"One more file. That's it."

We stand next to each other before the mirror, adjusting our bands and pulling on our wigs. Barbara has twenty-five years on me, easily, and it shows, but not too much. Well-preserved, I think. The main sign of Barbara's age is the puckering of small vertical lines round her mouth, evidence of a lifetime spent smoking. She smells of cigarettes now, the aroma of old smoke strong, layers on layers over years—the woman kippered in it.

Barbara's wig is yellowed at the front, too. Unlike mine, which is still box-fresh, white and evidently barely worn. Barbara looks askance at it in the mirror—I catch her eye.

"I only had a few years in the crown court before I left," I say. "I didn't get much use out of it."

"We'll make sure it gets properly broken in," Barbara says. "You've done excellent work on this so far. I'll make sure you're sorted out."

Ready, we walk out of the robing room together, black gowns swooping behind us. Jeremy is waiting in the front hall of the court building, his expression hunted. He's in a dark jacket and white shirt, all ready for the dock. He looks less comfortable in it than he did in the tweed jacket, a little as if he's borrowed his father's clothes for the big occasion.

"I think that chap's a journalist," he says, gesturing behind him at a man in an ill-fitting suit. "I recognize him—he was hanging around my flat last week."

Barbara looks over, shrugs. "Most likely," she says. "This is bound to attract some media attention. We've discussed it already."

Jeremy clearly has more to say on the subject, but his lips tighten.

"Zora should be here any minute," Barbara says. "Then we'll find a conference room, talk you through what's going to happen. I'm going to get a coffee right now. Do you want anything?"

Both Jeremy and I shake our heads, and as Barbara leaves

for the canteen, we move together to the back of the entrance hall. He keeps looking over his shoulder, evidently on edge.

"We should find a conference room, if there's one free," I say. "I can text Barbara where we are."

We walk down a long wood-paneled corridor, trying doors. We're about halfway along when there's a loud screech.

"Sir, sir! Look, he's here!"

It's a group of teenage girls, their makeup thickly applied, eyebrows stenciled on with heavy hands. I look at their fake tans and blink, aware suddenly of how pale and pasty I look. The girls flock around him, touching him on the arm, chirruping in turn.

"Sir, we've come to support you, sir. We don't want to see you going to prison, sir. We're here to show everyone what a great teacher you are, sir, how much we like you."

Jeremy looks like a trapped animal. He catches my eye and he's so clearly desperate to be rescued that I nearly laugh, though I'm well aware of how serious the situation is. I know what his bail conditions are. Apart from anything else, he's not meant to have contact with any pupils from Freya's old school. OK, technically, he hasn't sought them out, but they're definitely doing their best to make as much bodily contact with him as they can. If the prosecution sees him in this situation, it could make his bail position problematic to say the least.

There's an empty conference room just behind me. I gesture to Jeremy, beckoning him in, and when he doesn't move, I wade into the throng and take hold of him by the arm, dragging him into the room, whereupon I slam the door shut and wedge a chair against it so that no one can get in.

He stays standing next to the table, gray with fear. I face

him and put my hand on his arm again, but more gently this time. He inhales once, twice, then moves close in toward me, slumping his head down on my shoulder. I'm hesitant, stiff for a moment before I put one arm round him and pat him on the back. His breathing calms. Eventually he moves away.

"Sorry," he says. "Sorry. That really freaked me out."

"It's OK," I say. "I understand. That was pretty full-on." I smile, pat his hand. Turning away, I pull my phone out of my bag, about to text Barbara to explain, when she rings me.

I catch her up quickly, and within a matter of minutes, someone tries to open the door, the chair I've propped in the way crashing to the floor. I move hurriedly to clear the path and Barbara comes in. She rolls her eyes at me but makes no other comment about the girls outside.

When we have sat down at the conference table, Barbara clears her throat, starts talking.

She tells Jeremy what he can expect on the first day in court, where he'll sit, how little sway they will have over jury selection. Given his father is a judge, it's most likely he knows all this, I think, but he looks as if he's calming down as Barbara talks to him, color returning slowly to his cheeks.

"Will either of your parents be attending court?" Barbara asks.

"Yes," Jeremy says with a distinct lack of enthusiasm. "My mother will be here for the duration, I expect. She'll get here any minute. My father will turn up when we know what time we're starting. He didn't want to spend hours waiting, and they find it difficult to be in the same place as each other." Jeremy pauses. "They're both being very supportive, though," he continues, as if to counter any criticism.

* * *

We stay holed up in the conference room. Alexandra turns up soon after, directed by Jeremy, and she hugs her son and clings on to his hand. He looks more and more like a schoolboy in a borrowed suit. It's hard to think of him as predatory at all.

Jeremy's father is wise not to come in advance—by lunchtime we're still not in court. Barbara texts him to tell him about the delay, and he replies to say that given there won't be time now for anything substantive to happen, there's no point in his coming. Barbara relays the message to Jeremy, who greets the information with a shrug.

"And isn't that just typical of your father," Alexandra says, her eyes snapping with anger. Jeremy doesn't reply.

I keep checking my phone to make sure the school hasn't been in touch to ask where Robin is, in case Andrew has failed to take her in. Nothing. No news is good news, after all. At least the delay gives us time to get through all necessary discussions—Jeremy and Alexandra are pleased by the discoveries I've made in the messages from Freya's computer. Alexandra goes so far as to mutter *well done* at me, and Barbara declares herself ready to cross-examine, promising to *tear that girl to shreds* in the witness box. I imagine how much Freya must be dreading her court appearance, and I suppress a shudder, though I'm increasingly curious to see her in the flesh after spending so much time in her social media. Jeremy's anxiety doesn't fade, and a feeling of tension rises during the morning, especially when we have to leave the conference room at lunchtime and we're mobbed by the teenage girls who have inexplicably been waiting to catch a sight of their idol.

"He's hardly the Beatles," Barbara mutters, but she takes hold of his arm and walks him through to the court canteen.

The prosecution team fills another table in the room, and Barbara gestures at them in a friendly way, but the two sides do not interact.

By the time we're finally called into court at half past two I'm ready to throttle Alexandra. She's one of the most opinionated women I've ever had the misfortune to meet, sounding off about everything, from the way that the defense should be won to her disapproval of working mothers. I keep my tongue under tight control, but it's a relief when we get to leave her in the public gallery while Jeremy is sent into the dock. The judge comes in and tells us that in her view, we're not going to get very far with proceedings today. She apologizes for the delay, and says that she will ensure that progress is made tomorrow.

"So that's it?" Jeremy says after we leave court.

"Such a waste of time. And money," Alexandra says. "All those people standing around like that. Something should be done."

"That's what years of austerity does," I say. She shoots me an evil glare.

Barbara holds up her hand. "No need for any unpleasantness. This happens on occasion. More than we'd like to think. But it should get going properly tomorrow."

We say goodbye to each other, shaking hands. If I'm quick, I'll be in time to pick up Robin at the end of school before she has to go to after-school club.

The journey up to school is the first time I've had to think all day. I'm furious about Andrew, the way he's just waltzed back in, whisked Robin away again. I've been scared all day that he's taken Robin, that he's not going to bring her back this time.

If I get her back—no, *when* I get her back—I'm going to get legal advice, file for divorce. I'm going to block him from being able to turn up and take her whenever he likes. This can't happen again.

Anger builds up in me, hot and strong. School can go fuck itself, too. So what if these women don't want to know me? I don't want anything to do with them either. I get off the tube with fire in my belly, rather than the usual slug of dread lodged cold and clammy in my gut. I've driven it out, salt on its tail. I'll wither the lot of them.

But something has changed. Something's different. I've gone expecting a fight. I don't get it.

"Hi, Sadie," says one mum.

"Hello," says another.

A group of them smile at me, actually smile, and wave, their faces open and warm as I pass.

What the fuck? I can't make sense of it.

"Afternoon," says a third.

I'm confused. It's like I've ended up in an alternative reality.

"Sadie," Julia says, walking up to me. "I hoped I'd see you. Do you think we can talk?"

It's gone from strange to completely incomprehensible, cracks in the space–time continuum.

"Julia," I say, trying to keep my voice neutral. "What do you want to talk about?"

"We've got off to an appalling start," she says. "I think we should try and start again."

I have no idea how to reply.

"Jessica told me all about last week, your name on the board. School captains together!"

I blink. "Oh, come on. That makes no difference, surely."

"It makes all the difference. You deserve the place—or rather, Robin does. It all makes sense now. But honestly, you should have told us all right from the start. It would have saved so much trouble."

"So much trouble?" I say. I nearly squeak, I'm so taken aback.

"If I'd *known*, you see, I would have realized you weren't some interloper. Of *course* Robin should be here. Even if she didn't start at the school earlier. You're part of the school family," she says, gesturing around her in an expansive way.

I'm still at a loss for words, but Nicole then approaches and joins in.

"I told you Julia was lovely, didn't I?" she says. "It's going to be all right, now. You'll see."

"Honestly, yes," Julia says. "I do hope you'll accept my apology. I can be rather territorial at times. And of course, we are under so much pressure with the exam. It's such an important term. But of course, you know all about that, don't you? You've been through it all yourself."

Can this actually be happening, all the weeks of hostility smoothed in one simple apology? Surely no one can switch as quickly as this—it must be some kind of trap. But before I can say anything, Robin comes through the gates. She doesn't see me at first, and she's clearly unhappy, her shoulders drooping and her mouth downturned. She stands looking around for a moment, and when she sees me, her face lights up a little—but only a little.

She trudges over to me. I give her a quick hug, and we start to move away. Julia stops us.

"Wait, wait a minute," she says. "I think we should all go for tea. A little welcome party. Make sure we've moved on from any misunderstandings."

"What's going on, Mom?" Robin says, growing rigid in my grasp.

"Julia thinks we should all be friends."

Before Robin can reply, Julia breaks in. "I think you and Daisy are going to get on really well. It'll be good for her to be friends with someone who's as clever as she is. She needs the competition."

I catch Nicole's eye over Robin's head. She raises an eyebrow. "I know you don't think Pippa is much of a match for Daisy," she says, her voice dry.

"That's not what I meant," Julia said.

Nicole laughs. "It's fine, Julia. I know what you meant."

At this point, Daisy and Pippa turn up. They look surprised to see Robin and me with their mums, but Julia doesn't waste any time on background explanation.

"We're all going to go out for tea," she announces.

"What about homework?" Daisy says.

"Let's not bother with that tonight," Julia says. "You do lots of homework. Tea will be much more fun."

Robin and I are being pulled along by an unstoppable force. I look at her, wondering if we should make a break for it, but she's talking to Daisy and Pippa. A little hesitant, perhaps fearing ridicule, but as I watch, the other girls both laugh at something that she's said, not unkindly, but properly, and as Robin realizes that they're not teasing her, joy starts to emerge on her face, the tentative beginnings of a smile.

"Are you coming?" Julia says, and I look once more at Robin. I'm desperate to get her home and find out how the weekend has been. I'm also desperate not to hear anything about it, to pretend that it hasn't happened in the first place. Robin looks at me pleadingly.

"Can we go, Mom? Pippa says it's the best hot chocolate in the world."

I should refuse, but I don't have the heart to say no. I haven't seen Robin look so happy in weeks. I swallow down my reservations. It's only a cup of tea. What harm can it do?

"Yes. Let's go," I say. "It'll be fun."

27

The rest of the afternoon passes in a whirl. Julia's a force of nature, whisking us down the road and taking over the back of a nearby coffee shop and ordering cakes and tea and hot chocolate all round before I can blink.

"Now, you girls sit and chat nicely," she says, when all the plates and cups have been laid out in front of them. "I'm going to have a lovely chat with your mum, Robin. Get to know her properly."

Robin looks as overwhelmed as I feel. I'm not entirely clear what part I'm expected to play in this new drama, but I drink tea and eat cake, listening to the chat, watching Robin as she does the same, her face relaxing more and more as the other girls talk to her. Finally, she laughs, and with that, a knot of tension deep inside me lets go.

"I really wish you'd said you were an old girl," Julia says again. "It would have made all the difference."

"I don't see why it should make the slightest difference," I say. "We shouldn't have to prove that we belong."

Julia's mouth tightens. Nicole shifts on her chair, and the children stop chatting, looking over at the adults with concern on their faces. It grabs at my throat to see the worry back on Robin's face. I want to take the words back, cancel the challenge I've presented to Julia. But at the same time, I refuse to leave it all unmentioned.

"It's been very difficult," I continue, resolute. "It's hard enough moving to a new place—new at least to Robin—without encountering such hostility. There's been some really nasty stuff that's happened." I'm thinking of the dead robin, though I don't spell it out.

Julia's lips tighten even more, her eyes staring over into the middle distance as if she's weighing it all up. I glance over at Robin, who is staring straight at me, her eyes puppy-like—*don't spoil it, don't argue, let this be good, please.* It's up to Julia now. The pause stretches out, each second lasting longer and longer, time looping and spiraling while we wait to hear her response.

Finally, she focuses back on me, opens her mouth. I close my mind to Robin's imagined whimpers, lift my chin. I'll face this head on, whichever way it turns.

"You're right," Julia says. "I was too hostile. I'm sorry. Can we start again?"

I should mention the maggots. They're lingering in my mind. But around the table the tension is gone. Robin's face relaxes and she turns back to the other girls. I know that if I keep going now, refuse to accept Julia's apology, Robin will be livid with me. I can't face upsetting her any more.

"Sure," I say. "We can start again."

Robin laughs, and Daisy and Pippa laugh too, and some of my anger subsides. I want Robin to be accepted. Maybe I should have the moral courage to tell Julia how despicable she is. I don't. But even if I've accepted her apology, it doesn't mean I trust her. I'm going to keep a close eye on her.

I smile. "It must be very strange to have someone new join in Year Six. Especially with these awful tests looming. I can understand it's difficult."

"Thank you," Julia says. "I really appreciate it. I mean, look how well the girls are getting on. It's so much more pleasant when we can all be friends." She leans back, gestures expansively to Nicole. "Don't you agree, Nic?"

Nicole nods, smiles, a serene expression on her face. She says to me, "I told you it was all going to be OK, didn't I?"

"You did."

"Just so funny to think that we were at school together," Julia says. "It's a shame we were so many years apart. I don't suppose you remember me at all, do you?"

"Not in the slightest, I'm afraid—nor Jessica. Four years is just that bit too much."

"Yes, of course," Julia says. "We don't remember you at all, either. I suppose the years never mixed. It's not much different now."

At that moment my phone pings. I read the message from Barbara. *Early start tomorrow—judge says we can sit from 9:30. See you at 9.*

"Work?" Julia says.

"Work. My trial. They're sitting early tomorrow."

"It must be *so* fascinating. What are you working on at the moment? Such an interesting job, to be a criminal barrister," Julia says. I look at her with surprise that she knows what I do. Someone must have mentioned it. Maybe Robin. "Are you working on something big at the moment?"

I can't resist the opportunity to show off. "Well, I guess it is quite a big trial. But I'm not playing any major part in it. I'm just the junior. And I've come in very late—most of the work has been done already. It's a teacher who's accused of having had a sexual relationship with his pupil."

"Did I read about that? Wasn't there something in the *Standard* yesterday?" Nicole says with great enthusiasm. "There was a photo of him. It's that girls' school in central London, right? He's gorgeous."

"Oh, I know *all* about this," Julia says. "A daughter of a friend of a friend is there. The girl in question is a little bit...loose, shall we say. They say that she likes making up stories about people. The feeling is that it's a disgrace the case has got this far. He's the son of a judge, or something. It's very odd."

I have to piece through the remarks fast to work out what I can reply to and what I can't. I'm keen to question Julia more on her comment *She likes making up stories about people*, but I don't want to draw attention to it overly, or say anything too detailed about the case.

"Well, I'm acting on his behalf. And the senior barrister who's representing him is very good. I'm sure she's dug out all of this already."

"Is he as good-looking as the photo?" Nicole says.

"I can't say I've noticed," I say. "He's my client. He's very young, too. I haven't really been looking at him in that way. Besides, his eyes are very close together. But I suppose you could say he was good-looking."

Nicole laughs. "Lucky you. I thought he had such kind eyes from the photograph—they didn't seem too close together at all. And what's wrong with fancying a younger man? Look at the Macrons."

I laugh it off, but Nicole's teasing continues, though Julia stays aloof. It's not unkindly, gentle prods and smirks. I'm enjoying it, being in a group of women again. I've missed my mum friends so much since I've been back in London.

Before I realize the time, it's already half past six. The party breaks up—homework and music practice call. Robin has been enjoying herself too, and we make our way home together both in a better mood than we've been in for ages.

"Did you enjoy yourself, then?" I say.

"Yes. This afternoon was fun. I enjoyed people talking to me properly."

"I know exactly what you mean."

Robin runs off upstairs, and although I should ask about the weekend with Andrew, whether she's had fun, I'm happy to leave the subject well alone.

28

Swept up in the tsunami of Julia's social acceptance, it becomes very clear that Robin's experience of school is going to be completely different from now on. The word has spread overnight. I wake to several messages from various mums asking if Robin would like to come to their houses for playdates. I show Robin and she rolls her eyes at the infantilizing terminology, but she's happy at the attention, nonetheless. I'm asked to a number of drinks and coffee mornings, and in one more formal email, if I'd like to join the flower-arranging committee. I blink at that one. I'm about to put down my phone and get ready for the day ahead when another text arrives. This time it's from Zora.

> *Got some potential info on this Julia—I spoke to Sophie and she thinks she remembers more, a Julia who was bullied really badly—she was bucktoothed and she smelled a lot. Developed bad acne later on, too. Guess she's making up for it now xxx*

For a moment the information doesn't compute. Julia doesn't have an air of victimhood at all. She certainly doesn't have the empathy. But as I consider it, pieces start to fall into place. Her perfect teeth, perfect complexion, perfect everything. Her hope that I don't remember her from school. Despite everything she's done, I start to feel a tiny bit of sympathy for her. Maybe we're not so different, under it all—I had a pretty miserable time too. Even though my response was to get as far away as I could from it, perhaps it's not so strange that Julia wants to reclaim her past, reinvent it. I won't say anything. She's being friendly now; it's going to help Robin's life immensely. But I haven't forgotten what's happened, and I hug the knowledge to me.

Robin is practically bouncing by the time we get to school, skipping a little higher every time we pass a girl who says hello. Now we're on the inside, I can see quite how isolated we were. I'm met at the gates by Julia and Nicole, almost as if they've been waiting for me, and they draw me into warm embraces before trying to get me to join them for coffee.

"I can't, I've got to get to court," I say. "Another time, when it's all over."

"Of course, off to represent Mr. Sexy," Julia says, winking.

"Hardly." I laugh.

"What time will you finish?" Nicole asks.

"Around four, I think."

"You won't be here in time for pickup?" Nicole says.

"No. Robin's going to after-school club. We've got it all worked out."

"I think we can do better than that," Julia says. She turns to Robin. "Would you like to come home with us this afternoon? You and Daisy can do your homework together."

Robin nods, enthusiastic. I remonstrate—it's too much,

too soon. But Daisy starts talking immediately to Robin about what they can do when they've finished their homework and, again, I don't have the heart to say no.

"Then that's all set," Julia says. "She can come back to ours, and you can pick her up from there. That'll take the pressure off a bit, until the trial is over. Nicole, don't you agree?"

"Yes, great idea. And she's welcome at ours, too. I know Pippa would love it if she came over."

I have reservations, but Robin is so enthusiastic I shut them down. There's no denying it'll make life easier. After-school club only runs till half past five, and if the trial runs over at all, I'll be late.

"It's really kind of you both," I say. "It'll make it much easier. I know I need to make better arrangements, but in the meantime..."

I travel to court with a lighter heart. I'm still cynical about the fact that our acceptance into the fold has been based on such a superficial premise, but at this stage I'm not going to fight it. I'm just grateful that Robin has friends at last. A maggot of doubt crawls across my mind and I stamp on it. I'm keeping an eye out—they're not turning into our new best friends. Not yet.

I run into Jeremy at Elephant and Castle, loitering in a doorway with a hunted look on his face.

"I saw some of them on the tube again," he says. He doesn't need to explain who.

"We'll plow through them," I say, "and find a conference room again."

Sure enough, the teenagers are waiting at court, flicking their hair at me as I try to pass through them, nearly asphyxiated by the heavy stink of cheap perfume rolling off them.

At least I'm prepared for the onslaught this time, keeping my chin up and fighting my way through. We find the same conference room as the day before and bar the door shut. As the tension lifts we start laughing.

"Why on earth are they here?" I say.

Jeremy looks solemn; the laughter shuts down immediately. "It's an all-girls school," he says. "They get silly around male teachers. And you know how hysteria can spread around girls. I'm just a craze to them. They don't realize it's my life." The solemnity grows with each word he speaks, the air in the room becoming heavier.

"But don't they have lessons?"

"You'd think," he says. "But they're sixth formers. They have free periods in the morning. They'll be gone by lunchtime, at least. And they'll get bored soon, anyway. As soon as they realize I'm ignoring them."

"Good."

"Thanks for walking me in. I don't think I could have done it without you." He smiles.

"No problem," I say. "All part of the service." Without putting my bag down, I go through it, looking for one of the files, but I'm being clumsy and I drop it on the floor, spilling the contents everywhere. I kneel down to pick them up and Jeremy kneels too to help me. He's close now, very close. For a moment, I feel the warmth of him and Nicole's jokes echo through my mind. I certainly do not fancy my client. I stand up quickly, slightly rattled. My phone pings, and I snap back into myself. It's Barbara, five minutes away.

"I must go and robe up," I say, smoothing down my skirt. "Barbara will be here any minute. And we're on at half past nine, don't forget. It's an early start today."

I open the door and walk out of the room with such speed that I catch the teenagers unawares, thumping one of them on the ankle with my wheelie bag as I go.

"Ow," says the girl, and I turn and mouth *Sorry* at her. But I don't mean it.

SUNDAY, 12:30 P.M.

At long last it's my stop. I get up and push my way through the standing passengers, head down, ignoring the concerned comments, protests, as I thrust myself at the door of the bus, first to get out. I'm running along the pavement, my feet pounding—one, two, one, two—anything to get there now, right now.

I can't run, though, I never run, and a sharp pain is building up in my right side, insistent. I'm trying to ignore it but I can't. I have to stop. I lean against a garden wall, trying to get my breath back, the pain finally receding.

My phone beeps and I look at it. After looking as if it had died, it's come back to life, Lazarus-like. The screen is mostly obscured by the crack but I can just make out the text. Zora.

Have they arrived yet? Is she home?

I can't reply. It's too much. I start running again, but I have to stop, the stitch building up once more, and I lean back against the wall and wail NO, NO, NO, THEY HAVEN'T.

A touch on my shoulder. I jump, shrinking back before I see it's a community police officer, his high visibility jacket jarring yellow in my eyes.

"Is everything all right?" he says. "Are you feeling OK?"

I don't have time for this. I can't waste breath reassuring him when everything is not OK, not OK at all. I shake my head.

"She's gone," I say. "She's gone. I have to find her."

I take in a deep breath and the stitch has gone so I shrug him off—"Fine, I'm fine"—and then I'm off again, at the end of the road and turning the corner before he has a chance to react.

29

Finally, it begins. Jeremy takes his seat in the dock, prosecution and defense barristers to left and right, Barbara at the front, me in the middle, Zora at the back, nearest to Jeremy in case he needs to consult her during the course of the proceedings. On the other side, the prosecutor, Edward Kayode. He's on his own, no junior, no CPS representative. But I know that the lack of backup on the prosecution side won't be an issue to him. Nearly twenty years' experience and deeply competent, he's described in the Legal 500 as a "highly charismatic advocate, with an in-depth knowledge of his cases that is second to none."

We all rise as the judge enters. We bow toward the front of the court. The judge bows back, and we all take our seats. As proceedings begin, ripples of noise from the public gallery start to make their way into the body of the court. I look around at the teenagers who have taken up seats in pole position at the front of the public gallery. Alexandra is sitting at the other end of the front row, her face a mask of disapproval. I can't see anyone who could be Jeremy's father at this point.

Jeremy is looking distracted, his attention caught by the

activity at the back rather than where it should be, on the judge. I wonder if he might be looking for his father. The clerk of the court has to call his name out twice before he reacts, leaping up to confirm his name and address.

Zora opens her notebook and starts scribbling a note, ripping out the page and handing it to me. *I am finding the father impossible*, it says. *He keeps emailing me, telling me what to do. Then he can't even be on time to support his own son.*

I read this, turn and catch Zora's eye. We raise our eyebrows at each other. I know it'll be a lot easier for the defense team if he isn't there, drowning us with his expertise, but I worry that it'll have an adverse effect on Jeremy. I take another glance at him. He's staring down in front of him—pale, drawn.

Out of nowhere the thought comes into my mind—he *is* good-looking. In his suit there is something attractive about him. And he's young. Very young. As I look at him, I start to get the strangest feeling that I've met him before, his face suddenly familiar against his white collar and dark jacket, his hair slicked over neatly to one side. He looks up and catches me staring at him, one corner of his mouth raising in a smile. The sense of familiarity fades. I smile back, return to my notes.

The jury panel files in. Time to pay attention to proceedings. Their names are read out, and, in turn, they take their seats. Zora is looking at Jeremy to check that he has no reaction to any of them—he gives a small shrug at each one in turn. He doesn't know them, evidently. The jurors are told that the case will last a little under two weeks, and that it relates to a school in central London, giving its name and precise location. If any of the jury members have any connection to the school, they must declare it now. They all shake their heads. The jury is set.

As they are sworn in, I look hard at each of their faces. It's the right mix for the purposes of a trial like this. Eight women, covering a range of ages and ethnicities, four men. Given it all hangs on the credibility of the complainant, this is a good balance; women are harsher on female complainants, at least in my experience. Harsher on other women, full stop.

Administrative procedure out of the way, Edward Kayode, the prosecutor, gets to his feet, and lays out what he says the prosecution case will be to the jurors. They're looking alert, all except one man to the far left of the back row, whose expression is less than enthralled. He perks up noticeably when Edward comes to the specifics of the indictment, the three occasions on which he says the prosecution will be bringing evidence that the defendant had sexual intercourse with the complainant. Even the dispassionate way in which the details are laid out, clinical in terminology, isn't enough to slake the hungry look on the juror's face.

My throat tightens and I turn away, trying not to show the repulsion I feel. It'll be to Jeremy's benefit. *Well played, my son*, words I can hear that juror saying the moment Freya turns up in the witness box. It's horrible. But if it helps the defense…

I keep taking notes.

Jeremy is even more pale by the time the court rises for the day.

"It sounds appalling," he says as we walk out of court. "They're going to convict in an instant."

"Don't panic," I say. "It's meant to sound like that. They're bound to put it in the strongest terms they can. They have to set up their narrative. This is probably their best moment, before any witnesses come along to spoil their neat little story."

"I suppose," Jeremy says.

"And the jury aren't against you. I can tell that."

"I didn't want to look at them," he says.

"Well, you should. A couple of the older ladies were smiling at you. And the bloke at the back is very much on your side. He looks almost approving of what they're saying you've done."

"God, people are awful," Jeremy says. "But what if Freya is convincing? The police obviously believe her—they wouldn't have charged me otherwise. What if the jury believes her too?"

"Have faith," I say. "OK, the prosecutor is damn good. But Barbara is good too. She's one of the best. She's been doing this for years longer than he has. She's like a Rottweiler when it comes to cross-examination. You'll see."

Jeremy laughs then stops, his face solemn again. "It's very sad. I feel awful that it's come to this. I hate to think what Freya must be suffering."

"That's a laudable sentiment," Barbara says as she catches up with us. "But think about what she's putting you through. That's pretty unforgivable."

"Nothing should be unforgivable," he says. "We should always strive to see both sides of the story."

I'm struck by his understanding, but Barbara does not look convinced, one eyebrow raised. She starts to say something, stops. "Let's see how this all pans out," she says in the end. "Then we can start thinking about forgiveness."

Jeremy nods. By this time, we're at the door of the robing room. Zora appears and we stand in a tight circle at the side of the corridor. At least we're not being crowded by hormone-struck teenagers. They have all left, as Jeremy predicted.

"Your father called, Jeremy," Zora says. "I told him where we were up to."

Jeremy's face twitches. He takes out his phone and looks at it. "He hasn't been in touch with me," he says. "I guess he must have been busy. And I suppose there wasn't that much to see yet."

"No," Zora says. "This was just the opening, and we all knew what would be said. Given he's funding the defense, I'm sure he'll come to see that his money is being properly spent." She pauses, before continuing. "And be there for you, too."

Jeremy leans against the wall next to him, shutting his eyes briefly before rolling them up to the ceiling.

"I'm sure he will," he says. "He must feel under a lot of pressure. It's hardly an ideal position for him to be in, his son being prosecuted for something like this."

"At least the press hasn't got hold of the connection yet," Zora says. "In some ways it might be better if he doesn't come into court at all. There's already publicity enough around this."

Jeremy nods. He and Zora say goodbye, Alexandra too, and Barbara and I go into the robing room. We don't discuss the case. There isn't much to say. No surprises yet. I hope there will be no surprises at all.

Barbara leaves first. I'm a few minutes behind her. I text Julia to see how everything is and receive a reply almost immediately. *All good here—getting on with homework and about to eat pasta for tea. Such a lovely girl! She's welcome any time J xxxx*. I text back to thank her before gathering up my things.

The courthouse is closing for the evening, the corridors now deserted, only a faint whiff of the stew the canteen served for lunch remaining. I'm distracted, thinking about Robin, hoping her day has been better, hoping her new friends are there to stay, when someone takes hold of my arm from behind me and my heart leaps into my throat. A man's voice says, "Sadie." I don't recognize him at first; my hair has fallen over my eyes, obscuring my vision as I turn toward him.

"Sadie," he says again, and now I realize it's Jeremy. Even though I should be relieved, the fright he's given me lingers. I smooth back my hair and take a breath.

"Jesus, you nearly scared the life out of me."

"Sorry," he says, stepping back. "Sorry. I didn't mean to."

I laugh, a little awkward now the fear has passed.

"I wanted to talk to you," he says. "I wanted to see how you thought today had gone."

"Barbara would have been happy to talk to you. Or Zora," I say.

"I know," he says. He pauses for a moment, laughs. "I have to be honest, Barbara scares me a bit. I don't like asking her questions in case she thinks I'm being stupid. Also, I think she's going to pass it on to my dad."

I smile. "She can be a little imposing, I guess. But she would answer any questions, stupid or not. And she would respect client confidentiality." I start walking toward the exit of the building.

Jeremy's shoulders are slumped. "I suppose I should ask her," he says, all laughter gone from his voice. "It's difficult, though. She's being very professional, but she must think I'm an idiot to have ended up in this situation."

"I'm sure she doesn't," I say. "You're bound to think the worst because this is all so stressful for you. But at least it's started. It's better than all that awful waiting. It must be."

"It is," he says. "I just want this to be over. Whichever way it turns out, to be honest."

We leave the court building and walk down the steps at the front. I wonder if he wants to go for a drink. I imagine the evening now, chat about the case, about the entrance exam, about his father and my mother and how hard it is to live up to a parent like that. Jeremy has the same air of being a disappointment to his family that I've always felt. I can almost taste the wine on my lips, the easy camaraderie of a decent claret. But I hold back.

"I have to go," I say. "I need to collect my daughter."

Even though dusk is falling, I see his smile fade. "Of course," he says. "It's late."

"It is. At least it means the journalist has fucked off."

He nods. "Thank God. And he wasn't here this morning, either."

"Though don't be too excited about that," I say. "There was a journalist from the Press Association in court. Barbara pointed him out to me. It will be reported."

"I know," he says, "At least they're not door-stepping me… yet. It could be worse."

"It could. Anyway, I must go. I'll see you tomorrow. Remember court is sitting at ten, not nine thirty. Though the earlier you are, the more likely you are to avoid the press."

"True," he says. I'm about to start walking away when suddenly he launches himself at me and hugs me, his cheek against my neck, skin to skin. I don't relax into the hug; I feel very aware of myself, my hands big and clumsy as I reach behind him and pat him firmly on the back, once, twice, three times until he lets go. I back away, one arm held up as if in salute, and walk fast round the corner to the tube.

Later that night, when Robin is asleep, I call Zora. We'd exchanged texts about Julia, but so far I haven't had a chance to tell her about Andrew's visit. Now I fill her in.

"What did he want?"

"I have no idea," I say. "Wanted to see if we were doing all right without him."

"That doesn't make any sense."

"It doesn't," I say. "Anyway, at least the trial has got going now."

"Yes, it's good. You're doing well. Barbara is pleased with you."

"That's something. Maybe it's looking up. You're wrong about the school, you know. I think it's going to be OK. It's turned a corner. People have finally started being friendly. Robin is happy."

"I'm sorry, what? People are being friendly? You said they were terrible."

I'm glad now I didn't tell her about the dead robin. She wouldn't rest until I'd gone charging into school to kick off even more trouble. "It's been pretty awful for Robin. I'm just grateful she's a bit happier now."

"OK, sure. But do be careful. You don't need these women, you know."

"I wish that were true. I really do. But I do need these people. Terrible or not, I've got to suck it up. It's important for Robin that we get on OK. It's only superficial, you know that."

"I suppose so. But I don't think you should trust these women after the way they've been treating you."

"I know. I am being careful. But they're making an effort now, so I have to play along."

I end the call. I know Zora has a point, but I don't want to burst the first bubble of happiness I've had for weeks. I go to bed worrying, but as my anxiety calms, my resolution crystallizes. What I said to Zora is true. It is what it is. I'm not going to forgive Julia for her previous hostility, but I am going to give her a chance and stop regarding them all with such suspicion.

It's not like I have much choice, anyway.

30

Robin is still happy the next morning when she wakes, and my mood has lifted during the night. There were no dramas or unpleasantness at Julia's house yesterday, and seeing Robin so cheerful confirms my resolution to make the most of our new beginning. I go to court with a lightness of step I haven't felt in weeks. Even the sight of a photographer lurking in the car park at the front of court doesn't bother me. At least not until he raises his camera, the long lens poking at me, worrying away at the mask of solemnity I plaster on.

It's a relief to get through the main entrance. I take in a couple of deep breaths while waiting for Security to search my bag, passing through the metal detectors. I expect to see Jeremy in the hall, but he's not there. I go straight into the robing room. Barbara is late, arriving only a few minutes before we're due in.

"Had a text from Edward Kayode this morning," she says. "He's going to make an application to adjourn today."

"Why?"

"The complainant is ill. Apparently." She rolls her eyes.

"What's wrong with her?"

"A migraine. There's a note from her doctor," Barbara says.

"Right. Can't he get on with one of the other witnesses in the meantime?"

"That's what I said. That's what I'm going to say to the judge."

I pause. I know that tone. "I can hear a 'but.'"

"Yes. But I think the judge will allow the adjournment. I'd ask the same. Their whole case hangs on her testimony. It's got to be made center stage," Barbara says, throwing her wig on her head and shoving her glasses straight.

"You're going to object, though?" I say, rushing to keep up with Barbara's long strides toward court.

"What do you take me for?" Barbara says with a snort. "I told him it was the most outrageous demand I'd ever heard, and that every effort should be made to end the agony for my client."

"Did he reply?"

Barbara comes to a halt. "He was extremely impertinent," she says, but she's smiling. She digs into her bag and pulls out a phone, calling a message up onto the screen. "This is what he sent."

I peer at it. The reply is a single emoji, the small yellow face rolling its eyes up to heaven. I laugh.

"Exactly," Barbara says, and we enter court with seconds to spare before Her Honor Judge Chynoweth makes an appearance.

Exactly as Barbara has predicted, the case is adjourned for that day. As Barbara puts forward her arguments against the application, it's clear that the judge is not impressed, her expression hardening. She gestures to Barbara to sit down.

"I've heard enough, Miss Carlisle. The case is adjourned.

We all know the importance of the complainant's testimony. Though it would be preferable if she is able to attend tomorrow," the judge says, "or I will need a further letter from her doctor. This case needs to progress."

Edward nods in agreement, and we are all dismissed until the following day. I leg it out, pleased I'll have the day to myself and also that I'll be able to be at school in time for pickup.

I decide to surprise Robin at the school gates, but when I arrive at pickup, I'm taken aback to see Nicole's face fall at the sight of me. The expression fades fast, though, a smile appearing in its place.

"How lovely! Robin will be so pleased," she says. "We didn't think we were going to see you until much later."

"Finished early today," I say. "So I thought I'd come. I can just take her home now."

"Ah, that's what I was worried you'd say. Pippa will be so disappointed if Robin doesn't come—she's been looking forward to it. Why don't you come back too? I could see what Julia is doing. Let's have a girls' night in!"

I smile but I'm a bit taken aback by Nicole's intensity. By the other mothers, too. The last few weeks have been a nightmare from which I've woken, but not yet fully. *Hi*, one says, *Hello, good to see you*, another. *We must get Robin round one afternoon, such a lovely girl*, a third. I see Julia in the middle of a cluster of women, and as soon as she catches sight of me, she waves, all the others waving too, taking their cue from their puppet master. I'm touched at last with the fairy dust of Julia's approval.

Julia comes over and approves the plan. I'm swept up with

her, with Nicole, the darts of envy cast by all those excluded from this blessed crew falling harmless at my feet, held off by the protection of Julia's charm. Robin and I walk along the street to Nicole's house, hand in hand, and I can see from the smile on Robin's face that she feels the same exhilaration.

Nicole opens a bottle of Prosecco as soon as we get into her house, and the girls disappear upstairs in a gust of giggles and whispers. I take hold of the glass that Nicole thrusts at me, condensation chill on my fingers. The bubbles catch in my throat, and I cough, thinking I'm about to humiliate myself by choking again. But Nicole starts to laugh, and Julia too. The cough passes and I take another sip, and another, drunk not on alcohol but on the headiness of early friendship, all the promise of evenings like this to come.

An hour later and we're two bottles down. They've given me the gossip about the teachers and other mums, how both of their marriages broke down, but they survived. I'm drinking it all in, though I don't share much about Andrew, only that we're separated. I tell them I've been invited to become part of the flower-arranging committee and they laugh, telling me not to touch it with a barge pole.

"They've no idea what they're doing," Julia says. "One of them did a day course at some florist in Marylebone and since then it's been bloodshed over the placing of a single rose."

Nicole snorts. "What Julia means is that she ran it very well from Years One to Three, but then some new parents turned up in Year Three and took over, claiming greater expertise. They'd sabotage the arrangements that we did. It stopped being worth it."

I look at Julia in wonder. "I can't imagine anyone getting the better of you," I say.

"I choose my battles," Julia says, taking a sip of Prosecco. "It all started to get unpleasant around the time that Paul and I were dealing with our initial separation. I take my involvement in the school very seriously, but I wasn't going to waste energy arguing about hydrangeas." She sits up, as if reminded suddenly of something. "Didn't they have that maths test today?"

Nicole nods.

"Girls!" Julia calls. She stands up and walks out to the bottom of the stairs, calling up again. "Girls, can you come down? I need to talk to you."

There's a thunder of footsteps from above and then the three girls appear. Daisy stands tall and earnest at the back, her eyebrows knitted in a worried expression. Pippa also looks tense. Only Robin seems relaxed. The room has tipped off-kilter, somehow, the mood shifted.

"How did everyone do in the maths test today?" Julia says.

Robin's expression remains unchanged. Pippa shifts from foot to foot and Daisy turns a dull red, blotches appearing on her neck. No one replies.

"Seriously, girls. How did you get on?"

Robin looks at me, her head tilted to one side in inquiry. I shrug, nod.

"Eighty-two percent," she says. "But we did fractions last year at my old school."

Daisy has gone even more red, and Pippa's almost jumping from foot to foot now, her movements increasingly jerky.

"That's very impressive," Julia says. "How about you, Pippa?"

Pippa squirms and mutters, "Sixty-nine percent."

"But you struggle with fractions, don't you?" Julia says. "That's not bad."

Pippa's face relaxes a little. She moves over to where Nicole is sitting, hovering beside her, and after a moment Nicole puts an arm around her, squeezes her tight.

"And you, Daisy?" Julia says. She's smiling but there's ice behind her eyes. I'm feeling nervous and I haven't even sat a maths test.

"Seventy-seven," Daisy says, looking down.

"Sorry, darling. What was that?" Julia says, strong emphasis on the word *darling*.

"Seventy-seven percent," Daisy says, more loudly. She pushes her hair back off her face, walks up close to her mother. "Seventy-seven percent! Not eighty. OK? Are you happy now?" Mother and daughter stay nose to nose before Daisy bursts into tears and runs out of the room, Pippa in tow. Robin hovers for a moment, looking at me in a confused way, before she follows her friends.

"It's really not that bad," Nicole says. "It was better than Pippa's mark."

"That's not the point," Julia says. "Of course it's better than Pippa's mark. But she should be getting over eighty percent, easily."

I sit back in my chair, spectator to the two drunk women as they glare at each other, all friendship seemingly forgotten. I'm holding my breath, and it's only when Nicole laughs that I let it out in a long, silent sigh.

"You take all this far too seriously, you know," Nicole says to Julia. "It's going to be fine."

"You don't know that for sure," Julia says. "I don't want to take anything for granted."

"Oh, come on," Nicole says, in a way that suggests she's done this many times before. "You know she's going to be just fine. She's been top of the year all the way through. She's a dead cert to get through, we all know that."

I think it's safe to interrupt. "Is it really that bad?"

Both women look at me with surprise.

"Don't you know anything about the process?" Nicole says.

"Not yet," I say. "I guess I could have found out, but I've been so overwhelmed with moving and the case and everything."

They laugh, but there's a note of incredulity there, sharp at the edges.

"Oh, for your obliviousness," Julia says.

Nicole laughs. "Julia has approached this like a military campaign. She's been putting Daisy through boot camp since Year Four, at least."

Julia shrugs. "Life's a war," she says. "And this is a battle I intend to win. You have to think about the long game. GCSE results, A levels. Oxbridge. It's very competitive." She pauses, sighs. "I know you think I'm mad, but I'll do anything to make sure she gets through to the senior school. She might seem a shoo-in with the marks she's getting, but it's so important. Daisy loves Ashams so much." She sounds as if she's going to burst into tears.

"And the scholarship," Nicole mutters. "Daisy has always been top of the class."

Julia smiles in a modest way. "I'll settle for her getting through to the senior school, you know. That's the only thing that matters. The scholarship really isn't important."

I blink, given the vehemence with which she'd discussed it in the headteacher's office, but I'm not going to bring that up again, not when it's all going so well.

"I'm surprised you sent her to Ashams, you know," I say. "A friend of mine reminded me about the bullying." As soon as I've said it I regret it. It's the Prosecco, taking the edge off my defenses. I push the glass away from me.

"What bullying?" Julia says, in a voice that's almost level.

"I was talking to someone from my year. She said you were quite badly bullied. Sorry, I wasn't going to mention it..." I wish I had just kept my mouth shut.

"I don't like talking about it," Julia says with a deep sigh. Nicole leans over and puts a hand on her arm. "I've left that all behind me. But yes, it was a very difficult time and my grades suffered. I don't want to see Daisy go through the same thing. I just want her to be happy. I mean, really, the scholarship isn't important in any way, not really. As long as she gets through to the senior school I'm absolutely fine with it."

I catch Nicole's eye. We're clearly thinking the same thing. We don't believe a word of it. Daisy has to be the best, or she'll suffer for it.

31

I'm dressed for court and about to leave the house with Robin the following morning when I receive a message from Barbara. The prosecution has provided a second medical letter, and the complainant is still ill. Court has been adjourned until the following Monday. I'm not going to argue with the unexpected bonus of a long weekend, spending time with Robin after her weekend with Andrew. I wonder if he might turn up again unannounced, and I feel a shiver of fear, but then I remember his last words to me before he left, that he wanted to see that we were doing OK without him. He gave no sign that he was planning to come back any time soon. I'm going to put him out of mind, at least for the next couple of days.

The forecast is good, and I want to tackle the garden and the ivy that grows uncontrolled up the front of the house, plant the bulbs I've been planning. Robin has been complaining more and more about the spiders that are finding their way into her bedroom in search of warmth—cutting the foliage back from around her window may be one way to deal with the issue.

I change quickly into jeans before taking Robin up to school. She's quieter than usual.

"You OK?" I ask.

"I was just thinking about last night," she says. "It was a bit weird how pushy Daisy's mom was being with her."

"I didn't like it much. I know it's important that you do your best, but it did feel quite full-on."

"Daisy gets really stressed about it," Robin says. "We were talking about it in the café at the start of the week."

"Well, I promise I'm not going to go nuts. As I say, you keep doing your best."

Before I can say any more, Nicole and Pippa have joined us. The girls run off together.

"Thank you for having us last night," I say. "Lovely to sit and chat."

"I'm so pleased you could come round," Nicole says. "I'm sorry that it all got a bit strained. Julia is really bothered about the exams. Too much so. I do try and tell her to calm down, but she never listens to me."

I look at her as she's speaking, trying not to compare her with Julia in my mind. Nicole is small, mousy, a bit stooped; too ready to laugh at Julia's jokes. Julia's practically four-dimensional, crackling with energy. I'm not surprised that she won't listen to Nicole.

"It's Daisy I worry about, really. She must be under so much pressure. Pippa told me she's been in tears quite a bit this term," Nicole continues. "Julia is one of my best friends, but I do think she should dial it back a bit."

"So you've tried talking to her about it?"

Nicole laughs, a short bark. "I did once, at the beginning of term. She nearly bit my head off. And then Robin and you appeared...Maybe you could try? She really likes you; she said so after you left."

I feel surprised, but I'm not going to argue. Whether she likes me or not, I have no enthusiasm for the idea of talking to her, tackling her about the way she spoke to Daisy the night before.

Right then, Julia appears, Daisy behind her. Julia kisses both of us in greeting, while Daisy hovers in the background. She's not looking well, bags under her eyes and her face pale and drawn. She shifts from foot to foot. Julia turns and looks at her.

"You'd better go in," she says, "or you'll be late. And remember, you need to do better today."

Daisy nods, mute, and turns and runs into school.

I steel myself, open my mouth ready to say something, anything, in defense of the poor girl, but Julia pre-empts me.

"I bet you think I'm terrible," she says, "but that girl really does need pushing. We've all got our own way of doing things. She's not like your Robin—she doesn't have any drive of her own. I have to make sure she keeps up to scratch."

"She did seem very upset last night," I say.

Julia looks at me, her eyes very blue and cold. "All families are different," she says, in a way that shuts down any further reply.

"You do very well," Nicole says, clearly deciding she's going to calm down the situation.

Julia continues to look furious for a moment before her face softens. "You've only just got here," she says to me. "You haven't got it yet, the pressures of the senior school exam. It's not like it was in our day. When you do get it, you'll understand why we have to push them so hard."

"I know we're very new to this," I say.

"You are. But you'll understand soon enough. Look, why

don't you all come to mine tonight? The girls can do their homework together, then watch a movie; we can have a chat, and we'll make sure there's no upsets. Not like last night."

I should be thrilled by the invitation. Back into the inner sanctum, an opportunity for me fully to redeem myself after the humiliation of the first time I went to Julia's house, a time that feels light years away. But I can't face it. The night I have planned involves pizza and a film, and I have no intention of giving up on this idea.

"I'm so sorry," I say. "That does sound lovely. But Robin and I have plans for this evening already. Another time, definitely."

"What plans?" Julia begins to say, but her phone starts ringing and she has to answer it, barking instructions down the handset at whatever unfortunate is at the other end. I seize the opportunity and run away.

After a day spent happily hacking down plants, I arrive early to collect Robin, planning to scoop her up and run before Julia can push the invitation on us again. When I see Nicole in the distance my heart sinks, thinking it's no use, but I pretend to be engrossed in my phone. Fortunately, Robin comes out on her own, one of the first girls to leave. I grab her hand and we get to the bus stop as fast as we can. I explain the plans for the evening somewhat breathlessly to Robin as we go.

"Are you happy with that?" I ask as we sit down on the bus. Robin doesn't reply, leans her head against my shoulder. "I'll take that as a yes."

32

Saturday morning.

I wake up, tangled in the duvet. Hot, sweating. The phone is ringing. I fumble through the bedclothes and track it down. It stops ringing as I pick it up, but starts again. Nicole.

"Jesus Christ, you have to wake up, please wake up. Something terrible has happened, something terrible." Nicole is shouting down the phone, her words almost incoherent, she's talking so fast, sobbing, her voice shaking.

"What's going on?" I say, pushing myself upright in bed.

"It's Daisy," Nicole says, howling.

"What's Daisy?"

"She won't wake up. Julia tried, I tried. But she won't wake up. The ambulance is on the way. Please come. You have to come. I don't know what's going to happen."

The phone goes dead. I'm fully awake now. It's later than I thought—nearly eight o'clock. I leap out of bed and throw on some clothes. Nicole's distress is contagious—all my reservations about Julia are on hold; she needs my help, and I'm going to give it. Robin is fast asleep and for a brief moment I wonder if it would be safe to leave her, shield her from the situation, but I put the thought out of my head. She might be sensible, but she's far too young. Andrew, too—what if he comes back when I'm not there? I wake her up and tell her to dress, and we run out of the house.

Before we reach the bus stop, I see a black cab, its light on. I flag it down and we get in. I push my hands hard down against the seat to assert some control over myself, trying not to scream *faster faster faster* at the driver. I keep checking my phone, calling Nicole back every now and again to no avail.

At last we get to Julia's street, a journey that feels as if it's lasted hours, though in reality it was only fifteen minutes. We pull up on the other side of the road from the house, the same spot that the taxi dropped me all those weeks ago when I went to the party. I remember Daisy at the front door, so careful to establish that I was a proper guest, and the thought of that earnest little girl, her tight smile, sends a pang straight through me.

There's an ambulance directly outside Julia's house. The front door is wide open. I reach out for Robin's hand, her fingers cold, gripping hard to mine. We cross the road together. People start to appear out of the front door. Two paramedics carrying a stretcher between them, a man at the front, a woman at the back. For a moment, it looks as though the stretcher is empty, and the band of fear round my temples loosens its grip, but it takes hold again tenfold when I spot the small face, pale above the blanket wrapping the body. Daisy's face. At least not a body. Her face would be covered. Surely her face would be covered.

Robin sees Daisy at the same time and cries out. I pull her in closer and together we watch as the stretcher is placed inside the ambulance. When it's safely in, the male paramedic closes the door, leaving the woman inside with Daisy. Then he gets into the driver's seat and sets off, sirens wailing.

"Where's Daisy's mom?" Robin says. "Why isn't she with Daisy?"

"I don't know, sweetheart. She'll be going on soon after, I'm sure," I say, trying to sound reassuring, though it's far from how I feel.

I'm transfixed by the car that's parked outside Julia's house, revealed by the departure of the ambulance. A police car. No one inside. I might not know for certain why Julia hasn't been able to go with Daisy, but I have a sinking feeling that this might well provide the explanation.

Slowly, we make our way up the steps to the front door. I come to a standstill, Robin pinned to my side. There's darkness in that house, I can feel it beating its way out. We could leave now.

"Sadie, Sadie!" Nicole's voice cries out from inside. "Sadie, thank God you're here. It's terrible. Come in."

My desire to leave passes. Nicole's crying, tears streaming down her face. I can't leave her to cope with this on her own. Whatever "this" is. I loosen my hold on Robin.

Together, we step into the house.

Nicole's hovering by the drawing-room door, Pippa at her side. The place feels very different now; the gilt has worn off. The door is shut, and there's a rumbling of voices.

"It's the police," Nicole says, speaking so quietly that I strain to hear her. She repeats herself, mouthing the words in an exaggerated way. "The police."

I move forward. "Why are the police here? Why isn't Julia going to the hospital?"

Nicole tells the girls to go to the kitchen and have a snack and draws me into the front room. Green walls, dark wood furniture; somber already.

"It's awful," Nicole says. "So awful. I'm so glad you're here. I didn't know who to call."

I give her a hug. Nicole slumps against me, weeping onto my neck. She pulls away, straightening herself up and sniffing, wiping the trail of snot away with her sleeve. She sits down on one of the ornate chairs and takes a deep breath. "We came round last night, right? You were invited too?"

I nod.

"We thought the girls would like a sleepover, since they've been working so hard. A chance for Julia and me to catch up, too. We haven't seen as much of each other this term as we'd like." Nicole's voice is low. I have to lean in close.

"We ordered in pizza. The girls ate theirs in front of the TV. We sat in the kitchen and drank a couple of bottles of wine."

"Like Thursday then," I say.

"Well, yes. Like Thursday. But Julia was a lot more relaxed. At least, I thought she was. She said she'd talked to Daisy and they'd worked out a plan. It was all going to be fine. Daisy was going to pull it together and would be getting better marks from now on."

I raise an eyebrow. Nicole catches sight of it.

"You're right," she says, answering my unspoken question. "You're right. Her marks are brilliant anyway."

"How was Daisy?" I desperately want Nicole to get to the point of what's happened to put Daisy in an ambulance this morning, but I don't want to rattle her by rushing her through the story.

"She wasn't great, in retrospect. Really nervy, complaining of a tummy ache, headache. She couldn't settle, even though they were watching *Mean Girls*. She kept coming down, wanting to talk to Julia. I think she was worried about something."

"What?"

"The tests. Julia being angry with her. I don't know. But I wish I'd seen quite how ill she was getting." Nicole takes in another deep breath. The volume of her voice is sinking even further as she gets closer to the end of the account. "In the end, she went to bed early. Pippa stayed up a bit longer, chatting to us, before she went up too. I did suggest we leave, but by that stage I'd had a bit too much to drink." She looks at me as if for absolution. "You know how it is?"

I nod again. "I do. Friday night. Of course I know how it is."

"We could have got a cab back, but Julia made up a spare room for me. We went to sleep. It really wasn't that late, either. About eleven, I guess. Pippa woke up early and came through to me. She told me that Daisy was still flat out. We went down to get some breakfast, and Julia went to get Daisy."

There's a long pause.

"What happened next, Nicole?"

She looks at me, white as a sheet. "That's when the screaming started."

33

Nicole doesn't say any more, but sits silent, her face drawn with shock. I want to ask her what happened next but every time I start to speak, she raises her hand to hush me, as if she's trying desperately to hear what's going on in the rest of the house. Julia is with the police for what feels like hours, though it's less than twenty minutes. She comes out of the living room and in to us, her face tearstained, hands clenched. I hear heavy footsteps climbing the stairs—the police can't have left yet. Julia won't speak to either Nicole or me. We go into the kitchen and Nicole makes a cup of tea for Julia and tries to get her to drink, but she pushes it away.

Finally, Nicole asks, "Do you want me to go to the hospital with you?"

Julia is looking at her phone. She looks up at Nicole, her expression blank. "They've told Daisy's dad. He's going to be there. I know he'll be on his way. I don't want to see him."

"But Daisy..."

"She's unconscious, Nicole. You saw her. They can't wake her up. She won't know if I'm there or not. It won't make any difference to her."

"She might be able to hear you," Nicole says. "Don't you want to see her?"

"I said no!" Julia is standing now. My fingernails are jammed hard into the palms of my hands, trying to control my shock at Julia's reaction. No one speaks for a moment, the silence palpable, vibrating between us, before it's broken by Pippa's entrance, Robin behind her. She goes straight to Nicole's side, strain apparent on her face, too.

"This is all your fault," Julia says, turning on Nicole's daughter. There's so much venom in her voice that it could crush Pippa to the floor under its weight. "You should have woken. Then we'd have found her sooner. If she dies, this is all on you."

Pippa bursts into tears. Nicole steps forward, eyes blazing, before she makes an effort visibly to control herself.

"You're saying this because of the shock," she says. "You know that's not true."

"How the fuck should I know what's true and what isn't? They both went to bed absolutely fine. And now your daughter is fine and mine is in a fucking coma. Who the fuck else should I blame?"

Every time Julia swears it jolts through me. Pippa visibly sways under the onslaught. Nicole puts her arm around her.

"I know you've had an appalling shock," Nicole says, "but this is insane. You can't blame Pippa for this. God knows what's happened—the hospital will run tests. It could be anything. You mustn't jump to conclusions."

"Why not? The police are jumping to conclusions. That woman officer, she said something about a possibility of an overdose, toxicology reports. They're going to search the house." Julia sits down abruptly, covering her face with her hands.

"What are they looking for, Julia?" Nicole says, chill, insistent.

She raises her head from her hands. "I don't know, all right," she spits. "I don't fucking know! My daughter is unconscious in hospital and they won't even let me go and see her. I have to stay here under some sort of guard while they tear my house apart, and instead of it being me with her, her own mother, they're letting that bastard Paul go and see her instead."

Nicole is looking grave. "You really don't have any idea what they're looking for?"

"Of course I don't! Just because they found a pill box by the bed...It's vitamins, all right!" Julia is yelling now. She gets up and paces over to Nicole, right up close to her face. Pippa shrinks away. Nicole stands her ground and finally Julia backs off, sitting back down, slumped at the table.

"Do you want me to go to the hospital?" Nicole says. "I can report back."

Julia shakes her head. It looks as if her anger is now spent. "There's no point. They won't let you in. She's going to be in intensive care. The paramedics promised that the hospital would call me."

A female police officer comes into the room. "Mrs. Burnet," she says, "we're going to make a start in your bedroom. Is that OK?" She's pulling on a pair of disposable gloves.

"Nothing I can do to stop you, is there," she says. Then she looks over at me, her expression sharpening up. "You're the lawyer. Can I stop them?"

I'm caught in her gaze, a rabbit in headlights. "I don't really deal with cases at this stage...I think that if you say no, they will have to apply for a search warrant. It's not completely certain they'd get it, but the chances are they would. Under the circumstances, maybe it would be best to call a solicitor?"

Julia waves a dismissive hand. "Let them search. I don't care. And I don't care about seeing a solicitor. They'll see I've done nothing wrong." She looks again at me, her expression even more sharp. "What are you doing here, anyway?"

"Nicole asked me to come," I say.

"How strange," Julia says. "Well, the show's over. You might as well go."

I look over at Nicole, who shrugs, her face neutral, though there are hints of pink rising on her neck.

"I thought Sadie might be helpful," she says.

"I just don't know what I'm doing. I don't think anyone can help at this point," Julia says. "You should go, too. All of you. I might have to put up with the police in my house, but I don't have to tolerate all of you. Get out of here. Please." She walks out of the room, slamming the door behind her.

I turn to Nicole. "We should go."

"I don't like to leave her like this." Still, Nicole stands and picks up her bag. Pippa already has her overnight bag with her, and we all file out of the house. Robin is close by my side, her eyes wide.

"At least the police are here. They'll keep an eye on her," I say. They're standing by the steps. I turn to look at the house. The morning is dark, clouds hanging heavy, and the basement light is on. I can see Julia clearly from the street, moving through a series of sun salutations. I pull at Nicole's arm, gesturing at the basement. We watch Julia stoop in downward dog pose. A male police officer comes out of the house. He asks us both for our names and contact details, which we give. After he's written them down, I turn back to see if Julia has stopped. She's now balancing on her head, her feet straight up perpendicular from the floor.

"I've never seen that before," the police officer mutters.

"Someone doing yoga?" Nicole says.

"Someone standing on their head while their kid's in a coma," he says. He stares for a second more, before moving back into the house.

34

I keep Robin close for the rest of the weekend. I resist the temptation to call Nicole or Julia to ask how Daisy is, taking the view that they will be in touch if there's any news. The whole episode has left me unsettled, worried about the effect it might have on Robin.

We work in the garden together, watch films. Robin has nightmares on the Saturday night, coming through into my room, but she's calmer by Sunday evening, exhausted by all the work we've done hacking down plants, cutting them back. The front windows are less obscured by ivy now, more light coming into the rooms, though the disadvantage is that it shows up even more clearly the terrible state of the paintwork and the stains on the wallpaper.

"It could be a really nice house, though," Robin says, looking around the living room early on Sunday evening. "I like it more than Julia's house. It feels more homey."

I look at the stains, the gas fire, the tatty mantelpiece that stands empty since I put away the figurines. "Really?" I say.

"Really, Mom. We're making it our own. Like they say on that singing program. If we just decorated it some more, it would look great. We could even sort out your old bedroom."

"We'll see, sweetheart. We'll see. Anyway, it's time for bed." I give her a hug. "It might be quite difficult tomorrow, you know. We haven't heard anything yet about Daisy. There's probably going to be some news."

Robin hugs me back.

The following morning it's in and out at school. Even though I'm desperate to find out what might be going on with Daisy, with Julia too, I've had a text from Barbara confirming that the case is going ahead today. The complainant, Freya, is fully recovered from her "migraine" (the quotation marks loud in Barbara's text) and the court will certainly be sitting. I hope that even though we're early, we might still see Nicole, but she isn't at the gate. There are clusters of parents whispering quietly together. It's very subdued. News has clearly leaked out.

I say goodbye to Robin, tell her not to gossip to anyone, and leg it to the tube, not wanting to be late on such a significant day in the trial. As I go, I write a text to Nicole, asking if she will still be able to take Robin after school. *Totally understand if not up to it*, I say, *but could you let me know so I can book her into the after-school club*? As I enter the station, Nicole messages back saying *Yes of course—I'll catch you up then. Hoping to get into the hospital today. No word from Julia.*

I go down the escalator, losing signal. However concerned I am for Daisy, I'm going to have to park it for now, concentrate on the case. Barbara will need proper notes from me, and for me to go through again all the cross-examination evidence that I found in the social media messages. I need to have my brain switched on—no distractions.

* * *

"Sadie," Jeremy says as soon as he sees me. He takes my hand, shakes it. Alexandra is standing beside him, and she smiles too, though it doesn't reach her eyes. This is going to be a stressful day.

"You doing OK?" I say to him, and he nods once, his face tight.

At this point Barbara appears. "We'll robe up," she says, "and meet you outside court."

Jeremy nods.

"Let's see what we get," Barbara says as we make our way to the robing room. "If they've dressed her up in something sensible, we've got an issue. If she's chosen her own outfit, we might just be OK."

A ripple of noise from the public gallery greets Freya's entrance into court. Her outfit is restrained enough, a black top and skirt, but she's gone heavy on the makeup, foundation and eyeliner applied so thickly no trace of her youthful complexion is left visible.

I look closely at her as she reaches out to take hold of the Bible, swearing to tell the truth and nothing but the truth. I move my gaze from her face to the hand that is holding the book. Given the effort she's made with her appearance, I would have expected a manicure, gel extensions or the like. But her nails are chewed nearly down to the quick, the skin around the nails red and swollen. And when I look back at Freya's face, I now see past the war paint, past the mask that I recognize because it's one I put on myself when I need the reinforcement, albeit with a lighter touch. I can see Freya's eyes are red, too, and her lip trembles as she takes the oath, her hand shaking as she gives the Bible back to the usher.

I lean my head forward, looking through the brief, engulfed in pity for the girl.

Once I've recovered myself, I look over at the jury. They do not look friendly. They turn between Jeremy, in the dock, and Freya, in the witness box, and their faces shift from each to each, a softening toward the clean-cut, smartly turned out young man, today in shabby chinos and worn-in blazer. He's the ideal client—no need to tell him to dress sensibly. From a defense point of view, the setup is ideal, the weight of opinion, at least for now, firmly on their client's side, their case all but won. But thinking about what Freya is about to experience, the mud through which Jeremy's own name has been dragged, it's hard to think any victors at all are likely to come out of this situation.

SUNDAY, 12:48 P.M.

Around the corner, down the hill. This isn't a bear hunt, though. I don't know if I'll get through it.

One step after the other. I'm half-running, half-walking, the stitch still catching at my side. And the closer I get, the slower I'm going, until I come to a halt. I'm so focused on getting there, breaking down the door, finding her and bringing her out. But what if she's not there? What if I've got this wrong?

Maybe he's got her. Maybe he's come back and he's taken her. Maybe he found a way to get to them somehow and they've plotted together and he's got her and he's going to take her and I'll never see her again and…

Stop! I have to stop this.

One step at a time.

One foot in front of the other.

I can see the house, right there, just there, and I'm going to be there and I'll ring the bell, I'll knock on the door, and she'll come running out and she'll hug me and it'll be good, it'll all be fine.

All shall be well.
All shall be well
and all manner of thing shall be well.
I'm nearly there. Just a few more steps.
Then I'll find her.

35

The prosecutor takes Freya through her evidence gently. At first her voice is low, but after the judge asks her if she can speak a little louder, she becomes more audible. She looks at Jeremy directly from time to time as she talks through the early days of what she describes as her relationship with him. I have to admire her courage—it would have been open to the prosecution to make an application for special measures, methods by which the girl could be spared this direct confrontation with him, giving evidence from behind a screen or even by way of a video link, but Barbara told me that morning that, according to the prosecution, Freya had said she didn't want them. She wanted Jeremy to see what the effect of his behavior had been on her.

They met when she was fourteen, Freya says, when he started teaching her history lessons. History became one of her favorite subjects, and he brought it to life. Edward asks her to expand on what she means by this, and she says that one of the things he did that she really liked was to recommend novels set in the same period as they were studying, because she enjoyed reading those stories. Edward asks if there was anything in particular about the novels that she noticed.

"They had a lot of sex in them," she says, looking down at her hands.

"Can you elaborate on that?"

"The first ones he recommended, they were ordinary stories, but then they got more like love stories, with a lot of sex scenes."

"What did you feel about that?"

"I didn't realize history could be like that—I thought it was really boring. Kings and queens and battles. I didn't know that it could feel like real life, that someone like Elizabeth the First would think about sex, too."

The grooming continues over two terms, Freya describes. The light erotica of popular historical fiction is replaced by more explicit material, books Jeremy told Freya to buy or take out of the library. She'd write book reports for him, extra homework for the first time ever. It's not just the first time she's found history interesting, Freya says, it's the first time that any teacher has taken her seriously, seeing beyond her superficial appearance to acknowledge an academic worth she didn't know existed in her before.

"How did Mr. Taylor make these recommendations to you?" Edward asks.

"He'd talk to me at the end of lessons. Sometimes he'd find me in my classroom or we would have a chat in the corridor."

"At what sort of times would these conversations occur?"

"During the school day. Until the time we had tea in the staff room after school had finished. That was the first time."

"Can you tell the court about what happened there? What was the date, do you recall?"

"Of course I recall," Freya says, her voice cracking for the first time. "It was the day I lost my virginity. I think I'd remember that, don't you?"

Edward Kayode pauses for a moment, giving Freya a chance to compose herself.

"You've said you remember the date—what was it?"

"It was June of last year, that's the first time that we met outside school hours. The sixteenth of June."

"In your own words, can you tell the court what happened?"

The date relates to the first count of the indictment. They met outside the school gates by chance, Freya says. Jeremy had given her a copy of a book, *Fanny Hill.* The prosecutor picks up a sealed plastic bag containing a book and asks for it to be handed to her—she looks at it and nods.

Returning to the evidence, she says that Jeremy asked her what she had thought of his latest book recommendation. Freya had found it very full-on.

"What do you mean by that?" Edward asks. Freya's sangfroid has finally cracked, her cheeks bright pink. She picks up the glass of water that has been provided for her and drinks from it, swallowing loudly. My fists are clenched with the tension as Freya tries to calm herself to get to the most difficult part.

"I mean it's rude," she says. "Really rude." She seems to be gathering strength from somewhere. "I mean, obviously you see stuff on the internet all the time. You can't escape it. Boys send it, you see on your phone. Hardcore, whatever. But the fact that he had recommended this book to me, the way it describes sex. It felt really personal. Like he was trying to tell me something."

"What kind of thing?"

Every member of the jury is watching the girl intently. Freya pauses, the flush back up her neck, her cheeks blotched with red. "I began to wonder if he was trying to tell me he liked me."

"Liked you in what way?"

"In a...a sex kind of way. If he fancied me."

She returns to the chance meeting. She had left school a little late, she said, because she had been trying to finish off some geography coursework in a rush. As she went through the gates, she ran into Jeremy. He was coming back in, explaining that he had left something behind. He asked her about the book and she had blushed and said it was rude, but after he pressured her a little more, she'd admitted that she'd liked it. She went into school with him as he collected what he needed, and they found that the building was deserted. He took her into the staff room and made her a cup of tea, and then he asked her to show him her favorite passage from the book. She had balked at that, so he took the book from her and found what he said was his favorite passage before reading it aloud to her.

After he had finished reading it, he asked her if she wanted him to do to her what had been described in the passage. She wasn't exactly keen but wasn't reluctant, either. She allowed him to kiss her, undress her, give her oral sex (after some hesitation, she says she enjoyed it) after which they had full intercourse. He had worn a condom and his actions were all very gentle.

Freya's voice is becoming quieter and quieter as she recounts this, and the judge has to ask her to speak up on more than one occasion, her voice kind but firm. I'm trying not to react, but I feel her embarrassment. I'm trying not to imagine Robin in her place. I look over at the jury to try and read their reactions—their faces are neutral, as if they're trying to make it easier for the girl, too. There's a huge disconnect between Freya's harsh appearance, the don't-fuck-with-me eye makeup, and the tremor in her voice, which is audible to the whole court. When she gets to the end of this part, the judge orders the court to rise for a twenty-minute break, and the relief on the girl's face is evident as she leaves the courtroom with the representative from Witness Support.

"She's coming over better than I thought," Barbara says, "but I don't think we'll have too much of a problem rattling her. This is all too pat—textbook grooming. She's obviously been reading blogs online."

I nod. It is pat. But that could also be because it's true. I push the thought out of my head—this isn't how I should be thinking.

"Go and check on Jeremy," Barbara says. "See what he has to say so far."

I go back to the dock. The security officer lets me into the custody section at the back of the court house where Jeremy is sitting before court resumes. He is pale, his jaw set.

"Are you OK?"

"It's just so upsetting to hear," he says. "I did my absolute best for that girl. And she's twisting it all to get at me. Talking about those books, it's ridiculous."

"You didn't give them to her," I say.

"There's an internet full of proper porn," he says. "Why on earth would I be falling back on a load of old overwritten erotica to seduce a teenager? It doesn't make sense."

He has a point, I think. "I suppose not." Before I can say

anything more, I feel my phone vibrate in my suit pocket. "Sorry, I should just check..."

It's a message from Nicole. *Daisy is still unconscious*, it says. *Toxicology tests pending. Overdose suspected.*

I take a sharp intake of breath at the word *overdose.*

"Is everything all right?"

I look up, slightly surprised that despite the stress he's facing, he's noticed my concern. I hesitate for a moment before answering his question.

"It's one of my daughter's friends," I say. "She fell ill on Friday night—she's been unconscious since then. It looks like she might have taken an overdose."

"That's awful," he says.

"You've enough on your plate. I shouldn't be talking about it."

"This is serious, though," he says. "I understand how worried you must be." He pauses for a moment. "Your daughter goes to Ashams, doesn't she?"

"Yes, that's right."

"Year Six?"

"Yes."

He pauses again, carries on. "Look, I probably shouldn't say anything. It's just gossip, I don't know anything concrete. But one does hear things...I'm still in touch with teachers from my school. We talk about things."

"What things?" I say, sharply.

"It's very competitive, isn't it?"

"Yes, that's what I'm told."

"And places are incredibly hard to come by?"

"Yes. That's certainly the impression I've been given."

There's a long pause. "What I heard...and, look...

I don't know if this is true. I heard that they have problems all the way through. The parents are incredibly pushy and even though the school does its best with the kids, they can't protect them from everything."

I feel a spurt of alarm. "I'd say that's fair—I've found the staff very good so far. The parents, well, that's a different story. But we're settling in a bit better now," I say.

"Well, that's good." Another pause. "Look, that wasn't all. It's just...I was talking to someone about it just the other week. It had stuck in my head that your daughter is there." He is looking worried now.

"And?" I try to sound calm but my hands are starting to shake.

"I didn't think anything of it at the time," he says. "Accidents happen. But now there's another one..."

"Another what?"

"Another child in hospital," he says.

"Who was the other one?"

"It was last year," he says. "I don't know exactly what happened, but—"

He's interrupted by the security guard. "Time to get back into court, sir."

I have to leave, but I need to hear the end.

"What? What happened?" I hiss at him.

Jeremy stands up, straightens his tie, ready to go back into the courtroom.

"She died," he says. "I don't know how, but she died."

A chill runs through me. I walk back into court, following Jeremy. His words in my ears.

Fear lodged cold in my throat.

36

The next part of Freya's evidence is a blur. Slowly, I come back into the room. She recounts the other two occasions on which she alleges she and Jeremy had sex; once in an empty classroom, the other back in the staff room after hours. She felt special being singled out, she loved talking about books to him. He suggested *Fifty Shades of Grey* to her as a more modern book that she might enjoy. They messaged each other in the vein of the two main characters. He had even tried to persuade Freya to send some photographs of herself posing naked to him, although she had refused.

Now I'm fully engaged. I'm swinging away from my sympathy toward Freya. After all, if there's one thing I'm familiar with, it's the contents of Freya's social media and messaging accounts. And there is no trace of these exchanges anywhere. The prosecutor, Edward, is clearly aware of this too.

"By what means did you message each other?" he asks, after she has described an exchange that has left the jury pinch-lipped.

"We used an app called Viber," she says. "I had it installed on my iPad."

"Are you able to show the court these messages?"

She looks down, shakes her head.

"I'm sorry, I'll need you to speak your answer," Edward says.

"No," she says. "I can't show the court. The app was on my iPad, not on anything else, and I lost my device last summer."

"What do you mean by lost it?"

"I must have left it at school or on the bus. I couldn't find it. Also, we only ever did secret chats."

"Can you tell the court what a secret chat is?"

"It deletes all the messages as soon as they are read. Jeremy—Mr. Taylor—he was really strict about it. We couldn't message in any other way."

Freya looks over at the dock to where Jeremy is sitting. I turn around to see that he does not meet Freya's gaze, his head lowered. It startles me when Freya calls him Mr. Taylor. It makes her sound so young. I look around the courtroom, wondering where her parents are sitting. If it were Robin, I'd be going spare watching my daughter having to deal with this. If it were Robin, I'd want to kill Jeremy with my bare hands. At least she's safe at school right now. As Freya should have been...

"Did you communicate by any other means?" Edward asks.

"No. Only like that. And the occasional email about homework via school. But there was nothing in them—they were just normal."

"How did you email?"

"On my laptop computer."

"Were there any messages on your phone?"

"No. It's just a basic Nokia, not a smartphone. He wouldn't text me on it, though, because he didn't want to leave an electronic trail. That's what he called it."

"I'd like to clarify this for the court—you had a laptop computer, a mobile telephone and an iPad, is that right?"

"Yes."

"Isn't it unusual that you would have an old Nokia rather than a smartphone?"

"You tell my mother that!" There's a ripple of laughter around the court, a break in the tension. Even Freya smiles. "I used to have an iPhone, but I broke it too many times. My mum said I'd have to make do with the Nokia until I proved to her I could look after it. I was about to get a new phone when I lost the iPad."

"When do you say that you lost the iPad?"

"Last summer."

"And you didn't try and download the communication app Viber onto your laptop?"

"He told me not to. He said it was safer only having it on one device."

Edward shuffles through his paperwork. "Did anything happen to the phone and laptop?"

"The police took them away. I don't have them any more. My mum got me another Nokia because she was so cross about it all."

Edward signals that he has finished this line of questioning, and the court rises for lunch. We eat sandwiches in the canteen. Jeremy is tense, but Barbara is relaxed.

"Don't worry," she says. "This is genuinely at the worst it can be for you. Once I start cross-examining it will all be fine. And the jury aren't looking impressed. Don't you agree, Sadie?"

"It's true," I say. "I don't think they liked the suggestion that she'd lost the iPad at all. Or this self-destructing message service. All a bit too convenient."

Jeremy nods. He looks at least partly reassured.

"I'm going to tear this whole story down, Jeremy," Barbara says. "You have my word. We are not letting her get away with it."

I leave a little before the others to go to the loo. The teenage girls are standing in a cluster in the corridor. They've hung on to see all of Freya's evidence. As I pass by the group they stop talking, starting again as soon as I've turned toward the bathroom.

"She's such a liar," one of them says. I stop walking, unable to resist the temptation of eavesdropping. "I know she'd shagged at least three people before she says this happened."

"You don't know that, though," another one says. "That was just gossip."

"It wasn't just gossip. Emma told me. Her brother knows the boys."

"Emma gossips all the time. She's always making things up."

"I can't believe you're standing up for Freya. Look at what she's done to Mr. Taylor."

The other girl is having none of it. "What about 'I believe her'? You're always going on about that. We're meant to believe the victim. You're only standing up for him because you fancy him."

"I do not."

"You do so. And it's disgusting. He's way older than you."

This last remark is said at high volume and is met with incoherent shouts, sounds of rapid movement. A scuffle seems to be breaking out amongst the girls, heading ever closer to where I'm standing listening. I put my head down and walk on, my mind whirring.

* * *

Once we're back in court, before the judge returns, I get my phone out and text Nicole to ask if there's any news. *Nothing*, comes the answer almost immediately. *I'm so worried. I'm going to drop in at the hospital this afternoon on the way to pick up Pippa. Do you want me to collect Robin?*

I turn to Barbara. "Are you going to need me after court?"

"No. I just want to make sure that you've gone through all the messages that we have with a fine-tooth comb."

"I think I've put everything down in that document I gave you. There is nothing about Jeremy, or to him. No corroborating evidence. It seems almost incredible that there would be nothing. I don't buy this iPad story."

"Neither do I," Barbara says. "And by the time I've finished cross-examining, neither will anyone else in this court."

I message Nicole back. *If you wouldn't mind taking Robin back to yours, that would be great. I won't be late*, pressing send just as Her Honor Judge Chynoweth comes back into court.

Edward seems invigorated by the short break, bounding up to his feet as soon as it's time for him to start the examination again. Freya does not look so cheerful. Her makeup is still mostly in situ, but there are smudges around her eyes, as if she's forgotten the mask she's wearing and rubbed her eyes, smearing the eyeliner. She looks tired, drooping as she stands. The judge notices this too and asks if she would like to sit down as she gives her evidence, but she shakes her head.

Edward begins again. "You've described those three occasions when you were intimate with the defendant and a series of very personal messages that you exchanged. You've said the last of those incidents took place in the first week of July, just before the end of term."

He pauses and Freya nods, says yes.

"Did you have any discussions with the defendant about the continuation of the relationship into the summer holidays?"

"Yes," Freya says. "I thought it was going to keep going. I wanted to go to his flat."

"And did you see him in the holidays at all?"

"Only once." Freya is looking upset now, her shoulders hunched.

"Can you tell the court about that occasion?"

She bows her head before taking a deep breath. "We had been messaging lots, the first week of the holidays. He said we should arrange a date to meet up soon. We had to be careful, but we would make it work. Then I lost my iPad. I couldn't find it anywhere. So I couldn't message him."

"Did you try and get in touch with him by other means?"

Another long pause. Another deep breath. "Yes," Freya says. "I did. I went to his flat."

"Had the defendant given you his address?"

"No, I found it," Freya says, her voice low.

"You found it?"

"The last time we…I was with him, he went to the loo to flush away the condom. He left his wallet on the desk. I took a photo of his driving license. So I had his address." Her voice is very strained at this point.

"Why did you take a photo of his driving license?" Edward says.

"Because it had his photo on it. I wanted to have that. And I guess I wanted his address. Just in case." She straightens herself up. "I didn't mean to do it, but I couldn't help myself."

"And did you do anything with that address?"

"Yes. I went there. I wanted to ask if I could have his phone number so I could message him now that I'd lost my iPad. My mum was really cross, and she wasn't going to let me get another one, and so I couldn't use the app any more."

"Let's return to the day you went to his address. Was he there?"

Freya pauses. "He was there. But he was really angry with me for coming round. He said it was stupid and immature of me. So I left." Freya sounds cross, as if the memory is still raw.

"How did that make you feel?" Edward says.

"Horrible. I'd thought we had something special."

There's a pause while Edward goes through his papers. I'm furiously noting this all down. I can see by the upward tilt of Barbara's head that she considers this evidence important, and I want to be thorough in my transcription.

He starts up again. "Did you see him again that summer?"

For the first time, Freya actually starts crying, a couple of sobs escaping from her before she puts her hand over her mouth. She rubs at her eyes with the back of her other hand. Now she looks closer to the schoolgirl she really is. Though it isn't making the jury members look any more sympathetic. They're shuffling in their chairs, and one woman checks her watch.

The court usher gives Freya another glass of water and she drinks from it. The judge asks if she is all right to continue or if she needs a short break.

"It's OK," she says. "I can keep going." She lifts her chin. "I did see him again. It was in August. I'd been staying at my dad's house in Surrey, but I was getting bored and he was never there. So I decided to go back to my mum's. I just left early one morning because his stupid girlfriend was there again and I don't like her. I got the train back into London, but instead of getting the tube home, I decided to go back to his flat, see if maybe I could see him. I'd ordered him a book, a special copy of *Fanny Hill*, and I wanted to give it to him. I thought maybe he would like me again if I gave him a present."

"I see," Edward says. "So when you went to his flat, what time was it?"

"About nine."

"You weren't expected at home?"

"No. I hadn't told my mum. I just went straight to Jeremy's."

"What did you do when you got there?" Edward prompts.

"I was going to ring on the bell, but I felt too nervous. So I sat on a wall opposite his flat and I waited to see if he came out."

"And did anyone come out?"

I look up at Freya and feel a chill as I watch the girl's face. For a moment it's entirely bleak. Slowly she turns to Edward.

"Yes. Jeremy came out."

"Was he alone or was he with someone else?"

Freya looks straight at Jeremy. "He was with someone else. A girl. I don't know who she was." I glance at him but, as ever, his head is lowered.

"What were they doing?"

"He was saying goodbye to her. She looked like she had stayed the night—he was in a dressing gown. He kissed her for ages and then she left." There's an expression almost of triumph on her face, swiftly replaced by sadness.

"And what did you do?"

"I kept my head down. As soon as he shut the door, I ran over and pushed the book through his letter box, then I left."

"You still wanted to give him a present, even after you had seen him kissing someone else?"

"I thought it might make him feel guilty," Freya says, deep sadness in her voice.

"Was it soon after this that you told anyone about what had happened between you and the defendant?"

"Yes. I told my mum, but she said I was making it up. Then I called the police myself. That's when it all kicked off." She gestures around her at the courtroom before her head droops, as if she's overwhelmed at the thought.

37

Court adjourns shortly after. Freya's testimony for the prosecution has been concluded.

Barbara is all set for cross-examination. She repeats her instructions to me to double-check the files of printouts. Jeremy seems calm now that the evidence has been laid out. He leaves almost as soon as we are all dismissed from court. I say my goodbyes and leave, too. I want to ask him about the rumors he's heard from Robin's school, but it's not the time.

Nicole hasn't texted again, so I make my way up to north London as fast as I can, the tensions of the courtroom giving way to tension about Daisy, about Julia, about Robin.

I reach Nicole's house and she comes to the door. I hear the sound of children's laughter upstairs. At least Robin is happy, not thinking too much about Daisy or what might be happening. There's a smell of cooking, fragrant and enticing. The house is warm, curtains drawn against the autumn dusk, and when Nicole moves forward to give me a hug, I'm drawn into the embrace of her home.

Nicole is flushed from cooking, a slight smell of fried onion in her hair. When she moves away from me, it's clear how much pressure she's under. Her jumper is stained and her hair hasn't been brushed for some time.

"Is there any news?"

"Nothing. Daisy is in a coma, with an aspirant pneumonia—they say that she must have slipped into unconsciousness from the drugs before vomiting and choking on that vomit. She was close to death when Julia saw the state she was in. She's suffered a loss of oxygen, leading to a hypoxic brain injury and, on top of this, she breathed in some of the sick while she was unconscious and it's led to an infection in her lungs. The next few days will be critical. They don't know how she's going to be when she wakes up, what level of brain function there might be. If she wakes from the coma at all..." Nicole says the last words in a whisper.

I feel the word reverberate through me. *Coma.* "I hadn't realized it was so bad."

"It's not something I could really text," Nicole says. "I wanted to tell you myself."

She draws me through into the living room and sits down on the sofa, patting the space next to her. "I have no idea how it happened, or what Daisy might have taken, but they seem to be suggesting a drug overdose."

"Where would she have got drugs from? What kind of drugs?" I can't stop asking questions.

"They don't know yet. They're running tests. And as for where... Well, that's why the police were searching Julia's house."

I push on. "How long had she been unconscious?"

"Pippa didn't realize anything was wrong—she woke up very early and came straight through to my room. She just thought Daisy was asleep. It was when Julia went in to wake her later that she realized there was a problem, that Daisy wasn't right. She was unconscious, and there was vomit round her mouth. She wasn't breathing. I did CPR on her, and the ambulance arrived really quickly and took over. Her brain was starved of oxygen for a period of time—they don't know how long. It's really serious."

"You said she was unwell during the evening on Friday?"

"She was…agitated. She said she had a tummy ache and a headache, but I thought she was just in a state." My new friend looks nervous. "That last maths test hadn't gone so well, and she was still upset from the really low score she got."

"When she got seventy-six percent?"

Nicole looks at me. "The score Julia thought was low. That one."

"Daisy does seem to be under a lot of pressure."

"She is," Nicole says. "I mean, Julia really does love her, but she holds her to incredibly high standards." She gets up from the sofa, paces around the room a couple of times, stopping in front of the mirror over the mantelpiece and pulling at her hair. "All this stuff we tell them, be *your* best, not be *the* best. I'm not sure Julia has got that memo yet."

I laugh, though there's little humor in it. "It is competitive."

"Sure." Nicole sits down next to me on the sofa. "That's why I called you. I know it must seem odd, because we've only just started talking to each other. But you seem far more normal than the others. It's gone a bit mad. Especially this year, all the pressure to get through to secondary school…"

We sit in silence for a moment. Despite my concern, I'm a little flattered that Nicole has seen me as a source of normality.

"I guess we've avoided the worst of it, coming in so late on," I say.

"Well, that's one way of looking at it. You're not exactly seeing any of us at our finest. It all used to be so lovely, but it's got so fraught..."

I'd almost forgotten what Jeremy said to me earlier in court, but this comment reminds me. "I heard something. From someone outside school."

"Go on?" Nicole says.

"There was someone who died?"

Nicole is twisting the ends of her hair. "I'm not really sure..."

"No, I'm not sure either. And he did say it was all probably gossip, but..."

Nicole opens her mouth as if to say more, before she's interrupted by the doorbell. She gets up and rushes to the front door. There's a murmur of voices. It's Julia, and I go out into the entrance hall to join them. She's pale, with dark circles around her eyes. When she sees me, she gives me a half-smile before taking her coat off. "I could murder a drink."

We go to the kitchen and Nicole opens a bottle of white wine, dumps three glasses on the table, and sloshes the wine into them noisily.

"So, how is she?" Nicole asks.

"The same." Julia drinks half her glass down in one gulp. "Exactly the same. She's just lying there all white and tired with a tube down her throat. It doesn't even look like her."

"I wish you'd let me see her," Nicole says.

"I know how much it's going to distress you," Julia says. "I'm just trying to protect you." She takes another drink, tops up her glass. "And they don't want too many visitors. It's disruptive. I mean, it is Intensive Care..."

Nicole pats her on the arm. "It's so awful," she says. "You're dealing so well with it."

"What choice do I have? Paul came in to see her today. He was really upset."

"Was it OK? Seeing him, I mean?" Nicole asks.

Julia pinches her lips together, shakes her head. "He was as much of a selfish shit as ever. He had a real go at me, said I hadn't been looking after her properly, that he was going to go for custody as soon as she was well enough to go home."

"What did you say?" Nicole asks.

"That it wasn't the time or the place. The only important thing was that Daisy pulled through safely."

"Did he agree?"

Julia drinks again, lowers her glass. "He told me to stop being such a fucking hypocrite. That I was playing the perfect-mother role again and it made him sick because I was very far indeed from being a perfect mother." She puts her face in her hands, her shoulders starting to shake. Nicole rushes over to her and pulls her into an embrace where Julia stays quiet for some moments, then the only sound to emerge is a muffled sob. I watch them, full of sympathy for Julia. She might well be awful, but it's such a horrible situation it's impossible not to feel sorry for her.

"He's such a bastard," Nicole mutters into her friend's hair. The thought of Andrew comes into my mind, how unkind he's been to me, and my sympathy for Julia grows even more.

A timer goes off on the oven. Nicole releases Julia and goes to turn it off before pulling out a huge fish pie bubbling with a golden cheese crust. My mouth waters.

"I thought we might need something comforting tonight."

Julia goes over and gives her a hug. "You really are amazing," she says. "You're such a huge support, Nicole. You too, Sadie." She turns to look at me. There's genuine emotion behind the Botox. "We didn't get off on the right foot, but I know I can count on you."

"And Robin's been so wonderful with Pippa," Nicole says. "It's been such a comfort to hear them laughing upstairs. She's been brilliant at distracting her."

"I wish I could be so easily distracted," Julia murmurs. I try not to be offended.

The girls come downstairs and Nicole serves up spoonfuls of pie. We all sit around the kitchen table. I eat hungrily—it feels like hours since lunch in the canteen with Jeremy—and Robin and Pippa do too, but Nicole and Julia both push the food around their plates with their forks.

"Daisy would have eaten the whole thing by now," Julia says with a sigh.

"Such a big appetite," Nicole agrees.

"Not that big," Julia says, the sigh replaced with something sharper. "Not like Pippa here—she's on seconds already."

"Pippa..." Nicole says, "you know you should ask before you help yourself to more." She takes the plate away from her daughter, even though Pippa is still halfway through a mouthful.

"Sorry," the girl mumbles, starting to blush.

"That's OK, darling. Just remember, though, you really don't need to eat so much."

Robin looks over at me as if to check that it's all right for her to keep eating, and I nod at her before reaching for the serving spoon and giving myself another helping, too.

"Oh, I do envy you, not caring about what you eat," Julia says, and I blink. "I wish I could let go of some of this control. But, you know, even in a time of such huge stress, I just can't let myself shovel food down like that."

I have a forkful of food held nearly to my lips. I catch Nicole's eye before I lower the fork slowly.

"Oh, Julia, you're so brave," Nicole says. "You're just marvelous. I would be in pieces by now."

I murmur in agreement, pick up my plate and Robin's, pile them on the side by the dishwasher.

"We'd better go," I say. "I don't want to impose any more. And I do need to do some work."

"Very happy to have Robin tomorrow," Nicole says. "Any time."

She sees us to the front door. As she hugs me goodbye, she leans close. "I keep saying it, but please don't mind what Julia says. She's under so much stress. It's very hard."

"I can't even imagine."

The thought of Daisy lying unconscious in hospital is not far from my mind. I hold Robin's hand tightly all the way home.

38

There's no news the next morning, either. *Situation still the same*, Nicole texts. *Robin welcome as ever tonight.*

I send a quick reply thanking her for the update. Thinking back to the conversation with Jeremy the previous day, I do an internet search—*Ashams girl dies*. Nothing other than hits that relate in a positive way to the school for the first few pages on Google. No negative information, no mention of a dead girl, just story after story about their bursary scheme and philanthropic work in the local community, and multiple articles about their stellar academic results. I keep plowing through but Robin comes in and I have to get ready to leave with her.

"Are you sure you want to go to their house again?" I ask her on the way in to school.

"Yes, I like them," Robin says. "It's OK, Mom, I promise."

I don't argue. I can't, really, given that I've got no after-school alternative arranged.

"When this trial is over," I say as we reach the school gates, "I promise we'll sort things out properly. I'll find you an after-noon nanny if I have court. I'll get it all arranged."

"Maybe Dad will have moved here by then," Robin says casually. I blink.

"Is he thinking about that?"

"I'm not sure. He said something when he was over. I don't know. Anyway, don't worry. I like Pippa and Nicole," Robin says, and kisses me goodbye.

I see Nicole in the distance but she's glued to her phone and doesn't look up, so I make my way to the tube, grateful not to have to chat. I'm thinking about what Robin has said about Andrew, that he might move back. It's not a problem I want to deal with right now—I like him being out of sight, out of mind. I know I'm going to have to deal with it all sometime. Just not now.

The tube journey works its usual magic of compartmentalizing my concern about Daisy, replacing those tensions with concerns about the trial and how Barbara's cross-examination will proceed. By the time the tube is going under the Thames, I've put Daisy and Julia and Nicole right into the back of my mind. Now I'm flicking through my files in my head. I know I've gone through all the messages thoroughly, and there is definitely no sign of the Viber app that Freya mentioned yesterday in court, but I'm still worried that I might have missed something. I can't think what, though. There's no trace of the alleged relationship between Freya and Jeremy, either on the laptop Freya was using for her messaging and social media, or on the basic Nokia.

The missing iPad, Viber—it does all feel too pat, as Barbara said. Freya can say what she likes about it, but with no evidence to back it up, it's worthless. It's threadbare, the prosecution case. Even though Freya came over better than I anticipated, the jury still did not look convinced.

The train pulls into Elephant and Castle, and I make my way to court.

After fifteen minutes of Barbara's cross-examination of Freya, the jury look even less convinced. I keep a close eye on them throughout, looking away only to write down the salient details of the answers that Barbara elicits. Zora is scribbling away behind me as well, ensuring we have a complete note of the evidence.

It's not so much about what Freya says in reply, but more the narrative that Barbara creates through her questions. I can see why Barbara is so highly sought after as an advocate. Her tone is sympathetic, non-judgmental. She sets Freya at her ease. It's clear Freya has had a difficult time with her family—yes. It's hard when parents divorce—yes. Freya was resentful toward her mother for throwing her father out when she discovered his affair—yes. Freya thought her mother should have given him another chance—yes. Freya found it tricky living with her mother sometimes—yes. But having said that, it wasn't easy living with her father, either—no.

The girl is on guard, fingers clenched tight over the edge of the witness box, but as Barbara takes her far away from questions to do with Jeremy, Freya seems to be relaxing a little, some emotion breaking through the carapace of make-up she's again plastered on.

She must have felt very alone sometimes—yes.

She found it hard to get attention—yes.

She resented it when her mother spent time with other people instead of with her. A long pause. Yes.

And, conversely, she was happy when her mother paid attention to her—a vehement yes.

Her mother was very good when something was upsetting Freya—yes.

She could be very supportive if there was a problem—another strong yes.

But otherwise was quite preoccupied with her own life—yes.

Fair to say that Freya had problems at school—yes.

She'd lost some friends over the years—yes.

She had caused a lot of problems in school over the years too—a sheepish yes, eyes flicked to the gallery.

But the defendant—Mr. Taylor—had been helpful. Yes. He had. Very helpful. Freya nods.

She developed strong feelings for Mr. Taylor as a result. A long pause. Yes, but not...

"Yes or no, please," Barbara says.

"Yes."

And so it goes on. I know what picture Barbara is painting. She won't take long over it. Freya the lonely child, acting out to get attention, distressed by her parents' divorce. The moment she's given any attention by a teacher, she latches on to him. And when it all goes wrong...

Barbara moves off on a small tangent. She's holding the list that I put together of the lies Freya told. She pauses for a moment before proceeding.

"Did the police take a laptop away from you, specifically a Hewlett Packard?"

"Yes."

"Was there a Facebook account on there in your name?"

"Yes."

"Did you message a friend called Susie?"

A long pause, a nod. "Yes."

Barbara clears her throat. "Did you ever message Susie to tell her that a boy at another school had sexually assaulted you?"

Edward rises to his feet. "Your Honor, I must interrupt this line of questioning by my learned friend..."

The judge holds up her hand. "Be careful, Miss Carlisle."

"Yes, Your Honor," Barbara says. "There is a point to this." She turns back to Freya. "Did you ever send a message to your friend Susie to that effect?"

"Yes."

"When you made the complaint, did you believe it to be true?"

A very long pause indeed. Freya looks down at her hands, back up at Barbara again. She looks very exposed. I turn to look at Jeremy. For once he's looking up at Freya, his expression intent.

"Please can you answer the question?" Barbara says.

"No," Freya says. "No, I didn't believe it to be true."

"Did you say it for attention?"

"No," Freya says. I'm watching her intently. Her voice says no, but her face says something else entirely.

"Did you say it for revenge?"

"No," Freya says, but she looks even more troubled.

"Are you sure about that?" Barbara says. Even though she's on the attack, her approach is still gentle. There's a sympathetic tone to her questions, a tilt of the head.

Freya looks at her, defiance bristling from her. The two stare at each other, woman and girl, but it's Freya who looks down first. "Yes, I said it for revenge."

"Because he didn't want to enter into a relationship with you?"

Silence. Another battle of attrition fought, lost.

"Yes, because he didn't fancy me."

A phone goes off in the public gallery and the judge shouts and it's only at that moment that I realize how high the tension has grown in the courtroom. Barbara turns to me. There's a pulse beating in her neck. Few words may have been spoken but this part of the war definitely belongs to the QC. The jury can clearly sense it too—for once, they're fully engaged, some of them writing notes. Their expressions have changed as they look at Freya, now full of cool calculation. *She's done it once, what's to say she's not doing it again…*

Barbara brings another piece of paper out. She's moved on from what I've unearthed. She has exactly what she needs from the witness—anything else on the subject would detract from the effect that's been made.

"You told the court that Mr. Taylor had given you books to read?"

"Yes."

"And you've named some of the books—one of them was *Fanny Hill*?"

"Yes."

"Mr. Taylor didn't recommend that book to you, did he?"

"He did. Yes," Freya says, indignation rising in her voice.

"He recommended some books to you about the Tudors, is that right?"

"Yes."

"And when it was pointed out to him that there were some sex scenes in the books, he changed his recommendation, didn't he?"

"No, he didn't. He started with books by Philippa Gregory, and then they got worse. More sex."

"You found *Fanny Hill* somewhere else, didn't you?"

"No," Freya says, almost in a shout.

"And you hit on it as a good prop to use in manufacturing this story, didn't you?"

"I'm not manufacturing anything!"

Barbara nods as if satisfied with that answer. "Turning away from the book for a moment. You developed a crush on Mr. Taylor, didn't you?"

"I, no. Yes. I mean…"

"Let me clarify what I mean," Barbara says. "He paid you attention as a teacher, and you developed inappropriate feelings for him."

"No! It wasn't like that. You're twisting it!" There's red rising in her cheeks, a dull flush on her neck.

"But those feelings weren't reciprocated, were they?"

"They were!"

"You tried to get Mr. Taylor's attention, but he made it clear to you that he had no interest in that way."

"That's not what happened."

"And the hurt of that rejection was compounded by your discovery that he was in a relationship."

Freya has started to cry now, small sniffs and the wiping of sleeve across face.

"He dumped me. Yes, it hurt," she says, very quietly.

"And that's when you told the police that he had been in a relationship with you?"

"Yes."

A long pause from Barbara, as if she's making sure the jury has the point she's making.

I have to hand it to Barbara, it's all very effective. She clarifies that there's no trace of the iPad to be found, and that there is only Freya's word that there was any correspondence between her and Jeremy at all. Finally, Barbara asks a couple more questions in which she spells it out a little more clearly that she's suggesting Freya is making the entire story up in revenge for Jeremy's rejection of her. The bubble of Freya's self-confidence is completely popped. She's crying uncontrollably by the time she leaves the witness box, the shreds of her evidence all around her.

And it's been done with sensitivity. There's been no suggestion that Freya is sexually promiscuous, no attempt to put her moral values on trial. A portrait has been deftly drawn of a fractured relationship between parents and daughter, the girl desperate for love and attention, but unable to find it without acting out and lying. Edward's face is somber as he leaves court at the lunch break, when the cross-examination is over.

He knows the damage that has been done to his case.

39

I check my phone as soon as we're out of court, but there's nothing, no message from Nicole or Julia giving any update about Daisy. The longer that Daisy is unconscious, the worse the prognosis will be.

Sitting down at the canteen table with my coffee, I flick through the apps on my phone, unsure whether I should ask for an update or whether I should wait.

"I think the prosecution case will finish today," Barbara says, sitting down opposite me. "Tomorrow at the latest."

"You think?" Jeremy says. He's to my left. He looks at my coffee. "Aren't you going to eat anything?"

"I'm not very hungry."

"Oh, it's that poor girl, isn't it?" he says. "Is there no news yet?"

"None," I say, clicking at my phone again.

"What's this?" Barbara says.

"It's one of the girls in Sadie's daughter's class," Jeremy explains. "She's in a coma. It's very concerning."

Barbara raises an eyebrow.

"She's at Ashams, you know," Jeremy adds.

"Yes. Terrible parents there, by all accounts. Though aren't they all." Barbara shovels the rest of her sandwich into her mouth. "I have to make a call. See you back in court."

The rest of the afternoon passes without detriment to the defense case. Edward calls a girl called Asha, who is supposedly a friend of Freya's, but her evidence doesn't really progress the case much. Freya had dropped hints to her about a secret relationship but had not gone into much detail. I look at the girl's statement and can see that, for whatever reason, she's playing it down. When she made her statement to the police, she was adamant that Freya had actually discussed Jeremy by name with her, but she says now that she can't remember. Edward is clearly frustrated, but he can't push it too far.

Barbara cross-examines her, but only very briefly, to clarify that Freya never said with whom she was carrying on the secret relationship. She also asks if Asha had speculated at all about it—when the girl replies that Freya was known to invent boyfriends and bad situations to make herself look interesting, Edward's shoulders visibly slump. There are no further questions.

At the end of the day, the whole defense team, apart from Jeremy's mother, sits in the conference room while Barbara outlines the next steps. She's proposing a submission of no case to answer, as in her view, the case is paper thin.

"Do you think it'll succeed?" Jeremy says. "Will this finally be over?"

"It should do," Barbara says. "But the judge may take the view that as it all hangs on the credibility of the witness, it should be a matter for the jury to decide, so the trial will carry on. We'll have to see how it goes."

She stands, signaling that the conference is over, and she and Zora leave the room. Jeremy catches at my arm as I'm about to follow.

"Do you have time for a quick drink?" he says. "I know it's all looking positive, but I'm completely terrified. It would be really helpful just to calm me down."

I'm not sure. I don't want Barbara to think I'm acting inappropriately. I'm worried about Robin, too, but something about the way he's asked the question tugs at me. He's doing his best to seem calm, I can see that, but there's a tension humming underneath, and looking at him more closely, his eyes are rimmed red, a furrow deep by his left eyebrow.

"Let me check a couple of things," I say. "I may have to go home. Give me a few minutes and I'll let you know. OK?"

"OK," he says. "I know you have a lot of demands on you, but it would really help."

I head over to the robing room and change. Barbara is checking her emails.

"Jeremy has suggested a drink," I say to her. "I think he's quite worried."

"He doesn't need to be," Barbara says. "But I suppose it's stressful." She looks up. "Good idea. Go and calm him down. All part of the service."

I text Nicole. *Any news about Daisy? All well with the girls? I've been asked to have a drink with the client—does it work for me to pick up a bit later tonight? xx*

No problem at all, comes the reply. *And no news. Robin is distracting Pippa from worrying so that's good xx*

We walk toward Blackfriars together, stopping finally at a pub on The Cut. I ask for white wine and Jeremy goes up to the bar while I sit at a table near the back of the room. It's filling up, tired office workers in crumpled suits. No children in here, no groups of mothers. I look around with a sense that time has run away from me; the last ten years I've spent in America raising Robin all slipped away, the habit of court and drinking after work so easily resumed.

Jeremy sits opposite me and puts a bottle of wine down on the table with two glasses.

"It was cheaper than by the glass," he says. "Made more sense."

"Thanks."

He fills the glasses and I take a sip and then another, the alcohol smoothing its way through me.

"Is the little girl all right?"

"I don't know," I say. "I really don't know. It's so strange. The mother is a bit odd, too."

Jeremy nods. "I know exactly what you mean. I've met pretty much every type of parent doing this job. Some of them are completely nuts. I always do my best to keep my distance. I feel really sorry for some of the girls, the way their parents behave."

"Is that why you were trying to help Freya?" I say, before thinking. I pause and take another sip of wine. "Sorry. We shouldn't discuss it."

"It's fine. Freya was having problems at school, and there were a lot of meetings. She didn't have any parental support. They weren't interested, either mother or father, particularly once they'd split up. I tried to engage with her mother, but it didn't get very far. It was as if she'd given up on Freya. I guess divorce is always hard on kids."

"That's what I worry about, the effect on Robin." It doesn't feel like I'm talking to a client any more. I look down at the table and pick up a coaster, tearing it into tiny pieces.

"Freya's parents went through a very nasty divorce, from what I understand. I thought my parents were bad, but hers were terrible from what she said. It doesn't need to be like that, though," he says. "I didn't realize you were getting divorced." He looks at my left hand. I follow his glance, twist my wedding ring around.

"We've only separated recently," I say. "That's why Robin has started at Ashams. It's been... difficult."

The bar is full now, all the tables occupied. Jeremy's voice has got lower and I've had to lean closer to hear him. A man pushes past the back of my chair and it jolts me forward. I bash Jeremy on the forehead and he jumps back. I rub the bump and we both start laughing.

"Let's not talk about Freya any more," he says. "Let's have another drink and you can tell me the whole story."

The ice is broken now. I'm starting to relax. I might not have sought this change in my life, but now I have a proper trial, a future career. Robin is starting to make friends; I'm starting to talk to people. And Jeremy is beginning to relax, too; he knows the case isn't in the bag, but it could all be over the next day.

There's almost a celebratory feel to the night, the conversation rapidly moving from Andrew to lighter, more fun topics. The first bottle is soon finished, another bought. We order food and before I even realize the time, it's after eight o'clock. I check my phone. Nicole has texted—*Robin can stay if you like—we've enough uniform spare for tomorrow. They're having a lovely time Nxxx*

"I should go," I say to Jeremy. "I have to collect Robin. Though Nicole does say she can sleep over tonight."

"Then stay," he says. "Have some more wine. You deserve a break. It can't be easy doing everything on your own."

I look at my phone, at the wine, at Jeremy. I text *Thank you xx* to Nicole and settle back down until the pub closes at eleven, and we are asked to leave.

"Thank you," Jeremy says as we stop to say good night at the tube station. "I feel much better."

"I had a lovely night too."

He leans forward to kiss me on the cheek. I turn and we lock eyes. It's only when I feel the touch of his lips against me that I'm pulled back into myself, suddenly only too aware that he is my client. I drag myself away, wave as I run to hail a taxi with its light on, and he waves back and disappears into the tube. I sit in the cab, prodding my conscience. It might not have been strictly appropriate, but the evening was encouraged by Barbara, and the client has gone home happy. As am I, despite everything else that's happening. I did ask him again about what he'd said about the dead girl at Ashams, but he hadn't known any more, and it had been a relief to spend the evening talking about books and films and music, forgetting all about my worries for a while. I travel back home with a smile on my face, falling asleep the moment my head hits the pillow.

40

My good mood has faded by the morning. The house is too empty without Robin.

I wash and dress quickly, eager to get out, before it hits me that without the school run there's no need to leave for court so early. I make another coffee and wander around, unable to settle. All I can see are the flaws, the cracks in the walls, the holes in the floor. I've done a lot to the place in the time we've been here, but it's not enough. It'll never be enough.

Just like I was never enough for Lydia. Usually I ignore the thought of the pile of destruction in my old bedroom at the top of the house, but right now it lies heavy on me. I try not to imagine Lydia's triumph that she'd be bound to feel if she knew that my much-despised marriage has ended.

I pick up the photograph of my father from the shelf and look at him, wondering if it would all have been different had he lived past my infancy. Lydia rarely talked about him, and then only to complain about how inconsiderate it had been of him *to die like that and leave her all on her own to manage when he was the one who wanted a baby in the first place.* So much resentment, so much blame. He is smiling in the photograph, hair brushed neatly to one side, and

I smile back at him. At least he wanted me, even if Lydia didn't.

I still can't work out the motivation behind Lydia's legacy to Robin, grandmother to granddaughter. Was it purely to assert control over us? It wouldn't surprise me. But rather than being destructive, it's actually provided the thing that I so desperately needed, the route to escape from Andrew. Robin is happy, too. If my mother was hoping otherwise, she'd be disappointed.

I've just put the photograph down when my phone rings.

It's Andrew. The last person I'd expect to be calling me. It's the middle of the night in New York, let alone anything else. I take a moment to answer, nerves grabbing me around the neck. Anger, too, that he thinks he can just contact me like this, out of the blue. There's a delay on the line, a silence of a few seconds before some crackling noises. Then the sound starts to fade in and out, before the line cuts out entirely. I try calling back once, twice, but no reply. All the peace of mind I've built up collapses. I send a text, *What do you want?* and wait in vain for a reply. Different answers to my question dance around my head, none of them good. Andrew moving here, instigating a divorce, demanding custody of Robin.

I push it all away and make my way down to court, but try as I might, thoughts of his call continue to distract me. I watch the proceedings for most of that day from a point in the courtroom high above my own head. Edward and the officer in the case read the transcript of police interviews out loud, their voices droning, *No comment* repeated like a mantra. At one point I almost nod off, jerking awake with a sense of falling.

The only time that I'm fully engaged is when the police officer is asked about seizing the laptop and the fact that no iPad was to be found. The officer confirms to Barbara that Freya's phone is a basic Nokia, with no internet access, and that her laptop is a PC, running on an outdated version of Windows.

"Many teenagers are very technically proficient," he says, "but that was not my impression of the complainant. Her devices are very out of date."

"Was there anything on the laptop to indicate that an iPad might be connected to it?"

"Nothing at all. I mean, there wouldn't need to be—it's no longer necessary to sync them with a computer."

"But there is nothing to suggest that she actually had an iPad, is there?"

He pauses, shrugs. "Only her word for it."

"And is there anything to show that she used the Viber app to communicate with the defendant as she alleges?"

"Nothing there at all," the officer says.

"So there's nothing to support her account that this is an app she used?"

The officer shrugs again. "No. Nothing other than her account."

Barbara only has a couple of questions left in cross-examination.

"Did you seize every electronic device you found in the possession of the defendant?"

"Yes."

"And did you find any messages from the defendant to the complainant?"

"No. We didn't."

That concludes the prosecution case. I scrutinize the jury and they don't look impressed, at least not to me. Three women on the front row, their mouths tight, I can almost picture them knitting as the tumbril rolls past. Edward looks underwhelmed, too. He knows it can only get worse from here.

The afternoon has worn on and I'm stiff from sitting all day—I try to stretch my neck out without making myself conspicuous. Barbara rises to her feet.

"Your Honor, there are a few matters of housekeeping I'd like to address in the absence of the jury. Given the time, might I suggest that they are dismissed for the day?"

The judge agrees, telling the jury to return tomorrow at the usual time. They troop out, looking over at Jeremy and the public gallery as they go. I follow their glance to see Freya sitting there, right at the front.

She's sitting on her own.

The excitement of Jeremy's fan club has died down and now there are only a couple of teenage girls in court, glaring at Freya. She's leaning against the balcony of the public gallery, knuckles clenched white. I turn back, bowing my head.

"Your Honor," Barbara continues once the jurors have gone, "I'd like to make a submission of no case to answer." The judge nods, inviting her to continue. "I intend only to address you in brief. You are, of course, aware of the test as laid out in *R.* v. *Galbraith.* I am not suggesting that there is *no* evidence that the defendant has committed the offenses as outlined on the indictment. My submission is that what evidence there is, is inherently weak to the point of making it nonexistent. We have essentially heard only from the complainant, and I would submit that her version of events is entirely vague and unsubstantiated by any external corroboration.

"There is no evidence whatsoever from any other source that supports the existence of the alleged relationship. Despite her assertion that there was a trail of correspondence between her and the defendant, no trace of this has been uncovered, either on any of her devices or on the phone of the defendant, which was also examined in detail by the police. I appreciate that my learned friend will argue that Your Honor should take the view that the complainant's reliability goes to the heart of this case, and thus that it should rightly be put before the jury for them to decide upon it, but in my submission there simply is not enough for the jury to consider. This is essentially a borderline case in which I would invite you to exercise your discretion to dismiss the case."

Edward shakes his head throughout, and when Barbara has finished, stands up.

"I will be even briefer," he says. "I am grateful to my learned friend for stating in advance my reply to this submission. The credibility of the complainant is indeed at the heart of the case, and it is only proper that it is deliberated on by the jury at the end of the defense case, not dismissed at this point."

"I am inclined to agree, Mr. Kayode," the judge says. "However, there is merit to Miss Carlisle's contention that there is no other supporting evidence in this case." She looks up at the clock—it's half past three by now. "Given the time, I am minded to consider this application overnight."

She shuffles her papers together and stands. Court is dismissed for the day.

Barbara and Zora confer outside the robing room. They both look thoughtful as I approach them.

"We're discussing how best to play this," Barbara says. "As I said at the start, Jeremy has a lot of character references. We have two of them prepared to attend court. We had provisionally arranged for them to attend on Monday, but the bishop has emailed and he can now only come tomorrow. I'm thinking of asking the other if he can come tomorrow as well."

"What if the case is thrown out?" I say.

"Better to be prepared."

"You'd call them before he gives evidence?" Zora says.

Barbara nods. "Not orthodox, I grant you. But it'll set the tone."

"The judge might not like it," Zora says.

"Perhaps not, but if the bishop is only available tomorrow, what choice do we have?" Barbara says. I look at her closely, suspicious of the timing, but her face and tone are entirely innocent, her smile bland.

I get the feeling that Jeremy might be hovering in the hope of another drink, but I leave as fast as I can, desperate to collect Robin. The tube can't come fast enough; I get to the school gates with minutes to spare. It takes me a moment to realize how tense the atmosphere is, something strained in the groups of parents who cluster together even more tightly than normal. I look around to see if there's anyone I recognize and eventually find Nicole, deep in the heart of a circle of concerned women. I make my way over and touch her on the shoulder. She gives me a quick hug.

"There's a photographer there," she hisses into my ear.

"Where?"

"There." Nicole points discreetly. It takes me a moment to

spot the man. He's standing on the opposite pavement, camera with zoom lens in hand.

"Why is he here?"

"There's been a leak," Nicole says. "It's turning into a scandal. Look."

She pushes a copy of the evening newspaper into my hands.

"IS THIS HOTHOUSE KILLING CHILDREN?" says the headline, emblazoned above a photograph of the school. I scan through the piece. *Questions are beginning to be asked about the academic pressure at the highly prestigious Ashams School following the hospitalization of a Year 6 girl in circumstances yet to be explained. The matter is currently under investigation by the police. This leads on from the death by drowning last year of Zoe Leonard, whose…*

Nicole pulls the paper back out of my hands before I can finish reading. I look at her.

"It's awful that they've dragged it up again. Her poor family. She was a little girl in Pippa's class last year," Nicole says. "It was a terrible accident—she drowned when the family were away on holiday. Their only child. Absolutely devastating."

"That sounds horrific," I say. "Why hasn't anyone told me about this before?"

Nicole looks away for a moment, looks back. "You have to understand, it was awful. They're from overseas—her father's something high up in the diplomatic service, they went straight back home after it happened. It upset everyone so much; the children especially…"

"Hi, Mom," Robin says from behind Nicole, who stops talking immediately. She moves aside to let Robin reach me.

"You OK, sweetie?"

"Yeah," Robin says. She doesn't sound entirely sure. "Can we go home now?"

"You don't want to come for hot chocolate with Pippa and me?" Nicole says.

I look at Robin, who shakes her head. "I'd like to get home," she says again.

"I think we'd best get off," I say. "Thanks so much for having her."

Pippa walks ahead with Robin as we head off from school. They have a quick chat before she stops to wait for Nicole. She's looking tired, eyes heavy and hair uncharacteristically greasy.

"She's really worried about Daisy," Robin says after they've gone. "I've been trying to cheer her up, but she feels really bad."

"Have you heard anything about a girl called Zoe?"

"The one who died? Yes, they were talking about it earlier. It spooked me a bit."

I stop walking, turn to my daughter. Robin is pale, a bit shaky. "Why did it spook you?"

"I think it's her place I took. Her locker. They said no one had joined the school until I did. Dead girl's shoes..."

I can't think of an answer to this. I pull Robin close to me and give her a long hug, waiting until she's finally calm before letting go.

41

Once Robin is in bed and asleep, I open my computer to do some further research on Zoe. But I can't find out much more. A holiday gone wrong, a brief Associated Press report, no journalist named who I could contact. Perhaps because the parents are foreign nationals, perhaps because it happened abroad, but the story hasn't warranted even a short paragraph other than in the report about the challenges that the school is facing. The emphasis in that story is far more strongly on Daisy's ongoing coma and speculation about the cause, with extraneous detail about the fact that Julia and her husband, Paul, divorced two years ago in an acrimonious split, which ended up in court over the division of assets.

I message Nicole asking if she knows any more about it, but I receive no reply. I think about texting Julia, but I'm not sure whether she would find it intrusive. I'm sitting alone in the living room, the house quiet around me, and I know if I go upstairs and stand outside Robin's room, I'll hear her breathing, little sounds of sleep and the creaking of the mattress as she turns. Without bidding, the image of Daisy on the stretcher comes into my head, and my imagination takes it further, into a hospital bed, the girl surrounded by tubes and machines with flashing lights. And from there it goes further still, to an unknown villa in an unnamed country, a dark pool and the still body floating on the top of the water, the screams of the mother as the child is found.

I hug my knees close to me, holding myself safe against the intrusion of the thoughts, the horror of it, until my phone beeps and breaks the spell.

Nicole. *I'll tell you about it when I next see you properly. Can't text. I'm so sorry for Julia. Bad enough without the press poking in too.*

How is Daisy? I reply.

Nicole takes a moment to compose her answer. I can see the gray dots dancing at the bottom of my phone screen. *Still the same. All very worrying.*

We sign off and I go to bed, though I don't sleep for hours, my thoughts unsettled, veering from Daisy to worrying about what Andrew might be planning and back again. In the end I take my duvet and some cushions through to Robin's room and make a nest for myself on the floor, matching Robin's breath in, out, in, out, and in time, I sleep.

Robin is slow to dress and eat breakfast in the morning. She's dragging her feet deliberately, but I do my best to ignore it. It's only when Robin complains of a sore tummy that I say something.

"Are you worried about going in?"

"No," Robin says immediately. A long silence. "Yes. A bit. It's just with all this, and the English test too..."

"Try not to worry about the test," I say. "As long as you do your best."

"But I don't think I can do my best," Robin says. "Not when

I'm thinking about how I took the place of a dead girl. I'm probably using her locker. Maybe it's haunted."

I don't know whether to laugh or cry. "Just try and get through it. And don't think of it like that. Even if it was her locker, it wouldn't matter. You know there's no such thing as ghosts."

"I suppose." Robin shrugs.

"So there you are. It's OK. And Daisy is going to be OK, too. I promise."

Robin hugs me and finishes her breakfast off more cheerfully. I sip my coffee, hoping to God I've made a promise that can be kept.

Drop-off goes smoothly enough. We arrive at the same time as Nicole and Pippa, so the girls run into school together. I was planning to ask Nicole more about Zoe, but she's looking tired and pale and I don't want to press her.

"Are you OK?"

"I didn't sleep well," Nicole says. "It's brought it all back to me. Pippa's been really unsettled too. God knows what effect this will have on the tests."

"Surely that doesn't matter right now?"

Nicole shakes her head. "I suppose not," she says. "But they've worked so hard. I hope it doesn't all fall apart."

"I'm sure it's going to be fine."

Nicole takes hold of my hand and we stand together for a minute. "You're right," she says. "I mustn't let it get to me so much. The girls are well, that's the main thing. Imagine being poor Julia..."

"Is there any news?"

"Nothing," Nicole says, withdrawing her hand. "Daisy isn't

worse, but she isn't better, either. And until she wakes up, there won't be any way of knowing how affected she is."

I shake my head. Streams of people are moving past us, parents and children going into school, but it's as if we're on our own island, isolated from everyone else.

"I've said it before," Nicole says, "but I really don't know what I'd be doing if you weren't here. I know we've only been friends for a few weeks but it feels like so much longer. I've always found it tricky, making friends with the other mums. So it's lovely to have met a kindred spirit. It's made such a difference, having your support. And Robin is so good for Pippa, too."

"You've been a big support to me, too," I say. "I don't know how I'd have managed this trial. Robin is really enjoying being friends with Pippa. When I think back to the start of term, how much everything has changed..."

"We will just have to stick together, and we will weather all this," Nicole says. "Now, don't you have to get to court?"

I laugh, say goodbye. I'm still concerned, but Nicole is right, I need to focus on the trial now, nothing else. By the time I get to Inner London Crown Court, my worry about Daisy is packed away, pushed down. I'm ready for the day ahead.

SUNDAY, 12:57 P.M.

The house is shuttered up, its face closed to invasion. I hammer on the door until my knuckles are bleeding. Every part of me aches, my arms, my knees from the shock of the fall, my head throbbing. I'm screaming, "Let me in, let me in!" *at the top of my voice, but no one comes to the door. It's quiet; dead inside.*

I need to calm down, regroup. Plan what to do next. I stand back and examine the building closely. No chink, no opening. Every window is covered. There's a door at the side that leads into the garden and I go to it, test its handle, shove at it a few times, but to no avail.

"Can I help you?" a woman says from the pavement and I turn, a shock of hope and relief running through me. But it's not her—it's an older woman, glaring at me.

"I'm a friend," I say, approaching the woman hurriedly. "Do you know where she is?"

"I'm sure that if she wanted you to know where she was, she'd tell you," she says with immense hauteur. "Thumping on her door like that and making so much noise is not the way to behave."

"I'm looking for my daughter," I say. "I think she's got my

daughter." I'm trying to hold it together as I speak to the woman. I know I look crazed. But I can't hold the tears in now, great jags of sobbing, snot bursting from me—it's stress, worry about my daughter's whereabouts, emotion so uncontrolled it can only leak out like this. All of it caught up together, brought to a head by the woman's icy words.

She takes a step back. "If you don't get away from this house, I will call the police," she says. "I'm on the Neighborhood Watch scheme for this street and you are behaving very suspiciously."

I look at her, searching for some trace of humanity, any help at all, but there's nothing there: cold, hard, mouth pursed tight shut. The woman starts reaching into her bag as if to pull out a phone, and I turn and walk away, head lowered, controlling myself with some effort.

I'll be back, though. Whatever I have to do, I'll do it.

I'm going to find my daughter.

Whatever it takes.

42

Jeremy and his mother are both edgy when I get to court. They're standing in a huddle with Zora and Barbara.

"It's the hope that kills you," Alexandra is saying. "Do you really think there's a chance the case might be over?"

Barbara shrugs. "It's possible. But best to proceed on the basis that we will have to put up a defense."

We're approached by two men who look to be in their sixties, both wearing suits. One of them is impeccable in his tailoring, his jacket well fitted, his silk tie a tasteful hue; his look is formal, his manner assured, but he has a weak chin and a petulant mouth. The other is less sleek, but with a greater air of gravitas. An ecclesiastical air, at a guess. It must be the bishop. The character witnesses have arrived.

Zora introduces me to them. The less tailored is the bishop, as I had assumed, the more suave a headmaster, recently retired, from a boarding school in Oxfordshire. They both embrace Jeremy, their voices sympathetic.

"I'm sorry my father can't be here," Jeremy says, "but he sends his regards."

"Bloody useless man," Alexandra interrupts. "His only son is on trial and he hasn't shown his face."

"Please," Jeremy stops her. "You know he's stuck on a case himself." He turns back to the two men. "I know he's very grateful that you've been able to make the time to attend. I'm grateful too."

"Of course, dear boy. Very happy to say a few words on your behalf," the bishop says. The headmaster nods his agreement.

"I'll have to ask you to wait outside court," Barbara says. "And with any luck, you won't be needed at all. But if you don't mind sitting here, I'll let the court know where you are so that you can be called if necessary."

Both men nod and sit down. We go into court. Zora and I stand together at the back of the room while the others take their places.

"You look tired," she says. "How is everything? Is Robin's friend doing OK?"

"I don't really know. There doesn't seem to have been any improvement. Robin's putting on a brave face, but I can tell it's bothering her."

"I told you that school was a bad idea..."

I shoot her a sharp look, and she puts up her hand in a gesture of apology. "Sorry, I know. I get it. Anyway, talking of dreadful parents..."

"Funny the father hasn't made it to court at all," I say. "Though if he's anything like the mother, it's probably as well."

Zora rolls her eyes and laughs. I take my seat behind Barbara, ready for court to begin.

"Will Your Honor be minded to rule on the submission of no case to answer that I made on behalf of the defendant yesterday?"

"Yes, I was getting to that."

Barbara murmurs an apology, but the judge carries on regardless.

"I have considered your application carefully and while I appreciate the merits of what you had to say, it's undeniable that this case stands and falls on the credibility of the complainant. In my judgment, this is a matter that must therefore be considered by the jury, and on that basis, I am dismissing your application. The case will proceed." She pauses. "However, I regret to inform the court that due to an unexpected personal commitment, I will have to adjourn the case today at lunchtime, to recommence on Monday morning."

Barbara rises to her feet. "In light of that, Your Honor, perhaps it would make sense to call only the two character witnesses who are here in attendance today, and wait until Monday to call the defendant to give evidence."

Edward Kayode stands. "I have no objection to that course of action, Your Honor."

The judge nods in agreement. While the first of them is brought into court, Barbara turns back to me and mutters, "I can't say I'm overly surprised. It's a shame, though. I was hoping we could put him out of his misery today. I'm convinced they're going to acquit, but I suppose they have to go through the motions."

I nod. She's right. I glance back at Jeremy. He's staring straight ahead, his expression blank, only a faint twitch at the side of his face an indication of the disappointment he must be feeling.

Barbara takes the headmaster through his evidence first, every line he delivers measured, polished, honed to perfection. It's praise, but not hagiography, a little criticism of Jeremy's impetuous nature as a youth thrown in to temper his account, render it more impressive. The jurors nod along, approval on most of their faces. Edward is doing a good job keeping his face under control—I can quite imagine that he would otherwise be rolling his eyes.

When asked if he would like to cross-examine, he stands up.

"Just a couple of questions," he says. "You've known the defendant since he was born?"

"Yes."

"A family friend, you said?"

"Yes."

"Is that a friendship with the defendant's mother, or his father?"

The headmaster looks irritated. "His father. We were at school together. I've known him almost all my life. I wouldn't hesitate to vouch for him or for his son."

Edward nods. "But of course. How old were you when you first met?"

"Thirteen."

"So that would mean the friendship is one of over fifty years, am I correct?"

"Yes."

"A school friend?"

"Yes. As I've said."

"Was it a boarding school?"

"What does that have to do with anything?"

"Yes or no, please," Edward says.

"Yes, a boarding school."

"Great loyalties are engendered at boarding school, aren't they?"

"Well, I mean. If you're suggesting that I would put loyalty to my friend over telling the truth about his son, then..."

"I'm simply establishing the facts of your relationship with the defendant," Edward says. He looks over at the judge. "No further questions, Your Honor."

The bishop is just as impressive, his voice mellifluous and calming. What he lacks in grooming he more than makes up for in serenity. When Edward cross-examines him in the same vein it feels almost like an affront that the clergyman should be thus challenged. He hides his irritation better than the headmaster, but the good effect of his testimony is left tarnished, a small smear left on the glass of piety. With a few words Edward has conjured up the sense of a clique, a faction bonded on the playing fields, loyal to each other above all else. He's good. But is he good enough?

It's only half past eleven when both witnesses have finished. Barbara reads out two more letters from character referees—one Jeremy's chaplain from his former school and another, a business executive, who states that he is a friend of Jeremy's father from school. It's obvious that Edward wants to raise his eyebrow at this, but he's too professional to grimace at the jury. He just nods his head at the conclusion of each, and I watch as a couple of jurors make notes. Court is adjourned until Monday, when Jeremy will give his account.

We convene outside: Barbara, me, Alexandra, Jeremy and Zora. Jeremy is looking strained, his mother angry beside him.

"It's outrageous that this case is going ahead," Alexandra says. "You should have argued harder."

"I was convinced she'd throw it out," Jeremy says. "Freya's evidence was a joke."

"I think the jury will agree," Barbara says, "but the judge is right that her credibility is the point at issue. You must hold your nerve for a few more days."

"Does this mean I have to give evidence?" Jeremy asks.

"We've discussed this," Barbara says. "It's entirely your decision, but you know my opinion is that you will make an extremely good impression on the jury."

"I really don't want to. But Dad thinks I should, too. It would be really helpful to go through it all again beforehand with one of you, though."

"Of course. Why don't we do it now?" Barbara says. "We can go back to chambers."

"Yes," Alexandra says. "You need to make sure you're properly rehearsed. I think I should come too—after the disaster of that so-called application I've lost a lot of faith in you, Barbara. You clearly need close supervision."

Jeremy shuffles his feet, panic in his eye. "I'm sorry," he says, "I can't. I told Dad the case had finished up early today, so we're meeting for lunch."

"I thought *we* were going to go for lunch," Alexandra says. "It would make a change to eat with you somewhere other than this place." She gestures around her with an expression of revulsion on her face. "I've had enough of being south of the river to last me a lifetime."

"I'm really sorry, Mum. I can't. I promised Dad." There's anguish in Jeremy's voice.

"As if promises mean anything to that man," Alexandra snorts. "Well, as you clearly prefer the idea of his company to mine." She turns with a flourish and struts off. We all stare after her, slightly stunned. After a moment, Jeremy recovers himself.

"Dad does think I should practice my evidence, too. Is there any chance we could do tomorrow at some point?"

Zora shakes her head. "I'm sorry, I've got arrangements already," she says.

"I'm not free either," Barbara says. "How about you, Sadie?"

I think about Robin and suppress my initial reluctance. I'll sort Robin out somehow. It won't take long. "Sure," I say. "I can spare a couple of hours in the afternoon. Maybe we can meet in chambers?"

"Thank you," Jeremy says. "Let's swap numbers and we can confirm the exact time in the morning."

Zora and Barbara are both smiling at me, pleased that I've resolved the issue for them, and I don't want to disappoint them. I type Jeremy's number into my phone on his dictation, texting him *hello* so that he has mine, and we all say goodbye.

43

I sit on the tube with my eyes closed, trying to rationalize my fears, put it all in some kind of order. At least Robin is OK, I can hold on to that. But have I put her in danger, sending her to this school? One incident threatening the life of a child might be regarded as misfortune, but two? The train is approaching a station and, making a sudden decision, I get up. I change tube line and make my way to a stop I do not usually visit.

When I'm out of the station I message Nicole. *I was going to visit Daisy. Do you think that's OK?*

Nicole's reply comes back almost immediately. *Yes, go in. It's floor 7, room 20. I'm sure Julia will be pleased to see you.*

My steps slow as I come close to the hospital, the gray of its concrete looming high above me. I nearly turn around and walk away, but I stop myself. It's all very well for me—I can escape the misery of it, hide from the reality that Julia is facing for her daughter. But that's no way to behave. I set my jaw and walk in through the front entrance, finding my way up to the seventh floor.

It's a private section of the hospital, a reception desk immediately through the doors. I approach and ask one of the staff where I should go. He points me in the right direction. I explain who I'm visiting but he's not interested, just nods, smiles. It's fine to go through, don't worry, is his clear message as he turns back to his computer. I walk over, take a deep breath and knock on the door.

There's no reply. The door is ajar and I push it open without a sound. The room is in darkness and I make my way slowly down a short entrance into the main room. There's a small lamp glowing at the side of the bed, the blinds shut over the window at the far end of the room. The only other source of light is the blinking of the machines that I guess must be keeping Daisy alive.

Now I'm standing next to the bed, I see a small figure shrouded under the covers. There's a woman sitting next to the bed, head bowed, hands outstretched on the sheets.

Julia.

"Hi," I say, my voice soft. There's no reaction. "Hi," I say again, more loudly this time. Still nothing.

I walk around the bed to where Julia is sitting and put my hand on her shoulder, a gentle touch at first, my grasp becoming firmer, though she doesn't react. Finally, just as I'm about to give up, she turns to me, her face drawn.

"Sadie," she says, in a voice that seems to come from far away. "Sadie."

"I wanted to come and see Daisy. Is that OK?"

"It's OK," Julia says. "You can see her."

I look at the bed. There isn't much of Daisy visible. Every part of her not covered by sheets is hooked up to the equipment. Her face is obscured by a plastic breathing mask, and there's a rhythmic pumping sound from one of the machines nearby.

"Is she going to be OK?" I say, the words bursting out before I can stop them. Julia's face tightens, a flash of something that could be fear, could be anger at my clumsiness. She looks away, back at her daughter.

"I don't know," she says, "I really don't know."

She says no more. I stay for only a few minutes longer and with a final clasp to Julia's bony shoulder, I take my leave, the weight of the room heavy on me as I go out of the hospital and make my way home, shaken to my core to see Daisy so ill.

Despite spending the afternoon scrubbing the house and rearranging the tattered furniture, something of this weight still hangs over me as I go to school to collect Robin. I've messaged Nicole to say that I'll be there, suggesting coffee before pickup, but she hasn't replied. When I see her at the school gate I wonder if she'll want to talk to me, but she's friendly as ever, apologizing for the lack of reply and showing concern for the report that I make of my visit to the hospital.

"It's grim," Nicole says. "I feel so bad for them. There's nothing else we can do, though. Just be supportive when Julia asks, that's all. When she gets out there'll be more to do."

"I suppose so," I say. I'm about to continue, question Nicole as to what she really thinks of Daisy's chances of recovery, but we're interrupted by a group of other mothers, flocking around Nicole to ask what the most recent news is. I back up, letting Nicole fill them in until the girls come out of school. Robin's face lights up to see me.

"How was your day, sweetheart?" I says.

"It was OK," Robin says. "I got through the test all right."

"That's good," I say. I turn, ready to leave, when I see that

Pippa and Nicole are having a very intense conversation on the side of the pavement. Nicole is waving her hands and it looks as if Pippa is crying.

"Is Pippa all right?"

"She did really badly in the test," Robin says. "Like, below fifty percent badly. She's incredibly stressed."

I look at them again, feeling sympathetic. We turn to go when Nicole calls after me.

"Sadie! Hang on. I want to ask you something."

We turn and wait for them to come over. Pippa is tear-stained, her eyes pink, but Nicole is looking excited.

"I've had a brilliant idea," she says. "I think that what these girls need is a break. A little trip to the seaside."

Pippa starts to look a little bit more cheerful. Nicole continues.

"I have a holiday house in Aldeburgh, on the Suffolk coast. I've just thought, why don't I take the kids up for the weekend? You could come too?"

"I'd love to," I say, "but I've got to work tomorrow."

"Oh, Mom," Robin says, disappointment leaking out of her.

"I'm sorry," I say, "but I have to go to a meeting."

"It's OK," Nicole says. "I'm very happy to take her. Honestly, it's no trouble at all."

The girls both say "yes" at the same time. Robin looks at me, her eyes pleading. So does Nicole.

"You'd be doing me a big favor," she says. "Robin is such a good influence on Pippa. She's so calming. Can you spare her for a couple of nights?"

"I don't think..." I start to say. I don't want to let Robin go away, keen to keep her close.

"Please, Mom. It'll be so much fun. Please."

"Please," Pippa says too. She's stopped crying, her face tense with expectation. "I'd love it if Robin came too. I like Robin."

It's too much. I can't deal with the pressure they're putting on me. I don't have the heart to cause so much disappointment. "If you're sure," I say to Nicole. "You've had her a lot recently. I don't want to impose."

"It's not imposing, promise," Nicole says, reaching over and grasping me by the hand. "Thank you." Her voice cracks as she says this, and I can see that there are tears in her eyes.

I smile. "It'll be lovely for Robin to see the sea. Some fresh air is just what they need."

44

After some discussion, we decide that Nicole will take the girls the following morning. Robin and I have a quiet evening; pizza and television. She pulls out the clothes she'll need for the trip to the seaside. It's very peaceful.

The next day we're up and out before eight. Nicole and Pippa are both delighted to see us, and I wave as they drive away down the road. I've got the whole weekend clear now, nothing to do other than the meeting with Jeremy this afternoon. I should be pleased.

I walk away from Nicole's house, looking at my phone to check for messages, when I catch my foot on an uneven piece of pavement. I fall forward, regaining my balance only at the last minute, but even as I stand back up it feels as if I'm still falling. Without Robin there, it's as if I've come untethered, my sense of gravity off somehow. I try to shake my head clear, scraping my hand along the rough surface of the stone wall on which I'm now leaning, grounding myself with the feel of it, breathing in once, twice, to get myself back to center.

It's fine. I'm fine. Robin's fine. We're both fine. I stamp

home, breathing in through my nose and out through my mouth in rhythm with my steps.

Later in the morning I message Jeremy, suggesting we meet in chambers at two. He replies shortly afterward, saying that he's hurt his knee going for an early-morning run, asking if I'll go to his flat instead—*I can barely stand, let alone walk*. I feel a distinct lack of enthusiasm at the idea of trekking across London rather than simply going into chambers. I don't have anything better to do, though, so I message back and ask for the address.

After some thought I find an outfit that's about right for a weekend conference—tidy, but not overly so, black on black with a colorful scarf. Barbara has texted with some last-minute reminders for me to give Jeremy about keeping calm, taking a minute to answer questions; I'm all ready. I make my way down to south London on the tube to his flat, a part of town I haven't visited for years.

It takes me a moment when I get out of the tube station to orient myself, the streets unfamiliar. I take my phone out of my bag to check the map for directions to Jeremy's flat and see the battery is nearly flat; I forgot to charge it overnight. I concentrate on memorizing the route.

While I'm looking at the map, a message arrives from Zora, swiftly followed by a second. *Isn't this Andrew's firm? Hope all is well* says the first. The second is a link to a news story. I glance at the headline but then the phone battery drops from 2% to 1% so I go straight back to the map, no time to waste.

The phone holds at 1% of battery nearly all the way there. I try not to check it too many times, but the streets are identical, terraces on terraces of similar houses. As I turn onto Jeremy's road, the phone gives up the ghost. I walk halfway along the road, ring the bell, 74B. I've made it.

It takes a while for Jeremy to answer the door. I hear slow, heavy thumps from inside, as if someone is making their way with difficulty down a flight of stairs. When he finally gets there, he's red in the face from the effort he's made, leaning against the doorframe with lines of pain tight around his mouth.

"Sorry I couldn't be faster," he says, gesturing at the knee brace he's wearing over a pair of pajama trousers.

"It doesn't matter at all," I say. "Sorry to drag you downstairs."

"Come in," he says. He gestures me through in front of him, and I climb up wooden stairs into the second-floor flat. He comes up behind me, holding tight on to the banisters. I turn to see him pause, as if it's too much for him, before he grits his teeth and keeps going up. Standing to one side, I let him go first into the front room, a living room that's full of plants and books and light from the two tall windows. It's a room that puts me immediately at ease.

He lowers himself onto a big sofa, and I take a seat on an armchair that sits perpendicular to him, opening my bag to take out his statement.

"Hang on," he says. "We don't have to get straight into it. Let me get you a drink first."

He stands up again, very slowly, and starts to hobble through into the back of the house.

"I'm fine," I say, "honestly. I don't need anything. I think we should get on."

"Well, I need something," he says, "if I'm going to have to think about all of this."

He keeps going, leaving the living room. There's clinking and banging, as if he's trying to find something in a cupboard. I reach instinctively for my phone, only to be reminded that it's flat. I walk to the door.

"Do you have a charger I could borrow?" I say. "My phone's dead."

There's silence for a moment, before Jeremy answers, "There's one plugged into the wall."

I find it but it's the wrong charger. "Mine's an iPhone," I call out. "Do you have an Apple charger?"

Another pause before he replies. "I don't think so."

"Are you sure? My phone's completely dead."

He sighs, the long exhalation audible from the kitchen, and then says, "Try the drawer in the coffee table. Just at the front."

I go back to the coffee table, a large, low wooden number, with a drawer taking up most of its width. I slide it open, but can't see a charger. I rummage through. There's piles of papers and receipts, old tickets to play performances. I try to pull the drawer out as far as it will go, but it's stuck on something and I can only get it out halfway. I stick my hand in and start digging, amazed at the amount of crap in there. At last I feel the end of a charger, a wire. I tug at it to get it out but it's stuck on something. I pull harder, dig deeper. The end of the wire is stuck so I pull at it and the drawer together with such force that the drawer comes out of the table completely, scattering its contents all over the floor, the charger lying on top of the pile.

I pick it up and plug it in at the wall in the corner, connect my phone. Jeremy comes back into the room, a corkscrew in his mouth, a bottle of wine stuck under his arm, and two glasses clutched in one hand. He's supporting himself against the wall with the other hand. I help him, taking the glasses and the bottle of wine and putting them down on the coffee table. He looks askance at the mess all over the floor.

"Sorry," I say. "It was all stuck." I move toward the mess of stuff I've spilled over the floor but he gestures me away.

"Just leave it," he grunts, taking his time to sit down on the sofa. Once he's down he takes the corkscrew out of his mouth and reaches for the bottle to open it.

"I won't, thank you," I say. "It's a bit early in the day for me."

"Call yourself a criminal barrister?" he says, laughing. "Come on, don't be a bore."

He pours wine into both glasses, the red liquid sloshing nearly to the top. They're big glasses, too; over half the bottle has gone into them. He pushes one over to me, spilling a drop over the side onto the table as he does so. Picking up his own, he takes a deep swig, the wine staining his lips.

"Come on," he says. "It's not going to kill you."

His tone is aggressive. He's trying to put on a smile, but it's not reaching his eyes. And looking more closely, I see they're bloodshot and red around the rims. He pushes the glass at me again, with more force, spilling some more. I'm beginning to wonder if this is his first drink of the day. I haven't seen him like this before. I pick up my glass and take a small sip, put it down again.

"Shall we make a start?" I say.

"A start on what?"

"Discussing your evidence," I say. "I have a copy of your

statement here, if you'd like to have a look." I try to pass it to him but he bats it away.

"Not now," he says. "I'm really not in the mood. It's too stressful."

"Nonetheless, we do need to go through it all."

"Nonetheless. *Nonetheless*," he says, even more of a jeer in his voice. "Now you're sounding more like a barrister. Put the work down for once in your fucking life and have a fucking drink."

He's pissing me off now. I gather my papers back together, put them in my bag, and stand up. "I'm going to go," I say. "This doesn't seem to be the best time for you right now."

He subsides back on the sofa, his head slumped between his hands.

"Don't go," he mumbles. "I'm sorry."

Anger is coursing through me. I've given up a weekend away with Robin for this. But his pose is so abject that I feel a twinge of sympathy.

"It's a very difficult time for you," I say, "I do understand that. But you should try and calm down. Getting this stressed isn't going to help. Why don't I make a cup of tea? Or some coffee?"

"Fuck tea," he says. "Fuck coffee." The fight's gone out of his voice, though. It sounds as if he's close to tears. I perch on the coffee table near where he's sitting, put the bag back down. I'm in two minds as to whether I should reach out a hand to pat his arm, perhaps, or rub his shoulder. I'm about to pat him on the knee when he launches forward at me and grabs me tight, the stubble on his chin rough against my neck.

I stiffen immediately, shocked at the suddenness of his

movement. I try to pull away but he doesn't let go, pulling me instead over from the coffee table onto his knee. I'm pushing against his arms, kicking out at his legs, but he's strong, much stronger than he looks. Much stronger than me. My heart's hammering hard against my chest, panic, fury rising fast, and I thrust out against his arms.

"Let go!" I shout. "Let go of me."

I get some purchase on the floor and push up hard, bashing his chin with the top of my skull hard enough to knock his head backward. He lets go of me, very suddenly, and I spring up. Stopping only to grab my bag, I make my way fast to the door.

Jeremy's crying properly now.

"I'm sorry, I'm sorry," he says. "I'm sorry. I didn't mean to scare you." He tries standing up but collapses back down again, his knee clearly paining him.

"You can't behave like this," I say. "I'm not here for any social purposes. It was to go through your statement."

"I just thought..."

"You thought what?"

"I thought you might be interested," Jeremy says. "You went for a drink with me. And you're kind. Everyone keeps shouting at me. Telling me what to do."

"I'm sorry if I've given the wrong impression," I say. "I should never have gone out for that drink with you in the first place. But this really is just work."

He sobs, his shoulders shaking.

"I don't want to be on my own," he says. "I keep having nightmares about going to prison. I'm terrified."

"You're not going to go to prison," I say. "It's more than likely that you're going to be acquitted."

"You can't promise that, though," he says.

"No, I can't. It's up to the jury. But juries don't like convicting people like you."

"What do you mean, people like me?"

I look around the flat, all the signs of affluence. Velvet curtains, solid wood floors. Designer Scandinavian chairs. None of it readily achievable on a teacher's salary. I look over at Jeremy, the way that his shoulders are drooping, the self-pity oozing from him along with the booze.

"Nice, middle-class, white men like you. They'll look at you and decide they don't want to destroy your life. Maybe you did do it, but they won't care about that. We both know that Freya wasn't a great witness, and even if she'd been brilliant, they still don't like convicting when there's no other evidence."

Jeremy leans forward, picks up his glass of wine and drains it. He looks into the empty glass, his expression equally empty. He kicks hard at the pile of stuff from the drawer that's lying at his feet. The stack collapses, and everything scatters across the rug.

"Maybe they should care. I felt really sorry for her up there," he says. "When Barbara was cross-examining."

I blink. This isn't what I was expecting. I look over at him to see that he's staring at the floor, his face tight, the look in his eyes intense, almost fearful. It's as if he's seen a predator, a snake that's about to strike. I follow his gaze.

There's a book on the floor. A hardback. The cover is face-down. Jeremy starts to move toward it, but some instinct in me is strong and I move fast, getting hold of it just before he is within reach. I move to the door before I turn it over to look at it.

Fanny Hill—Memoirs of a Woman of Pleasure. A small red book, the title printed in gold. I open it and look at the inside page. *Can't wait to reenact this again. All my love Fxx*

I look from it to him, back to it again.

He subsides back on the sofa.

"It's not what it looks like," he says.

I'm still. Still as the snake I thought he saw. "What does it look like, Jeremy?" I hiss. He's silent.

Little prickles of shock are sparking on my skin, the hairs on my scalp lifting.

I'm thinking about Freya, about the vilification she's undergone. I'm thinking about the way that the jury looked at her, tight-lipped. I'm thinking of myself as a girl, starved of any attention by my mother, and how easy it might have been for someone like Jeremy to weasel his way in, someone purporting to be kind, understanding, all the qualities so missing from my life. I was lucky. Much luckier than Freya.

Jeremy has moved forward, his elbows on his knees, his hands clenched together. His face is strained.

"She was fifteen when you started grooming her, Jeremy. Fifteen," I say. "Does that not mean anything to you? Are you so devoid of shame that you can sit there and tell me you think this is OK? Does it not keep you awake at night, the thought of what you've done, the lies you told?"

"Don't..." he says.

"Why the fuck not? It's about time someone said it. You've destroyed that girl's life, twice, firstly to entertain yourself, secondly to protect yourself. It's repellent behavior."

He's crying now. It's as if I'm looking at him for the first time, all his charming mannerisms finally seen through the prism of truth.

"You're a stinking coward," I say. "This is appalling."

He puts a hand up as if to stop me, lowers it. "You don't understand," he says.

"I don't want to understand," I say. My phone starts ringing, a shrill insistent sound. It grounds me properly for the first time since I recovered after saying goodbye to Robin this morning. I shake my head and go to my phone, pulling it free from the charger. I turn to face him.

"If you don't tell them, I will. You've put me in an impossible situation."

"Do you think they don't already know?"

I'm transfixed. I look at him, expecting to find a smirk, but his face is a mask of misery.

"Who knows?"

"Who do you think? My father, Barbara. It's stitched up beautifully. Can't have me blackening the family name. At least it isn't my father's name—I gave that up when he walked out on us. I wish I hadn't now—no one can accuse His Honor of having a pedophile son."

"Zora?" I say, almost in a whisper.

"Oh, no," he says. "We kept the solicitor out of it. Need-to-know basis, after all." He laughs, but it turns into a sob.

I'm unmoved by his tears. I want to throw the book at him, smash him in the face with it, but instead I place it in my bag. He lunges to his feet, injury seemingly forgotten, and blocks the door, grabbing my bag from me and pulling out the book. I stand motionless and he collapses back on the sofa, giving a cry of pain as he bends his knee. I turn and look at him. He can do what he likes with it, deny it as much as he likes—I've seen it now. He knows I know. Then I walk out of the room, down the stairs, slamming the door behind me.

45

I turn it over and over in my mind all the way home. It's not a confession, not as such. But this is hard evidence which I shouldn't withhold from the court. I don't know how to approach Zora, though, to tell her she's been so misled by the QC she's instructing. I should speak to the Bar Council, ask their advice as to the appropriate course of action. My heart sinks at the thought. I'm so tired already.

I wait till I'm home and have made myself a coffee before I look at my phone again. There's a number of missed calls. Four from Jeremy—he must have tried to call while I was on the tube—and I block his number immediately. I will not be speaking to him again. And one from a U.S. number, not one I recognize. While I'm looking at it, it rings again, and I answer. It's Andrew.

"Sadie," he says. "There's something I need to say."

Now I'm overwhelmed with exhaustion. "You know what, Andrew? You don't get to do this now. I'm tired. I'm really tired. I've a massive work problem and one of Robin's friends is in a coma. I've enough on my plate."

"OK. OK. I get it. I just wanted to say this." He plows on. "I know there's a lot to explain. I know it's been really difficult. But it's not what it seems. I want you to believe in me, whatever is said. And I will explain. But I can't yet."

"No," I say. "No. Not now. I'm too tired." I end the call.

I look again at my phone, remembering Zora's text for the first time since I went to Jeremy's flat. The question about Andrew's work makes no sense on its own so I open up the link that Zora has sent. It takes me to the Reuters website.

DOJ charges property firm founder, former executives in Ponzi scheme

(Reuters)—U.S. federal prosecutors charged the owner and other executives of Seacliff Securities on Thursday with orchestrating a $250-million Ponzi scheme involving 2,000 victims.

Seacliff Securities. Andrew's firm. I skim through the rest of the article, but they don't name the executives. I try to call him back, anxious for an explanation, but the number rings out, and when I try his mobile, it's dead.

I call his number again, but as I do so, there's a loud knocking at the front door. Putting the phone down, I go to the door and open it. I'm on autopilot, my thoughts miles away.

Julia enters the house, shaking and weeping. Under any other circumstances I'd feel self-conscious about the state of the house in comparison to her mansion, but she isn't noticing anything, she's so upset.

"I didn't know where else to come," she says. "They've kicked me out so Daisy's dad can visit. I couldn't bear to be on my own."

I bring her through to the kitchen. I'm trying to think of

what to say to get rid of her, though I know I should be more compassionate.

"Can't you visit together?"

"Not possible," Julia says. "We can't be in the same space. Not since the divorce. You know it went to court."

I nod. Looking at Julia under the light, it's clear she's in a very bad way, and I feel more compassion, thoughts of Andrew disappearing in the face of her misery. Her hair is greasy and unbrushed, her face sallow under the harsh overhead light. All her normal poise has gone out of the window. She's lost weight, her face haggard now. Her rings hang loose, and as she twists her hands together, over and over, a ring falls off, rolling onto the floor. She's oblivious, but I pick it up. It's heavy, a shiny gold ring, plain, with two sideways Ts in the middle, facing each other. I roll it around in my hand.

"I can't explain what's happening," Julia says, "but they're trying to set me up. I know it." She speaks with urgency, leaning across the table toward me. Her breath is sour, fetid with nights unslept, anxiety.

"Set you up?" I say. "Who is trying to set you up? For what?"

"They're going to say it was all my fault," Julia says. "But I didn't do anything wrong. I swear it. I've been doing my best."

I move around the table and put my arm around her. She's stiff at first, but then leans into me, before tensing up again, jerking so hard that she dislodges my arm.

"You've got to believe me, Sadie. I haven't done anything to hurt Daisy. Honestly."

I try to make eye contact with her, fail. I want to try and engage with Julia properly, get her attention, give her reassurance, but she's too much on edge.

"I know you haven't," I say. "Of course you haven't done anything to harm her."

"I know they're going to blame me for everything. That's why they won't let me see her," Julia continues, as if I haven't spoken.

"I thought that was because your ex is there?"

Now she looks at me, eyes blazing.

"That's what they *say* the reason is. But they'd say anything, wouldn't they?"

"I think you're completely overdone. You're exhausted. You need some food, a bath and a proper night's sleep."

Julia keeps staring at me, holding my gaze for so long that my eyes start to water. I blink and look away. Julia laughs, a harsh sound that holds no amusement in it.

"Any minute now you'll make me a cup of tea," she says.

I open my mouth, shut it. Open it again. "I'm sorry. There's nothing I can say that'll be of any help. But if you can't be at the hospital, wouldn't it make sense to get some rest? You must be exhausted."

"I am exhausted," Julia says. "Completely exhausted."

"You could stay here if you want. Robin is away tonight. It wouldn't be any trouble."

Julia leans back, her expression softer.

"That's very kind," she says with a smile. "I wouldn't want to impose, though. I'll go home—it's for the best. Where's she gone?"

"With Nicole and Pippa. They've gone to the seaside for the weekend."

Something shifts in Julia's face, the warmth gone, as if a light has been flicked off behind her eyes. But it's only for a second, for such a short time that I wonder if I've imagined it, as Julia turns to me, smiling once more.

"You've been very kind to me," Julia says. "I'm sorry we didn't get off to the best start. Once Daisy is out of hospital, I hope that we'll become much closer."

"So do I. And I really hope that's soon. How is she doing now? Has there been any improvement?"

Darkness reappears in Julia's eyes, a distance reopening between us. For a moment she looks entirely bereft.

"I don't know," she says. "I just don't know. They say they're doing everything they can, but..."

It's the end of the conversation. Julia's shut down, as if she came here under some kind of spell, which has now broken.

"I'm sorry, I shouldn't have come," she says. "I don't quite know what I was thinking. I'm going to go home. You're right, I should get some rest. And have a bath."

She gets up and gives me a quick hug, walks out of the kitchen before I even have a chance to stand up.

"Your ring?" I call out. She comes back. I put it in her hand, and she looks at it.

"I bought this to cheer myself up," she says. "Tiffany. My favorite. Funny how little it means now." She pushes it into her pocket and strides out. I call goodbye, but I hear the front door shut behind her.

After sitting for a moment, trying to work out what the purpose of the visit has been, what's actually going on, I give up and return to my phone. It's Andrew I want to find out about. I flick quickly through the messages from Jeremy, deleting them before reading after a quick glance ascertains that they're all variants on *sorry, got carried away.* He certainly did.

At that moment a text comes through from Nicole.

Robin has left her phone behind, in case you were trying to text her. She noticed earlier but I forgot to tell you—sorry if you've been trying to get hold of her Nxx.

A jolt goes through me. Despite missing Robin so much, it hadn't even occurred to me to text. I'm just not used to her having a phone. I run upstairs to look and sure enough, it's sitting on the corner of a shelf, battery long drained. A bittersweet feeling runs through me. It won't be long before Robin has to be surgically removed from her phone, like other teenagers I see on the bus, engrossed in their little screens. At least Robin's still a child at heart, no matter how grown up she sometimes seems.

I go back downstairs and pick up my phone to text Nicole, but instead I'm overwhelmed by an urge for human connection, a word with Robin. I ring Nicole. She replies after a couple of rings but sounds distracted, her answers to my questions short, although she's friendly. The conversation doesn't last long.

"I'd better go," Nicole says. "I need to sort out some food for the girls."

"How are they doing? Can I have a word with Robin?"

"They're out playing on the beach at the moment," Nicole says, "but I'll send some photos later. They've had a great afternoon. I think they're really happy."

"That's brilliant," I say. "You know, my meeting has actually finished. I could always come up too?"

"That would be great," Nicole says. "It's quite fiddly to get to without a car, though. There isn't a station in the town."

"Oh, right. I guess I could hire a car, but..."

"Why don't you have a relaxing evening and then you'll see Robin tomorrow. We can arrange a trip another time."

"OK." I'm about to tell her about Julia's visit, how stressed she was, but Nicole has finished the call and I don't have the energy to call her back and recount it all. I want to look online for information about Seacliff Securities, find out what the hell is going on.

Much later that evening, when I'm sitting on the sofa, still fighting my way without success through numerous internet searches, my phone beeps. It's a message from Nicole, *All tired out!* it says. The words are attached to a photograph of Robin and Pippa asleep together on a gray sofa. They're lying feet to each end, their heads meeting in the middle as they share a big cushion as a pillow, blonde hair and brown entwined, cheeks flushed as if from running around outside. I zoom in on Robin's face—it's relaxed in sleep, corners of her mouth lifted as if in a smile. A tension eases in my chest. At least she's OK. That's one less problem to worry about.

I make more efforts to find out what the hell is going on with Andrew, but the Reuters report is the only one I can find. It's not being reported by any other news agency. I try the Seacliff Securities website, but it looks just like normal. The office number clicks through to an office-closed message, but given it's a Saturday afternoon in New York, that's not so unusual. I think about calling round some of Andrew's colleagues, but I can't bring myself to do it, break the silence of months to ask…to ask what, exactly? Who has been arrested? Is it a fraudulent organization? It's too much to comprehend.

I decide to go upstairs, hoping there might be more information available in the morning. I close up the house, check the front door is double locked before I finally get into bed. I look at the photo of Robin for a long time before falling into a fitful sleep, filled with fleeting visions of her running away from me along a rocky shore, long brown hair blown out behind her in the wind.

46

I jerk awake from a nightmare in the early morning, rushing through to Robin's room to check on her before remembering that she's not here. I return to bed, problems pushing into my mind, jostling out any benefit from my brief sleep.

Andrew. Has he been arrested? If not, where is he? And what the hell is the story with Seacliff and the Ponzi scheme? If he has been involved in something like this, it makes perfect sense, providing an explanation for his behavior over the last while. But I don't know how to deal with the idea that he might have committed a criminal offense. I might be separated from him, but he's still Robin's dad. It's unthinkable.

Then Jeremy. The book. I'm going to have to do something about it, though I don't know what. Again, I remind myself that I need to speak to the Bar Council advice line and ask for their opinion on it. Also think about reporting Barbara for her unethical conduct. I should never have gone to his flat in the first place.

I roll over, ready to get up. Time to face it all. But before I do, I look at my phone. There's a message from Nicole, sent around 6 a.m.

Robin's got homesick. Julia came up for the evening, but

she's driving back with Robin first thing this morning. She'll drop her with you. Hope that's ok Nxx

I call Nicole immediately, who picks up almost as quickly.

"What happened?" I say. I'm alert. Not anxious, but alert.

"Oh, poor Robin. She had a terrible nightmare, woke up screaming and crying. Inconsolable. She just wanted you. We calmed her down, gave her a drink. Julia said she'd bring her back this morning, and then we let her get back to sleep."

"What time did they leave?" I'm trying to stay calm but I can feel my heart rate rising, memories still haunting me of the last time I didn't know where Robin was, those awful hours.

"About seven," Nicole says. "So they should be with you pretty soon."

"I didn't realize Julia was going to visit. She didn't mention it yesterday."

"Oh yes, she mentioned she'd seen you. Well, you know how upset she was. She got back to her house and she just couldn't cope with being there on her own, without Daisy, not being able to go into hospital and see her, even. So she thought it would help to come up to us, see the sea. I really wanted to say no, but she insisted."

"I wish you'd asked me before sending Robin off with her," I say.

"I did message. But Robin was so excited about coming home..."

I feel the reproach in Nicole's words. Robin can't even cope with one night away. She's disturbed everyone. "I'm sorry," I say. "I thought she'd like it. I suppose it all got too much for her."

"Well, it's as well that Julia was here."

"Thank you for having her," I say, and the conversation ends. As soon as I've cut the call to Nicole, I phone Julia's mobile. There's no reply. I try again, and still it rings out. Nothing to worry about, though, I reason. Julia's driving. Maybe it's not hooked up to hands-free. She's got someone else's child in the car with her—she's bound to be driving carefully, more carefully than usual. She won't want the distraction of the call.

It's not even eight yet. I lie back down in bed and my eyes grow heavy again. I fall asleep, my phone still in my hand until another nightmare pulls me from sleep just after half past nine, dread looming over me, horror close.

No call from Julia. No sign of them. Where the fuck are they?

I put the phone down, make coffee, go through to the bathroom and shower. When I flush the loo, the handle comes off in my hand, the decrepit plumbing giving up the ghost at last, and in frustration I throw it at the wall, in the direction of the bathroom sink. It clips the mirror over the sink with enough force that it breaks it, the crack spreading.

I'm not superstitious, but I look at the damage with dread, tentacles of it uncoiling through my gut. I know I'm being stupid. There's nothing to worry about. There's bound to be a good explanation for everything. I need to distract myself, stop being hysterical. Too much pressure. I'm under too much pressure.

Moving with sudden decision, I go downstairs and find a roll of bin bags. I'm going to clear up my old bedroom, put all the debris into the rubbish and start again, rip out all of the traces of Lydia's spite and fury. This is Robin's home now, and I'm going to make it perfect. It's time to stop putting it off.

Taking a deep breath, I head upstairs again and into the room, facing the chaos head on. I open up the first bin bag, shovel in scraps of paper and shreds of fabric, the ruins of all my childhood. Every now and again I find a page that's escaped destruction, a paragraph from a much-loved book. I'm not lingering over it, though, filling one bag, then the next. I'm in a frenzy, anger at Jeremy, at Andrew, worry about Robin, and underneath it all, a drumbeat of defiance against my mother. *Fuck you fuck you fuck you* as I scoop and bag, scoop and bag. *I'm not like you; I love my daughter. I take your hatred of me and I spit on it. Fuck you.*

This frenzy soon fades. I might have started off immune to the hostility that pulses in the room, but soon enough it beats me down.

It's nearly ten. Julia hasn't called back. I still don't know where Robin is. I go back downstairs and pace from room to room. Waiting. And as I wait, the word *Tiffany* comes into my head, a pale blue box, a bird crawling with maggots. A cold hand grips my guts.

Part 2

SUNDAY, 1:00 P.M.

I stumble back to the bus stop from Julia's house, knees and head sore from where I fell over. I know my head is still bleeding but I don't care. Adrenaline has numbed me. The shock will hit at some point, but now I welcome the pain, the sting of grazes, distracting me from the darkness in my head. My imagination is going deeper into places I've never wanted to visit, my fears spiraling out of control.

I should be at home, in case Robin has somehow made it there. There's no point pacing the streets when I don't have the first idea where my daughter might be. I need to sit down, take stock, speak properly to the police.

At the thought of the police, the memory of my earlier phone call crashes into me, my hysteria. They'll have me marked down as a troublemaker, a time waster. It'll be hard to get them to take anything I say seriously.

Do I even know what Robin was wearing yesterday? I need to put a description together for the police, that's for certain. I can see it now.

MISSING: Ten-year-old girl, 4 ft 9 inches tall with shoulder-length brown hair, blue eyes. Robin was last seen wearing...

What? What was she wearing? I wasn't with her—how can I know? It's not Robin anyway, the description so cold and two-dimensional. It says nothing of the child she really is, warm, loving. And brave. So brave. She's dealt with this move across the Atlantic, from everything that was known, familiar, all her friends at the school where she was so at home. She's negotiated our separation, all the weeks of not seeing her dad, the move to London, the new school, trying to make new friends, the state of the old house…I've put Robin through so much. I don't even want to think about what's blowing up with Andrew.

It's going to be different now. As soon as Robin is home again, back with me, it's going to change. I'm getting my house in order.

Determination replaces my despair. Enough wallowing now. Time to go home and sort this shit out.

I'm nearly at the bus stop when I hear a woman calling.

"Sadie, Sadie!"

It's Jessica. She's dressed in running kit, her cheeks flushed. I want to ignore her, but she's coming closer, hand outstretched.

"I thought it was you," she says, taking hold of me by the shoulder. I stiffen, her touch unwelcome.

"I was on my way home."

"Over this way for coffee with someone?" Jessica says, her eyes beady with curiosity.

"Something like that," I say. "Anyway, I'd best be off." I try shaking Jessica's hand off but she takes a closer hold of my shoulder.

"Is everything all right? You don't look very well."

I take a moment to reply, unwilling to show her any weakness, putting my chin up against her beady gaze. "I had a fall," I say, gesturing at the mud on the knees of my jeans. "Tripped over a paving stone."

"Ah, OK. Popping in to see Julia for coffee, maybe? Or Nicole?"

Her face is hungry. I didn't think about the effect my newfound friendship with the women would have. Jessica's jealous. I can't even begin to deal with that right now.

"I popped over to see Julia, but she wasn't there."

"Well, she's got quite a lot on her plate at the moment," Jessica says, the tip of her tongue darting out, moistening the corners of her mouth. She leans forward toward me. "I know she's terribly popular, but she does seem to attract a lot of bad luck. That poor daughter of hers..."

I don't want to engage at all. I want to walk away as fast as I can from this woman, her face more and more predatory. But I can't help myself. I want to know what she means.

"Bad luck?" I say, my voice quiet. So quiet I'm not even sure Jessica will hear me. But she's focused so avidly on me, she doesn't miss a word.

"Bad luck. At least, that's what some people might call it. That little girl on the edge of death in hospital. They're saying she might have been drugging her?" Jessica hisses. I feel the woman's breath on my cheek, warm and stale, unclean. I try to move backward but the claw tightens. "And of course, there was that other little girl, Zoe. You must have heard about that?"

"I know there was an accident," I say. "What does that have to do with Julia?"

"Well, she was there, of course. Didn't you know?"

"Where?"

"On holiday with Zoe's family. When it happened. When Zoe drowned."

A jolt of shock passes straight through me. My face twitches.

"Oh dear," Jessica says, "you really do look pale, Sadie. I don't see why it should come as a shock, though. Where Julia is, bad things happen. You must have heard the stories at school."

I look at her in complete surprise, not even trying to hide it. "School? No, nothing. I don't remember a thing."

"About how much of a bully she was? It was legendary."

"I never heard a word. Bear in mind she was a couple of years below me, though—I wouldn't know. My friend says that she heard Julia was bullied a lot."

Jessica starts laughing, a sound of genuine mirth. She has to take her hand off my shoulder to wipe her eyes, and I step back. I want to get away from her.

"Your friend is wrong," she says. "Your friend is very wrong indeed. She was a complete bitch. She and her cronies bullied one girl so badly she left—I was friends with her little sister."

"How come you keep sucking up to her now, then? If she's so awful?" I say.

The predatory expression fades from Jessica's face, her lips tightening. She wraps her arms around herself, warming herself against the memories.

"I'd never want to piss her off," she says. "She scares me. I'm nearly forty years old, and Julia Brumfitt still scares the shit out of me."

I'm chilled to my bones. I start to back away, desperate to escape.

"Isn't Robin with you?" Jessica calls.

I don't reply. I turn and keep walking, icy with terror.

47

I will the bus to speed up as it trundles home. But when I climb off, my steps are suddenly reluctant.

I'm torn.

I'm almost scared to rush to see if Robin has arrived. My fear is that the house will be closed and empty as I left it, the lights off, no life there to be found.

But right now, Robin might be standing on the doorstep, knocking at the door. She might be shifting from foot to foot, upset that I'm not in. I speed up. I'm not even sure that Robin took a coat with her, I wasn't paying enough attention to what she packed. She'll be cold and tired and upset. I'm nearly running now.

Another thought intrudes. What if she's not there... What if there's no one waiting, no little figure eager for my return. My steps slow, speed up, slow, until I'm around the corner at last, nearly at the house, and there's someone at the door, a figure moving around, a figure that I know really is too tall to be Robin, but still it could be her, it could be her... I break into a full run.

I burst through the front gate, calling out Robin's name at the top of my voice. And a voice replies. But it's not Robin.

"Sadie," Zora says.

At the sight of her, I burst into tears.

"I don't know where she is," I say. "I don't know where she is."

Zora stays quiet, waiting for me to continue, and with the worst said, the rest of the words come out.

Once I've filled Zora in on it all, I spring into action. I call Nicole and ask her again to repeat the sequence of events earlier in the day. I also take a note of the address in Aldeburgh and get her to tell me exactly what Robin was wearing when she left. Nicole seems surprised by how angry I am but answers my questions without demur. I call Julia again, too. *Where the fuck are you? Where the fuck is my daughter? Call me now.* After that, we sit at the kitchen table, tense with concentration.

"Is there anyone else you can call?" she says.

"No. Robin left her phone here. There's no way of getting hold of her."

"Right," Zora says. "It's time to involve the police. I don't care what that woman says about waiting, about it all sorting itself out. Julia should have brought Robin back here hours ago. We can't wait any longer."

I'm paralyzed for a moment. It's all too real. Then I overcome it. I nod, once, and I call 999, dealing with the operator with force and efficiency, far more effectively than earlier. She says that officers will come to the house shortly, to interview me, and the call ends.

That job done, the fear comes back. It's too much for me, all too much. I go upstairs to Robin's room, lie down on her bed, close to her pillow, the teddy bear she left behind. The smell is a comfort, at least for a moment, and I wrap the duvet close around me, enveloping myself in the traces that Robin has left behind. Zora is clattering crockery downstairs, clearing up, and I put my head under the duvet, wrapping it close around my head. I shut my eyes, willing it all away, and Robin back by my side.

I wake with Zora's hand on my shoulder, a gentle shake. The room's dark. I sit up with a start.

"I thought I'd better wake you," she says. "Though I really wanted to let you sleep."

"I should never have gone to sleep in the first place," I say. "I can't believe I did that."

"It's the shock, I expect," she says. "You were curled up in here like you were hiding."

I push her words away, and the duvet, getting to my feet. I've regained strength from this moment of retreat.

"What news?" I say. "Is there any news?"

"Nothing," she says.

"The police?"

"Not here yet. I suppose they're not sure that she's missing yet."

"Or that she's been taken," I say.

"Or that she's been taken." Zora sounds heavy, her voice flat. As exhausted as I was an hour ago.

I look at her.

"We mustn't assume the worst," she says, though her expression belies her words.

"Thank you," I say.

"For what?"

"For coming and helping. Staying with me. I couldn't do this on my own."

"You shouldn't be on your own," Zora says. "Andrew should be here."

"Andrew," I say. I haven't even thought about him. "I can't get hold of him. I read that story you sent me, but I've no idea what's going on."

"Jesus. As if there isn't enough...I guess it might explain his behavior, if he was involved in a fraud..."

We're both silent for a moment. I know it's a dark cloud looming huge on the horizon, but right now I'm turning away from it. Andrew cut himself off months ago—I'm all cried out on him, all thought out, too. Robin's the only person on my mind.

We sit together in Robin's room, and we wait while evening falls and night grows dark.

48

I wake up with a start. I'm confused, fear grabbing at me. I've been dreaming that I've lost something very important, and I jerk up with a jag of panic. It takes me a moment to orient myself—still in Robin's room, the streetlamp outside the window glowing orange. There are glow-in-the-dark stars on the ceiling and I can see one in the corner, its pale green phosphorescence glimmering quiet against the light from the street.

My neck hurts from the angle at which I've fallen asleep. I stretch it one way, then the other, before full consciousness hits and I jump up, looking for my phone. I was holding it when I fell asleep at 2 a.m., exhaustion and stress too much for me. Even though four hours have passed since I last checked, there's nothing.

No sign of Robin, either.

Zora is asleep too, lying across the bottom of Robin's bed, her feet still on the floor.

A motorbike revs loudly as it drives past the street and she wakes up, jolting upright in the same way that I did. She looks around, her face slack with sleep and shock.

We gaze at each other through the orange glow.

"Anything?" Zora says, and I shake my head.

"Nothing. It's nearly six. We need to call the police again."

"Yes," Zora says. "They have to take this seriously now. Robin's been gone for nearly twenty-four hours."

We're both silent then, trying not to consider that the first twenty-four hours when a child goes missing are the most important.

Zora sits next to me while I call the police again, very insistent that Robin's disappearance now has to be treated as a matter of urgency. I hang up, turn to Zora.

"I think they've got the point," I say. "They promise they're going to send someone out very soon to take descriptions from me, get the story. They're getting on to it."

"Good," Zora says. "That's good." She pauses for a moment. "Any word from Andrew?"

"Nothing." I'm silent for a while, running through the other issues I've ignored, problems too big to put off any more. "We're due in court this morning at ten, Zora. Or at least..." my voice trails off. "I'll try Andrew again. But his phone has been dead since Saturday."

I move back into my own room to call him, unable to cope with an audience, even Zora. I stand just inside the door, hesitating for a moment before making the call. This time it rings, though there's no reply. I think for a split second, leave a message.

"I don't know what the fuck is going on. And I don't care. Robin is missing. You need to come here now, wherever you are. Your little girl is missing and I don't know what to do."

I lower the phone and stand looking into the room for a moment. My mother's old room. Full of my mother's possessions, the kitsch of years, which I've tuned out for all the time we've been there, focused only on making the rest of the house a home for Robin. Returning to my childhood home should have been to a refuge, a place of safety, but it's proved anything but. Every day has been a struggle against Lydia's rejection, the rejection of me by the mothers at the school gates. And now the only person who matters to me is gone.

If I get Robin back—no, *when* I get Robin back—I'm starting again. I'm going to break the trust, take possession of what's mine, what's Robin's. Ripping it all out, slashing it all down. Robin and I, we'll sit down, work it out, where we want to be, what we want to do. And nothing will stop us.

"There's no way I can go to court," I say to Zora. We're downstairs in the kitchen, drinking coffee. Jeremy's confession is ringing loud in my ears and I can't tune it out any more. I've put Zora's role as my instructing solicitor out of my mind all weekend, so desperate have I been for her support, but I can't ignore it now.

"Might it help to do something else?"

I look at her scathingly. "Are you being serious? I can't possibly. I have to talk to the police. What if she comes back? She'll need me."

"The police are going to be here really soon," Zora says. "You'll have more than enough time to talk to them before you need to leave."

"I'm not sure..."

"I think that being normal, sticking to a bit of a routine, might not be such a bad idea. We can both go down. It won't take you long to come back up if anything happens. You'll have your phone—they will be in touch immediately if there's any news. I'm worried about you. The stress of this. It might be good to take your mind off it for a little bit."

I'm falling off the side of a cliff, straight down into a dark hole. There's a rushing in my ears, my heart beats a rapid syncopation, each beat a syllable of Robin's name, *RO-BIN, RO-BIN*. Then I catch myself. Getting into a state isn't going to help the situation at all.

"Maybe I should," I say.

"I'll be there if it gets too much. And you can always turn round and come home."

For the first time since I realized Robin was missing, I feel something other than terror for her whereabouts. I feel guilt. Shame that I haven't been open with Zora about finding the book. I didn't say anything to begin with because I wasn't sure how to handle it, and then it got swept away by everything else until it was too late. I'm worried about what to do, how best to handle the situation. It's been pushed out of my mind by Robin, and now it's too late. I should have told her immediately. But if I'm honest, I was scared to. Scared that she might also be involved. That she might have been lying to me too. I should have trusted her, though, told her immediately.

Now I don't know how to tell her at all.

I shower, dress in a suit. While I'm getting ready I make a decision. I'm going to tell Zora, regardless of the complications it causes to the situation. As soon as I'm ready I go downstairs.

"Zora, there's something I need to tell you," I say as I walk into the kitchen. She looks up at me.

"What?"

"I'm sorry, it's something I should have told you before. It's about Jeremy."

"I'm not sure I..." she starts to say, when there's a knock at the door. Despite knowing the police are due, I can't help but feel a leap of hope, dashed as soon as Zora opens the door and I hear the sound of adult voices.

The two women take their seats at the kitchen table, introducing themselves. Both detective sergeants, one called Hughes, one Labinjoh. They're sympathetic, gentle, but there's steel in their eyes, and they take down notes with an air of purpose that I find reassuring. There couldn't be a greater contrast with the way that my call was received the day before.

I explain what I know, that Nicole told me Julia was driving Robin home, that they left the previous morning, and that I've been unable to make contact with Julia ever since. They nod, write down some more.

"One of our Suffolk colleagues has been to speak to Nicole, in Aldeburgh, so we have a good sense of the timeline. We've an alert out on the car in question—we're doing everything we can to locate your daughter."

"It's a shame you didn't take it more seriously yesterday," I say, the words blurting out before I can stop them. I don't want to antagonize them, angry as I feel.

"We have a transcript of your call to the emergency services yesterday morning," Hughes says, looking at me. "I take your point, but there was insufficient to go on at that stage."

I remember about my incoherence as I spoke to the operator. The detective isn't wrong. "There was my second call, though. You should have paid attention then."

The detectives glance at each other. Labinjoh clears her throat. "There was an incident in Wood Green. A double stabbing."

She doesn't explain further. She doesn't have to. I'm well aware of the budget pressures on the Metropolitan Police, the stress the force is under, the cuts to numbers of officers.

I nod. "You can appreciate that I'm under a great deal of strain."

"Of course. I'm sure we'll have more news very shortly."

They leave. It's nearly nine o'clock. If I'm going to go to court, I have to leave now. Zora can sense my hesitation.

"Come on," she says. "Let's go."

I stand at the door for a moment more, undecided, before taking a deep breath. We set off down the road toward the tube, scanning each car in turn as it passes in the vain hope that I'll see Robin safely on her way home.

49

As we travel down to Elephant and Castle, worry about Robin roils in my mind. Zora looks troubled too, her face drawn. She doesn't refer to my earlier comment about Jeremy, and it doesn't come back to the front of my mind until we're nearly at court.

Now it's roaring up. I don't care about Jeremy at all now, regardless of my role on his defense team. I do care about Freya, though. It could so easily have been me. And I care about Zora. I don't want her career to be affected by this, either.

The more I think about it, the more my rage mounts, all the pent-up stress from Robin's disappearance feeding into it. Forget talking to Zora—it's Barbara I want to see. Leaving Zora in my wake, I stride into the court building, through to the empty robing room. I pull my wig and gown out of the bag before stuffing them back in and pacing round until Barbara arrives a few minutes later. She nods good morning.

"We need to talk about the meeting on Saturday," she says. "I've just been told."

I look at Barbara in a way I've never done before, scorn writ large across my features.

"What about it?" I say.

"His father has had to spend the whole weekend persuading him that he shouldn't plead guilty. I can't believe what a mess you made of it."

"What a mess *I've* made of it? Surely you must see how wrong this is? He should be pleading guilty. We certainly can't represent him."

Barbara shrugs, no trace of apology in her face. "Do grow up," she says. "You know that's not how it works. The prosecution needs to prove the case against him, remember? I know you're being all dewy-eyed and idealistic, but seriously, think about it. He's got his whole future ahead of him. Not to mention his father's own reputation as a judge. Pretty poor show to have a son done for a sex crime. It's up to the prosecution and so far they've done a dismal job, wouldn't you agree?"

"Because you're misleading the court," I say. My voice is loud enough that a couple of barristers who have just opened the door into the robing room take one look at the situation and retreat, shutting the door fast behind them. "I can't believe you'd be so blatant about such a huge ethical breach."

"Get a grip," Barbara says. "You have to look at it as a whole. Freya is as much to blame as he. She made the first pass."

"She's a child, Barbara."

"Are you telling me you weren't sexually active as a teenager? I'm over twenty years older than you and I most certainly was. I'd have been grateful to have someone mature like him around, rather than those horrific fumbles from boys my own age. Don't be so wet about it."

"This is unbelievable," I say, hissing the words at Barbara in fury. "I'm off the case."

Barbara laughs. "It's not like you've had to do much, let's face it. You spent a bit of time going through the evidence, but that's it. Your job is done."

"Go ahead and defend him—you're doing it without me. Let's see what the Bar Council has to say about it. I'm going to make sure that Zora knows all about it, too."

Barbara's eyes narrow. She glares at me, an expression on her face that has probably never failed before in its exertion of power. I stand for a moment, brain pulsing with rage, before I pick up my bag and storm out of the room.

It's only when the door has slammed shut behind me that I realize I haven't thought about Robin for the last few minutes. And with that, my rage disappears, pushed out by cold fear again. I shouldn't be here, propping up a rotten defense for a toxic defendant. I should be looking for my daughter.

I put my head down and walk straight back out of the court building. I see Zora and Jeremy, an older man beside them, but I keep on walking, even when Zora calls my name. I'm at the end of the car park when I feel someone pull at my shoulder, hard enough to shake my stride. It's Zora, with Jeremy and the other man behind her. I glance at the older man, look a little closer. It's a face I haven't seen in years, the family resemblance clear between father and son. Men who would be good-looking if their eyes weren't so close together. Suddenly I'm back in the alleyway twenty years ago, his hands hard on my breasts, his breath sour in my face. My kick hard to his groin. I look at them both with horror.

"Where are you going?" Jeremy says.

"I'm off the case. I can't continue to defend you."

"But..."

"You shouldn't continue to defend yourself," I say to Jeremy.

"But it's up to you. I'm sure you'll do exactly what *he* tells you to do."

"Hang on a minute," Jeremy's father splutters.

"Hang on a minute nothing," I say, spitting out my words. "It all makes sense, him using his mother's surname, not yours. But like father, like son. You never took responsibility for any of your shitty behavior. Why would he?"

"I'm nothing like him," Jeremy says, full of outrage.

"Ask him about how he behaved toward pupils. Ask him how many he felt up in the pub. Ask him about the official complaints," I say. "Go on, ask him. He'll say he doesn't have the first idea what I'm talking about, but give it a go. Ask him how he used to behave in the nineties. How he behaves still, most likely." My anger has given me wings. I'm soaring above them, rage coursing through me pure and cold.

"How dare you make such allegations?" His Honor Judge Michael Forest says.

"I was the same age as he is now when you groped me up in that alleyway and I had to boot you in the balls to get you off me," I say, pointing at Jeremy. "You treat him like a child but you were quite happy to try it on with me, weren't you? Lording your seniority over me and the other pupils, all those nights round Temple. I know you don't remember me, but I told you to fuck off. I had to kick you hard to get rid of you. And I was terrified for months that you were going to tell my pupil-master. No fucking wonder your son is such a disgrace."

"How dare you?" Forest says.

I turn around and give him the finger. "Fuck off, you lecherous shit. I'm out of here."

I walk off. Zora runs after me.

"What the fuck is going on?" she says. "What's happened to the case?"

"I'm sorry, Zora." Then I pause. "Had you forgotten about that shit? What he did to me?"

She looks away.

"Seriously? You'd get me to represent his son? I can't believe this."

"I knew you needed the case," Zora says. "I thought it was more important to get you back to work."

"I told you I didn't need your charity," I say. "Especially not for a case like this. Not when they knew he was guilty as sin from the start. I bet you knew too."

"What are you talking about?" Zora says.

"I found the copy of *Fanny Hill* that Freya gave him in his house," I say. "It's so obvious."

"Why the hell didn't you tell me sooner? You've had the whole weekend," she says. My rage fades. She's right.

"I'm sorry. It all felt so complicated. And then Robin..."

"We'll talk about this later," Zora says. "You get home. I'll sort it out."

50

Before I get much further, my phone beeps. I come to an immediate halt to look at it, oblivious to the woman walking behind me who is forced to dodge around me at the last second, hissing at me to watch out for other people.

I've got like fifty missed calls from you. Is everything OK? Went off-radar for a bit but back now—come round for a coffee if you like. Julia xx

I have to read the message through three times before I can take in what it's saying. But even when I've absorbed the words, I can't begin to comprehend it. The insouciance of it, the casual way Julia says she's been *off-radar*, as if I haven't been desperately trying to reach her for the last thirty-six hours, as if the police aren't trying to find her. I don't understand. All hostilities forgotten, I turn back to catch up with Zora and show her my phone. She comes with me immediately, leaving Jeremy and his father quarreling in the middle of the car park.

"You need to tell the police," Zora says, but I'm already doing just that. As soon as I'm off the phone I book an Uber, type in Julia's address. We wait for it to arrive.

"Did the police say it was OK for us to go there?" Zora says as we climb in.

"Fuck the police," I say. "I want my daughter."

The cab moves slowly through the morning traffic. I dig my nails into my hand so hard they pierce the skin, but the pain brings a strange comfort, stigmata of my desperation.

As soon as we arrive, I fling open the door of the car and jump out, running straight to the entrance. Zora is close behind. I bash on the front door and after a moment it opens. Julia is standing in the hallway, a confused expression on her face.

"Where's my daughter?" I say. "What have you done with my daughter?"

"I don't know what you're talking about," Julia says. "What's happened to Robin?"

I lunge toward her and Zora steps in fast to pull me back. I struggle hard for a moment, bringing myself back under control.

"Please, Julia," I say, lowering my voice with an effort. "Please tell us what you've done with Robin."

"I haven't done anything with her," she says. "I haven't seen her for days."

"But..."

"Look, you'd better come in. I have a lot of very nosy neighbors," Julia says, drawing us inside. We stand in the hall. "What's going on?"

"We were told that you were bringing Robin back from Aldeburgh yesterday," I say. "Nicole says you were driving her home. And we've been waiting and waiting but nothing. No Robin. And now you're saying..."

"I'm saying I have literally no idea what you're talking about," Julia says. "I'm sorry."

I look at her closely. She appears to be genuinely confused, but that doesn't mean anything. Her clothes are creased, her hair not as sleek as usual, but she looks pretty much as normal. It's unreal, as if I've dreamt the last days, the darkness into which I've been sucked since Nicole told me that Robin had gone. Any minute now Robin might run up the steps and over to me, grabbing me in a big hug.

"That's not what I've been told," I say. "I want Robin."

Julia starts to speak again, her face earnest, but I can't hear what she's saying. There's a buzzing noise in my ears, a heavy rushing, and stars dancing in front of my eyes. I've felt like this before, and I know what it means. I'm about to pass out. Staggering over to the stairs, I sit down heavily and put my head in my hands.

Zora is shouting now, and Julia crying, and the noise is making my head spin worse and worse. I start shouting too, but I'm so dizzy that I can't keep upright, slumping instead against the wall. The air is fraught with anguish, the absence of Robin a shard of pain stabbed deep into me.

At that moment, at the point when everything might explode, there are knocks at the door. Loud, assertive, followed immediately by the voices of the police officers that had attended my house that morning. I open my eyes and see there are three uniforms behind them. I sit up cautiously. "Julia Burnet, I am arresting you on suspicion of the attempted murder of Daisy Burnet. You do not have to say anything, but it may harm your defense if you do not mention when questioned something which you later rely on in court. Anything you do say may be given as evidence. Do you understand?"

Zora has backed off, standing next to me by the stairs, and Julia's face is shocked and pale, mouth open as if to speak, no sound coming out.

Another man and woman come through the door. They're wearing white forensic suits. DS Labinjoh addresses Julia again.

"We have obtained a warrant for the search of your property, which is going to take place now."

They lead Julia out. Zora and I follow, my feeling of faintness overridden by shock. As the police are putting Julia into the car, I gather my strength and run over to them.

"What about Robin? She denies knowing anything about her. Where's my daughter?"

"Our inquiries are well in hand. We will contact you the moment that we have information. In the meantime, I'd ask you to be patient. I can assure you that we are doing everything we can to find your daughter."

I stand back and the police get into the car and drive away with Julia. I'm close to tears. Zora takes me by the arm.

"Let's go home, Sadie. Come on, let's go home. They know where to find us. And maybe Robin's there now, too."

I look at Zora, hope blazing naked in my eyes. I take her arm and we stumble together, clinging to each other for support.

51

Hours pass. Nothing happens. We sit, we pace. I make a phone call to the police every hour, on the hour, until I'm told very firmly to stop it.

"We've got nothing to go on but Nicole's version," I say, the words bursting out of me.

Zora sighs. I can't stop the speculation, the loops of hopeless repetition.

"There's no reason for her to lie," Zora says. "And what's more, the police have checked it all out. You heard them—they told us so. They've been to the cottage. They've had a proper look."

Zora's words are certain. But I'm still not convinced. Rationally, I understand Zora's points. But if the police hadn't told us to stay put, I would have been straight up like a shot to find Nicole, pin her against the wall and ask her exactly what's going on. Maybe everything she said was a lie? Maybe she made all of it up? Perhaps Julia never went to Aldeburgh in the first place, never saw Nicole or Robin?

But I can't go there in my mind. It's a black hole around which I'm skirting all the time. If Julia didn't take Robin as Nicole said, then I have no explanation for her disappearance, no clue as to where she might be, and the thought throws me into such a void of despair that I can't countenance it for even a second.

"I should make us something to eat," I say, trying to break the cycle of worry. I haven't eaten properly all day.

I scramble eggs, make toast. The bread is moldy, but only at the edge so I cut off the crusts, throwing the spoiled parts in the bin. I put a plate of food in front of Zora and sit down to eat my own, the mouthfuls sticking to the back of my throat. I manage to force half of it down before giving up.

Zora is the same. She's got through a bit of it, but with the same lack of enthusiasm, pushing it around her plate before giving up too. I pick up our plates and start washing up. Maybe it'll calm me down a bit to tidy up. We should talk about the case, but I can't bring myself to care.

Once I've finished the washing-up, I sit back at the table and look at my phone. There's a text from Nicole.

Back in London now—I kept Pippa off school today. Let's have coffee tomorrow after drop-off. Thinking about you. Nxx

I show it to Zora, holding my phone out wordlessly to her. "What do you think?"

"That the police were happy for her to leave Aldeburgh. If they'd thought there was something to suspect, there's no way they'd have let her go," Zora says.

The black hole in my mind recedes a little. "Maybe you're right," I say. "But we still don't know where the fuck Robin is..." My voice cracks, my chin trembling. I've run out of self-control. Hunching my shoulders over, I burst into tears, great sobs jagging out of me.

I'm crying so much that I don't register the knock at the

door at first. They keep on banging, though, and I run to the door to find the two detectives there.

I take them through into the front room, trying to pull myself together a bit, though it must be obvious what kind of a state I'm in. They look at me with kind expressions across the room as they each sit in one of the ancient armchairs. I fight an urge to explain that this isn't really my house, that I'm doing it up, so they don't judge me on the state of it. Not that they care. I just want to break the silence, keep movement going around me so that I don't crack up again.

DS Hughes clears her throat.

"We've had some developments," she says.

My head shoots up.

"We are limited in the information that we can give you at this stage," the detective continues, "but as you heard earlier, the investigation into Julia Burnet has taken a new turn. We have received certain evidence that has turned the situation surrounding her daughter, Daisy, into an attempted murder inquiry."

"What evidence?" I say.

The detectives look at each other, and DS Labinjoh nods at DS Hughes to continue.

"We have received the results of the toxicology report on Daisy. It's showing significant quantities of modafinil and also of diazepam."

"What does that mean, exactly?"

"It means that she has been receiving improper amounts of medication, that weren't medically necessary. Modafinil is usually prescribed for sleep disorders, to manage conditions like narcolepsy, but it's misused by some people. It's easy enough to get hold of it online. Students sometimes take it to stay focused and awake for long periods of time so that they can get work done."

"Why would Daisy be taking that?" I say, aware as soon as I say it how stupid the question is.

DS Hughes is kind enough not to sneer. "That's not the hypothesis on which we're working. Our theory is that someone has been giving that drug to Daisy, perhaps in an attempt to enhance her performance at school. Have there been any exams recently? Or tests of some importance?"

I can't control my shock. "The entrance exams for the senior school. It's just an exam at the beginning of next term for entry to the senior school. I mean, it's a competitive school, but drugging your child? That's insane." I get up and stride across the room, back again, trying to get myself back together. I can't sit still any longer.

"The diazepam wouldn't help with focus, though, would it?" Zora says. She's also looking shocked.

"No," Hughes says. "Quite the reverse. And that's the second part of our hypothesis. That the tranquilizer was given in an attempt to calm the child down, after an overdose of the stimulant."

Her words fall into the silence of the room like stones in a pool. I feel a reverberation around me.

"How could you do that to a ten-year-old?" I say.

After a moment, Zora says, "This is all very terrible, but what does it have to do with Robin?"

I sit back down next to her. Fear is gnawing at my guts.

"We've received evidence to suggest that Julia was taking these exams very seriously," Hughes says. I nod in agreement. "We've also received information that Robin, your daughter, was scoring very highly. Is that right?"

"Yes," I say. "She's very bright. She enjoys tests. I wasn't putting any pressure on her, though."

"That's not what we're suggesting, Mrs. Roper. Don't worry. We think there may be a connection, though. If Julia thought that your daughter was some competition to Daisy, perhaps? Likely to take her place?"

"I'm sure Daisy was going to get her place at the school, no problem."

"Or perhaps there was some kind of prize?"

I stop, think. "The scholarship. There is a scholarship. But surely..."

Again the detectives look at each other. DS Labinjoh speaks for the first time. "We want you to look at something, see if you recognize it." She reaches down into a black briefcase that's at her feet and pulls out a clear plastic bag with something small inside. I recognize the bag as the kind the police use for evidence in trials, and I swallow a whimper.

Labinjoh pulls on a pair of disposable gloves. She reaches into the plastic bag, removing the item, holds it up to me.

It's a soft toy. A little one. A knitted meerkat, wearing a green vest and black trousers, a safety pin through its ear. The toy Zora made for Robin all those years ago, from which she's never been parted. I leap up and try to grab it from her but the detective moves it out of my reach.

"Do you recognize this?" she says to me. I'm still trying to get to it. "Please, don't touch it. This could be very important evidence."

I sway where I stand. I feel hands on my arms, guiding me backward to my seat, pulling me down and keeping hold of me. It's Zora.

"Yes," I say. "Yes, I recognize it. It's Robin's meerkat. Where did you find it?"

Another long pause. Another look shared between the detectives. I'm thrumming with the tension in the room.

"In Julia's car," Hughes says. "Right underneath the front seat. Was it something Robin carried around in her pocket at all?"

"Yes," I say. "She always had it with her."

"We're working on the theory that it fell out somehow, and no one spotted it."

"And where is Robin?" I say, my voice very quiet.

"We don't know," she says. "But I promise you, we are going to find out."

52

The detectives leave soon after. They've given me firm instructions to stay put, not to try and do anything, no appeals on social media, nothing. They are on the case—they're certain that Julia is implicated and they will discover Robin's whereabouts very soon. Their confidence seems unshakable, no chink of doubt, but my terror is unassailable, too, claws hooked deep into me. I'm out of energy, though. The day has drained me.

"You should go to bed," Zora says.

"I can't sleep."

"You need to rest, at least. It's no good if you fall apart."

"I suppose."

"Have you heard anything from Andrew?"

"Nothing," I say. "I told you he didn't care."

Zora doesn't react. She doesn't have to. "Go on, go and get some sleep. I'll wake you if anything happens."

I go upstairs into Robin's room, lying down on the small bed. I want proximity to the daughter I love, not the mother who hated me. But until my daughter is home, I will never have the proximity I want. I lie awake for hours, tracing patterns between the glow stars, my heart sore.

I sleep in the end, just before dawn, but I'm dragged from sleep by loud knocks at the door. I jump up immediately, certain it must be the police, bringing Robin home to me. Moving fast, I miss the top step, and fall headlong down the stairs, bashing my head on the banister at the bottom. I lie for a moment, my leg twisted under me, before there's another bang at the door and Zora opens it. I get to my feet, stumble, head and knee both throbbing, but I don't care, it doesn't matter, I've heard Zora's voice talking to someone and it must be Robin, surely it must be Robin.

"Are you OK?" a man's voice says, and I look up. It's Andrew. Not Robin. And the disappointment fells me.

My estranged husband and my best friend help me through to the kitchen. Zora takes herself off upstairs, muttering something about having a shower.

Andrew slumps down, glancing around. "This place needs some serious work."

"I know."

"But you've made it comfortable, you know. It feels more like a home than it ever did before. Or it would if..." He doesn't finish his sentence. I can't breathe properly, the air sucked out of the room by all the things we're not saying.

"We're not here to talk about home improvements. What's going on, Andrew?" I say. "I saw the news report, the arrests. Why are you here?"

"For Robin," he says. "For you."

"You're fucking that other woman. You don't care any more," I say, my voice flat.

"That's what I needed you to think. So that you'd go."

"I don't understand."

"I wanted to explain. When I called..."

"Right," I say.

"I know it hardly matters now. But I hope it will, soon. I needed to get you out of the country safely. You and Robin."

"What do you mean?"

"It's a big fraud—you saw that, from the arrests. They've nicked all the top bosses. The investment company, it's a Ponzi scheme. I didn't realize to begin with, but over the last few years it's become increasingly obvious to me. I've been gathering evidence, cooperating with the Securities and Exchange Commission."

"I don't understand..."

"I knew it was going to blow. There were going to be arrests, a lot of publicity. I thought I might be arrested too, at least to begin with. I was worried about visas...the lot."

"Who the hell was that woman, then? All those mysterious phone calls?"

He looks at me pleadingly. "She was my attorney. The only person I was allowed to speak to about any of it without fucking up the investigation. They wouldn't let me tell anyone. Your mother's legacy...well, to begin with, of course, I thought it was a terrible idea. But that was before I realized the full extent of what was happening at work. It started to look more and more like a lifeline. And when the place for Robin came up...I knew I'd never be able to persuade you. I had to get you to leave me—it was the only way."

"You did all of that on purpose? Cut me off, wouldn't look at me for all those months? Made me think you were sleeping with someone else. That you'd take Robin away from me?"

Andrew nods, his face ashen. "I'm sorry."

"It's the worst thing anyone has ever done to me. How am

I meant to believe anything you say now? Why couldn't you just tell me?" I look at him, only the other side of the kitchen table but he might as well be a thousand miles away. He puts his head in his hands and his shoulders shake. I make no move to comfort him.

He looks up at me at last, his cheeks wet. "I couldn't. I wasn't allowed to tell anyone. I did this for your own good, I promise. I just wanted to protect you both."

There is no room for this anger right now, but through the fear for Robin that's all-consuming, I have a cold certainty that if we ever get to the other side, Robin safe back with me, there will be a reckoning, and my rage will be mighty.

I don't say anything else. I've no interest in anything other than where Robin is. Andrew isn't even real to me right now; I'm numb to all the hurt he's caused, though I know that underneath the thought is starting to grow that if he hadn't done all of this, Robin wouldn't be missing now...

Zora comes back downstairs and joins us. She explains the situation in full to Andrew while I keep checking my phone. When she's finished we sit for what feels like hours more, the silence beating heavy around us, walking to the front room to look out of the front window, back again. At last I receive a call from Nicole.

"I'm at the hospital with Daisy," she says. "Why don't you come in and see us so we can talk properly?"

I relay the conversation to Zora. I don't look at Andrew. "I can't go, though, can I? What if something happens here? The police told me to stay put."

"I think you should go," Zora says. "You might find out something useful. I promise I'll call if there's any news at all."

Daisy is still in the same room in the hospital that I visited before, the same machines still beeping around her, the mask obscuring her face. Nicole is sitting beside the bed, Pippa with her. The moment that I walk into the room, Nicole leaps up and runs over to me, grabbing me in a hug. I hug her back. We embrace for a moment before Nicole lets go.

"I'll never forgive myself," she says. "I should never have let Robin get in the car with Julia. I should have realized what kind of a state Julia was in."

I look at her closely. This thought has come into my mind more than once, too, how much blame I should attribute to Nicole. But at the same time, what Julia is accused of doing is unthinkable.

"How was this to be predicted, though?" I say. "You couldn't have known Julia was so crazy that she'd drug her own daughter and try to take out the competition." As I say the word *competition*, I start to shake, the reduction of Robin to this, solely a barrier to someone else's ambition, to be knocked down at will.

Nicole hugs me again. "I'll never forgive myself," she says into my hair. "I'm so sorry."

I sit down on a chair at the end of Daisy's bed, next to where Pippa is sitting. Pippa is looking hunched and cold, muffled in an oversized hooded top. She's clutching something in her hands and I look more closely to see it's a small stuffed bear, the fur worn at the edges. Despite all my own sorrow, my heart goes out to the girl. She's sitting here beside one friend, unconscious in a hospital bed, and waiting for news of another one.

"How are you doing?" I say to her.

Pippa twitches. She looks up at me, only briefly, and then turns her concentration back again to her bear, twisting it in her hands. Her hair is greasy, the marks of a comb through it visible near her parting. As I'm watching, she reaches her hand up and starts scratching at her scalp, worrying away at something. Eventually she brings her hand down and I'm horrified to see that where she's been scratching, there's a bloody patch now visible, dark against the blonde hair.

"Your scalp," I say. "It's bleeding. Are you OK?"

Pippa hunches even more over her bear, her face stricken. She doesn't reply. Nicole moves beside her and puts her arm around her, looking down at her.

"She's fine," she says. "Pippa just picks a bit at her scalp when she's unsettled, that's all. It's been a difficult time for her. For us all."

I nod. There's nothing I can say to that. Watching Nicole holding Pippa, I want to cry. There's nothing I want more than to be able to hold my daughter, too. I can almost feel Robin's solid warmth, smell her hair.

Nicole is looking over at Daisy. She doesn't realize I'm watching. Something in her face shifts, a sharpening of her features. She looks completely unlike herself for a moment, a stranger to me. Then she turns and smiles, the warmth returning as suddenly as it left, the sudden contrast giving emphasis to the bleak darkness that was in her eyes before.

A man walks into the hospital room, his footsteps loud.

"Paul," Nicole says. "How are you doing? Daisy's been OK. No change."

Paul. Julia's ex-husband. I look over at him. I remember the way that Julia talked about him, an uncaring, unfeeling man who treated her with such cruelty, a monster who drove her to court in the end to get a proper financial settlement for her and Daisy.

It's not how he comes across. He looks comfortable and tweedy, a geography teacher rather than the investment-banker shark I'd been led to expect. Still, I know better than to judge by appearances. He might look pleasant, but that gives no assurance as to what he's really like. As he comes further into the room, I can see distress on his face, deep-set bags under his eyes from many sleepless nights.

"This is Sadie," Nicole says, introducing me. "She's Robin's mum. You know, the girl who..." She doesn't finish the sentence. It's clear she doesn't need to. Sympathy has swept across Paul's face and he's taken my hands between both of his.

"I'm so sorry," he says. "You must be going through hell."

I'm warmed by the empathy in his voice. He knows what I'm going through. Even if his daughter is here physically in the bed, she's lost too, her return as uncertain as Robin's.

"I feel so sorry for both of you," Nicole says.

Paul takes Nicole's chair, nearest to Daisy, and Nicole joins me down at the bottom of the bed. Pippa goes and sits on the floor in the corner of the room, picking up a book. I squint over in idle curiosity. *Hard Times*. I blink, surprised.

"Is there any news?" Nicole says. She doesn't say about what, but it's clear that she means Julia.

Paul nods. "I've just spoken to the police. The search of the house has turned up packs of both modafinil and diazepam, with her fingerprints on them. They've charged her with administering drugs to Daisy. I can't get my head around it. I had no idea she was so worried about Daisy getting into the senior school. Or that she cared so much about the scholarship."

"Nothing about Robin? She's not said anything?" I burst out.

"I'm so sorry, Sadie. She won't speak at all," Paul says, and the kindness in his voice nearly breaks me. "But there's something else, too. They're also looking into a death that happened eighteen months ago, a little girl who drowned."

My head jerks around. He must be referring to Zoe. Jessica had said Julia was there.

"The parents have never been fully satisfied about the circumstances surrounding her death. And Julia was on that holiday. Now that some motivation has been established, the police are asking her about it."

"That was so terrible," Nicole says, her voice very low. "Pippa was on holiday with them too when it happened, though she slept through the whole thing—Zoe sneaked out at night, to practice her swimming. That's what they reckoned, anyway." She looks pale at the thought. Then she shakes her head, as if to throw it off, looking over at Pippa sitting on the floor with her book. "Pippa, sweetheart, you'll wreck your eyes reading in the dark like that."

Pippa gets up, stretches. "I'm hungry, Mum. Can we get something to eat?"

"I'll take her down to the canteen if you want," I say. Desperate as I am for information, I'm more desperate, suddenly, to get out of there, away from all the intensity of emotion. If I don't escape the room I'll explode, the pressure in my head unbearable.

"Oh no, it's fine. I'll take her," Nicole says, and she stands up ready to leave. At that moment, however, a doctor comes in. She wants to speak to Paul about Daisy. He turns to Nicole.

"Would you stay with me? I don't always keep all the details in my head—it can be a bit overwhelming."

Nicole looks from Paul to the doctor to Pippa, then to me. She shrugs her shoulders as if in defeat, then looks at me. "Would you mind taking Pippa down, after all?"

53

Pippa's starving. She eats all of her cheese and ham sandwich before I've even touched my coffee, and she nods enthusiastically when I ask if she'd like another one. She's halfway through that, too, before she speaks for the first time.

"Thanks," she says. "We didn't have time for supper last night. It's been really strange." She doesn't elaborate, opening the can of Coke I added to the order and taking a large swig. I watch her as she eats. Even though Robin has been friends with her from the start of term, this is the first time that I've ever looked at her properly. She always faded into the background when Robin and Daisy were around. Funny, almost, that the one who sparked the least life is, at this moment, the one with the most. I shudder at the thought, fear for Robin overwhelming me once more.

"It was a fun day on Saturday," Pippa says. "I liked having Robin around. I was sorry when I woke up and she wasn't there."

I blink. I can't believe I've not thought to question Pippa sooner about it. Stress is making me slow, stupid.

"What do you think happened, Pippa?" I say, as gently as I can. "Do you have any ideas?"

"I don't know, really. We spent all day running round on the beach, riding up and down on bikes. No work, for once. Then we had supper and Robin went to sleep and Mum carried her up to bed and I went to sleep, and when I woke up she wasn't there."

Asleep on the sofa. That must have been the point when Nicole took the photo and sent it. Unusual for Robin, though. But not unheard of.

"Do you remember seeing Julia at all?" I say.

Pippa looks blank.

"Daisy's mum?" I prompt.

"Oh yes. She had supper with us. Mum says she left early in the morning. Before I woke up and saw that Robin was gone, too."

Nothing new. Nothing to cast any light on the situation. "Did anything unusual happen when she was there? Anything at all?" I ask, unwilling to give up hope that the girl might have at least some clue as to Robin's whereabouts.

Pippa shrugs. "It was such a fun day," she says again. "Mum even let us go in the secret house." A long pause, and Pippa's face slowly flushes, tears starting up in her eyes. She picks up her Coke but her hands are shaking and she drops the can and it falls over sideways onto the table, spilling what's left. Pippa picks up a handful of napkins and tries to mop it up but she's being inept about it, the mess spreading further.

"What's the secret house, Pippa?" I say. The world has stopped moving around me. Everyone has vanished, just the girl in front of me and the long, dark trail of liquid on the table, dripping slowly onto the floor.

"I shouldn't have said anything. It's a secret."

"I promise I won't tell anyone," I say. "But I do love secrets. Especially secret houses. It sounds really exciting."

Softly, softly...

"Mum found the key, finally," Pippa says. "It's been missing for years. Nearly as long as I've been alive. But she found it and we all went in and looked, but we went out again really fast because it was full of dead flies."

"Where is it, this place?"

"You promise you won't tell?" Pippa says.

"I promise," I say. I have no intention of keeping it. Nothing is more important than Robin. "Please, tell me where it is."

"It's at the back of our house by the sea. It looks like a garage, but it isn't. It's like a little house inside."

Very carefully, I check whether Pippa wants anything else to eat or drink. I take her upstairs, not rushing her, not doing anything to show that she's said anything of any importance at all, chatting to her about tests and Christmas and any other subject I can think of while we wait for the lift, keeping my voice soft and calm. It seems to work. Pippa chatters away to me all the way back up to the seventh floor, where I deliver her to Nicole.

"I'm going home now," I say. "Andrew texted, and he's sounding terrible. I need to go and be with him."

"But we haven't had a chance to catch up," Nicole says.

"Why don't you pop round later?" I'm backing out of the room, trying not to look as if I'm rushing. Nicole is smiling at me, hugging Pippa close to her, the model of a loving friend, a loving mother. There's nothing I want more than to believe that she's as kind as she looks, but every instinct I possess is telling me to get out, now, and find out what the hell the significance of the secret house is.

Paul smiles at me too, a friendly smile, and he comes over and hugs me quickly.

"I'm so sorry about your daughter," he says. "I'm thinking about you all. Wishing for her safe return."

I look at the small figure in the bed. "I'm thinking about you too," I say. As soon as I'm out of the door, I'm running, straight for the lift.

54

I call the police on the way home, telling them I've essential information. They take it seriously. And after a journey that lasts only minutes, but feels like hours, finally I'm home, through the door, face-to-face with the detectives, Labinjoh and Hughes, Andrew and Zora hovering behind.

"I've just talked to Nicole's daughter," I pant. "She says there's a separate part of the house. A hidden part. She called it the secret house. Have you checked there?"

They look at each other, back at me. Hughes speaks.

"I can't say that we have," she says. "This is not information we had before."

"But don't you think it's worth checking out? Maybe Robin's in there."

They look at each other again. "It all seems a bit tenuous," Labinjoh says. "But..."

"Tenuous? What's fucking tenuous about it? I thought you said you'd leave no stone unturned."

"If you'll let me finish," Labinjoh says, "we'll put out a call to the local police now. And we'll drive up there, too. Just in case."

I'm so keyed up that I open my mouth to shout at her again before realizing what she's said. "Oh, OK," I say. "You'll go."

"We'll go now."

They march down the path, purposeful. I suddenly run after them. "Can I come too?" I say, trying not to plead. "If Robin is there, she'll need me."

"Get in," Hughes says, gesturing to the back of their unmarked car, an unremarkable saloon. With no hesitation, I do what I'm told, slamming the car door behind me.

The car may be ordinary in appearance, but it's clearly had something done to soup up its performance. Labinjoh drives it fast, cutting through the traffic of north London, gliding along the North Circular and out onto the A12 with little trouble. Hughes asks me to repeat everything that Pippa said and she relays the information down her phone.

"There's a shortage of officers right now," she says. "There's been an incident in Ipswich; an explosion in a factory. Everyone's on call there—potential fatalities. We'll just have to be quick."

Without warning, Labinjoh slams on the sirens. I'm jolted backward in my seat as the speed picks up, faster and faster. I wasn't sure they were taking this seriously.

I was wrong.

Slung from side to side as we screech through interminable roundabouts, I try to clutch on to the car with my left hand, and my phone with my right. As we swerve through a turning to the right across a dual carriageway, the phone vibrates in my hand. I look at the screen—a text from Nicole. I try to open the message but the car pulls out to overtake a tractor without warning and the phone flies from my hand into the other side of the car, out of my reach.

We're there, though, we're nearly there, and we drive past a golf course, a long street of houses, a church on the left. I barely have time to take it all in before we're screeching across a main road and past a pub, turning right into a narrow residential road, one back from the sea front. We come to a halt beside another pub, close to the entrance to an alleyway.

"Here?" I say.

"Here," Labinjoh says.

Between the pub and the alleyway is a small building. Across the width of it is a wooden garage door, a smaller door is cut into it, but the structure has a low wall in front of it, behind which a number of wheelie bins are lined up, blocking the whole entrance. We stand for a moment looking at it before Hughes pushes through the gate and disappears down the alley. There's a shout a few seconds later.

"There's another door here," she says. Labinjoh runs after her, and I'm close behind. At the end of the alley, at the back of a house that I presume must belong to Nicole, there's a side door leading into the small building with the garage door. The detectives take it in turns to push at it, but it doesn't budge, and there's no reply when they thump on it, asking if anyone is inside. I'm shouting too, calling out Robin's name, an edge of desperation in my voice.

The detectives give up on the door and return to the car. I move forward to take their place and thump at the door a few more times, beating my fists against the wood, until the police come back and push me out of the way, down the alleyway back toward the road. Hughes is carrying a small battering ram, the kind that I've only ever seen on TV police dramas. She shouts a warning, runs and swings it at the door once, twice, and suddenly it's open and they're in, the ram dropped to the ground with a clang.

Hughes is in first, Labinjoh straight after. I'm at the back. But when I hear Hughes shout out I leap forward, pushing Labinjoh out of the way, and follow Hughes up a flight of stairs to see her kneeling on the floor next to a pile of rags. A pile of rags surrounded by hundreds of dead flies. Drifts of them, more than I've ever seen gathered like this in my life before.

I'm focusing on the wrong thing. The flies don't matter. Because Hughes is doing something with the pile of rags, sorting through it, lifting up blankets and scraps of material. She pushes the whole lot back and bends down and it's now that I see what she's found.

Who she's found…

I run over and kneel down beside her, next to my daughter as she lies on the floor, her lips blue. I start to sob, a keening sound, as I reach out and takes Robin's hand.

It's cold.

AFTERWARD

I'm as cold as a corpse.

The flowers are white and the coffin is white too, little pink flowers painted all over it. She'd have liked it. Pretty, just like she was. A tear slides down my cheek. Another. I can't remember a time now when I haven't been crying.

I clutch my hands together as the reading begins: Jesus, suffer the little children. *It's the wrong way round. The little children suffer. How they suffer. Forced to sing and dance on command, live out their parents' hopes, dreams. Fix all their failures.*

I'm sorry, I'm so sorry.

I look at the spray of flowers on top of the white painted box. Not lilies, the waxen petals heavy and cloying, but bright, cheerful sunflowers, freesias, sprays of green ivy woven through the flowers, bright against the white paint, a delicate scent spreading through the church. All her favorite flowers.

The readings stop and the hymns stop and now there's nothing left to stop the conveyor belt moving the coffin into the flames. They take off the flowers, putting them carefully on the floor, and I want to scream at them to stop, no one cares about the flowers, just get her out of the box, get her out.

I don't scream. I bite my lip so hard it bleeds.

The curtain pulls back, the coffin moves through the gap.

The curtain closes. The scent of freesias sticks in my throat. I get up, walk out of the crematorium, into the sunshine that's bright and warm, but my eyes are dark and I stumble, fall.

55

"I know you have other things on your mind," Zora tells me over the phone some time later. "But I thought you'd like to know what happened in the trial."

I shrug.

"He pleaded guilty. To every charge. There was uproar in court."

"Right," I say. "Right. Well, that's something. I didn't think he'd have the courage." It feels as if all that happened a lifetime ago.

"He went into the witness box to give his evidence, and instead of saying what we'd rehearsed, he told the court that everything was true."

Something stirs inside me, a small twinge of emotion. "And what happened?"

"The judge asked if he was changing his plea, and he said yes. He also yelled out to the whole court that it was down to his father and his QC that he'd kept the plea of not guilty going for so long."

"Wow," I say. I can almost imagine it, their faces puce with rage, their professional integrity torn to pieces.

"I didn't know anything about it, you know," Zora says.

"I want to be absolutely clear with you about that. I would never have carried out a defense on that basis."

"I know," I say. "Jeremy did say it was his father who was the main instigator of this. Not that Barbara did anything to counter it."

"Protecting their own," Zora says. "No integrity."

"That poor girl," I say.

"Yes, that poor girl."

We're both silent for a moment. I think about Freya, how bravely she gave her evidence. Then I take in a breath.

"I'm sorry I didn't tell you I found the book. It was incredibly stupid of me. I should have known better. It was all very...difficult." Remembering that terrible weekend, I suppress a shiver. "So what happens now?" I say.

"He'll be sentenced in a few weeks. And I've made a complaint to your chambers and to the Bar Standards Board about the way this has been carried out. Frankly, I'm appalled."

"Good."

"He'll have to do his own mitigation, too. Or get someone else. We're off the case," Zora says. Another pause. "I don't know what your plans for work are, Sadie. If you want to go back into that chambers. Or if you were interested in a job with us. But we always need good people. There are lots of trial opportunities, and it might be more flexible for you. In any event, I've told David I intend to instruct on every possible occasion."

I consider this for a moment, file it away. I'll think about it in time. Not now.

"What's happened to Freya?" I ask. "Did you see how she reacted?"

"I heard her crying in the public gallery," Zora says. "I looked round and saw her. Something you might be pleased to hear, though. Her mother was with her, with her arm around her. I think they might be all right."

"Good," I say. I'm about to hang up, but then I stop. "Zora, I just want to say thank you. For everything you did. You've been a fantastic friend. I don't know when I'll feel up to it, but I'd love to work with you. But can we make sure we're not representing any more arseholes?"

Zora laughs. "You know I can't give that guarantee."

"True. Very true."

56

Robin stirs. She's waking up. I lie next to her, looking at her face as she gradually opens her eyes. She's slept in my bed since we got her home from hospital, though she's starting to play on her own a bit more. She still hasn't gone back to school, though she says she's nearly ready.

I find the warmth of her presence a comfort, too. My frayed nerves are starting to heal, my cortisol levels sinking back to normal. It's a mammalian instinct, this need to lie in a pack, back to back against the night. Sometimes I lie awake in the dark, listening to Robin breathe, and I imagine what it must have been like in that dark outhouse. Robin doesn't speak about it, can't remember. Or won't. I hope that she never woke and tried to seek comfort, looking for me and finding no one there.

I read about an experiment once, baby monkeys ripped from their mothers and caged with a wire frame as a surrogate, unmoving and unmoved by their cries. It cut me to the core, the cries of the baby monkeys so loud in my mind it was deafening. My own mother was that hard, that unyielding. I would try time and time again to speak to her, get her to notice me. But I was too often a disappointment, never good enough. My mother could spend weeks in the same house as me, cooking for me, washing my clothes, but never once making eye contact with me.

Once Robin wakes up fully, we get dressed and go upstairs to my old bedroom. It's time. We discussed it the night before. We're going to be quick, brutal. It's got the best view in the house, high up in the eaves. I look out over the garden, at the pots of bright cyclamen I've planted up for the winter. There'll be daffodils there when it's spring, crocuses and snowdrops, too. Perfect for Robin. We'll reclaim the space, break the stranglehold of hate. And it doesn't take long to finish the job I started all those weeks ago.

"Do you want me to take that rubbish down?" Andrew asks as he climbs up the stairs. "I've got rid of four bags already from your room."

I hand him the junk that we've sorted so far and I listen to him thudding his way down to the front door, his feet heavy on the stairs. *Your room*, he'd said. He's still on the sofa in the living room. It's for Robin's benefit he's here, that's all. That's what I'm telling myself, anyway.

Robin has been digging through drawers on the other side of the room. We've got past our initial horror at what Lydia did, finding it almost funny now.

"She must have hammered at this bit with a shoe or something," Robin says, showing me the crushed plastic head of a baby doll. One of the eyes has gone entirely, the other is sticking out of its socket at an alarming angle. "It's amazing."

We continue to work in silence. I find some pages of *Where the Wild Things Are* that are more or less intact and I try to piece them back together, thinking about how happy

I would have been to be in a home where I was loved, best of all.

"Mom," Robin says, breaking my concentration. "Mom," she says again. "Look at this."

I look up. She's holding an old shoebox. "What's that?"

"It was in the bottom drawer. It isn't damaged at all."

"Wow, probably the only thing in this room that isn't," I say and we both laugh. Robin picks her way across the littered floor and hands the box to me and we look at it together. "I'm almost scared to look inside," I say. "What do you think it'll be? A dead toad? A severed toe?"

"Maybe it's an ox's heart full of nails, like the witches used to make," Robin says, her eyes round and ghoulish.

It's tempting to leave it, throw it straight into a rubbish bag and never think of it again. But I know the thought of it will haunt me. I take a deep breath, get a grip on myself. I know full well the depths of my mother's malice—there's nothing she can do now that has the power to hurt me.

"Come on, Mom, get it over with," Robin says, and I brace myself, take off the lid.

"Oh," I say. And "Oh," again, my hand flying up to my mouth to cover it, winded.

"What is it?" Robin says. "Here, let me see."

She reaches into the box and pulls out the matryoshka doll that I remember from so many years ago. I watched my mother smash it into pieces, the tendons in her neck straining with the force as she wielded the hammer.

"I thought you said it was broken," Robin says. The doll has come out of the box in one piece. I take it from her and trace my fingers over the joins, the small smudges of glue.

"She must have mended it," I say, and there's a ripple in the air somehow, a loosening.

"This is going to be a lovely room," Robin says, and she stands close to me and hugs me.

"I'm sorry," Andrew says, later that day. I look at him.

"I know."

"Do you think you'll be able to forgive me?"

I keep looking at him, and he looks back. We hold the gaze for a long time.

"Will you go back to chambers?" Andrew asks, later still.

"One of us is going to need to earn some money," I say. "Now you've turned supergrass and had your boss arrested and lost your work visa."

"We can make it work," he says. "It's your turn now. I'm here."

"I'm not sure," I repeat. "I don't know if I want to stay here, either." I gesture around at the kitchen. "Not that we can go back to the U.S."

"Over my dead body. Anyway, even if we could, I'm not sure Robin would let that happen," Andrew says. He laughs. After a moment, I laugh too.

"What's so funny?" a voice says from the front room, and then Robin's there, in front of us. Still pale, still a bit underweight from the time she spent in hospital. But all right. Completely all right.

"Your mother is suggesting we move back to America," Andrew says. "I wasn't sure you'd be up for the idea."

"No way!" she says. "I'm not moving again. I like it here. I like school. Can we stay?"

I look at them both and smile. It's as if none of it ever happened. The shadow has passed from Robin, though I don't think I'll ever be free of it myself, the touch of Robin's hand so cold on mine those weeks ago still lingering on my skin.

It all moved at such speed after we found Robin that it's taken me a while to process exactly what happened. An ambulance arrived and she was bundled into it. From the lowness of her temperature, the traces of blood on her head, I was convinced at first that she was dead, but a faint pulse was detected. It took some weeks for her to make a full recovery, however, and for the tranquilizers with which she'd been drugged to work their way out of her system.

"If you'd found her any later, it would have been too late," one of the doctors in hospital said to me. "Or if she'd been given any more. She's been lucky, all things considered."

I look at her now, bouncing around the house with Andrew. Very lucky indeed. Not like poor Daisy. Her funeral was one of the saddest events that I've ever attended. It broke my heart to watch Paul at the front of the crematorium, head bowed in despair, Nicole next to him. They're growing close, Nicole and Paul. It seems to be bringing him some comfort.

I can't begin to imagine how Julia must be feeling. But nothing about her makes any sense. It's unimaginable that someone could have been so eaten up with ambition for their child that they would be prepared to kill the competition. But this is exactly what's happened.

Julia is currently remanded in custody charged with the involuntary manslaughter of Daisy, and the false imprisonment and attempted murder of Robin. Nicole's text to me at the time that we found Robin in the secret house was to tell us that she'd lost the keys to the building; Julia had visited the house some years previously and knew about the rooms at the back. She must've pocketed the keys when she had the chance. Nicole didn't think to mention it before—it simply didn't occur to her that Robin could be hidden there.

Fibers from the clothes Julia was wearing were found by forensics all over Robin's clothes, her fingerprints on the keys that were eventually found in Julia's handbag, and on an empty packet of tranquilizers of the sort used to drug both Daisy and Robin, thrown away in the bin outside Julia's house, with Julia's name on the label.

Julia is pleading guilty to the involuntary manslaughter of her daughter, the police have told me. She says she's devastated, that she'll never forgive herself for what happened. She's said not guilty to any charge relating to Robin. So far. But she's provided no alternative explanation. It probably doesn't matter to her any more in the face of Daisy's death. She seems to have given up any real attempt to defend herself.

The police are working on the theory that, overcome with grief and guilt at Daisy's coma, she decided in the heat of the moment to take Robin, blaming her for disturbing the balance of the class. Once she got Robin up first thing on the Sunday morning, she gave her a spiked drink and bashed her over the head before hiding her in the property next to Nicole's house.

I'll never know what was going through her head, though I've tried to work it out. To drug Daisy—well, there was a logic there, in a dark, twisted way. Julia's drive to succeed was ruthless. It was clear she'd stop at nothing. Until Robin came into the class, Daisy was guaranteed to win the scholarship, be recognized as the best. Robin kept beating Daisy in the maths tests—maybe this was why Julia kept giving more and more drugs to her daughter, artificially gearing her up, calming her down, until it all went too far. She must have thought it was all Robin's fault. So when she saw her chance to take her revenge on Robin, make her suffer as much as Daisy, she grabbed it with both hands.

I look at my daughter now. The resilience of youth. She's bounced back entirely, only a small mark on her head. No other scars. Nothing. She won't even have to do the senior school exams—Ashams has been so shaken by the scandal that they've suspended the entrance procedure for girls currently at the junior school. Admission to the senior school will now be automatic.

"While this is an extreme example of the dangers of competitive parenting," the letter that arrived from Mrs. Grayson said, with remarkable understatement, "we are anxious for the future not to encourage an atmosphere that lends itself to any behavior of this kind."

Good for Robin. Good for Pippa.

Too late for Daisy, the poor child put under such deadly pressure by her mother, stuffed full of performance enhancing drugs in Julia's vain attempt to make her shine.

And too late for Zoe. There won't be any charges there. But it's only because of lack of evidence. The police told me that Zoe's mother is convinced that Julia was behind her daughter's death, somehow, Zoe's place at the top of the class too much of a challenge to Julia even when the children were only in Year 4.

I look at Robin. I know just how lucky we are.

* * *

Pippa comes around to play later that day. She's going to sleep over. As soon as she arrives the girls run upstairs together, giggling. They're thick as thieves.

Nicole gets out of the car and hands over Pippa's bag at the doorstep. I know I should ask her in, but I'm speechless at the sight of her, prettier than I've ever seen her before, hair newly cut and colored, lipstick on. "Paul is waiting in the car," she says. "We're going away for the night. To a hotel in the Cotswolds."

There's a beat, a pause, before I come up with a reply. "I hope you have a lovely time," I say in the end.

Nicole's halfway down the path before she turns, comes back.

"I do hope Robin will be back at school soon," she says. "We miss her. You, too."

I look at her blankly.

"We can't wait to get you volunteering for the Christmas Fair! I've taken over from Julia, now—I'm head of the PTA. Given how closely I worked with her, the decision was unanimous," Nicole says.

I wave as they drive off. Her words are bright, but they tinkle like ice.

An image flashes unbidden into my mind. Nicole, this time. Her face as she looked at Daisy in the hospital. Eyes dark with an emotion I didn't recognize at the time. But now I wonder. Could it have been envy? Did she hate the girls who got so much better marks than Pippa? Did she covet Julia's position in the school? Could she have drugged Daisy and tried to kill Robin, leaving Julia to take the blame? She had motive, method—opportunity.

I shake my head. I'm being stupid, drawing connections

where there are none. I know what the story is—there's no need to complicate it.

"Can we make a cake, Mom? Is that all right?" Robin says, all pink and excited, Pippa behind her.

"Yes, of course you can," I say.

"Thanks, Mom," Robin says, running out of the room. Pippa is close behind. But before she goes out, she turns to me.

"I like Robin," she says. "She's not like Zoe or Daisy—they showed off all the time and made me feel stupid. Robin doesn't, though—she's my friend. She'll always be my friend." She looks at me, unblinking, her eyes intent.

There's no logical reason for it, but chill fingers pass through me. Then Pippa smiles and they melt. She's a child, just a child. I go through to the kitchen and turn on the oven, ready to help.

EPILOGUE

No one ever remembers me. Maybe I don't exist.

Mummy says I'm real, though. Mummy sees me. She sees everything I do. We do everything together. Solve every problem together.

I'm a part of her, she says.

They don't think I'm as clever as the other girls. Though they're wrong. I like hiding it so they don't notice. They know I can do some things better, though.

Running, jumping. Swimming.

Zoe, I said, Zoe. Just a bit deeper. You can do it.

Don't be scared.

I'll help you.

I didn't help her. She never helped me. I didn't like her.

But I helped Robin. I made sure she'd be found. Even though Mummy said no, Robin would only end up being nasty to me too.

Mummy's wrong. Robin's kind to me. I hope she'll always be kind to me.

Robin's my friend.

Acknowledgments

Second novels are difficult, and this book has been no exception. My deepest of thanks to my editor, Kate Stephenson, at Wildfire for her endless patience and skill in bringing the best out of this book, and to my agent, Veronique Baxter, for her great knowledge and support through the whole process. It has been brilliantly copy and line edited by Karen Ball and Julia Bruce—my thanks to you both.

I am very lucky to be published by Wildfire in the UK and Grand Central Publishing in the US, the best in the business—I am very grateful to the team at Wildfire, and to Seema Mahanian and the team at Grand Central. Thanks in particular go to Andy Dodds in his support of me through the publication tour of *Blood Orange*—I loved visiting so many great US bookshops, and I can't wait to come back again as soon as I can.

Dr. Rosie Baruah gave up some of her valuable time off from treating patients on the Covid-19 frontline to give me information about the effects of drug overdoses, and Anya Waddington was extremely helpful in her advice about entrance procedures for secondary schools—my deepest thanks to you both. Any mistakes, in these or any other areas, belong to me alone.

I was given reassurance, advice and encouragement at the earliest stage by my first readers—thanks so much to Jemma Arvinitis, Louise Hare, Laura Joyce, Amanda Little, Maxine Mei-Fung Chung, Kate Simants and Trevor Wood.

I've stolen your names and taken up a lot of your time moaning about the difficult second book syndrome—thank you, my friends. Susan Chynoweth, Norma Gaunt, Kristian Glynn, Katie Grayson, Sarah Hughes, Femi Kayode and Sandra Labinjoh—I can't wait to see you all in person rather than on a computer screen. A special thanks to Sarah Pinborough, too, for all your support during this first time of publication—it's very much appreciated.

Helen Chatwell—thank you very much indeed. You know what for. Ruth Davison, you were a glaring omission from the Acknowledgments of *Blood Orange*, but again, thank you very much indeed. You also know what for.

To all teachers, everywhere, you have my unqualified respect and gratitude. And, in particular, everyone who has ever taught my children. I hope I have never been as difficult as any of my fictional mothers at the school gate. I'm glad that world lives only in my imagination…

I never expected that my first novel, *Blood Orange*, would reach as many readers as it has, and I'm very grateful indeed to every single one of you for picking it up and giving it a go. I have loved seeing it being discussed in book clubs and reviewed by bloggers—you're all amazing and I really appreciate all the work that you do for the best of reasons, the love of books and reading.

My family has given me a huge amount of support over the

last year while I've written this—my parents, Bill and Jenny, my brother Alex and niece Amelia and nephew Ali, my parents-in-law, Ian and Cathy, and my brother-in-law Oli, thanks so much to you all. I'm very glad to have a normal family with no strange legacies in place.

Finally, to Nat, Freddy, and Eloise. I couldn't do it without you—you're the best lockdown companions I could ask for. I love you all.

Charlotte Knee Photography

Harriet Tyce grew up in Edinburgh and studied English at Oxford University and law at City University in London before working as a criminal barrister for nearly a decade. She completed her MA in creative writing at the University of East Anglia. Her debut novel, *Blood Orange*, was published by Grand Central Publishing. She lives in north London with her family.